The Gold Flake Hydrant

The Gold Flake Hydrant

GREG MATTHEWS

NAL BOOKS
NEW AMERICAN LIBRARY
NEW YORK AND SCARBOROUGH, ONTARIO

PUBLISHER'S NOTE

This book is a work of fiction. Names, characters, places, and incidents either are the product of the author's imagination or are used fictitiously, and any resemblance to actual persons, living or dead, events, or locales is entirely coincidental.

Library of Congress Cataloging-in-Publication Data

Matthews, Greg.
  The gold flake hydrant.
I. Title
PR9619.3.M317G65 1988   823   88-1364
ISBN 0-453-00584-5

Designed by Leonard Telesca

First Printing, July, 1988

1 2 3 4 5 6 7 8 9

PRINTED IN THE UNITED STATES OF AMERICA

1

It came down the hill sideways, this giant orange garbage truck sliding on the ice. The driver never should've come over the top of Crestview that fast, not without knowing if the down side was visited by the grit truck lately, which it wasn't, and as soon as he started down his wheels kind of slid out from under him, and in around two seconds he's coming down sideways with his engine revving like crazy and the back wheels spinning, all eight of them, which only made the situation worse in my opinion.

I'm down at the bottom, halfway across the intersection there, so I've got a terrific view of the whole thing. I knew soon as I heard the garbage truck coming over the top of the hill he's going way too fast for icy conditions, even before I saw the orange roof and the pickup arms and smokestacks. I stopped right there in the middle of the intersection, maybe not a smart thing to do but there wasn't any traffic around that early, just me and the garbage truck coming over the hill above me, and I thought, "Too fast," even before I saw the grille and bumpers, and it was satisfying in a way to see him start to slide as soon as he's over the crest because it proved I'm right.

The cab drifted to the left and the back end swung way out and before the driver's got time to figure what's happening the whole five tons or whatever is sliding sideways downhill, rattling and banging and the engine revving like a Sherman tank. I could see the driver spinning the wheel but it's too late, because the truck's coming down faster and faster, the back end ahead of the cabin now, and that's what hit the first car parked along the curb, the back end, just swiped it like you'd swat a fly and that red Chevy got shunted backward onto the sidewalk with its hood all buckled and the windshield popping out and disintegrating in midair like a little storm of ice crystals.

The garbage truck kept coming down Crestview, heading straight for me, turned completely around now, I mean it's coming down backward, this big greasy orange wall coming at me like a locomotive and I'm stranded on the tracks it seems like, just standing there not able to move, and it's getting bigger and bigger, but then it starts turning some more and the back end kind of wandered over the other side of the street and sideswiped a Plymouth this time, just shoved it easy as can be right off the street and kept on coming like nothing happened at all, with the smokestacks really pouring out black stuff, the little lids on top of the pipes standing straight up. "Move . . ." I told myself, but I couldn't, I don't know why, something like the rabbit and the snake I guess, so I just stood there like an idiot with this garbage truck fixing to cream me in around five more seconds, getting bigger and bigger, going sideways again now, only it's the other side this time, and right about then the driver must've panicked and hit the pickup lever, because they started coming down from alongside the cabin, those long steel prongs for lifting dumpsters, and when they got low enough they rammed through this old Falcon's windows and started pulling it down the hill with the truck, like they're dancing together, this big orange man and little blue lady, and the pronged Falcon slammed into a Buick and that started the garbage truck swinging back the other way again, the back end whipping around, but before it came around completely the Falcon came off the prongs at the front, jolted loose by the Buick I think, and now the truck's coming downhill backward again and I'm *still* standing there hypnotized. I bet I would've been squashed like a bug if the truck didn't all of a sudden swing sideways again and run backward against this Tercel at the curb. This time, instead of being deflected by what it ran into and keeping on downhill, it plowed that little Tercel right under the big square orange back end, pushed it up across the sidewalk and into a tree and that stopped the whole show right there, because it's a big tree, one of those hundred-year-old types, and the bottom branches that hung over the street got snapped off by the truck backing the Tercel up against it, garbage trucks being tall the way they are, and then everything quit moving.

I went on over. My heart's jumping around and my legs are shaking like Jell-O now that I know I won't get flattened after all. Maybe they were jumping and shaking all through the whole thing and I was too busy being hypnotized to notice. The Tercel was a total mess, like it was sat on by an elephant, squashed under the garbage truck's ass that way. There were people coming out of their front doorways now, wondering what all the crashing and crunching was about, and didn't they just squawk when they saw what the truck did to their cars! It must've missed at least a dozen on the way down, but the five it got made Crestview look like a tornado came through. Everyone's got their pajamas and robes and stuff on because it's only 7:20 or so and it all happened while they're pouring milk over their cornflakes and buttering their toast or blueberry pancakes or whatever.

They got really pissed at the driver, who's still in the cab and staring at nothing it looks like to me, dazed I guess. Somebody opened the cabin door and asked him if he's okay and he just says, "She got away from me . . ." like his wife ran off with another guy. "She got away from me . . ." he says again, but it isn't enough, not when you've creamed five cars like that, and some guy with rubbers on over his slippers and an overcoat around his robe is asking him, "What happened? What happened?" like it isn't obvious what happened to anyone with half a brain, but he keeps wanting to know, "What happened?"

Then they all spotted me, and seeing as I'm the only one apart from the driver who's fully dressed they figured I must've seen the whole thing, which I did, so now they're all asking *me*, "What happened? What happened?"

"It got away from him," I said.

I could've told them he was going too fast, but why should I? They've all got insurance I bet, and the garbage truck guy's already shook up enough without having irate car owners suing the Sanitation Department and making him lose his job, which might really make his wife leave him, and I didn't want to be responsible for anything like that, uh-uh, so I said it again, because people when they're pissed off and confused and panicky need telling two or three times before stuff gets through to their brains. "It just got away from him. It wasn't his fault or anything. The hill hasn't been gritted yet. It slid right out from under him."

They swallowed it pretty fast. I don't think they wanted to blame the driver, I mean he's right there in front of them, and you have to be kind of an asshole to blame someone who's right there in front of you for whatever happened. It's much easier for everyone if somebody or something that's somewhere else can be blamed, because that way it isn't so embarrassing and no one starts throwing punches or reaching for a gun or anything. So they all agreed it's the Streets and Highways Department who's to blame for not gritting the down side of Crestview early enough in the morning, and they all stood around swinging their arms and agreeing about the grit and waiting for the cops to get there, and someone brought out a cup of coffee for the garbage truck driver to calm him down some. I think a stiff whiskey would've done the trick better, but the cops might want to breathalyze him even if it's only breakfast time, you never know. Anyway, he got coffee. So did I. They wanted me to stay around because I'm a witness. It was that decaffeinated crap, but I drank it to be polite. I'm that kind of guy.

The cops came and I told them the bullshit about how it wasn't the driver's fault, he was only going slow but the wheels slid out from under him anyway, and about fifteen people told the cops it's the Streets and Highways Department's fault for not laying grit early in the morning to prevent accidents like this from happening, and the cops took my name and address and everyone went back inside except for a few who had their clothes on by now and wanted to see the truck get up off that poor little squashed Tercel, kids mainly. Kids love seeing things that are smashed up. They were very envious of me because I saw it all actually happening, lucky me!

One of the cops says, "You the same Weems that got in trouble at Harry's?"

He means did I slit my wrist at Harry's Highway Haven five months ago. What a delicate cop.

"Yeah."

"How's things nowadays?"

He's trying to be friendly. Maybe he's one of the cops that got called to the scene when I did it. If he hasn't seen me since, it's no wonder he doesn't recognize me. I had a Mohican haircut dyed red back then, and now I just look like any other kid. I've got a hunting cap with earflaps on anyway.

"Okay."

"Getting your grades?"

"Nah. I quit school."

"Working?"

Now I don't think he's friendly anymore, just plain goddamn nosy. Who's he think he is, asking personal stuff like this?

"Not yet. I've been looking."

"Well, good luck. Jobs aren't easy to find."

Amen, Dick Tracy. Tell me something new.

"Thanks."

"We might be in touch if there's an inquiry about this." He means the garbage truck smashing all those cars. "There probably won't be, but there might."

"Okay."

"Stay loose," he says, and goes back to the squad car with the shotgun clamped against the dash and starts talking into the mike, but I can't hear what he's saying, maybe getting a computer check on me from the station, just to make sure there's no connection between me opening my wrist at Harry's Highway Haven five months ago and the garbage truck creaming five cars this morning. Maybe he thinks I made it happen to get my own back on the world, suicides being very fucked-up people, you know. Well he's gonna be disappointed, because since all that stuff happened I've kept my nose so clean it's shiny. I'm an A-1 citizen around town. Mr. Inconspicuous. John Cypher.

The garbage truck driver came over and said, "Thanks."

We both know what he means.

"That's okay."

"I appreciate it."

"Could've happened to anyone," I said, meaning anyone who drives like a total moron when the road conditions are shitty. I'm betting he's so shook up about it he'll be a more careful driver from now on, so there's no need to get him in trouble with the Sanitation Department over what he did with their big orange truck. Basically what I'm doing is I'm playing God. It's a good feeling, parceling out judgment like that, but it's kind of tacky too, in a way, because this guy's in my debt now, morally speaking, and I don't want anyone to be in my debt about anything, anytime. I don't want power over people any more than I want people to have power over me. I wouldn't know how to collect a moral debt in any case. It'd get to be a stale debt, just waiting around to be collected.

"Well," he says, "let's see if the bitch starts up again after all the excitement."

He got back in the cabin and fired up the engine and pulled out slow. The Tercel got left behind easy enough, not snagged under the rear bumper like you'd expect. It looked kind of funny when it was under the truck, but on its own it just looks like a mess. The lady who owns it is looking very upset, but I figure she's got insurance. If she didn't she'd be howling. Then three tow trucks came up Crestview from the intersection, so someone must've called them to come haul the smashed cars away to the body shop, except the Tercel, which I bet goes straight to the junkyard to get squashed even smaller in the compactor till it's just a little block of scrap. I hung around awhile, watching the truck crews hook up the cars and work the winches and haul them away. There's two more tow trucks now, so everyone got taken care of. Those things come racing to accidents like vultures, they really do. Then I got bored and went on home.

Peggy was already through eating breakfast and not too happy about me not being there to eat it with her. She's been like that since my sister Loretta left home and got married a little while back. She hates to eat alone, Peggy, and I screwed up her whole morning by not being there to munch alongside her. I could take it or leave it, this mealtime togetherness bit, but Peggy thinks it's a big deal. "Maintaining the family unit," is how she puts it, which isn't how she talks at all so she must've heard it on the tube. Anyway, she was pissed at me.

"Where were you?" she says as soon as I'm in the door, still with my cap on even.

"Out," I said. Sometimes I like to get her riled, just to make life more interesting. My life is very boring.

"You know what time breakfast is, Burris."

"I got held up."

"By what?"

"The James gang. They took every cent."

She doesn't think it's funny, so I told her about the garbage truck slipping and sliding down Crestview.

"I don't believe it," she says. Boy, is she mad, and just because I wasn't there to eat with her, I mean we don't even *talk* or anything over breakfast generally, so what's the big loss? And I don't like it when she says I'm lying, because pretty often I'm actually telling the truth, like now.

"You must've heard it from here, all those cars getting smashed up. It's only four blocks away."

"I didn't hear a thing," she says over her shoulder. She's looking for her bag with the car keys in it. Every morning she looks for it, this big ratty shoulder bag. You'd think it was invisible the way she can never find it. I could've told her it's behind the door where she hung it last night, but she's got me irritated by calling me a liar, so she can turn the house upside down for all I care, and be late for work. Peggy works down at the Wishee-Washee Laundromat nowadays. She's the manageress.

"Help me," she says, getting all frustrated. You know when she's frustrated because she grabs hold of her hair and pulls it all out of her face so she can see that pesky bag better, only it won't help her this morning because she needs X-ray vision to see it behind the door. I kind of swivel my head this way and that, pretending to look for the damn bag. She doesn't think I'm sincere, though, because I've got my hands in my pockets, which makes me look very laid-back, not a frantic bag-seeker like her. She lets go of her hair and says, "Don't just stand there, *look* for it." She's got enough hair to stuff a double mattress, Peggy. She dyes it too, because the yellow-white color it really is makes her look old, she thinks, so for the past month or so it's been reddish-gold, *auburn* it says on the bottle she gets it out of. She doesn't look anything like the girl on the label.

"Burris, help me find my *bag*."

"It's behind the door."

She grabbed it and left, just like that, no good-bye or anything, just to make sure I get the message that she's in a bad mood about me not being there for breakfast. Sometimes she's

not like a mother at all, more like a cranky big sister, most of
the time in fact. I heard the Impala start up out in the driveway
after a few grindings and coughings, then she's gone. Now
there's just me. The house is mine.

I fixed myself waffles, then after I ate them I felt guilty
because they're bad for you, so I had some All Bran as well,
just to do the right thing by my body. Burris Weems, Sports-
man of the Year, says be kind to your bowels with All Bran.
A good reaming is the road to good health, boys and girls, so
shovel this healthy stuff inside you and your asshole won't
grow over from lack of use. Then I had coffee with real caffeine
in it, and orange juice to balance the caffeine's bad effects.
Breakfast is a juggling act. Then I stared at the wall for a while.

It's my job to clean up the house. I've got no problem with
that. Fair's fair. Peggy goes out to work and I stay home and do
the housework. It's easy enough. But I didn't feel like getting
started on the dishes just yet. I just wanted to stare at the wall
for a while, feeling kind of blank, I don't know why. This blank
stuff is getting to be a big feature of my life just lately. All I
have to do is stop concentrating on what I'm doing for just a
few seconds, very easy if what you're doing is the dishes, and
right away I'm staring at nothing with my hands still in the
suds with the rubber gloves on and the scouring brush in one of
them, but I don't even know it's there because I can't feel my
body anymore. All I am is eyes, staring and staring, but no
matter how hard I stare I'm not even *looking* at anything, like
my eyes are open but not *seeing*. I stay that way for I don't
know how long, not seeing, not even *thinking*, and then some
little thing brings me back, the dishes settling in the sink with
that underwater clunking sound they make, or a car passing by
in the street, any little thing at all and *bingo!* the spell's broken
and my eyes kind of crank down and see my hands in the
dishwater and I wonder how long it's been since I was scrub-
bing the crap off the plates, entire *minutes* I bet, missing minutes that flew out the window forever.

The other day I switched off the vacuum cleaner and was
just about to reach down and unclip the bag, but I didn't do it,
I just stood there instead, looking at the cord stretching away to
the socket in the wall. The cord's plugged into the bottom

socket, and the top socket looks like a little sad face looking back at me. We looked at each other for the longest time. I practically fell asleep standing there next to the vacuum cleaner, and what was going through my mind was nothing, *nothing at all*, just a silent, silent nothing. Zero.

And it's not just when I'm doing household chores. That stuff only takes an hour a day on average, so I've got plenty of time to spare, but what do I do with it? I stare at things and think about nothing. It's happening more and more, but I'm not afraid of it. It's a very curious phenomenon, and if it keeps on happening often enough I might get to figure out what it is and what it means. It's a very peaceful kind of problem. There is no heavy drama involved here.

So I sat at the kitchen table doing the staring thing for a while, then the back screen door banged in the place next door and snapped me out of it, and I thought to myself: "Time to tape again." Up in the attic is a bunch of tapes I made last summer, along with the Little Sony recorder I stole from Radio Shack, all bundled up with rubber bands and double-wrapped in plastic bags to keep the dust off. I didn't ask myself why I wanted to start taping again, I just went and put the coffee table from the living room under the hatch that you have to climb through to get to the attic, and put a chair on top of the table so I can reach it. The hatch hasn't got one of those counterbalanced ladders you can just pull down. You have to grab the sides and boost yourself into the attic like the bomber crews had to do to get in their planes in WWII, except you do it headfirst, not legs first like they did. I only weigh one twenty-eight so it's easy enough, even for a wimp.

The Sony and tapes were where I hid them. I left the used tapes up there and came down with an empty one and the recorder, then closed the hatch and put the furniture back where it's supposed to be. Then I went in my room and sat on the bed, which is where I am right now, looking out the window at all the snow in the backyard. I put the new tape in the machine and told it about the big orange garbage truck that came over the hill.

2 Can we talk?

My life is like that little Tercel that got squashed this morning. My life has been sat on by circumstances. First there was the short leg. I won't go over that again. Having a short leg seems like no special deal right now. I mean I wish it was the same length as the other one, and sometimes I have these fantasies about getting together a stack of money and having this fancy operation to make them the same, which they can actually do but it costs plenty, messing around with bone grafts and all.

No, the big problem is, *Who the fuck am I and where am I going?* I've tried to figure everything out over the past few weeks and gotten nowhere. Once everyone in town knows you tried to kill yourself, nothing can ever be the same as it was. The way it was was already bad enough, me being the school geek et cetera, but after the wrist-slitting business in Harry's Highway Haven I got to be a double-geek, on top of which I still had to repeat the semester like they told me I would before summer vacation, which I did, I repeated it, and flunked all over again, and *why* did I flunk out two times in a row? I'll tell you why. I flunked because I figured I didn't need any of that boring education crap because what I planned on being was an actor. Yeah, an *actor*. Can you believe it? *I* can't believe it now, but I believed it back then, which is why I didn't do any studying and thought school was a big joke, which I still think it is, but that doesn't help unless you *become* what you planned on becoming, or at least keep on *believing* you'll get to be what you want to be, this career that you don't need schooling for, which is how I see acting. I mean, it's all instinct and pretending and stuff, right? You've either got it or you haven't, and getting A's in biology won't do squat to make you a better actor, so why bother?

It was just pathetic, it really was. I took down the picture of Charlotte Rampling in my room and put up a poster of James Dean, you know the famous picture of him walking along a New York street in the rain, all hunched over with this big old overcoat on and a cigarette getting wet in his mouth? I put it on the wall and looked at it and looked at it and it was like I *was* old Jim, way over there in New York City, waiting for my big break on Broadway that'd lead to a movie role, and meanwhile I'm hunching along through the rain looking hopeful as hell about things, with two legs the same length and a terrific profile and a big successful future ahead of me, just like Jimbo, only I'll drive more carefully than he did. What an incredible, stupid, moronic *fantasy*! Only a grade-A conehead would've thought that way, and it was like I'd shoved my head in a pencil sharpener because I *believed* it, actually believed it'd *happen*. What a clown! For months I lived on that dream and felt pretty damn cocky about things, which is why I didn't bother with homework et cetera. Why the fuck should I do boring stuff like that? My grades took a nosedive, then went underground like moles.

So just before school shut down for the Christmas break it was obvious to everyone that wild man Weems had gone and done it again, blown his opportunity for advancement, and the principal had me in his office and asked me what happened and I told him I'm just dumb, I guess, which he said he didn't believe, and he said he understood that things must be tough for me after my big trouble with suicide and all, and he's going to take that into account when he decides what to do about me, and what he went and did about me was he got in touch with Dr. Willett, who was my shrink at the Juvenile Psychiatric Counseling joint and Willett says I've got a high IQ, but what he also said was I'm screwed up because of my domestic situation—my old man getting blown away in 'Nam, he means—which is bullshit, because I don't feel anything about my dad one way or the other, frankly. No, what's fucked me up is all the stuff on those other tapes, the thing with Lee and

Diane and the way they ran out on me and left me to clean up their mess behind them. I'm talking about the very successful suicide by Diane's old man, Gene, who I put in the trunk of his own car and drove all the way home to New Mexico, only it all went wrong and I had to dump him like a sack of garbage out in the desert somewhere. They don't know about all that. No one knows about it except me, so anything they say about my psychological state of mind is horseshit, believe me.

Peggy and the principal and Dr. Willett all wanted to know why I threw in the academic towel that way, but I wasn't telling. "I just don't like school" is what I said, and when they kept after me—wanting to know why? why? *why?*—I practically went catatonic on them to get them off my back, and it worked. They quit asking and now school's out for Burris Weems forever. Get the picture? I flunked out this time around because I figured you don't need school to be an actor, only *now* I know I won't ever *be* an actor. There's a reason for that too.

The cause of my undoing, friends and neighbors, was a woman, namely Sandra, who's the daughter of Rick and Alice, who run Harry's Highway Haven. We saw a lot of each other through the fall, and *no*, in case you're *wondering*, I *didn't* get in her pants, but we liked each other okay. Then when I failed my repeat semester she told me I'm immature and on a one-way street to nowhere, blah, blah, and anyway she doesn't go for me so much now that I haven't got a red Mohican anymore. You know how guys are supposed to fall for girls just because they've got big tits? Well it seems like Sandra started dating me just because I had a weird haircut, the only one like it in Buford, Indiana, so I was *glamorous* or something dumb like that. She didn't care if I tried to kill myself either, because that just made me even weirder, and Sandra, she's the kind who wants a weird boyfriend because she can't stand the high school jocks most girls go for. I fitted the bill just right for a while there, but I cut off the Mohican and flunked my grades and she told me we're through, because flunking your grades is okay if you're a musician and you figure you're bound for glory on MTV, but I don't play a note, so I'm just a boring guy with a half inch of hair that flunked because he's a total dork, basically, which isn't glamorous at all, so I'm shot down in flames, James. I panicked, I really did, and I told her about how I was gonna be an actor, which up till then I never told *anyone* about, and you know what she says, the bitch? She says, "You couldn't be an actor. You're too goofy-looking."

Too goofy-looking! The big flaw in her argument is that there are plenty of actors who're goofy-looking. They play the goofy-looking roles. Not everyone can be a fucking hero, okay? But she wasn't bothered about the logic of it, just wanted to let me know I haven't got a prayer, not as an actor, and not as the guy she wants in her pants either. Crushing blow for the Weems ego, which was only just about recovered from being ditched by Diane back in the summer. Girls can be real bitches sometimes, I mean it. See, Sandra was already dating another guy, but I didn't find out till later. She was dating him and for all I know *fucking* him *before* she told me we're through. What a bitch! That's real dishonest, I think, and while we're on the subject of Sandra, I saw her a few days back with her new guy, much better looking than me, natch, and it was like having a pickaxe slammed into my guts. And it *still* hurts.

It's gotten so bad I've quit going out to the mall or any other place I might run into them, even quit going to the movies in case I run into *anyone* from school. That's how ashamed and humiliated and fucked up I feel about everything. I mean I never had any real friends in any case since way back, but I always felt like I could wander around town, like I *belonged*. Not anymore. I belong in the doghouse, definitely, and my weight's gone way down and I look so terrible Peggy's quit nagging me about getting a job and left me in peace the last week or so, which was smart of her because there were getting to be more and more times when I felt like taking a bread knife and cutting her goddamn head off.

Things are bad in general. Last Friday night I woke up from this dream about how Lee and Diane pulled up outside in Lee's beat-up old Dodge pickup and we all drove away together, but when we stopped so I could get out and take a leak they drove away without me, just left me there by the side of the road, which is when I woke up and I really did need to take a leak, and after I went and took it I came back to bed and bawled my eyes out, to be perfectly candid about it.

I've gone and sidetracked myself. . . . I was talking about Sandra and that bitchy thing she said, and how it made me quit believing I could be an actor. At first I told myself what the fuck does *she* know anyway, and kept on believing and staring at the picture on my wall, but what she said just wouldn't go away. It was always in the back of my mind. I stared at that poster of James Dean like some old Catholic lady staring at a picture of the Virgin Mary. I stared and stared at it and wouldn't let myself accept I couldn't be an actor just because I'm goofy-looking. What the fuck does *she* know! That poster got me through for a little while, but then the dream died. It happened last Saturday. I was crunching along through the snow and I decided I'd go sit down in the park and watch the squirrels dig up the nuts they buried in the fall, which is what I did, went to the park and sat on a bench, and all of a sudden I knew I wasn't gonna be an actor, not even a goofy-looking one. I felt very calm about it, which is surprising I think. It was like I didn't need to believe in that particular fantasy anymore. Maybe it was a healthy thing, dumping the dream that way, calmly, and making no big deal about it. Maybe it means I'm facing up to reality and all that mature stuff, who knows? The problem is, I haven't got anything to put in its place. So I won't be an actor, so what *will* I be? Good question. No answer. Maybe that's why I've been staring at walls so much, looking for the answer in magic writing on the wall, but around here the only writing on the wall is spray-can graffiti.

The problem, the way I see it, is separation. I've gone and separated myself from everything and everyone. I'm practically a hermit, Kermit. Everyone else *belongs*. They've got their friends, they go in and out of each other's homes, go to the same parties, go to the movies together, fuck each other, et cetera, and when they're older they'll go to college and join a fraternity or sorority and *belong*, or if they're weird they'll team up with other weirdos and go to weird bars and clubs and hang out there and shack up together and *belong*, and straight or weird they'll have a plan, a kind of picture of themselves in the future, and what they're doing is working toward the picture, making it *real*, and the ones with the same kind of picture'll marry each other, smart ones with smart ones and dumb ones with dumb ones, and they'll know other people the same as them and'll be in and out of each other's homes and swap partners when they're older and more bored, but still *belonging*, still inside the picture that they made into reality.

And where does that leave Burris Weems? It leaves him where everyone expects him to finish up—on a park bench, ha, ha! Even the fucking squirrels know what to do with their lives, but not our hero, no sir. Burris Weems gathered no nuts and now it's winter, Christmas practically, and Peggy's patience is wearing out, I can tell. She'd rather see me in a job, any kind of job, instead of doing the housework while she's down at the Wishee-Washee earning an honest buck, which she does every winter because it's too cold to stand outside the mall and sell those dopey velvet paintings she does. That's strictly a spring and summer occupation with old Peg, and she earns better money in the winter doing regular work. With that plus her veteran's widow's pension we make out okay, I mean the bills get paid and we don't starve or anything, but flunking out of school two times running means I have to go find a job after Christmas or I'll be the youngest bum in the Midwest.

While I've been yakking I've been watching this pigeon out in the yard. I put bread crumbs and stuff out there for the birds, and there's this pigeon pecking away with his little pinhead going up and down, up and down. Pigeons look real dumb because they've got these big bodies and little bitty heads, and this pigeon looks dumber than most because there's a cat watching him from over by the fence, and instead of flying away he's staying right where he is, pecking up those crumbs. The cat's got a problem that might help the pigeon, though, and what it is, he wants to get down on his belly the way they do before they wiggle their butt and spring at whatever they're after, but the snow in the yard's so deep he hates to get down into it that way. Cats are real finicky about getting their paws even a little bit wet and they shake them and shake them to get rid of the water, so how's this guy gonna cope with snow? He doesn't know what to do, the cat, and first he gets down like his feline instincts tell him to, and one second later he's up again with this real disgusted look on his face and his belly hair all hung with *wet snow*—yeccchhh!

Meanwhile the pinhead pigeon pecks on, and the cat's getting very frustrated, pretending to be uninterested by closing his eyes down to slits, like the sight of a pigeon feeding ten feet away is just the most boring thing in the world, practically sending him to sleep. He even looks away at other things in the yard, like he needs some visual stimulation to keep him awake, but really he's aware of every peck that pigeon makes, and he's trying to figure how to get the fucker without going belly-down in all that horrible white stuff. The pigeon is acting very unconcerned, even got his back to the cat now, that's how much of a damn he gives.

This is very interesting. Am I rooting for the cat or the bird? I could tap on the window and make the pigeon fly away, but I'm not going to. I'm an impartial observer. It's fang and claw versus beak and wing in nature's timeless drama, the struggle for supremacy et cetera. Uh-oh . . . the cat's gonna make his move . . . getting down on his belly like a sniper in a snowdrift . . . but now he's up again! He just can't stand it. Now he's gonna try again, but differently this time . . . scrunching his ass down in the snow but keeping his belly and front legs clear of the ground, not like a cat at all . . . his butt's wiggling now, tail flicking . . . this doesn't look natural to me. . . . He jumped! Again! The pigeon took off. It's all over. The cat jumped all wrong. He knew it before he landed. What he tried to do was leap over the snow in a couple of hops to get to the pigeon, but a cat can't be a kangaroo and he just ended up looking silly. He knows it too, you can tell by the way he's looking around. Tap on the window. He's looking up. Yeah, pal, I saw you make an idiot of yourself, you klutz. Go eat your Savory Morsels and leave the wildlife alone, whisker-face! He's not looking at me anymore, letting me know he doesn't give a shit. Now he's heading for the fence. *Booiiinngg.* Up to the top in a single leap, so there's at least one cat-thing he can do right. Ass and tail . . . gone over the other side.

You know what? It's a crazy thing, but watching that dopey cat made me feel better. Isn't that just the craziest? I feel *fine.* I think I must be one of those psycho types that has what they call wildly fluctuating moods. A few minutes back, going over all that bad stuff, I felt like shit, I really did, but now I'm okay again. Maybe it wasn't the cat. Maybe it's the Sony. Yeah, my Sony is a little psychiatrist. You just have to talk to it. Talk, talk, talk, that's one thing Burris Weems can do okay, with the right audience, namely me. Is this a case of split personality? I ask myself.

Nah, no way. You're just unusual, nothing weird about it.

Are you sure?

Sure I'm sure. Would I lie to you?

I guess not.

Let's go take a dump, Burris.

Okay. After you, Burris.

No, after you, Burris.

No, really, I insist.

Insist on a cyst on a blister, mister.

3

Peggy was in a lousy mood when she came home. A customer had her wash chewed up by one of the machines and said she was going to sue, even though there's a big sign on the wall that says customers wash their clothing at their own risk, so she's out of luck, legally speaking. But Peggy was pissed anyway.

"I pointed at the sign," she says. " 'Can you read English?' I said, but she kept right on bitching, a real head case. She overloaded, it was obvious. Naturally the clothes are going to get torn up if they're packed so tight the water can't circulate. I told her, but she kept right on saying she'll sue, she'll sue. She was just incredibly ugly too. Did you ever notice that really ugly people are generally the rudest, like being ugly gives them the right to be totally obnoxious for no reason?"

"Maybe it's some kind of twisted defense mechanism, you know, compensating for being ugly. *Over*compensating."

"Don't get psychological, Burris, please. She was a stupid, ugly bitch. If she comes back I'll tell her to take her stinking wash somewhere else."

She'd do it too. She can be very intimidating when she stokes herself up over something. It's a good thing I had her favorite chow lined up, which is chicken, or she might've turned some of the flame on me, not that I couldn't cope with it or anything. Living with Peggy you have to be able to fight back. She's a lot crankier now than she was last summer. I think that's because Mack, the guy that used to screw her on a regular basis, he sold his frame shop and moved to Oregon. She didn't say much about it at the time, but I figure he didn't ask her to come along, which must've stung plenty. So she's had a lot of problems to cope with just recently, her boyfriend taking off that way and her daughter getting married and moving out, which Peggy didn't want, and most of all her odious ingrate of a lazy bastard son Burris, the really big thorn in her side, practically a telephone pole sticking in her guts. So I'm only nasty right back at her when she goes too far and really asks for it.

I dished up and we started eating. No, I *don't* wear a fucking apron, in case you were wondering.

"Is this from Olsen's?" she says. That's a supermarket.

"No, Safeway."

"I thought so."

"What's wrong with it?"

"Nothing," she says. "Forget it."

"Safeway's chicken is just as good as Olsen's."

"I said forget it."

"Also cheaper."

"It shows, if you'll pardon me having an opinion on the matter."

"As a matter of fact, Olsen's and Safeway both get their chickens from the same farm. It was in the paper last week, all about how this chicken farmer, Biddle—I remember because it's such a stupid name—he's making plenty of bucks out of supplying both places with exactly the same chickens, but they aren't complaining because they both say Biddle raises the best chickens in the entire state, so they both sell exactly the same chickens. There's no difference."

"It must be the way they prepare them, then. Olsen's is better, but I'm not going to argue about it. I've had enough arguing for one day."

Incidentally it's all bullshit about Biddle and the chickens. I made it all up. I haven't got a clue where Olsen's and Safeway get their fucking chickens from. They could be delivered by UFOs for all I know. Mars Needs Women. Earth Needs Chickens. An intergalactic bargain is struck. Maybe they'll take Peggy to Mars and I'll get some peace.

The phone rang. I answered it as usual. When the phone rings Peggy just sits there like the king of the castle. I'm the dirty rascal that gets the phone every time.

"Hello?"

"Hi, I'm feeling horny. Would you mind very much breathing heavily down the line."

"Hi, Loretta."

My sister, the joker.

"How's things over at the asylum?" she says.

That's *my* place.

"Oh, about the same as usual. How's things at the kennel?"

That's *her* place.

"Crowded and noisy. Needs new straw. Is Peggy home?"

"Yeah, but watch it, she's in a bitchy mood."

"I'll be very unassertive."

I went back in the kitchen. That's where we eat, in the kitchen, unless there's something on TV we want to watch.

"For you."

"Thank you, O Gracious One."

I started eating again. Safeway tastes just fine by me. Peggy stayed out in the living room, yak, yak, yakking. She's got more yak than a valley in Tibet. Joke, ha, ha. Earth Needs Humor. I heard her say something about "the master chef," which must be me. Okay, lady, tomorrow night you get marinated breast of rattlesnake followed by crisp, lightly breaded, deep-fried tarantulas.

When she hung up and came back she says, "We're invited over for Christmas Day lunch."

I didn't want to go because Pete, that's Loretta's husband, he'll just give me a hard time about being a useless, selfish bum.

"Aww, shit," is what I said.

"I told her how thrilled you'd be. And don't say *shit* while we're eating."

"Shit."

The devil made me do it.

"Burris, I'm warning you."

"Okay, okay. Do we *have* to go over there?"

"Loretta and Pete and the kids are the only family we've got, chum, so be grateful."

"You go. I'll be grateful from a distance."

"Have I told you lately you sound like something from a very inferior sitcom?"

"No, I don't think so. You can tell me now if you like."

"The Noël Coward of Buford," she says, being sarcastic.

"Thank you, my dear," I said, very Noël Coward. "Shall we indulge in tiffin?"

"What's tiffin?"

"Beats me. Something English people do."

"Is it something sexual?"

"How should *I* know? I was never in England."

"Noël Coward was tutti-frutti, wasn't he?"

"An outrageous rumor, my dear."

I'm still doing Noël Coward. To be honest, it's the same voice I use to do Basil Rathbone, also Laurence Olivier.

"You don't sound anything like him, Burris."

"My good woman, who could possibly sound like *me*?"

"*Nothing* like him."

"How would you know?"

"I saw him in a movie, that's how."

"*What* movie?"

I think I've got her now. Peggy's got a lousy memory for stuff like this.

"I don't remember."

"Hah! Expect me to believe that? Boy, I could win every argument ever invented if I said, 'I saw it in a movie, only I don't remember the name.' Very convenient, if you don't mind me having an opinion on the matter."

"I *did* see him in a movie."

"Yeah? What happened in it? Bet I can tell you the movie if you tell me what happened in it."

"I don't remember except it had that tutti-frutti Noël Coward in it. I don't think he was even very witty. That's supposed to be what he does, isn't it, be witty?"

"Did. He's dead."

"I know he's dead, Burris. That's beside the point. The *point* is, I saw him in a movie so I know what he sounds like. Sounded."

"But you don't remember the name."

"No."

"I'm supposed to *believe* this?"

"It had Liz Taylor and Richard Burton in it!" she says, like she all of a sudden discovered $E = mc^2$.

"*Boom.*"

"What?"

"*Boom.* It's called *Boom.*"

"What is?"

"The *movie*. It's called *Boom*. Noël Coward and Dick and Liz."

"It wasn't called that. No one'd call a movie anything as dumb as *Boom.*"

"They *did*. She's a dying millionairess on this private island and Burton comes along and hangs around waiting for her to die, and Noël Coward was this guy that drops by for dinner."

"He drops by for dinner on a private island?"

"Yeah, by boat. *Boom.* I think it was his last movie before he croaked. Well?"

"Well *what*?"

"Is that the movie you saw, or what?"

"Maybe, but it wasn't called *Boom.*"

"It fucking *was!*"

I hate it when people don't admit I'm right. It really pisses me.

"If you use language like that at the table again I swear I'll put you outside. You do *not* swear in the house, you *hear* me!"

"I *hear* ya! You're only about five feet away for chrissakes! Oh, excuse me, can we profane the Lord's name in the house, or doesn't that count as swearing?"

"You can do what you like with Jesus, just don't go mouthing off with the other stuff, especially while we're eating. Do I make myself perfectly and absolutely clear on the matter?"

"Gee, I'm not sure, not absolutely positively. Would you mind repeating it?"

She looked at me like I'm something slimy and disgusting she found under a rock and says, "All those little neurons in your brain winking and flashing and storing up what Noël Coward's last movie was and who else was in it and what the goddamn thing was all about, and you can't even get through high school. Did you know American high schools are just about the easiest things in the world to graduate from, which is why this country's in such a goddamn mess, did you know that, Burris? The easiest schools in the world, and you flunked out, so don't patronize *me*, little man, don't look down your nose at your mother who *did* graduate from high school, don't you *dare*, you . . . little *shit!*"

I lifted up a hand and peeled out a finger.

"One—goddamn, but we'll excuse that." Second finger. "Two—shit. *Little* shit to be exact. What kind of role model is this that I should pay attention to what you say, huh? You tell me something, *shout* it at me even, and then you turn around and break your own *rules!* How's *that* for hypocrisy? And so *what* if you graduated. Where'd it get you, huh? Making change and sweeping up down at the Wishee-Washee Laundromat. Big *deal! Extremely* big deal . . ."

That's when she threw the bread at me, picked up the entire loaf of Dutch Crust and flung it across the table right in my face and slices went everywhere. We looked at each other with little daggers coming out of our eyes, shooting across the table like machine-gun bullets, lines of little daggers. I picked up the nearest knife, just reflex I guess. It was a butter knife. Peggy took one look at it and starts howling like a hyena, pointing at this stupid little knife in my mitt, about as lethal as a toothpick, and I started laughing too, it's all so crazy. I swear the both of us are totally psycho.

After all that weird stuff in the kitchen I snuck off and did some more taping to bring everything up-to-date, and I'm not through yet, because now I'm out taking a walk around town the way I like to do and I've brought the Sony along with me. Yep, I'm just a talkin' fool today, folks. Normal people take their dog for a stroll, but yours truly takes a recorder. Okay, for the record it's 9:32 P.M. and according to the thermometer we've got hanging by the back door it's a bracing 7 degrees Fahrenheit here in Buford tonight as I speak, and as I come around the corner of the house and go down the path to the sidewalk I'd estimate the wind chill brings that figure down to a tingling minus 15, so let's all dress sensibly if we're going out-of-doors.

I'm stomping along Westwood Drive through snow about a foot deep except where it's already been stepped on or driven over. There's whole stretches of sidewalk without a footprint, which just shows how people hate to walk anywhere unless they absolutely have to. People drive two blocks for a pack of cigarettes, they really do, but me, I like to walk, which is just as well because I don't own a car or motorcycle, probably the only kid in twenty miles that doesn't. *Crunch, crunch, crunch.* Snow looks so soft you think your feet'll sink into it without a sound, like into cotton, but it's crusty and crunchy like frozen salt. I've got the hood of my parka up over my hunting cap for protection because the air's really whipping along, pushing at me whenever I cross intersections where it can grab at me out there in the open. With the hood up and the bottom of it folded across my face and held there by Velcro patches you can only see my eyes. It's like looking out through a furry tunnel because the hood's lined with fake fur that cuts my vision to about forty percent of normal. If I want to see what's happening either side of the tunnel I have to turn my whole body because my head can't move in here. Also I've got on thermal underwear and thermal insoles inside my Red Wing boots, plus furry mittens. I look like Nanook of the North. No-Nooky of Buford, ha, ha. Incidentally, my Sony is tucked inside the hood right next to my mouth. Look, Ma, no hands! If anyone comes close to me they'll figure I'm talking to myself. Plenty of people already think I'm crazy anyway.

Peggy really had me worried back there. There's a couple screws coming loose up in the old attic for sure. Maybe it's menopause, even if she's only forty-one. Maybe not. Maybe she's just miserable and fucked up and that's what makes her so cranky. She's got a boyfriend that left her and a daughter that left her and a son I bet she wishes would leave her, ha, ha. No, really, she's got problems, I can see that, and one of them is cash. We'd be a helluva lot better off if I got a job. I'm genuinely ashamed about living off Peggy's money, I mean it, but whenever I think about getting a job and working alongside some bunch of dumb bozos that'll figure I'm dumb like them for working at whatever shit job they do—which is all I'll ever be able to get, not being a big-deal college graduate, not even a high school graduate—when I think about that stuff it knots me up inside, no kidding, and what'd be worse is when they figure out I'm *not* dumb like them because there's no way I'd be able to fake it, talking about the big game on TV and how we should do the world a favor and nuke the Russkies and Iranians et cetera. I mean guys like that are probably okay and all, probably treat their wives and kids okay and even wear Red Wing boots like I do, but they likely as not believe God looks pretty much like Uncle Sam and think America is just the greatest thing since female mud wrestling, all that red, white, and blue crap, and I just don't go along with it, not really, I mean I wouldn't want to live anyplace else, okay, but when they get out there on July Fourth in their Levi's and baseball caps with their kids on their shoulders and cheer the parade it makes me feel like a man from Mars. So I don't want a job. I couldn't hack it around guys like that, I just know I couldn't.

The thing is, so long as I'm not under direct pressure from Peggy to go earn a buck, I won't. I'm taking advantage of her, I know, but I won't stop unless I absolutely have to. I'm very honest about admitting to myself what a rotten stinking advantage-taker I am, which is probably a good thing because someone who kids himself about what he *really is*, is even more pathetic than me, frankly, but the trouble is, the pride I feel in being so honest gets kind of squashed by the stuff I'm being honest about, namely the raw facts pertaining to the way I take advantage. Who can be proud of honestly admitting he's an asshole? It's a real dilemma, Emma. Peggy and Loretta both nag me plenty, off and on, but not as much as they could, maybe not as much as they should . . . okay, *definitely* not as much as they should, and the reason for it is . . . they love me. It makes me cringe when I think about that, but I can't get around it. They made a very big fuss over me when I tried to kill myself last summer, which proves they always did love me even though up till then they kind of kidded me along like I was some kind of cute but pesky mascot they kept around the place, more like a couple of casual buddies than a real mother and sister. Yeah, they showed me how they really feel, and what do I do? I shit on them. Let's face it, I'm a real slime.

I'm on Timberland now, heading into town. Most of the houses along here have got colored lights strung up on Christmas trees in their front windows, or even on trees growing in the yard where the whole neighborhood can see, and they've got wreaths of holly on the doors and the kids have built snowmen and stuff, all the usual Christmas garbage. Boy, am I ever a Scrooge. Humbug! is right. You can't go in a store without having *White Christmas* or fucking *Jingle Bells* coming over the Muzak, and everywhere you look they're selling Christmas wrapping paper and ribbons, all red and green and gold, and those spray cans of fake snow for squirting over the Christmas tree. Who needs fake snow in Indiana? There must be a million tons of the real stuff piled up along every curb in beautiful Buford. I'm coming up on one right now, this long white sloping wall like you'd find along a new trench, but there's no trench, just the sidewalk on one side and the road on the other, with the curb and gutter completely buried. The snowplows push them up and people shoveling their walks add to them and they stay there till the thaw, with gaps kicked through them where people have to cross the streets and streaks of yellow down them where dogs take a piss. One thing I like about snow is the way it kind of sparkles under the streetlights. That looks pretty good I have to admit, and also I like the way tree trunks and light poles stand out against it, black on white like an old photograph. Snow is okay, it's Christmas that stinks.

I just tried to turn the tape off with my tongue. It didn't work. I read somewhere that astronauts have switches in their helmets that are tongue-activated, so that's why I tried it with the Sony, but it isn't designed for tongues. I'll have to take my mitten off and use my finger as usual. I'll talk some more when I'm in town maybe. Weems to Houston: From out here Earth is a big blue shiny Christmas tree decoration and the Milky Way's like silver tinsel. I'm looking for the plastic angel at the top of the universe. Nope, not there. My orbit is deteriorating . . . any second now I'll hit the stratosphere, then the atmosphere . . . things are getting hot, hot, *hot* . . .

See that falling star?

That was me, Houston.

10:29. I just now had a narrow escape. Here's how it happened. I was walking along Evergreen and wishing I could go in a bar and get drunk and forget what time of year it is, but I can't because I'm not old enough. I don't even look sixteen and a half if you want to know the truth, not even if I quit shaving for a few days. So I'm walking along and who do I see coming toward me? Only Sandra and the prick she's dating and screwing, that's who. If there had've been an alleyway between them and me I would've ducked in and hid behind the garbage or something, but there wasn't, and here they come, yakking to each other. Sandra's got on a red jacket with baggy sleeves, also a red beret. It looks great on her, the bitch, and prickface next to her looks good too, the bastard, with a ski cap and Navy surplus P-jacket and English boots.

They haven't seen me yet and there's only about five yards between us now, and I don't I don't I don't wanna have them see me walking all by myself but there's nowhere to hide, no alleyway, no doorway, just an empty wall to one side of me and the street on the other. Three yards and they still haven't taken any notice of me, yak, yak, yak, so maybe they'll go right past without seeing it's me, but I *can't take the chance*, so what do I do? I turned and faced the wall, stood there with the bricks a foot from my nose and stared at it, all the little flaky bits in the mortar and the bricks all chipped and cracked it's such an old wall, the back of the Farmers' Produce Market as a matter of fact, which has been there for around fifty years, stared and stared till I practically burned a hole through it. I'm listening with ears like radar dishes turned backward to pick up those two sets of footsteps coming closer and closer, muffled by snow, passing right behind me . . . I'm scared she'll stop and say, "Burris, is that you?" and I'll have to turn around and act surprised and say, "Oh, hi, Sandra. Hi. Paul," which is the prick's name, and Sandra'll say, "What are you doing?" and I'll have to say something very witty like, "Me? Oh, I'm just . . . looking at the wall." Please, *please* don't recognize me and stop and talk to me, *please* don't do that to me, Sandra . . . I'll forgive every shitty thing you did to me, dumping me and screwing someone more handsome et cetera if you'll just *keep walking* . . . *Crunch, crunch, crunch* . . . They're right behind me now, not stopping I hope . . . Nope, not stopping . . . going right on by . . . and I wondered why I felt like fainting, and found out it's because I was holding my breath, probably stopped breathing the second I saw them coming toward me.

Now that they've gone by without stopping I can breathe again. Aaaaaaaahhh . . .

"Did you see that guy?" says Paul.

"No," says Sandra.

"I think he was pissing against the wall."

She laughed, and I bet she turned around to see the guy pissing against the wall, namely *me*, but I didn't dare turn sideways to see, just heard her laugh. Then they crunched away. They didn't recognize me thanks to the hood. Why didn't I think of that before? All you can see are my eyes, and in overhead street lighting the bill of my cap'd put even them in shadow. I could've walked right by them and they wouldn't have known me from Adam. Why didn't I *think* of that! And Paul didn't *really* think I'm some bum pissing against a wall, did he? He must've just said it to get a laugh out of Sandra, the idiot. Well, he got one. She never laughed much at *my* wittiness.

I'm still staring at the bricks, like I'm paralyzed. I couldn't move at all, but I felt very calm about it, like the wall in front of me is the kitchen wall or the living room wall or my bedroom wall, all the walls I'm used to staring at and falling into a trance in front of. This could be dangerous, getting hypnotized by public walls. It's the kind of thing people notice and make remarks about, and I don't want people thinking I'm really crazy like Lennie the Loop who walks around town staring at stuff all the time, so I kind of cranked myself around and told my feet to start walking and headed down Evergreen like I was doing before I bumped into the happy couple. Jesus, of all the people to bump into. . . . Sometimes I wonder about stuff like that, whether it's destiny or something, bumping into people you don't want to bump into, or if it just happens that way because they happened to be walking along the street the same time as you, so it's just coincidence, just bad luck, and not something that *had* to happen because it was programmed to happen. I prefer to think it's coincidence, frankly. It'd be kind of awful if there really was this thing called the Hand of Fate that shoos you along like a rat in a maze with walls to make you go where it wants, this way, that way, around the corner and there's your cheese, ratface. Nah, there's no such thing as Fate. If there was, Sandra would've recognized me and it would've been real embarrassing. I think it was pretty clever of me to face the wall that way, very quick thinking on my part even if it wasn't strictly necessary because my parka hood covered my face anyway, I mean how about if it had've happened on a warm night when I didn't have a parka on, huh? Anyway, it's all behind me now.

So, where to next? The park, to see the Christmas tree I guess. I've seen it by daylight a few times already because they put it up on the fifteenth, but I haven't seen it at night with the colored lights and all, so that's where I'm headed now, talking into my hood where the Sony's tucked snug and warm next to my jaw. It's so close it'd probably record through vibration alone, never mind the actual sound. What time is it? 10:33. It's a funny thing, but no one's ever asked me how I got this watch, not even Peggy, which is just as well because I'd have to lie and say I found it on the sidewalk, or else say I got it off a dead man's wrist, namely old Gene. I think I'd lie.

I'll never tell *anyone* about Gene. When I get to heaven and St. Peter says, "Your old buddy Gene's waiting for you, Weems," I'll say, "Gene? Gene who? Gene Autry? Gene Hackman? Gene Wilder? I never met anyone called Gene. You've got the wrong Weems, pal." I wear the watch on my right wrist. On my left wrist there's a red-and-black leather band to hide my suicide scar. If you didn't know me you'd figure I'm left-handed because of the watch. I bet Peggy never asked about it because last summer she accused me of stealing a TV and I made her look pretty silly when I told how I paid cash for it when they bulldozed the Starlite Motel. She probably doesn't want to risk another mix-up like that. Peggy doesn't like to look silly. Hey, who does?

10:56 and there's the tree, all lit up. It's about forty feet tall. Okay, it's very pretty, very impressive. What more can I say? Nothing. There's bunches of people standing around gawking at it, not too many seeing as it's late. I bet lots of little kids got brought to the park straight after supper to see the lights on the tree, but they've all gone home now. I think I'll do likewise. Just this second I've started to feel very depressed about things. Directly after I saw Sandra and Paul I was kind of high, a delayed reaction to all the adrenaline that got pumped through me during the emergency situation, but now the adrenaline's gone and petered out in my veins and there's just the same old tired blood mooching along through the arterial system, bored as hell by the whole biological miracle, I mean it must've covered the course a few trillion times by now, right? Tired, wimpy blood. The corpuscles are snoring they're so bored with being inside Burris Weems. When that adrenaline buzz hit them it must've been like a flash flood racing through drains that two seconds before had just a trickle in them. But now it's gone back to being tired blood. I can feel it filling my feet, too weak to climb back up my legs to go through the heart one more time. I don't feel very good at all.

Time to hit the long and winding road that leads to my door. That's a line from one of Peggy's old Beatles albums. Whenever she's very depressed she plays all her oldies, I don't know why, it doesn't make her snap out of it, just puts her deeper into it from what I've seen. She sits there with a bottle of Southern Comfort and plays the old stuff, Stones and Animals and Creedence and gets drunk as a skunk, even sings along some-times, or tries to. Peggy can sing like a pyramid can tango. The long and winding road.

11:34. Almost home now, at the corner of Westwood and Crocus to be exact. There's Nonny on the corner, same as always. Nonny's a fire hydrant. Back in '76 with the Bicenten-nial it got to be a big thing around the country to paint fireplugs, remember? They got painted red, white, and blue so they looked like little Uncle Sams with stumpy arms. Loretta and I painted this one. She did most of it because I was just a klutzy seven-year-old. We gave it a red hat and a white face and blue and white stripes up the main section and red again on the screw caps, like gloves, then we painted the mouth and eyes in blue and there he was, this very patriotic little guy, and I called him Nonny, don't ask me why, but that's what I called him— Nonny, and there he is today, still with his red, white, and blue outfit, kind of flaked and faded now, and his red hat's piled with snow, his arms too. I bet he's been pissed on about a million times since '76 by the local mutts, but he keeps right on smiling, the dopey little bastard, and the smile stays there even when it's 101 in summer or 15 below zero in winter, smile,

smile, smile. Poor old Nonny. What the hell does he know? Smile and the world smiles with you. Unless you're a hydrant, in which case you just get pissed and snowed and rained and sunned on.

Crunch, crunch, crunch.

Up the walk to 1404 and through the door.

Home.

Message ends.

Update—11:49. Peggy wants me to help her at the Wishee-Washee tomorrow because there's always a big load of pay wash to do on Christmas Eve with people too busy to do it themselves, all busy rushing around buying last-minute presents et cetera. It'll be a real fun day, I can tell. I know what to expect because I've helped out a couple times before. Such is life.

And that's the way it was this Monday, December 23, 1985.

Stay tuned for our late-night movie, *Love Laughs at Andy Hardy*.

Love pukes on Burris Weems.

4

A very interesting day today, *very* interesting.

All morning I helped Peggy do the laundry about fifty thousand customers brought in, loading and unloading into the washers, then the driers, making sure the loads didn't get all mixed up, making change when the quarters-for-dollars machine broke down like it *always* does according to Peggy. She phoned the owner to come fix it, then says I can take five and go get some lunch and bring her back a burger with fries. I was out of there in around five seconds.

I can't stand laundromats in general, and I hate the Wishee-Washee in particular. There's this Chinaman painted on the front window, looking like they used to look before the Commies took over, with a long pigtail and a little round cap and his hands shoved up his sleeves and this big grin showing lots of buck teeth and little slit eyes. It would've got the Chinese citizens of Buford good and mad if we had any. And inside, the fake Chinese stuff is everywhere, the fucking *motif*, you know? There's plastic pagodas in relief on the walls and those fancy lanterns with the turned-up corners and tassels, which don't mix with the fluorescent lights, believe me, and worst of all is this totally dorky sign on the wall: WASHEE VELLY CHEAPEE—GETEE VELLY CLEANEE.

The guy that owns the place thinks it's A-1 terrific because it's all his idea. He's a big old guy with a wife that died a few years back and a couple of kids that grew up and moved away so he's lonely, Peggy says, which is why he comes on to her every time he visits the place. Peggy says he deliberately doesn't fix the change machine properly because it means she has to call him up to come fix it all the time, which gives him more chances to make a play for her. I don't know, maybe she's imagining it. She doesn't look all that enticing or anything to me, not since she started eating so much when Mack dumped her and went off to Oregon. Nowadays she's got this big lumpy butt that the whole world can see because she wears tight pants, but the guy that owns the Wishee-Washee, Mr. Blangsted, he's around fifty or so and I guess a guy that old and desperate can't be too choosy, so maybe it's the way Peggy says it is, with him doing his Romeo act in the storeroom out back where the hot air machine is.

The laundromat's on Covington, and just a few hundred yards down the street is a McDonald's, so that's where I went. It was packed like a lifeboat on the *Titanic*, but I got my order and squeezed into a seat by the window where I can look out at the wonderful inspiring scenery of the parking lot. All the cars have got snow on their roofs and trunks, but melted away on the hoods because the engines warmed the metal, and all the telephone and electrical cables slung overhead are spiked with icicles, and behind them is the sky, almost black, like the bottom of a battleship grinding across the sky.

You couldn't hear yourself think in there with everyone yakking and kids screaming. There's shopping bags full of presents under the tables and the tile floor's getting slushier by the minute from all those snowy, muddy boots. They put down cardboard sheets over by the doors, but it isn't working. I hated eating with all that noise pounding in my ears, but every place in town would've been the same, jammed with hungry shoppers and their kids. The lady at my table's got three little bastards that keep screaming and dropping stuff everywhere, more like animals than human beings, and she doesn't know how to make them quiet down and behave. A few quick karate chops to the backs of their necks would do it. Chop, chop, chop, and you'd have three very quiet, well-behaved little darlings with their faces resting peacefully in their Styrofoam burger boxes with no more squabbling over who gets the Ronald McDonald mug and who stole all the Chicken McNuggets when the other guys weren't watching, just three quiet kids. They're so cute when they're dead. No,

Your Honor, I don't call it murder, I call it justifiable homicide in pursuance of public peace and order.

I was almost through with my burger and just about ready to accidentally-on-purpose jab my elbow in the eye of the little prick next to me when I noticed this guy standing outside the window, practically with his nose against the glass he's so close. I figured he's looking for someone in here but doesn't want to come inside and look properly. He looked kind of familiar, dressed like a bum with a long overcoat and black wool cap and long, long black hair and a long black beard, like a pirate almost. I didn't recognize him till I saw his eyes weren't moving the way they would've if he was trying to see someone inside McDonald's, instead of which they're not moving at all, just staring straight ahead like a statue's eyes, and that's when I knew who it was, namely Lennie the Loop, champion starer of the Midwest. The reason I didn't know as soon as I saw him is because Lennie's been out of circulation eighteen months or more, back in the asylum I heard, and he's grown his hair and beard while he's away, I mean they were medium-long the last time I saw him back in early '84, but now he looks like fucking Rasputin! Even his eyebrows are shaggy and dangerous-looking. It's old Lennie the Loop for sure, doing his thing to a McDonald's window.

No one knows why Lennie stares and stares, but it's got something to do with him being a Viet vet. I heard he was a Green Beret and used to lurk in the jungle for weeks at a time, covered in leaves and mud, eating rats and monkeys and armed with nothing but a cheese wire. They say he'd sneak up behind the VC like a shadow and slip the cheese wire in a loop around Charlie's neck and pull the wooden toggles at the ends until the wire cut Charlie's head off. Lennie lived in a hole in the ground just like the VC did, and the hole was full of heads, and the jungle for miles around was full of headless bodies that made Charlie freak when he found them, his buddies and cousins and uncles all headless thanks to Lennie's cheese-wire loop. They say Lennie had to keep digging new holes for himself because the old holes kept getting filled up with shaved Cong heads, all packed in like coconuts with teeth, and when we got out of 'Nam, Lennie had to be sedated with a drugged dart like they knock over grizzlies with to tag them, and wasn't allowed to come to until he's back in the U.S.A. with his cheese-wire loop in his hand and this creepy black cape across his shoulders made from human hair.

He spent time in the army nuthouse before they let him loose to come on home to Buford, where he didn't get a hero's welcome or anything, just one day turned up in the street, this skinny guy with the staring eyes, and he grew his hair and beard till he looked like the kind of guy who'd hate what Lennie did in 'Nam, and wore his clothes till they wore out and never washed at all, everyone says, and he's lived all this time with his old man in the auto junkyard over on the edge of town and never done a lick of work to support himself, just lived on a disability pension the Army gave him. They also say that when he came home from the hospital that first time he found out his wife had been going around with some other guy while Lennie was over in 'Nam chasing Charlie with the cheese wire, and Lennie saw red about it but pretended he didn't know, and one night followed his wife and caught her and her boyfriend in lover boy's car and cheese-wired the both of them, then drove the car to his old man's junkyard and put it in the auto crusher with wifey and lover boy still in the backseat with their heads in their laps and pressed the button and watched the evidence of his crime get squashed into a block of metal three feet square which is now part of a girder in a skyscraper in Indianapolis. That's what they say. It's a terrific story. I bet it's all bull.

He stared and stared through McDonald's window, and the noisy little fuckers at my table noticed him at last and quit screaming and just looked and looked, and then other people started noticing Lennie and they quit making a racket too, and looked at this bum in the long overcoat and black wool cap standing outside the window until practically the whole place was quiet and looking at Lennie, and that's when it happened. Someone says, "Has he got a gun . . . ?" and a woman way over at the other side of the room started screaming before anyone could say, "No, he hasn't," just started screaming the place down, and that set off some more screamers and suddenly everyone's charging for the exit like the place is on fire, mothers with kids trampling over other mothers with kids and guys jumping all over the place shouting, "Has anyone got a gun! Who's got a gun!" and someone shouts back, "In the pickup! In the pickup!" which I guess is out in the parking lot somewhere and not a whole lot of use. "Call the police!" someone's yelling, and the girls and guys back of the counter are crouching down out of sight or else charging for the exit along with the customers. It was the most incredible panic, like something in a movie. Ever since that crazy fucker shot up a McDonald's in California, this has been a nervous place to eat.

I guarantee I'm the only guy that was still sat in his seat. I wanted to yell, "Hey, everybody, relax! It's only Lennie the Loop!" but I didn't say a word, and the reason for it is I was watching Lennie's eyes, trying to see if he's taking any notice of what's happening in here, but he might just as well have been looking across Grand Canyon his eyes were so still and calm. The thing about Lennie's eyes is he's got the kind of irises that don't have any color at all, just a line around the edge and the pupil like a dot in the middle, very unreal and spooky-looking, especially in a face like Lennie's. Just then he quit gazing across the room, which is two-thirds empty by now, and dropped his eyes, those circles of nothing, dropped them and stared straight at *me* . . . and it's like having a double-barreled shotgun pointing at you, no kidding. I couldn't speak or lift a pinky even, could only stare right back at him so hard it's like his face was coming closer and moving away all at the same time, that's the kind of eyes he's got, like diamond drills that bore into your skull and let in weird thoughts, for example—I thought the reason he's staring at me is because he knows that I spoke his name into the Sony last night, didn't say anything nasty, just mentioned him in passing, but I did it *last night*, and it's like that fact is written on my face and Lennie the Loop can read it there and wants to know *why* I was talking about him last night and he wants to know right *now*, and I better tell him or those diamond drills'll bore right through into my brain and turn it to mush like an eggbeater. It was very scary, believe me, and I only quit being scared when some guys came up on Lennie from behind and grabbed him and flung him down in the slush.

I got up then and ran outside. Three guys were sitting on

Lennie and frisking him for a gun. His black wool cap was in a puddle and I picked it up. There must've been at least thirty people stood in a half circle, watching Lennie get flattened and frisked in the parking lot. "It's Lennie the Loop," I told the guys sitting on him, but they didn't hear me so I said it again, and this time they did.

"You know this guy?"

"Yeah, it's Lennie the Loop."

"Who?"

"Lennie the Loop, you know . . ."

But they didn't know. Living in a town the size of Buford you figure everyone knows about a character like Lennie, but maybe this guy's a farmer in town to buy Christmas presents. None of the other guys seemed to know who Lennie is either, and they don't look like farmers, so it just goes to show how even someone as legendary as Lennie can go unnoticed in the crowd, which is real surprising. I figured *everyone* knew about Lennie and the cheese wire. The way I learned about him was, back when I'm in grade school, just a little kid, Lennie walked by the school yard one day and some kid said, "Hey, there's Lennie the Loop!" and told the story about the cheese wire and the VC and the car crusher. But none of these guys know who he is, and it looks like no one in the crowd heard of him either. I got annoyed about that, frankly. It's the kind of feeling you get when someone looks at a picture of the Pope or the President and says, "Who's that?" You can't believe they *don't know*.

"He a friend of yours?" one of the guys wants to know.

"No, I've just seen him around town. He wasn't doing anything wrong, just looking in the window."

"He was doing a helluva lot more than that," says another guy, the one sitting on Lennie's guts. Lennie's eyes were looking at the sky and he wasn't struggling or anything.

"He was just looking in the window," I said.

"These people didn't start screaming about nothing," says the guy. He's wearing a National Rifle Association cap. I bet he's the one that was yelling about having a gun "In the pickup! In the pickup!" I'm surprised he hasn't got it shoved in Lennie's face.

"Well . . . uh . . . yeah, they did as a matter of fact. I was watching him all the time and he didn't do anything except look in the window. He just looks a little scary, that's all. He didn't do anything wrong."

The guy shook his head, and there's this little smile on his face that says I must be a total idiot not to know what he knows, just some dopey kid that can't tell shit from clay. I hated him for that smile, I really did. That's when the cops arrived on the scene. They didn't have the siren on but the roof rack was winking and flashing, red and blue, red and blue. The cops came over and it's the same two that came to Crestview yesterday morning when the garbage truck smashed all those cars. The one that knows my name gave me a look that says, "*You* again?" but he talked to the guys sitting on Lennie, not to me, not at first.

"What's the story?" he says.

The NRA guy told him Lennie came up to the window and pretended to have a gun and got everyone panicky. Jesus, what a liar! The other two didn't back him up, though, just said they didn't know what the hell was happening, just knew everyone was screaming about the guy outside the window. The second cop started asking around if anyone saw a gun in Lennie's hand and a couple of women said they're positive they saw something. One said it was a pistol and the other one said Lennie had a sawed-off shotgun under his coat.

"He's clean," says the guy on Lennie's guts. Everyone talks cop-talk nowadays. "We checked him out good," he says.

Finally the cop that knows my name turned to me and wants my angle on the incident, which I gave him, and he must've believed me or else he knows about Lennie the Loop, not surprising seeing as it's the kind of thing a cop should know anyway, the local crazies et cetera.

"Let him up," he says. He should've done it sooner in my opinion.

The guys got off Lennie but he didn't get up. The second cop was telling the crowd to go on about their business now. The whole thing went and turned into a big nonevent. The guys that were on Lennie looked very dumb. Lennie still didn't get up, so the two cops lifted him onto his feet.

"You want to press charges against these men?" asks the first cop.

Lennie didn't even look at him, so the cop asked him again, louder this time, and Lennie shook his head once, the littlest shake, maybe an inch each way. The cop turned to the guys that tackled Lennie and says, "Next time look before you leap, okay?" The other cop thought his partner was being witty or something because he kind of snorted a laugh into his hand, and the NRA guy got pissed about that.

"Take a look at this guy," he says, meaning Lennie. "Would you walk up to a guy looks like that and ask him, 'Excuse me, you got a gun?' What kinda bullshit's that? *Look* at him. It was a citizen's arrest. I had a right. We *all* did. *Look* at this guy. There were women screaming and running around. . . . You can't tell me he wasn't doing *something*. I'd do it again. Wouldn't you guys do it again?"

The other two said they would, but they weren't pissed about the whole thing like the first guy. They just wanted to forget about it, you could tell. Nobody was looking at Lennie anymore, and Lennie wasn't looking at anything. The NRA guy kept on about citizens' rights with the cops, a real pain in the ass, and I went up to Lennie and held out his cap, but he didn't look at it.

"Uh . . . here's your cap. It's kind of wet. I'm sorry. . . ."

I don't know whether I meant I'm sorry his cap's wet or sorry about the way he got thrown down in the slush or what. I just felt sorry as anything, as if the whole thing was my fault, as if by speaking Lennie's name last night I kind of *summoned* him to McDonald's today. I don't know why I felt that way, I just did.

Lennie started walking away then, and cop number two says, "Hey!" but Lennie kept right on walking. I still had his cap in my hand. I felt like he'd rejected me, because he wouldn't take the cap. "Let him go," says the first cop. "Lennie's okay. He's harmless." So he *does* know about Lennie, which means he should've told the guys to get off his chest first thing, not waited like he did. Maybe he thinks crazies like Lennie don't care if they're sat on in a slushy parking lot and their coat gets soaking wet, all for no reason. Some example he's setting.

The NRA idiot was really getting steamed now because the cops didn't treat him and the other two like heroes. He even started talking about how his taxes supported a police force that not only got to crimes too late to do any good but also didn't appreciate the efforts of citizens like himself who tried to do their best to keep crime off the streets, blah, blah, blah. The cops shut him up by asking if he wanted to make an official complaint against them, which he didn't, because it'd be a waste of time, he says, so they just got back in their car and switched off the red-and-blue flashers and drove away.

NRA says to me, "You keep terrific company," meaning Lennie I guess.

"I don't even *know* him, and he wasn't *doing* anything."

This guy's a total moron, just won't admit he made an honest mistake about Lennie. The other two didn't want to be associated with him anymore and went back inside McDonald's, which was filling up again now, everyone going back to their cold burgers and fries, so there's just me and this guy left outside now. He looked real mad when the other two walked away, like they're deserting the ship or something, then he looked at me and says, "Someday your sister'll get raped by a guy like that, *then* we'll see." He really said that. He didn't know I've got a sister, might just as well have said mother or girlfriend, someone close you wouldn't want to see get raped. I couldn't say anything. I should've, but I couldn't. It's like this guy and me don't even speak the same language. He put another one of those satisfied, kind of pitying little smiles on his face when I didn't say anything, like he's just won a big debate without even trying, and he went and got in a Monte Carlo and drove off. So it wasn't him that had a gun in the pickup after all, even if he is an NRA member. I bet he's got one in the Monte Carlo's glove compartment, though. No kidding, what a fuckhead.

I got Peggy's lunch and went back to the Wishee-Washee. "About time," she says, and starts munching. I didn't tell her about Lennie. I still had his cap all wet and gritty in my pocket, so I stuck it in with the next wash to get it nice and clean to give back to him sometime. When it was done I didn't put it in a dryer. Never put wool stuff in a dryer. If I had've it would've shrunk down to something you could put on a pet monkey if you had one. What I did instead, I put it on top of the hot air machine out back so it'll dry through contact with the warm metal, not hot air. I gave that cap a lot of attention, even picked out all the long hairs stuck in the weave that the wash didn't get out. That cap is gonna be in good shape to give back to Lennie. It'll make up for things, I hope.

Mr. Blangsted came in around 1:30 to fix the change machine. He tried to look very professional with this big box of tools he brought in and slammed onto the floor like a fucking bomb to make everyone jump. Then he kind of slapped open the front of the changer after he unlocked it, the way a stable hand would give a horse a big hearty slap just to show he isn't scared of getting his toes stomped on. He talks loud too, Mr. Blangsted, so everyone'll know he paid plenty for this machine and it's making his life a *misery*, dammit! Goddamn pesky *machine!* A real performance, very pathetic. Mostly it's for Peggy's benefit, I can tell, so she wasn't bullshitting about old Blangsted having a hot dick for her. Even while he's facing the machine and tinkering with its guts he's looking around for Peggy, making sure she hears every word he says, probably hoping she'll think, "Oh, what a strong voice Mr. Blangsted has, so overpowering. . . . He's such a *man!*" What she says out the side of her mouth to me is, "If we could just get him to poke his dumb head inside the pipes he'd save a fortune on hot air," which got me laughing, and he heard and looks over at the both of us, very suspicious, like he's asking himself why the hell anyone would want to crack jokes and laugh without consulting him first, or at least crack them so he can hear them and give them a big hearty he-man's seal of approval laugh, which is no more than he deserves because he's got big fat arms full of muscle and still gets a boner every now and then even if he *is* over fifty, dammit! The poor old fart, he wants attention just like a baby. There's no one left at home to give him what he needs, so he's got to go to his own laundromat to get noticed. It's kind of sad.

Finally he fixed the changer and filled all the little chutes with quarters, then went in the back room to check out the hot air machine, which was working perfectly and needed him poking around inside it like the world needs a pull string around the equator to keep it spinning. But he didn't spend too much time in there because there's no one to hear him or watch him being macho, so out he comes again, and he's got Lennie the Loop's black wool cap in his big beefy hand.

"Who belongs to this?" he says, thinking it's a very original thing to say, very humorous, you know?

"That's mine," I said. "I'm drying it."

He opens the nearest dryer and throws it in with someone's service wash. He knew it was a service wash because of the name on a piece of paper stuck to the window. He wouldn't have done it to someone's wash who was standing right next to it. "Take forever to dry out there," he says, the big dumb bastard. He already had the dryer door slammed shut again, in fact he flung the cap in so quick the drum didn't even slow down, and now Lennie's cap is dancing around with J. Wolinsky's socks and T-shirts, getting shrunk smaller and smaller with all that hot air rushing around in there. You'd think someone who owns a laundromat would know you don't tumble dry woolen stuff, but I think it was just another way of showing he's the boss around here. I had to get that cap out fast before it wouldn't fit anything bigger than a shrunken head from Brazil.

"Excuse me," I said, and I opened the dryer door a few inches to make the drum quit spinning, but Blangsted slapped it shut again with his big meaty mitt. He's got these hands could crush cantaloupes, one per hand. He used to be a Marine. How do I know? Because the dopey bastard tells everyone at least ten times so's they'll know how proud he is of it. "Don't let the hot air out," he says, and he's got this tight little grin on his face. He kept his hand on the door, even if the glass must be pretty hot from all the heat on the other side, but maybe that's another way of proving what a tough guy he is. Blangsted is the kind of idiot who'd try to impress a date by holding his palm in a candle flame.

"It'll shrink," I said.

"Nah," he says, still grinning.

"It *will*. C'mon, lemme get it out."

"Hot air costs money," he says. "You know how much it costs me to operate these dryers in weather like this?"

"I just want my cap."

"Let it get good and dry, then you can wear it. You put a damp cap on your head you'll catch cold."

"Just gimme the fucking cap, okay?"

That changed his face. He's old enough to be one of those guys that think swearing is okay if no one but the rest of the fucking platoon can hear it, but swearing when there's women and kids around just isn't *decent*.

"You know, talk like that could get your mouth put in one of these washing machines," he says, very stern and squinty-eyed like some tough old sergeant in a movie. I bet he's got one of those little statues of John Wayne on his mantelpiece, or one of those plates you can get with Big John on them, the kind you see in gift shops alongside plates with Jesus and Kennedy on them. That's America's Holy Trinity—the Duke, Jesus, and JFK.

"I'm very fucking sorry," I said. "If you let me take my fucking cap out of the fucking dryer I won't do any more fucking swearing."

When I'm good and mad about something I can get very brave along with it, but only if I'm pretty sure there's no real chance of me getting involved in violence. I don't like getting into that physical stuff because I can't fight. I wouldn't know how to defend myself at all, frankly. You could beat me into submission with a banana peel if you were vicious enough. Old Blangsted wasn't going to punch me in the mouth or anything, not with witnesses around. He took his hand off the dryer window, probably had his palm good and scorched by then, the big idiot. I pulled the door open and waited for the tumbling to stop, then plowed through all the stuff inside till I found Lennie's cap. It was warm but still damp, so no harm done. When I got it out I left the door open, so Blangsted had to shut it himself if he wants to save his precious hot air. I crammed the cap in my pocket, because if I put it back where Blangsted got it from I just bet he would've knocked it onto the floor or behind the machine where there's around six inches of dust built up between it and the wall.

He's got that stupid grin back on his face now, and he gives a quick look around to make sure there aren't any women and kids close enough to get corrupted by what he says next, which is, "You're a fucking little pussy, you know that? I bet the only pussy you see is the one in the mirror." Blangsted should get together with the guy in the NRA cap. They'd be like brothers.

"Are you in the NRA, Mr. Blangsted?"

"I don't need to join that bunch to legally bear arms. Listen, why don't you help your mother by doing what's right. Why don't you do the right thing and quit pussying around, huh? Flunking school, where's that get you? Nowhere, and you know it. You're just deliberately pussying around because you can get away with it. She lets you, so you do it. You're a fucking selfish little jerk-off."

As a matter of fact, he's right. It's awful when someone like Blangsted is right about you. I couldn't think of a single thing to say, and he grinned even wider, the prick. "Just pussying around, wasting time, living off Mama, still tied to the old apron strings, huh, Burris? What a pussy."

I wanted to say something clever like, "Are you referring to the feline genus or female genitals, Mr. Blangsted?" But I couldn't speak. This guy really despises me, I can see that now, and how come he knows I flunked, anyhow? I bet Peggy didn't tell him. Someone must've put an ad in the *Buford Beacon*: "*Blot on landscape. Local boy flops again, unsuccessful suicide, unsuccessful scholar. Will be successful bum.*" I wonder how many other people around town hate me for being a useless flunker? I must've provoked old Blangsted pretty bad to make him come right out and call me a pussy like that, but *he* started it, so I think *he* provoked *me* to provoke *him*, if you see what I mean. He just wanted an excuse to call me a pussy. It's probably frustration because Peggy won't swoon into his arms and say, "*Take* me, you big lug." I'd take him. I'd take him to the top of the World Trade Center and push the fucker off.

"Pussy," he says again. He can't think of anything new. The situation was getting depressing, somehow. I wasn't even angry anymore, because what he said is true. I felt guilty as hell if you really want to know. All I could do was walk away and do more loading and unloading of service washes, which is what I'm there for after all. Blangsted had a few words with Peggy, then left, the big lump of hamburger.

Every time customers came in to pick up their wash they wished me and Peggy a Merry Christmas. It got on my nerves, all that Christmas cheer stuff, but I didn't have to tolerate it for much longer because the Wishee-Washee closes early on Christmas Eve like a lot of other places. At 3:30 we quit and locked the place up.

Peggy says to me when we're in the car and heading home, "What was Blangsted bending your ear about?"

"When?"

"This afternoon, over by the dryers. You looked like a couple of old ladies."

"Nothing. I don't remember. I was just being polite."

"But what was he saying?"

"I don't remember. The words went in one ear and out the other. He was probably telling me the story of his terrific life or something."

"He wasn't talking about me, was he?"

"Well . . ."

"Come on, I've got a right to know, Burris."

"It *was* kind of about you, in a way."

"What kind of way?"

"He wants me to make sure your bedroom window's unlocked tonight. He says he's got something to fill your stocking with."

She practically steered us into the oncoming traffic she laughed so much. "The fat old goat," she cackles. "He's got a nerve. He didn't *really* say that, did he? You're making this up, aren't you."

"No I'm not. He said he wants to examine the inside of your chimney, because it's probably all clogged up by now. . . ."

"Wait a minute, mister. Cut the dirty talk *right now*. He didn't say anything of the kind."

"I *told* you I couldn't remember."

"Burris, if I didn't need both hands for the wheel I'd swipe you, you little dirtymouth. What makes you think you can talk to your own mother like that anyway? You think any other mother in town would tolerate that kind of crap? I'm lenient, Burris, because I'm not some typical mother-type mother, but even *I* have limits. Don't you ever use language like that again, you hear me?"

"All I said was stocking and chimney . . ."

"And I know very well what you meant. You think I'm stupid, don't you? You think I don't understand when you use double meanings."

"Double entendres."

"Don't be so *smart*, Burris. To prove to the world how smart you are you need to graduate, which is something you won't be doing, am I right? Not only not graduating from college, not even graduating from high school. Do you know how dumb that makes you, mister? It makes you practically mentally retarded, the kind of guy who's lucky to get a job emptying garbage or sweeping up at the Greyhound depot, something challenging like that, so don't you *dare* patronize me. *I* graduated from high school, pal. . . ."

"I think we had this conversation last night. It gets very boring when you keep repeating stuff like this—"

Whap!

She took one hand off the wheel to do that, which is dangerous driving in my opinion. It was a pathetic slap anyway. It's hard to swipe someone who's sitting next to you. You need to be facing each other to deliver a real good slap across the chops. She had to backhand me as a matter of fact, and backhanding is just as painful for the backhander as the backhandee, because the little bones in the back of the hand aren't cushioned like your palm is. It hurt her, I could tell by the way she put her hand back on the wheel.

"Jesus, Burris, it's Christmas Eve. Goodwill and peace on Earth, okay?"

"Yeah."

"Don't sound so grouchy. You asked for it."

"Okay, I admit it, now can you *please* concentrate on the driving."

"There's nothing wrong with my driving."

"Hah!"

She really did concentrate for a little while, then she says, "I'm sorry I hit you. I'm a little bit tense. That damn Wishee-Washee is the pits."

"Yeah, I agree. Just in case we have arguments in the future, how about we carry a loaf of bread everywhere with us and you can throw it at me whenever I get on your nerves, you know, half a dozen slices for regular annoyance, a dozen when you're *real* mad, and the whole loaf on those special occasions when you want to strangle me."

"We'd have an astronomical bread bill."

"I guess so. Hey, we could use Wonder Bread! That's practically made of plastic. Reusable, see? You could pelt me with the same loaf over and over and *still* use it to fix holes in the roof."

Stuff like that kept her sweet until we got home. She was in such a good mood by then she even made supper for us both, but halfway through eating she went all quiet, and later on when I'm washing up she sat at the table and smoked a cigarette and stared at the wall. Like mother, like son.

Finally she says, "Let's go for a walk."

"A walk?"

"Yes, a walk. Let's go for a walk."

"Uh . . . okay. Where to?"

"Oh, just . . . around. It's Christmas Eve."

I hit myself this fake hit on the forehead. "By golly, you're right, it *is* Christmas Eve. I *knew* there had to be a connection."

"What I *mean* is, you and I used to go for a walk together on Christmas Eve."

"We did?"

"When you were little."

"Why?"

"Because it was *fun*, that's why. You used to love it."

"Did Loretta come too?"

"No, she always hated slippery sidewalks. Remember when she broke her ankle?"

"No."

"Well she did. I think she was five. She's never been confident in icy conditions ever since."

"When Loretta was five I wasn't even born."

"Let's do it, huh? Let's go for a walk on Christmas Eve like we used to."

"Are you *sure* I used to do this?"

"Burris, I'm not trying to *trick* you into taking a walk with your white-haired old mother . . . auburn-haired old mother, and if I *was*, which I'm *not*, I certainly wouldn't use sentiment to do it. I can't imagine anyone less sentimental than you, my little tin man."

"Wait a minute, is that an obscure reference to *The Wizard of Oz*? You know, the Tin Man without a heart? Actually he was quite sentimental even without it."

"What I *meant*, Burris, is. . . oh, forget it."

"What'd I say *now*?"

"Nothing. Forget it."

"Aren't we going for a walk?"

"No."

"Why not?"

"Honestly, kid, you've got this terrific knack for squashing a conversation with cleverness that isn't even very clever, just showing off. You do it all the time and it's *very* annoying."

"Well okay, I apologize. I don't understand what it is I'm supposed to've done wrong, frankly, but I'm apologizing anyway because it's Christmas Eve or something. Now can we go for a walk, or what?"

"You *really* want to go for a walk?"

"Yeah, I really do. You want it in writing?"

"Where did I put my big boots?"

So we went for a walk, Peggy and me, mother and son. We stomped and slid along for a while, with Peggy hanging on my arm like ladies do in old movies, only with us it must've looked dopey because she's a couple inches taller than me. But I let her do it anyway to keep her in a good mood. It's Christmas Eve after all.

"Another lousy night for the comet," I said. The cheery companion, that's me, always with something uplifting to say.

"It's a bummer," Peggy agrees, and we slipped and slid and crunched a bit farther down the block. "There was another comet when you were little," she says. "Seventy-two or three, sometime around then, Cooty or something."

"Kohoutek. Seventy-three."

"How do you know? You were only a baby."

"They mentioned it in the news a few nights back, said it was the last comet that was visible to the naked eye."

"Well my eyes must've been fully clothed, because I didn't see a damn thing. Halley'd better make up for it."

"Yeah, or you'll refuse to look at it next time around."

That got her laughing again. She'll be in a coffin next time Halley's Comet comes through this neck of the celestial woods. Hey, neat phrase, huh? Sometimes I do that, say something poetic like "celestial woods."

We kept on walking and turned up Benedict for a block or two, and that's where we saw it, this fucking awful abomination on someone's lawn. I haven't seen anything so bad since the miniature waterwheel up in Harland Heights that Lee smashed with his pickup last summer. What this particular abortion was is one of those nativity scenes, Mary and Joseph and some shepherds and the Three Stooges—excuse me—the Three Wise Men, plus cows and sheep et cetera, all about two feet high and bunched around this cradle with Jesus in it, and everything is *plastic*, but not only that, every fucking piece, every human and animal is *lit from the inside* by light bulbs up their skirts I guess, so the whole scene glows with this very soft internal light that's supposed to look very reverential and *holy* or something. How can something look holy with a light bulb shoved up its ass?

"Look at that unbelievable crap," says Peggy. She really got a kick out of seeing it, it's so incredibly funny, all that Christian shit. We stared at it awhile. Something that bad kind of hypnotizes you, no kidding.

"Look!" says Peggy, pointing. "Oh, Jesus, *look . . .*"

I saw it. A pink plastic flamingo over in the corner of the yard. You couldn't see it as easily as the nativity scene because the flamingo doesn't have an electric cable running up its leg into its keister. I looked into the other corner where it's dark, and saw what I knew I'd see. Yep, a plaster fawn sitting with its legs tucked under it, very cute like Bambi. I pointed it out to Peggy and she practically clapped her hands she's so worked up.

"I don't believe it . . . I bet there's a socket for a flagpole on the front porch so they can hang out the stars and stripes on July Fourth."

"Yeah, I bet."

"Burris, I think I'm going to be sick. I can't stand garbage like this. It makes me feel sick in a very real way."

"Let's go. I've had about as much as I can handle too."

We took a few steps, then she says, "No," and looked around us.

"See anyone?" she says. "I can't."

"Me neither. Why?"

"Get your ammo ready," she says.

"Huh?"

She's already squatting down, rolling snowballs. I got down and did it too. Boy, you never know the kind of fun you can have until you take a stroll around your very own neighbourhood.

"Coast still clear?"

"I can't see anyone."

"Ready?"

"Yeah."

We straightened up.

"Fire!" she yells, and we flung every snowball we had. *Splat! Plop! Bop!* Peggy got a cow and one of the Stooges, and I got a shepherd and knocked over baby Jesus' cradle. We must've made a heap of noise, because the porch light all of a sudden came on and the front door opened. "Run!" screams Peggy, and we did, bumping into each other, and I went down and she grabbed me and pulled me up by the parka and we went slipping and stumbling back down Benedict the way we came.

"Hey, you kids!" shouts some guy behind us. "Come back here!"

"Nah! Come an' get us!" screeches Peggy like a little kid would, and we both practically busted a gut listening to him screaming about how he's gonna call the cops, but we didn't wait around to see if he means it. We didn't quit running till we were back on Westwood and almost home again. Peggy had hiccups by then.

"Jesus . . . hic! That's the best fun I've had in years . . . hic!"

"We could go back later and *really* knock those suckers down!"

"Better not . . . hic! He'll probably be waiting up with a shot . . . hic! . . . shotgun. Oh, God, I've got a stitch now . . . hic!"

We kept moving, but slowly, Peggy with a mitten in her ribs. When we got to Westwood and Crocus I pointed.

"Remember Nonny?"

"Who?"

"Nonny, you know, the fireplug we painted, Loretta and me. That's him, right there."

"I remember. Nonny the little Republican, a million years ago."

When we got back inside we felt great. We watched a movie together and Peggy let me have a little Southern Comfort. When the movie was through we went to bed. I've talked to the Sony a long time tonight. It must be the booze making me run off at the mouth.

Merry Christmas, America!

May your plastic Jesus light up your life.

5

Christmas Day.

I gave Peggy a set of wind chimes. She gave me a bird feeder. She says I'm all the time throwing bread crumbs out for our feathered friends, so why not do it properly with seeds and stuff, which I got a two-pound bag of also. I wasn't very thrilled to get a bird feeder, frankly, but what did I expect—a Porsche? She liked the chimes I think.

> Twinkle, twinkle,
> Little chimes,
> You cost three dollars
> Less two dimes.

We got in the Impala and drove over to Loretta and Pete's on Moorland. We don't go over there very often. The last time was Thanksgiving. Pete and Peggy don't get along so good, the old son-in-law versus mother-in-law joke. Pete thinks Peggy's a real kook, "an old hippie-dippy" Loretta told me once, but she made me promise I wouldn't tell Peggy. Pete thinks that women old as Peggy should be like TV mothers, always fixing good stuff to eat and smiling at boxes of soap powder and always looking neat and clean, not slobby like Peggy. He hates the way she's always bitching about stuff, and swearing, and calling the President of our great nation Robot Ron. Pete voted twice for Reagan, so he hates that name. He's kind of conservative I guess, but at least he doesn't allow guns in the house. His brother killed himself accidentally when he was a little kid, fooling around with their dad's .45. Pete won't let his own kid have toy guns even, or a BB gun when he's old enough. He's got two kids by his first wife, Angie, who's nine and Chris, who's four. Pete works for the phone company. He's the guy you see sitting on the curb messing around with terminal boxes crammed with colored wires. He studies nights, boning up on cellular phones and all the modern gizmos that're going to replace the millions of miles of wire the system uses now. Pete wants to be ready for the future when it comes, jobwise. Enough about Pete.

We had stuff for the kids, a giant jigsaw of Yellowstone Park and a big picture book with dragons for Angie, and for Chris a flying saucer with wheels that runs around in circles and another big picture book, this one about fishes or something, the usual kid stuff but they liked it. For Loretta and Pete we had a bottle of Johnnie Walker—Red Label, not Black—and a fancy cake that cost around fifteen bucks, *very* fancy, Nancy. What we got in return was a *big* bottle of Southern Comfort for Peggy, practically a flagon, and a ten-dollar book voucher for me, "because you've always got your nose in a book," plus a fur hat. "Your old L. L. Bean cap is a wreck," says Loretta, and she's right. The new hat is terrific, very thick and warm with earflaps, like they wear in Siberia. It's not real fur but I bet it cost plenty. They could tell I liked it because I wanted to go for a walk around the block to try it out, but Peggy said, "Hold it right there, happy wanderer. You can test it later."

We had a big meal, the usual Christmas stuff, I mean we really pigged out, also a lot of liquor got drunk by everyone older than me. Finally I got a glass of wine, *one* glass. Angie and Chris had a glass between them, mainly because Peggy told Loretta it wouldn't do them any harm. Pete wasn't happy about that, but I guess he didn't want to look too straight and boring on Christmas Day, so they got half a glass each, which means I got only twice as much as these two very young kids, which was kind of humiliating. Then Pete must've decided he'll really blow Peggy's mind by being superliberated and gave me a Scotch on the rocks. "If it's good enough for Bogie, it's good enough for Burris," he says. It was very unlike him and I appreciated the effort he made to loosen up. Too bad it tasted awful. I drank it down, though, and felt pretty drunk about five minutes later. Burris Weems is a very cheap drunk. It was a friendly get-together and working out okay so far, not like I'd expected, probably like it was in a billion homes everywhere on Christmas Day. Angie caused a riot when she wanted someone to light a fart. She got told by one of her friends at school that you can set a fart on fire because of the methane gas in it, and she wanted to see it happen. Everyone howled over that, but no one offered to cut the cheese and show her. I made a mental note to try it myself when I'm back home. It's interesting that we all have this potential flamethrower in our pants. Road gangs could burn the brush back along county roads by igniting farts all at once, real teamwork required there I think. I was pretty drunk all right.

The Christmas gathering was working out okay because nobody mentioned the two forbidden subjects—Ronnie Reagan and me flunking out of school. Then bigmouth Angie lets the cat out of the bag. Maybe that should be the kitten, ha, ha, because what she said was, "Loretta's gonna have a baby," right in the middle of a conversation that had nothing to do with babies. She calls Loretta by her name, not Mom or Mommy, because Loretta prefers it that way even though Pete isn't crazy about it. The kids call him Daddy. I never called Peggy anything but Peggy, even when I was a little squirt, so it seems natural enough to me. "Loretta's gonna have a baby," was the bombshell Angie dropped, and right away Peggy and I looked at Loretta's belly, which is flat, so she won't look like a bowling pin for a while yet.

"When?" says Peggy, like someone kicked her in the guts.

"Oh, around August."

I did some fast arithmetic. Loretta must've dumped her pills on the honeymoon. They went to Florida. Pete's folks minded the kids.

"Why so soon?" Peggy wants to know.

"Best to do it early so my body can snap back into shape."

"It was supposed to be a surprise for later on," says Pete, looking at Angie, who didn't look very guilty or anything.

"Later on today, this month, next year? *When* later on?" Peggy doesn't look happy about the big news. Pete was pissed at her for not going all gushy and wetting her pants about the upcoming blessed event the way she's supposed to. Peggy never was a big fan of motherhood. She told me once that being pregnant was like carrying a couple sacks of groceries around with you day and night, and the actual birth is like crapping a watermelon, so you can see why she's not dishing out congratulations today.

"Was this your idea?" she asks Pete.

"To tell you today?"

"To get her pregnant so soon."

"It takes two, y'know . . ."

"She's only twenty-*two* . . ."

"Peggy, it was *my* choice. I wanted to do it soon so my body can cope with it better."

"This is just crazy, if you don't mind my saying so. You don't even have *room* for a baby in this place. The kids are still sharing a room and soon Angie'll want a room of her own. . . . It's crazy."

"As a matter of fact," says Pete, "we're thinking of getting a bigger house to take care of that particular problem."

"A bigger house? On one salary? You expect Loretta to keep driving a cab while she's pregnant?"

"I'll be quitting the job in a month or so."

"So where's the money coming from?"

There's a little moment of quiet around the table, then Pete says, "I'll also be getting a better-paid job."

"Doing what?"

"The same thing. In Phoenix."

Another little piece of quiet. Trouble's beginning to brew, Sue.

"Excuse me, did you say you're getting a new job in *Arizona*?"

"Right. Heart of the Sunbelt. It'll be great for the kids, perfect for a new baby. And there'll be a hike in pay."

"And when is all this happening?"

You could practically see icicles hanging off what Peggy says.

"Around March," says Pete, not looking very comfortable.

"Arizona," says Peggy, like they're moving to Antarctica.

"You know how I hate the winters here," says Loretta, who's looking worried. She doesn't want to upset Peggy, not on Christmas Day.

"They have snow in Arizona too."

"But winter doesn't last and last down there the way it does here. And the summers are drier. Desert air is drier."

"We're gonna have a cactus," says Angie. She doesn't understand that the big people around the table are squaring up for a fight. Me, I'm envious as hell about Pete's family going down to Arizona. I only saw a little bit of it along the Interstate when I was there in the summer, and I couldn't concentrate very much on the scenery or the lack of humidity et cetera because I was kind of busy disposing of a dead body and the dead guy's car, also having a nervous breakdown, but I can appreciate Loretta's point about the weather. Indiana is just too damn cold in winter. It must be even worse farther north, in Maine and New England, say, and sometimes I think people must be crazy to live up in Canada with the kind of winters they have up there. Indiana's weather *comes* from Canada.

Peggy's looking like someone said her house just burned down. She's very close to Loretta because they're two of a kind, both very sassy, and she'll miss her when she's a thousand miles away. I can see Peggy turning into one of those movie moms that're always on the phone to their offspring, offering advice that wasn't asked for and generally interfering, and running up a phone bill that always has the husband hitting the roof, except in our house there's no husband, just the roof. I'm sitting there saying nothing, watching the others, like I'm too scared to ask myself how *I* feel about Loretta leaving town. Okay, I'm envious about her heading for the sunny southwest and all, but how's it going to affect me? I mean I'm very fond of Loretta too, seeing as she's been a good buddy to me since forever, and when she goes it'll leave a hole in my life you couldn't plug with a skyscraper. Shit! Loretta's going *away*! Boy, marriage can really break up a family. All of a sudden I felt sick about the whole thing. I felt like I'm just a passive spectator while this stuff is going on around me, and Peggy's all alone, trying to hold back the tide, but she's drowning instead. Just a few minutes back she was all smiles and cheerfulness, mostly the booze I think, and now she looks about a hundred years old.

Pete went around the table refilling everyone's glass. I wanted to knock back another Scotch like Bogie, take the bad news on the chin and show nothing, but it was hard. Loretta's my *sister*. She was my sister before she was Pete's wife, and for a whole lot longer too. Pete's arm came over my shoulder, but he's refilling the wineglass, not the Scotch glass, so he figures I've had enough of the hard stuff, and I bet this is the last wine I get too. I wanted to turn my head and sink my teeth into his wrist, something adult and mature like that. It was a very strong feeling and I had to stop myself from doing it. I generally think of myself as being older than sixteen because of the very unusual stuff that's happened to me, but wanting to bite Pete made me see I'm not so sophisticated after all, which didn't make me feel any better. Some Christmas Day *this* is.

Angie and Chris got pissed off because the big guys were talking big-guy talk, also they had a gutful of food so they got bored sitting around the table and dragged me off to see the Christmas tree in the living room again because they think it's a very big deal. It looked okay I guess, with shiny, spangly decorations hung all over it, like Liberace disguised as a pine. "Terrific," I said. I already told them it was terrific way back when we got here, but they needed to be told again. Then they dragged me off to their room, which has paper streamers pinned up across the ceiling and those fold-out snowflake things, none of which we've got at our house, or a tree. At our house we've got the calendar turned to December and that's all. They showed me their stuff, the same stuff they always show me whenever I'm here, toys and records et cetera, and I told them how great it all is and how I wish I had stuff like that, which is basically what they wanted to hear, but really I'm on automatic pilot, going through the motions, easy enough to do when you're with kids that young who believe everything you say even if you're lying like hell.

I wanted to be where it's quiet so I could think about the big revelations that happened, but you couldn't find anyplace noisier than Angie and Chris's room. Maybe Angie's not so young, because she's got this picture on the wall of Blackie Lawless in his leather and feathers outfit with the buzz-saw blades on the sleeves, not what you'd expect a nine-year-old who still wears tiger-feet slippers to have over her bed. I bet Pete hates it.

Loretta wouldn't give a damn, probably think it was funny to see old Blackie snarling and sneering over this angelic little kid. It's a big mystery to me, frankly, how someone like Loretta teamed up with a square guy like Pete. But I have to admit she seems happy enough since they tied the knot, so there must be something about the guy I haven't noticed. Maybe he's got a big prong or something. To be very frank about it, I always thought she'd find a guy kind of like me, you know, a different kind of guy from the regular variety. Pete's pretty normal, I think, and so does Peggy. She told me one time she thinks Pete is "bursting with ordinariness," and "extremely average." I agree. Pete isn't even *half* weird enough for Loretta, but it's too late now. She's gone and married the guy and there's a kid on the way and the whole shebang is shifting to Arizona for a new life. She's doing it willingly, so I can't bitch about it I guess. But it hurts anyway. If I told any of the idiots at Memorial High I'm feeling sad because my sister's moving away they'd call me a wimp and a pussy, just like that meathead Blangsted. Guys aren't supposed to feel that way about sisters, maybe not even about a girlfriend. I'd get laughed out of town. Maybe they'd laugh me all the way to Arizona. Then Pete comes in and says we're going for a walk because "the gals" want to have a talk, just the two of them, so "the rest of us" have to leave the house. He looked at *me* when he said that, just to let me know I'm not supposed to go join the hen party going on in the other room, which I didn't like, because it's my mother and sister in there, *my* family, not his, and I should be in there with them to talk about this very distressing thing that got revealed today. But he's got my new hat in his hand, so it would've been pretty rude of me to tell him to leave his own house so us Weemses can talk together.

So the four of us got space-suited up for the great outdoors and went crunching down the walk and along Moorland to the playground, where Pete and I had to push the kids on the swings and tell them how terrific they are on the jungle gym, which Pete told them to get off after around ninety seconds because their mittens kept slipping on the metal, very smooth and icy. So they got on the spinner instead and we gave it a few shoves to get it moving. The grease at the hub wasn't frozen too bad so we got it moving at a fair lick and Angie and Chris squealed the way kids do when they're frightened but having fun too. When they had enough speed to keep them going a couple minutes more Pete took me to one side with this big fatherly hand on the shoulder which I had to keep from shrugging off, and he gives me this big talk about how it's a shame to break up the family this way, which is the understatement of the century.

"It's too good an opportunity to miss, Burris. A better wage and a change of scene, better climate. It's got everything. I can't keep my family from having a better life, and anyway Loretta's all for it too, you can see that. The problem is, Peggy doesn't go for it. We were pretty sure she wouldn't. You don't look too happy either."

"I'm okay."

"The hat looks good. You look like Ivan the Red."

I think he's confusing Ivan the Terrible with Eric the Red, but I didn't tell him. He already thinks I'm a smartass and a jerk-off as it is. He's never said so, but I can tell. No I am *not* paranoid, it's just that straight people like Pete don't understand people like me. Or Peggy. I think deep down he'll be glad to get away from Buford because it means he'll get Loretta away from her kooky family and everything'll be fine with him and her down in Arizona with the kids.

"You'll be able to see the comet down there."

"Well, maybe not from Phoenix iself. It's a big place, probably have too much pollution, but out in the desert, yeah, we'll get a good view come March or April, whenever the hell it's supposed to come closest. We'll go out and take a look, sure."

I already know Phoenix is a big town because that's where I dumped Gene's car, minus the license plate. That green Chrysler could be anywhere by now, or maybe it's still in Phoenix with a new plate and spray-job. Maybe Loretta'll see it around town without ever knowing her own little brother drove that car to Arizona with a dead man in the trunk and dumped the body out along I-40 somewhere east of Flagstaff, then headed on down to Phoenix to dump the car. No one on the entire planet knows I did that incredible thing. So far as Peggy knows, I disappeared for a few days and laid low with friends right here in Buford after she and I had a big fight. That's all a blast from the past. Forget it.

"You know," says Pete, "we don't like the thought of leaving while you still haven't figured out what you're going to do with yourself. Flunking out of school doesn't have to be the end of the world. You could always go back and try again, only this time give it your best shot. Is that something you'd consider, maybe?"

"No."

"That's not a very reasonable attitude, Burris. It's getting tougher and tougher to break into the job market without having graduated from high school at the very least. Pretty soon you won't be able to get a job delivering groceries without a college degree."

"I'm not interested in going back to school."

"But what's the alternative? You can't be a bum. Imagine what that'd do to Peggy. She's not what you'd call a regular mother in a lot of ways, and I don't mean any disrespect by that, but she wants her kids to succeed in the world just like every mother does. Unless you make some kind of move you'll disappoint her. You're all she's got left now, in a manner of speaking. You can't expect her to just go on supporting you forever, though."

"I know."

"So what's the answer?"

"Beats me."

"That's not good enough, Burris. You can't bury your head in the sand about this, and you can't take the other way out either."

He means cutting my wrist again.

"I *know*, okay? I *know* all that stuff."

"Well what are you gonna *do* about it?"

"I don't *know* right now!"

Boy, I really hated his guts for a moment there. The kids were watching us too. The spinner was slowed almost to a stop and they're watching me and Pete argue. They looked kind of shocked. Maybe they remember the arguments Pete and his first wife used to have. Loretta told me Pete's first wife used to break things, plates and stuff. Those kids really looked frightened, just because we're using our voices louder than usual. Kids don't like that stuff at all.

"You're going to have to figure something out, Burris."

I wouldn't even look at him, the prick.

"Sooner or later you'll have to face up to how things are in the real world," he says. He's right, but I wasn't going to admit it.

Angie came running over. She looks like a little Eskimo, all wrapped up in about three layers of clothing, so much it makes her arms stick out from her sides. She's got on a pink parka. It must've been chosen by Pete's first wife. Loretta would never dress a girl in pink, not even as a punishment. "Can we go to the park?" she says.

"It's too far, honey. We'd have to take the car."

"*Can* we, Daddy, *please* . . ."

She's acting younger than nine, just to get her way. This is the girl with Blackie Lawless on her wall? Now Chris comes over too, not wanting to be left out, wanting to do whatever his big sister wants to do. "I wanna go ta th' *park!*" Did I act like that when Loretta was my hero, following her lead all the time? I can't remember.

"Daddy, can we go see the tree?"

She means the big one in the park.

"You've seen the tree twice already."

"But not on Christmas *Day*. Can't we see it today, *please?*"

"I wanna see it *too!*"

"Look, I don't feel like driving all the way downtown, okay? The roads are slick. They don't sand them or salt them or anything on Christmas Day because the sandmen like to stay home and be with their families just like everyone else, okay? So it's not safe to drive today."

"Peggy and Burris drove over from *their* place."

"Only because they had to."

They all looked at me.

"It was very dangerous," I said. "We almost had an accident *twice*."

"Fibber," says Angie, disgusted.

I didn't deny it. I've done my thing for family unity. Pete can figure this one out on his own.

"Cut that out," he says. He doesn't want me thinking his daughter's bad-mannered or anything. As if I give a fuck.

"You want to go on the swings again?" he asks her.

"No."

He could've offered her a million. She wants the goddamn Christmas tree. It's a battle of wills. Nobody wins in a situation like this, I mean you can't give in to someone nine years old, and you can't just smack her in the face and tell her to shaddap! Not unless you're a total asshole, which I have to admit Pete isn't, not as a father, anyway.

"Hey, how about we build a snowman!"

They all looked at me like I'm a genius.

It took a half hour. Don't think you can't raise a sweat just because it's only twelve degrees. We scooped and dumped and patted and scooped some more until we had a snowman. To be honest, he was more of a snowlump, nothing like a man, nothing like anything really, but the kids thought he looked pretty damn nifty. Kids don't know shit sometimes. Anyway, it got them good and tired and when Pete says it's time to go home they didn't fight him over it, and a little while later we're in the front hall kicking snow off our boots.

Peggy and Loretta didn't look happy. All the good cheer that lasted through Christmas lunch had flown up the chimney, and the tinsel and stuff all over the place looked like it was put up for some kid's birthday party, only the kid ran under a truck on the way over here.

"I think I'd like to go home," says Peggy, and no one tried to make her change her mind.

Everyone faked a bit more cheeriness for the big farewell scene, and we waved like celebrities in a parade when I pulled the Impala away from the curb. Peggy was too depressed to drive. As soon as we're out of sight of Pete's place she says, "What a disaster. Was it my fault?"

"It was a big shock," I said, being diplomatic.

"Fifty megatons, kid."

I drove very carefully, about fifteen miles per hour. I thought Pete was bullshitting about the sandmen, but the street feels very slick under us. Then again, the Impala's got about as much tread on its tires as an old pair of sneakers.

"How do you feel about it?" I got asked.

"It's her life I guess."

"That's very philosophical, Burris, very specific."

"I don't think you need to be sarcastic. It *is* her life."

"I'm sorry," she says. Then she starts crying, nothing dramatic, just leaking tears down her face. She's getting these little pouches at the corners of her mouth, and the tears rolled over them and dropped off her chin, which is getting kind of flabby too.

"Aww, don't cry, willya . . ."

That was my big attempt at consolation. Burris Weems, he's so *sensitive*.

"She's only been married two *months*."

"Yeah. Quick work."

"Why to *him*? And then to get *pregnant* . . ."

"That's what people get married for."

"He's already *got* two kids."

"Maybe Loretta wants one of her own."

"At *twenty-two*?"

"You were only nineteen when you had Loretta."

"That's beside the point. I brought her up *not* to make the same mistake, and what does she do? She acts like some hillbilly who doesn't know where babies come from. She's throwing her *life* away. . . ."

"You mean her exciting life as Buford's only lady cabbie?"

"Do you want to see your sister disappear from our lives, Burris? Can you honestly say that's what you want?"

"No, but like I said, it's her life . . ."

"And look what she's *doing* with it!"

"She looks happy enough to me."

"But he's so *boring*."

She's not crying anymore now, she's so mad. Still another couple miles to our place. I hoped she'd keep quiet and let me concentrate on keeping the car on the road, but no such luck.

"It's my fault. I should've encouraged her to strive harder."

Drive, drive, drive, concentrate, concentrate . . .

"Are you listening to me?"

"Yeah. Hey, I heard a guy on the tube the other night, you know Benny the Bear who owns the Buick dealership on Oakland? He's got this commercial where he's dressed up in his coonskin cap, his trademark you know, and he's wishing his customers a Merry Christmas and a Happy New Year and thanking them for supporting his business in eighty-five, and he says, 'All of us here at Benny the Bear's have strove to do our darnedest to give you big buck bargains on our Buicks,' something like that. Can you believe it? *Strove*. What a dickhead!"

"Burris, if I might interrupt, what are you talking about?"

"You said you should've encouraged Loretta to strive harder."

"Yes, and so?"

"That made me think of Benny the Bear saying 'strove' in his dumb commercial."

She's sitting sideways now, looking at me like I'm someone she never saw before in her life.

"You don't *care* about her, do you."

"Huh?"

"Watch the road! I haven't got insurance on this bucket! And take that hat off, please. If I can't see your eyes under all that fur I'm sure you can't see where you're going."

"I can too."

"You're taking sides with them because you like the hat. That's it, isn't it. They've bought you with a silly hat that isn't even real fur. That's a very cheap sellout, Burris, *very* cheap."

"Huh?"

She comes close to flipping out sometimes, Peggy, and it looks like this is getting to be one of those times.

"Tell me honestly, do-you-care?"

"I already *said* so! Jesus . . ."

"That's what your lips say, Burris, but your voice says something different."

"What am I, a ventriloquist?"

"Answer the question!"

"I *answered* it! I don't want her to go, and yeah, Pete's ordinary but so what? What are we except a couple of freaks, huh? What's so wonderful about us?"

"Watch the *road!*"

"Why not leave her alone if she wants to be normal. Maybe that's what she was meant to be."

"You don't think that, you're just saying it."

"I'm not. It's true. When Loretta was with us she was a nut too, but now she's with a normal guy, she's normal like him and the kids, and it doesn't look to me like it's doing her any harm so let her *alone!*"

"I suppose when you leave home you'll get to be *normal* too. You're suggesting that it's *me* that made the both of you peculiar. Once out of my sight you'll revert to type, is that it?"

I was out of Peggy's sight five days last summer and reverted to a mental breakdown and suicide. I couldn't be normal, not ever. It's almost flip-out time for Peggy-O, gang. I just hope we can make it home before it happens. Flip-outs are best experienced indoors, away from the neighbors' eyes.

Soon as I parked in the driveway she's out of the car like it stinks in there and up the walk and unlocking the front door. By the time I'm out of the car and at the house she's gone and shut the door in my face. How's *that* for manners. She's sailing close to the edge, and it's only 4:08. I estimated she'd be totally flipped by midnight. I went straight to my room and got it all down on tape. I can hear the sound of plates in the kitchen. Chow time. Signing off.

We are back.

Supper was a very quiet affair. Peggy wouldn't look at me, like I'm not worth looking at. Okay, lady, I thought, if that's how you wanna play it. So I didn't say anything either. There's nothing quieter than just the sound of knives and forks. Total freeze-out.

I compromised a little by washing up without being asked. I could've just walked away from the table after we finished eating, but that would've led to confrontation, which I'd walk a mile to avoid right now. Peggy parked herself in front of the tube and I did the same, at the other end of the sofa. We watched whatever she wanted to watch, anything to keep the peace, Denise. But maybe I should've argued with her about the programs. It isn't like Peggy to sit there without making a sound. Maybe arguments would be better than silence. Usually when we're watching TV she makes remarks all the time, especially when she's drinking like she is tonight, really sucking down the Southern Comfort. She didn't offer me any, but she didn't object when I took a little nip for myself. Southern

Comfort is an okay drink in my opinion, definitely better than Scotch.

We sat there for hours. Peggy didn't say a word, and I didn't try to make her start talking. It gave me the creeps to watch her out the corner of my eye with her profile lit up by the tube, this profile that probably was kind of pretty twenty years ago but has gone all pudgy since from eating too much crap, also drinking too much. She's got a bottle of pudge on the coffee table in front of her. Finally I couldn't take it anymore and went to my room. I didn't say good night or anything. Why should I? She's the one that's gone into a trance, not talking and all. I'll talk when she does and not before. It's 11:36 now and the tube is still on out there, but not loud enough to keep me awake. I'm sacking out. Sometimes sleep is like escaping from prison. Your problems and nasty situations et cetera have to fly a holding pattern for eight hours or so.

This is Weems Control closing down for the night.

Out.

6

The day after Christmas has also been interesting.

I woke up around 10:30. When I got hungry enough I got up and went to the kitchen. Peggy wasn't around. I went to her door and listened, then opened it a couple inches, being very quiet. She's asleep still, snoring a little. I shut the door and went and fixed breakfast, breakfast for one, that is. She can make her own damn breakfast. Then I went out back and hung the bird feeder on a low branch and filled it with seed. I went back inside and waited by the window for birds to come flocking around, but they didn't show, I mean there's birds in the yard but they don't know what the bird feeder is because it wasn't there before, so they won't go near it, suspicious I guess. I waited a half hour for them to wise up but all they did was scratch around in the snow where I usually dump crumbs and stuff. Birds are creatures of habit and not very bright in my opinion, but it isn't surprising when you consider how tiny their brains are, like around the size of a pea or something. With a brain that size it's amazing they can figure out how to fly and peck and fuck.

I got bored looking out my window and decided I'd go take a walk. Peggy's still sacked out. I bet she has a real hangover when she wakes up. She'll be gulping down distilled water like she spent a week in the Sahara. She keeps this big plastic distilled water dispenser in the refrigerator because she thinks it's a surefire cure for a hangover, but from my observations I'd say it doesn't work, Kirk.

Sleep on, mother mine,
Your sanity is on the line.
Suck it up, then sleep it off,
uh . . .
With both feet still inside the trough.

Maybe that's a bit cruel. She's my mom after all, and she's got problems, one of which is me. Come to think of it, I've got problems too, and one of them is her. I don't feel like thinking about problems today. On with the new fur hat and out into the wilderness, my snowshoes leaving their lonely tracks across the frozen waste and the northern lights flickering overhead and wolves howling in the distance as the intrepid trapper traipses transversely across Transylvania . . . wrong country . . . goes a-lurching across Alaska? Careering across Canada? Forget it. I looked around for Mukluk, the Siberian husky that lives a couple doors down, but he isn't out in the yard or nosing the piss stains on the snow along the curb as usual. I wish we had a dog like Mukluk, but Peggy isn't all that crazy about pets.

I figured it'd be a good idea to go someplace high up and look across Buford, you know, a panoramic view of the snow-covered village, blah, blah, so I headed for the water tower, which is the highest point around. Harland Heights is almost as high, but that's way across town. The tower's only a mile and a half, stuck up on top of Crane Hill. I don't know why it's called that. I've never seen any cranes there. Cranes live along rivers, don't they? But I've never seen any down by the river either, in fact Buford is probably the most crane-free area in the whole of Indiana. It's a No-Crane Zone. Maybe someone saw a crane up on the hill a hundred and fifty years ago and so they called it Crane Hill. Pioneers probably didn't have a whole lot of imagination, too busy getting crops in the ground and so forth. Anyway that's where I aimed for.

There's fine powdery snow sifting down from the sky, so much of it you can't see the sky at all, just this grayness with white powder spilling out of it. There's no wind, so my nose won't freeze or anything, but every now and then I have to wipe away the cold snot that comes leaking out my nostrils. I've got a long hard streak of frozen snot along the back of my right mitten because of this. When it gets thick enough I'll chip it off. There wasn't anyone around. I bet they're all sleeping it off like Peggy, thousands and thousands of people all buried in their beds, the shades pulled down. They don't know that Burris Weems is stomping along their street on his way to Crane Hill and the water tower. Keep on sleeping on, gang. I like it when the streets are mine. Buford is *my* town today, and I'm checking it out while everyone else stays asleep like the people in the castle where Sleeping Beauty took forty million winks.

My Red Wings don't make a crunching sound today because there's a fresh new layer of snow over the old frozen layer, so it's very quiet, no traffic sounds in the distance, not even any planes overhead, just this whiffling noise my pants make when I walk. I felt pretty good gimping along the streets all alone, swinging the short leg a little to keep up a good steady pace and my breath huffing and puffing out in front of me like I'm a steam engine, the one in the kids' story that had trouble hauling the train over the mountain, The Little Engine That Could, huff-puff, huff-puff, I *think* I can, I *think* I can, but after I huffed and puffed it a few times it came out, a *fink* I am, a *fink* I am . . . so I quit thinking it. This little engine can't.

Then I got some company, this dog halfway along Walnut, a Labrador. He came up to me and started following along, sometimes dropping back to sniff trees and stuff where some other dog took a leak, and maybe squirting out a little of his own, about as much as you'd shoot from a water pistol with one pull on the trigger, then he'd catch up with me, even get ahead of me sometimes, sniffing and pissing and looking back at me to make sure we don't part company. We had a very casual relationship, me and the mutt. He didn't want to be petted and I didn't try. He just wanted to tag along with anything that moved, and I was the only thing moving in the whole town, it seemed like.

Then we started up Crane Hill. There's a few houses at the bottom, not too many, and the last one is about halfway up. You'd think property developers would've built homes all over the hill seeing as it's got a pretty good view, but they haven't. Maybe there's a city law that says they can't develop a hill

that's got a water tower on it or something, I don't know.
There's a lot of trees, though, and the pooch went bananas,
running around and sniffing like crazy, probably smelling rab-
bits, and I kept on going up the service road that leads to the
tower.

And there it was. It stands about a hundred feet tall I guess,
with this thick central column that swells out at the top to the
tank itself, which is something like a flying saucer and something like a hamburger bun. You could feed Ethiopia with a
hamburger this big, I mean it's *gigantic!* There's a catwalk
around the edge of the tank and spindly support columns that
go down to the ground seventy, eighty feet below. The tank's
at least fifty feet across, with millions of gallons inside that
supplies most of Buford. There's another tower across town but
it's nowhere near as big. This is the one, the tower of power.
You can see it even at night because there's a flashing red light
on top to keep planes away, also the whole thing is painted
white and they turn on these floodlights under it so it looks like
a giant white mushroom. There's a metal ladder goes up one of
the supports to the catwalk, and another ladder that curves
from there up to the very top where the light is.

While I'm standing by the chain-link fence around the tower
the dog caught up with me and started sniffing along the wire,
looking for other dogs' calling cards. That's when this idea
came into my head—Get inside the fence and climb the tower!
What a view I'd get from up there! I got all excited just
thinking about it. The trouble is, the fence is topped with
Y-brackets that hold six strands of barbed wire, hanging out-
ward and inward. You'd need a pole vault to get over, unless
maybe there's a tree around the other side that's close enough to
the fence it has a branch hanging over. In the movies there's
always a convenient branch. So I walked around the other side.
No trees within ten yards of the fence, just an access gate, also
made of chain link . . . but it hasn't got any barbed wire on
top! There might as well be none anywhere, because one
vulnerable point is all it takes for a determined thrill-seeker like
me to get over, and that's what I did, got over the gate in
around thirty seconds. Whoever built this fence should be shot
for dumbness.

Okay, now for the ladder. Grab the first rung and up I go. My mittens felt slippery on the metal, my soles too, so I took it slow, Joe. It was scary, but not all that dangerous, frankly. I made it to the catwalk easy, and stood up. There's a handrail around the edge of it and I walked all the way around the tank. The view was good, but not as good as it'd be from the top. I could see the dog still sniffing around way down on the ground next to the fence. I whistled and he looked up, but couldn't see me till I waved, then he starts barking his dumb head off, the first noise he's made since we teamed up. He quit after a while and I faced the next step in my incredibly brave and daring adventure.

I grabbed hold of the ladder that follows the curve of the tank's dome all the way up to the flashing light. It's not a real ladder with side rails and all, just these rungs like big staples welded directly onto the metal. I started up and right away my heart starts doing flip-flops inside me because this is *nothing* like climbing the first ladder, Here I'm completely exposed, like an ant on a melon. If I slip off these pissy little rungs I'll slide down the tank until I hit the catwalk, and if I can't grab that in passing I'll go right over the edge and fall eighty feet to the ground, and the dog wouldn't run for help like Lassie, he'd just fuck off home, and if the fall didn't kill me outright I'd die from exposure anyway. That what I was thinking while I climbed, not looking at anything except the rungs and the smooth white paint of the dome under my nose. Jesus, was I scared. My asshole clamped shut like the doors at Fort Knox and I kept climbing, climbing, climbing . . . up and over the polar ice cap, climbing and climbing to the North Pole . . .

The top. There's even a kind of mini Arctic Circle up there, this low rim of metal around the warning flasher and a thing like a submarine hatch with a wheel to turn to open it, probably so the maintenance crew can get inside if things go wrong in there. I crawled inside the circle with my arms and legs shaking like I've got a fever. I took hold of the hatch wheel to steady myself and pulled my hat off to let the cold air at my scalp. The light was flashing on and off, on and off. They leave it turned on all the time so a plane doesn't crash into the tower on a snowy day like today. It's two feet tall, a red plastic drum with a metal top and two lenses inside like the flashers on a cop car, turning around and around. It's powerful, with plenty of candlepower, strong enough to turn my parka and mittens red every two seconds, like they're on fire. My head got cold pretty fast because of how short my hair is, so I put the hat on again, and after I finally quit shaking I looked around.

If it hadn't been snowing I could've seen clear across town, but I couldn't see even a third that distance with all this whiteness in the air, and when I got up the nerve to stand, the view didn't improve all that much. Buford looked like a toy town being dusted with talcum powder. The only sound was a very faint whining from the little electric motor inside the beacon that keeps the lenses turning. I'm the tallest kid in town, even if I'm only five foot three. I felt like the king of the mountain looking down on his frozen kingdom. I am the eye in the sky. My subjects are all asleep. I'll wake them up when I feel like it. Me, I don't need sleep like ordinary mortals. I stand here always, watching, day and night, rain or shine, sleet or snow, it doesn't matter to me because standing and watching is what I'm here for. It's what I *do*. It's a lonely occupation. Loneliness comes with the job, Bob. It's the price you pay for standing on top of the tower of power. I can hack it, no sweat. There's really nothing I can't do. I'm standing on top of a giant mushroom filled with water, a mushroom so tall it's got a light on top to keep planes away. I sat on the light. Now it's my throne. No one ever had a throne like this before, a flashing red throne on the tower of power. I felt like I could stretch out my hand and blast a hole in the sky, punch a funnel up through the falling snow and let down a cylinder of golden light from way up above the clouds, up where the sun is, and everyone in the cylinder of light would wake up, only somehow they'd be different from the way they were when they fell asleep last night. They'd know things they didn't know before, and their lives would be changed forever.

Am I a weird guy or what? How come I think these crazy things? I'm Burris Weems, town gimp and flunk-out, and I'm on the municipal water tank, that's all. I can't even change a buck, never mind people's lives. It's sad but true. I'm nothing and nobody. The king of the mountain on his flashing red throne on the tower of power can't even rustle up a date. So much for high office. Still, I'm glad I came up here. How many other guys ever sat where I'm sitting, huh? Not too damn many I bet. I decided I'd leave my mark there the way kids do on highway flyovers, spraying their street names and love messages et cetera. I didn't have a spray can with me, but I had a pocketknife, the one with the yellow handle that used to be Gene's. I carry it around with me all the time because you never know when a blade'll come in handy, Randy. This'll be the first time I've used it since I cut my wrist with it last July. Some people might think it's kind of sick for me to be carrying around the same knife I tried to kill myself with, but it's too good a knife to just throw away, and who could I give it to as a present? Besides, I'm sentimental about stuff that belonged to Gene. I've got his knife and his watch, and back home in my room I've got his shades. These things are important to me. I got out the knife and opened the big blade, thicker and stronger than the little blade, and scratched my initials into the metal base of the light, then the date—December 26, 1985. It was hard work, and you'd need a spotlight to see what I've done, the letters are so small, but I don't care. *I'll* always know it's there even if no one else does.

I stayed there awhile longer, starting to feel cold because I'm not moving around enough, just staring across town and feeling kind of sad for some reason. I didn't want to think about climbing back down the ladders, and I didn't want to think about going home. I didn't want to think about anything. I just wanted to sit and stare out across Buford, just stare and stare like I'm facing the biggest wall in the world, even if I'm sat on the highest, most open perch in the entire county. I felt like staying up there forever, sitting on the light, getting colder and colder and gradually getting covered with snow and dying right there, frozen solid like a statue, the king on his throne. They'd have to chip me out with jackhammers, or else wait till spring.

Then I thought maybe I better get down off there before I really do get too cold to function, I mean if my fingers can't grip the rungs I'll be killed. I didn't want that. If I'm gonna die young I want it to happen where everyone can see, none of this lonely death crap, so it's down the ladders for yours truly while

I can still do it. As a matter of fact I was *freezing* by then, also very hungry. It's way past lunchtime after all.

I got down, no problem, and climbed back over the gate easy as can be. The dog wasn't around. I whistled but he was gone. I started back down the service road, and when I got to the bottom of Crane Hill there's the dog in someone's yard. When he saw me he started following me back the way we came, along Walnut. He followed and followed, and when we got to the place where we originally met I expected him to quit following, but he didn't, just kept right on padding along next to me or behind me or ahead of me. A couple times I told him to go home, but no dice, he kept on doing what he wants to do, the kind of mutt that doesn't respond to orders. I could've screamed at him and waved my arms to make him go away but that would've made me look stupid, so I let him follow me all the way home. I ignored him, thinking he'd get pissed off with getting no attention and head back toward his own place, but it didn't happen and like I said, he came all the way home with me. By the time we got to 1404 Westwood Drive he was practically stepping on my heels. What to do? I'm the kind of guy who feels responsible for anything I get mixed up in. This dog doesn't know shit about direction, so if I went inside and forgot about him he'd just wander around the neighborhood, totally lost, so I had to do something. That's when I saw the tag on his collar. I took a close look. He held still so I could read the address etched on it. Why didn't I see this before? He lives way over on Chester, nowhere near where I first saw him, so he was probably already lost, the dopey bastard.

I brought him inside so he wouldn't wander off. Peggy was out of bed at last, dressed even. She took one look at the dog and says, "No."

"I don't wanna keep him, just drive him home. Can I have the keys?"

"You want to drive a dog home?"

"Yeah."

"What's the matter, wouldn't put out on the first date?"

She thought that was just terrifically funny. Still, at least she's talking again. I got the keys and took the pooch back outside. When I opened the passenger door he jumped right in.

He even sat on the seat, like he *owns* the goddamn car. I fired up the engine and backed out, then drove very slowly over to Chester. The dog sat there looking out the front window, probably enjoying the ride, who can read a dog's face? When I got to his number, 1736, I parked and let him out. He knew where he was right away and went around back of the house. Did I wait around for thanks from his grateful owners? I did not, just left a silver bullet on the curb and drove away.

I decided now that I'm in the car and the engine's all warmed up and running smooth I'd take a little spin around town before I go home and eat, so I did that for a while, then the snow started coming down thicker, big flakes drifting down like chunks of cotton candy. Enough is enough. These are not good driving conditions. So I headed for home, concentrating very hard on the road even if there's no other traffic around, just a whirling whiteness ahead of me, when I heard this sound, *whump!* very close behind me, so I swung over to the curb and *whump!* it happened again, and *whump!* a third time. I killed the motor and got out to see what the fuck made those three explosions, and back along Champlin, which is the street I'm on, is this telephone pole with three of those big gray cylinders about the size of garbage cans on a platform way up near the top, transformers or whatever, and all of them had flipped their lids and were on fire, the top of the pole too. It was a very unreal thing to see, some kind of short-out I guess from icicles or snow, I don't know about electrical stuff, but the canisters and pole were really flaring up, and people were coming out of their houses to see what happened.

I went back to grab an eyeful along with the rest, and that's when I saw Lennie the Loop. He doesn't live around here so he must've been just passing by when the pole blew, same as me. I drove right past without seeing him on the sidewalk, I was concentrating so hard. He's standing there in his long overcoat with his black hair hanging down his back, staring up at the pole like Moses getting a message from the burning bush, and for once he's staring at something worth staring at. His head's covered in snowflakes, which reminded me I've still got his wool cap at home, all clean and dry and ready to give back, but frankly I'd forgotten all about it, what with that stuff about

Loretta leaving town and Peggy going catatonic last night and all.

"Keep away!" some guy shouts. "The wires'll melt and come down! Stay back!"

Everyone except Lennie did the smart thing and kept their distance, but not him, no sir, he stayed right where he was with this kind of enraptured look on his face, the part you can actually see above his mustache and beard, his head thrown way back and his face turned up to the sky so he can see that burning pole all he wants, and even though there's snow falling down in his face his *eyes don't blink*, I swear they don't, which is very creepy. I'm the closest to him and I didn't see him blink those ice-chip eyes even once. People are screaming at him to get out from under the wires now that they're smoking like crazy, melting away where they join the insulators on the cross-bars, which are burning like yuletide logs. I don't know if it's dumbness or a death wish that kept him there. People kept yelling at him but he acted like he can't hear a thing, like he's inside a bubble or something.

"Hey, Lennie!"

That got through. He quit looking up and turned to see who knows his name.

"The wires are coming down, Lennie. You'll get burned."

He stared at me like I'm a lobster with a top hat.

"C'mon, Lennie, move it, willya!"

He's still right where he was when I first saw him. This guy wouldn't budge for a Mack truck. What a crazy fucker! This lady is pushing me and saying, "Go get him, go *get* him." So I did, I went and got him, stepped right over and grabbed his sleeve.

"C'mon, Lennie. It's *dangerous*, you know?"

He pulled his sleeve out of my hand by turning his whole body around and walking away up Champlin in the direction I've got the Impala parked. I didn't wait around, just followed right along. I didn't want to lose him now, not after I actually *touched* him. I didn't even look to see if the crowd that's gathered around is watching us, or if the wires are coming down or anything, I only focused on one thing, the back of Lennie's coat with all that long black hair hanging down over his shoulders, speckled with snowflakes like the world's worst case of dandruff. I ran a few steps and caught up. Now I'm side by side with Lennie the Loop.

"Hey, Lennie, I've still got your cap. I cleaned it up for you. I've got my mom's car right here. We could go to my place and pick it up and then I'll give you a lift home. Boy, that pole's really something, huh? I bet it malfunctioned with the ice and all. Stuff like that happens every winter. This is the car, right here . . ."

But he kept on walking. He never once turned sideways to look at me while I was talking, and he isn't turning around now to see the car I offered him a lift in. He just kept walking, heading into the snowfall like Rasputin aiming for Siberia or someplace. What a fucking ungrateful prick! I could've got myself fried by electricity, going over and grabbing his sleeve that way. I probably saved him from the same thing. What a total asshole! I hope the snow on his dumb head gives him a cold that turns to pneumonia and he dies coughing gobs of yellow crap into a rusty tin cup, the arrogant fuckhead! Who the fuck does he think he *is*, anyway, some fucking king in disguise who's wandering around checking out how the peasants live? Well fuck *you*, pal! I hope you walk under a snowplow, you mental bastard! That's the kind of stuff I thought, watching him walk away. I could hear sirens by then, fire trucks racing to the scene of the blaze. Some fucking fire—the top of a single telephone pole. I was so mad about the way Lennie treated me I didn't even wait around to watch the firemen do their thing, just got in the car and drove home, muttering in my head about how he's a stupid fucking moron that doesn't even have enough brains to get out from under melting wires, the conehead.

"Deliver the dog?" Peggy asked when I came in.

"Yeah."

"There's a fire somewhere, I could hear the sirens. Did you see anything?"

"No."

"Probably someone's gas heater exploded. That happens every year."

"I guess."

"What's that look for?"

"What look?"

"Like you peed on your boots and found out they're sandals."

She laughed. That's the second time today she's laughed at her own joke. Last night she wouldn't say Boo, but today it's Dial-a-Yuk, and it means she needs professional help. Anyone who changes so fast is shifting too much furniture around in the attic, definitely. The smart thing to do is humor her, keep her smiling. Frankly, I prefer this kind of craziness to the silent kind.

I had a real bad gut-ache from not having any lunch. I fixed it with two giant ham sandwiches, then went to my room to see if those idiot birds discovered the bird feeder yet. Well, they hadn't, but the squirrels had, three of them. They hung on to the feeder's roof with their back legs and reached down to grab the seeds out of the tray, being very messy about it. They didn't want *all* the seeds, just the sunflower seeds, so everything else got dumped into the snow. They didn't give a fuck, just kept on scratching through the tray and scattering seeds everywhere until they found the ones they wanted, and they didn't even want to share with each other, the greedy little fuckers. They kept trying to scare each other off, and there was one that's smaller than the other two that probably wouldn't get much bigger, not unless they let him eat more. They're probably a family, but did they treat each other decently? No way, none of that all-squirrels-together attitude you'd expect them to show, nothing like it, just every squirrel for himself. Squirrels are a very low rodent in my opinion. If I had've been Noah I would've gotten them over to a porthole with some bullshit story about a secret store of seeds, then grabbed the little bastards and thrown them out into the flood. Oh my goodness, what a calamity! The squirrels have fallen overboard! Now there'll be no squirrels in the world. Dear me, what a terrible thing. Oh well, all the more room for monkeys.

I did some more taping to bring things up-to-date. Now it's evening. The squirrels have fucked off back into the trees. I'm hungry again. The refrigerator is calling me . . . food, *food!* I must have *food*, I tell you! Gimme some *food!*

"Burris!"

Peggy, right outside my door . . .

"Yeah?"

"What are you screaming about in there?"

"Nothing."

"What?"

"Nothing!"

"They have special places for people who scream about nothing, Burris."

She laughed, then went away. That's *three* times today. This is crazy. I bet she'd laugh her head off if I told her why the chicken crossed the road. It must be some kind of delayed hysterical reaction to being so miserable yesterday, but like I said before, a laughing mental case is better than a silent one, so I'm not complaining.

7

Today is the twenty-seventh. *Was*, I should say, seeing as it's just after midnight now. It was a Friday, but it didn't seem like one because most people didn't work today. Why go to work for just one day between the day after Christmas and Saturday? After breakfast I asked Peggy how come she hasn't hung up the wind chimes yet, and she says, "Wind chimes?" I hated her guts for a few seconds, then told myself she's not normal so it's dumb for me to get insulted because she forgot all about her Christmas present. I went and hung them up myself, out on the back porch so I can hear them from my room. There was a little breeze blowing and the chimes went *ting! ping! tong!* like they're supposed to. The squirrels didn't give a shit. They've already emptied most of the seed from the feeder onto the ground. What I think I'll have to do is get a second feeder and fill it with just sunflower seeds, so the squirrels will leave the first feeder, the one with mixed seed, alone. The seed on the ground'll go rotten before the local birds figure out they can eat it, that it isn't all split sunflower kernels down there in the snow. We can't afford that kind of waste at the Weems household.

Afternoon rolled around. I already put up the wind chimes and refilled the feeder so I had nothing to do. Peggy turned the TV on and sat there flicking from channel to channel, a few seconds here, a minute or so there, flick, flick, flick, back and forth. I can't stand it when she does that. She isn't really watching anything, just killing time with the tube, waiting for the day to go by. It's very depressing to see her do this. So far today she hasn't cracked a single joke, which could mean she's going off the deep end again. I could tell she wanted to be by herself. You can tell stuff like that if you share a house with someone for a long time. There's this message going from her head into my ear, *dit dit dit, dot dot dot*—Burris-I-would-like-to-be-alone-like-Greta-Garbo-so-please-go-away-thank-you.

"Can I have the keys?"

"Going somewhere?"

"No, I just thought I'd keep them warm in my pocket, you know."

"On top of the fridge. Don't burn all the gas."

I went and got Lennie the Loop's cap from my room. I'm gonna take it to Lennie's place and put it in his ungrateful hand, the creepo craphead. That's what kind of day it is, the kind when you have to do desperate stuff like this just to kill time and keep out of your own mom's way so she can become clinically depressed in the privacy of her own home and not have number-one son interrupting her chain of depressing thought. 'Tis the season to be jolly.

Today it wasn't snowing, not like yesterday. I drove over to the auto junkyard, way over on the edge of town next to the railroad tracks. That's where auto junkyards always are. It's practically a tradition. I guess you wouldn't want an eyesore like that in the middle of town. It covers a couple of acres, with a chain-link fence all around. Inside is about a million junked autos, all kinds, going way back to the sixties when everything was long and flat and wide and had chrome trim along the sides. They're stacked up four and five deep with their windows smashed out and their wheels gone, getting older and rustier, stacked up on top of each other like metal pancakes with a heavy sprinkling of sugar snow on top. Across the yard you can see the big crane they use to pick up the bodies and dump them in the crusher, and way behind that is the embankment where the railroad is, with a freight grinding west along it, dozens of double-decker flatcars crammed with the latest from Detroit, all bright and new like Christmas toys on a model train, hundreds of them, so new I bet their tires have still got those little threads of rubber hanging off their treads from imperfect molding, so new their odometers only show the few hundred yards it took to drive them from the factory to the freight yard to get loaded aboard the flatcars and sent west for car-hungry America to gobble up. Ten years down the line they'll be in junkyards like this one, getting squashed in the compactor and melted down to make new autos that'll go past here on the freights to car-hungry America. It's almost like plowing and seeding and harvesting, around and around.

There's a gate halfway along the fence with a tin sign on it: BIMMERHAUS AUTO WRECKERS—TOWING SERVICE —USED AUTO PARTS. I parked the car and went in. The gate wasn't locked. There's a wide track leading from where I'm standing away between the cliffs of stacked autos. The junkers are piled up in islands any old where with pathways in between, like canyons winding through metal buttes and mesas. It looked like the kind of place you could get ambushed by rust monsters, little orange goblins that eat fenders for breakfast. I followed the main track away from the gate. It's the only one with tire tracks on it, and it wandered to the left, then to the right, then went around an extra tall stack of autos, a pyramid of Chevys and Pontiacs and Fords with scrunched-in roofs and sprung hoods and empty wheel hubs, and opened out into a big space in the middle of everything.

There's a beat-up tow truck parked over on the edge, and over on the other side is one of those forty-foot mobile homes that're a nightmare to move on the highway, but this one won't be giving anyone nightmares because it's had the wheels taken off, so this looks like its final resting place. Next to it is one of those bulb-ended propane tanks on blocks, like a stranded midget submarine, and in front of that is a kennel, out of which came a Doberman. It started snarling like crazy and practically strangled itself with the leash that kept it tied to the kennel. I kept going, but slowly. I hate Dobermans. I wouldn't trust a Doberman that was muzzled and legless and chained to a block of lead. This one was completely nuts, with slobber flying out of its mouth like an oversudsed washing machine, and what made it look weird as well as scary were these two little white party hats on its head.

Then the door opens and this guy comes out, an old guy around sixty with a mackinaw coat and big old boots, and he tells the dog, "Hush up!" It kept on barking. Those little pointy party hats on its head are tied under its chin with a white ribbon. It looked like a dragon in a Sunday bonnet, totally weird. "Hush *up!*" the old guy hollers again, then he says to me, "Come on, he won't do anything. He's all bluff and spit while he's on the leash. *Hush up when I say!*"

The Doberman quit making a racket and did a couple of those messy dog snorts, like a bum blowing snot onto the ground. I came right up to the trailer then, and the old guy looked me over and says, "Help you?"

"Uh . . . yeah. I'm looking for Lennie."

"Lennie?"

"Yeah. He lives here, doesn't he?"

"What's your business with Lennie?"

He sounded very suspicious. I stopped a few yards away. The dog was still watching me with drool hanging off his lips. I really hate Dobermans. Now that I'm closer I could see those party hats were covering its ears, and I figured they're some kind of winter ear protectors. They say some breeds of dog have peculiar weaknesses because they've been paddling in the same old gene pool for too many generations, so Dobermans must have weather-sensitive ears, I figured.

"I've got his cap."

"His what?"

"His cap."

I pulled it out of my pocket, Lennie's nice clean wool cap. The old guy looked at it like I hauled out a Halloween pumpkin or something.

"Where'd you get it?" he wants to know.

"Outside McDonald's, last Tuesday."

"He drop it, or what?"

"Uh . . . no, it came off when they jumped him. He wasn't doing anything."

"Jumped him? Who?"

"A bunch of guys. They thought he had a gun."

He looked at me a long while. There's a long drool connecting the Doberman's snout to the snow. I wondered how long it'd take to freeze into an icicle.

"You better come on in."

Inside, it's very hot, and the old guy took off his mackinaw. I took off my hat before my brain started boiling.

"You born in Africa?" he says.

"Uh . . . excuse me?"

"You're gonna burn up inside that coat."

I took it off. He hung it on a peg back of the door along with his own. The air was real hot in there. I could smell what he had for lunch, namely pizza. I bet the pizza man had the shit scared out of him when he delivered. Or maybe it was a frozen pizza the old guy fixed up for himself. There's also plenty of empty Budweiser cans standing on the floor next to a big comfy armchair, and another chair not so comfy-looking a few feet away, which he points to.

"Take a seat."

We both did. There's a picture of Jesus on the wall, next to which is a calender with a picture on it of mountains and trees and a lake. It looks pretty much like the Yellowstone jigsaw we gave Angie for Christmas. Yellowstone is a very popular subject for photographs. You could point a camera anywhere in Yellowstone and get a good picture out of it.

"Where'd you get the hat?"

"Outside McDonald's."

"Not *his*, yours."

"It's a Christmas present."

"Looks like a Red's hat. Put a star on the front, that'd be a Red's hat."

"That's what I thought when I got it."

"Saw Chinese with hats like that in Korea."

"Yeah?"

"You bet. They had better hats than we did. A winter soldier isn't worth a damn without a good hat. Helmet's okay for when there's shrapnel flying around, but for day-to-day use you need a good solid hat, preferentially with fur. They had 'em, we didn't."

"That's too bad."

"Ever see a frostbit ear?"

"No."

"Ears freeze easiest, the end of your nose too. You can lose an ear okay, always cover it with a hat, but how'd you look with the end of your nose gone?"

"That'd be rough."

"That's what they did to Indian women that played around."

"Who did?"

"Indian men. Cut the nose off any squaw that played around in someone else's tepee. Married squaws, that is. Unmarried could do what they wanted."

"I didn't know that."

"I didn't know it myself till I saw it in a book, this picture of a squaw with her nose cut off. Looked real ugly. She was no prize beforehand, like Tugboat Annie, but what they did to her nose was cruel. I'd even call it unnecessary. A good whomping and throw her out, that's enough. When you bring knives into a marriage it's not good. And what man'd want a cut-nose squaw around the place? Would you want a wife with no nose?"

"Maybe cutting the nose was the same thing as divorce, so the guy that did the cutting didn't have to look at what he did for the rest of his life, I mean he'd cut her nose then . . . uh . . . ask her to leave. Then he could get a new wife with a complete nose."

"That could be the way they did it. The knife, then the boot. I didn't read the book, just the part under the picture. I believe you're right. It wouldn't make sense for a feller to cut off his wife's nose and still keep her around as his wife. It'd put him off his buffalo meat."

He thought about it for a while. It smelled like old underwear in there as well as pizza. I can see thermal underwear at the throat of the old guy's wool shirt, with white chest hair poking over it. The hair on his head was pretty white too.

"Are you Lennie's father?"

"Lennie's my boy."

"Uh . . . is he around?"

I've still got his cap in my hand. My own hat's in my other hand.

"Maybe. I haven't looked. What were you saying about a gun?"

I told him what happened at McDonald's, then I told him about the burning telegraph pole. "I offered him a lift but he just walked away."

"That'd be Lennie's way of repaying kindness. He can't have any kind of dealings with people, just can't cope with it. It's not his fault, it's what happened to him in the Army. I blame the U.S. Army for Lennie being the way he is. Before they got him he was a regular boy, a real rip-it-up tear-ass kid, had two things on his mind, cars and women, in that order. You know what they call him around town?"

"Yeah, Lennie the Loop."

"Right, Lennie the Loop, and you know why?"

I told him about Charlie and the cheese wire.

"Right again," he says, "and it's horseshit. Lennie was in the Ordnance Corps, handed out a million weapons but was never in the field of fire himself, never set foot outside of Saigon, just a pen pusher who had charge of issuing weapons from some big warehouse full of firepower. A clerk is what Lennie was. That cheese-wire story, that's just horseshit. I bet you heard it from some kid, am I right?"

"Yeah ."

"I knew it. Kids love to make up stuff like that. Makes life interesting for 'em, the boogeyman, you know? Lennie never had the kind of mental concentration you need to be a Green Beret. All that stuff about cheese-wiring heads is just horseshit, but you try telling Joe Public the truth and see how far you get."

"Uh . . . how about the car?"

"What car?"

I couldn't say, "The car owned by Lennie's wife's boyfriend that the wife and boyfriend got murdered and crushed in by Lennie the jilted husband." That wouldn't have been polite, pointing out the cheating element to the cheated-on murderer's father who I only just met. So I said, "I heard he squashed a car in the compactor."

"Oh, yeah, yeah, the car. He did that. That part's true. Lennie, he loved that car, a '62 Parisienne, pale green when he got it but Lennie wasn't having any pale green car, not him. He sprayed it black, four coats, inky black, then chromed the en-tire engine. That engine was so hotted-up it sounded like a goddamn fighter plane, even had chrome carburetors poking up through holes he cut in the hood. Goddamn thing looked like the Batmobile. He loved that car, *loved that car*! It was the biggest thing in his life. Every week he'd wax and polish it so good you could see yourself in it. When he got drafted Lennie left the car with Carol Ann, that's his wife he got married to a couple hours before he got on the Army bus, wife that *was*, she's dead now, and she couldn't drive worth a damn, shouldn't have been allowed behind the wheel of a nickel-a-ride toy car outside a supermarket, but he left it in her keeping and a month before he came home she plows it through a couple fences and into a Mayflower truck coming the other way. Had to bring it home on a flatbed trailer. Whole chassis was twisted like a pretzel. You couldn't fix it, not a car wrecked so bad, just a pile of chrome junk, bloody too, a real mess."

"Is that how she died?"

"Only went and lost her head, like when Jayne Mansfield crashed her car back . . . whenever. Lost her head. Decapitated."

"Jeez . . . How'd Lennie take it, when he got back I mean."

"Took one look and practically cried like a baby, that's how bad it was, then he got in the crane and picked up that black Parisienne and dumped it in the compactor and hit the crush button. He just couldn't stand to see that beautiful car the way it was. It near broke him. I was there and I saw the look on his face. That's when it started, so far as I can see, the mental disruption he had to go away for pretty soon after that."

"Uh . . . how'd he feel about Carol Ann?"

"He regretted he ever gave her the keys. He should've listened to me, he knew that. It was a lesson too late to learn."

He sat there shaking his head and pressing his lips together.

I had to know. "So it was Lennie's car that got crushed, not someone else's."

"Not just his car, his *life*, his pride and joy."

"And he didn't kill anyone."

"Say what?"

"Lennie didn't kill anyone."

"I told you, he was in the Ordnance Corps. Never left the base. He even put on weight in 'Nam. The modern Army, they have Hershey bar machines everywhere you look, Hershey bars and con-domes."

"And he didn't kill anyone when he got back home."

"Is that what they say, he killed someone?"

I told him and he got mad.

"More horseshit! Carol Ann didn't have a boyfriend while Lennie was gone. She was the plainest woman you can imagine. She was real proud to be Lennie's wife. No one else would've wanted her, a girl plain as that. That's a horseshit story if ever I heard one. Carol Ann was no cut-nose squaw."

"So you think it was just what happened to the car that made him change."

"I didn't *say* that, I said that's when it *started*, but not even a car lover like Lennie would've gone crazy over just a wrecked car, not even that Parisienne. I figure it must've been something else made him start behaving strange after he put the car in the compactor."

"Carol Ann maybe? Her dying and all?"

"No, I don't include it. He never paid her all that much attention when they were dating, never spoke a word to her if there was someone else around he could jaw with. Naw, that wasn't it. I asked the army psy-chiatrist what it was that did it, but those headshrinkers, all they can tell me is Lennie's a paranoid schizophrenic. That means he thinks the world's out to get him, and he doesn't see things the same way normal people do. What kind of help's that? I want to know *why* he's like that."

"Did they ask him?"

"Sure they asked him. They asked him a million times when he first went in for treatment in seventy-four and the same damn stuff when he had to go back just last year, like as if in ten years he's supposed to've figured it all out for himself and be able to tell *them*. All he said was, "I wanna go home." Nothing else, just, "I wanna go home." It's peculiar, because he was never happy here, not after he crushed the car. He'd just sit around and stare at nothing and go for a walk in the middle of the night and not want to talk about anything with me, his *old man*. Why would he want to come home?"

Sound familiar? He could be talking about *me!* I'm a paranoid schizophrenic! Lennie and I could be *brothers* practically. Now I'm really feeling weird.

Old man Bimmerhaus one by one picked up all the Budweiser cans standing next to his chair and shook them till he found the one that isn't empty yet. He's been neglecting his beer while he talked to me, and now he chugged down half a can till it's empty as the rest. He had them lined up like tin soldiers. Poor old Lennie, a lonely walker of streets just like me. It's very ironic the way I called him a creepo yesterday, I mean that's how everyone at Memorial High thinks about *me*. It's a very obvious case of the pot calling the kettle black when they're stood side by side on the very same red-hot range, both of us getting blacker by the day, black as Lennie's Parisienne, black as the bottom of a well.

"Me, I think it was something that happened over there."

"Huh?"

"I figure something happened to Lennie in 'Nam."

"You said he didn't do any fighting. He was never out in the jungle, you said."

"A soldier can go nuts *anyplace*. The Army's enough to send you nuts if you aren't already. I did a hitch at the end of the Big One, but I never got to see action. Then I went and re-enlisted when Korea came along. You could be proud of the uniform back then, not like it was later on. I got action in Korea, you bet."

He thought awhile about the action he saw in Korea. He wasn't telling any of it to me. I wondered when he's going to crack a fresh can and offer me one. He hasn't even asked my name yet. I only know his because it's on the gate, his name and Lennie's too. Lennie Bimmerhaus. I never knew. Lennie the Loop suits him better.

"Never been near a woman since he got back," says the old guy. "He liked to chase 'em before, but not since he got back. It's like he had his balls blown off or something, but they weren't. He hasn't got a scratch."

Boy, old Bimmerhaus must be drunk, talking about his son's balls with a kid he just met who he doesn't even know the name of. I counted the cans. Seven. That'll do it. Me, I get drunk on one. He doesn't sound drunk, though, I mean he's not slurring or anything.

"You lose anyone in 'Nam?" he asks.

"My dad."

"Army?"

"Yeah."

"What division?"

"I don't know."

"You don't *know*?"

"My mom never talks about it."

"You don't know what *division* he was in?"

"No," I said, feeling stupid.

"Jesus H. Christ," he says. "Don't you *care*?"

"Sure, I just . . . don't know."

It wasn't enough, I could see it in his face, so I said, "I'm thinking about going to Washington, to see the monument, you know. I bet that'd have his division on it. His name's Weems. He'd be down the bottom somewhere with the W's."

"It isn't alphabetical like that. It's arranged some other way. I haven't been there but I saw it on TV, and the names aren't alphabetical."

"Well, I'll find out when I go."

"You do that, and take your mom too. You owe him that much, don't you?"

"I guess."

"You bet you do. Anyone gets killed for nothing, you owe him something. And there should be another monument for guys like Lennie that came back but weren't the same. They made a sacrifice too. There's a part of Lennie missing. He lost it over there, I know he did, only he didn't know it himself till he got back here and saw the car twisted all out of shape like that. I figure that's when it hit him, whatever it was, whatever it *is*."

"The car was a substitute."

"Right! A *substitute* for whatever it was!" He really liked the idea. "You'd think the Army could've figured that much out. I told 'em about the car and they said it was 'symptomatic.' What's *that* prove? Doesn't tell you a goddamn thing. Those guys," he says. "Those *guys* . . ."

He crunched up the empty Budweiser can like it's an aluminum psychiatrist. We didn't talk for a little while. The place doesn't smell so bad now that I've gotten used to it. The human nose adjusts very rapidly.

"So Lennie isn't home," I said.

"Huh?"

"Lennie isn't home."

"I didn't look yet."

"Doesn't he live in here with you?"

"Hell, no. Think I could stand to have him sitting there saying diddly all day long? It'd drive me crazy, and Lennie wouldn't like it either. He's got his own shack out back. Come on and we'll take a look. Maybe he's home. What'd you want to see him about?"

"His cap. I brought it back."

"Right. Well, he's not used to visitors. You'd be about the first."

He clawed his way up from the chair and we got inside our coats. I put my hat on and he dumped a flannel fishing hat on his head, very inadequate I thought for weather like this, and out we went. The Doberman came sprinting out from his kennel when he heard the door, but he didn't bark.

"What are those things on his head?"

"Just had his ears clipped. Dobermans get born with regular floppy ears. You have to clip 'em to make 'em stand up the way they do. Had his tail docked too. It's not a real Doberman unless you do that."

"I think I'd leave a dog the way it was if I had one."

"I got this one for a watchdog, so he's got to look like a Doberman or there's no point. One look at those little ears and a thief'll scram. Regular ears make a Doberman look like an ordinary hound from a distance. A thief'd maybe ignore him and get himself all tore up, and then you can bet I'd get sued, probably have to pay the sonovabitch compensation. It's a crazy world."

"What's his name?"

"Who?"

"The dog."

"He's just a watchdog."

We stomped along between the stacked-up cars, then I saw one I recognized. "Hey, I saw that Tercel get squashed by a garbage truck just the other day."

"Hauled it in from Crestview myself," he says. "That one's good for nothing but scrap." Then he says, "Lennie hasn't got behind the wheel of a car or truck in ten years. He must've walked enough to walk around the world by now."

I thought about Lennie doing all that walking, all those Buford-sized circles he's been going around and around in all these years. I tried to figure out how many times I've seen him since I first got told he's Lennie the Loop, but couldn't do it, I mean I must've seen him dozens of times, but none of them till the McDonald's thing ever stuck in my head. Lennie the Loop was just something always in the background that you knew was there but didn't take any real notice of, like a billboard or the water tower. Until now he didn't *matter*. It's surprising that I haven't bumped into him more often just lately, considering how much wandering around town I've been doing myself. It's like Buford is one of those very complex hedge mazes, and Lennie and I are walking around in there, maybe just a few yards away from each other only we don't know it because the hedges are too tall and neither of us makes a sound. Me and brother Lennie, paranoid schizophrenics, both of us lost in the maze, and on the platform over the maze is the guy who's got a bird's-eye view and is there to guide you out if you can't make it, but Lennie and I don't even look at him. This is *our* maze and we'll wander out of it in our own sweet time, thank you very much.

"Got to hose the garden," says old Bimmerhaus, and turns away and opens his pants and starts pissing over a Galaxie that's already half rusted through. He says, "Twenty years, you won't see cars like this anymore, not even in junkyards. Know what the next thing's gonna be?"

"No."

"Plastic cars. En-tire body made of plastic. Durable, rust-proof, impact-resistant, you name it. Won't even have to paint 'em anymore, the color's right in the plastic, and the engine's won't be metal anymore either. Know what the engines'll be made of? Ceramic. You know what that is?"

"Pots and stuff."

"Right. They'll pour a mold and bake 'em in ovens like bread. There won't be any steel industry anymore. Hell, it's practically dead already. Plastic pipes, plastic cars, plastic this, plastic that. When they invent plastic girders that's the end of steel. Know what they make the wings for the latest jet fighters out of? Fiberglass, like a goddamn fishing boat, special fiberglass. All that plastic and ceramic and fiberglass they can make for a dollar a ton, so you think they'll bother to recycle it? No way. It'll be cheaper to mold and bake new stuff every time, and when the plastic cars and fiberglass planes get old you know what they'll do with 'em? Dump 'em in the ocean to make reefs for fish to live in. Nothing else they'll be good for, so they'll get dumped in the ocean for the fish to live in. The twenty-first century, that's when there's gonna be a lot of happy fish."

He shook himself and put the hose away. We started walking again and went past the crane and the compactor. The crane's claw was resting on the ground like a giant iron tarantula, and the compactor looked big enough to swallow planets. We kept walking and pretty soon came to another open space and there's Lennie's shack, a tiny little ramshackle place with a tarpaper roof like something south of the border, the kind of place you expected to see a woman with ten kids making tortillas out in front of.

"Built it himself," says the old man. "I'd have gotten him a second-hand trailer but he wanted to build a place for himself. He's no builder, Lennie, but it's not as bad as it looks. I've been inside when it's raining and the roof doesn't leak. Pretty warm in there too, got insulation on the walls and a Sears heater. He makes out okay. Well, he's not home."

There's a padlock on the door. He gave it a couple tugs to be sure.

"What'll I do with the cap?"

"Leave it on the doorstep."

"It'll get dirty."

"Naw, not if it's just snowed on. Snow isn't dirty, doesn't even get things wet till it starts to melt. Leave it right there where he'll see it."

So that's what I did. What I really wanted to do is give it to Lennie myself, from my hand to his hand, but it looks like I won't be able to do that. It was very frustrating. I wanted to ask him a pile of questions.

"Does he ever talk?"

"When the moon is blue he'll maybe say something. The Army told me he's got 'intermittent mutism' as well as the other stuff, but he's no dummy. I've heard him talk as recent as last fall, but it's rare. We're not close the way we used to be before the war. They told me if I tried to make him talk he'll most likely clam up all the way, so I don't push it. If he's got something to say he'll say it. I've gotten used to it."

We went back through the junkyard to the trailer, not saying anything. I expected to hear some more about the twenty-first century but plastic cars was all he knew.

"Want a coffee before you go?"

"No thank you. I've got stuff I have to do."

"If I see Lennie I'll tell him you called around."

How's he going to do that when he doesn't even know my name?

"Okay," I said. "Thank you."

"You bet," he says, showing me his dentures.

And I left. On the drive home I kept having this very anticlimactic feeling, you know? It took a fair amount of nerve to go visit like that I think, to kind of confront Lennie, and seeing as he wasn't there the whole trip was a big letdown. Still, I learned some stuff, like the truth about the car crushing and how old Carol Ann died et cetera and that was pretty interesting. All in all, it wasn't a total waste of time.

Things hotted up when I got home.

"Where *were* you all this time?" Peggy yells at me, which was very unreasonable because I was only gone around an hour.

"Nowhere," I said, which was the wrong thing.

"Keys," she snaps, sticking out her mitt. I handed them over and she says, "You can just go nowhere again till I get home."

"Where are you going?"

"Loretta's."

She never calls it "Pete and Loretta's," which would've been more accurate. It's always just "Loretta's." It was okay by me. I don't mind being stuck at home by myself. That's what us schizo hermits *do*.

"Make yourself some supper and don't set foot outside this house until I get home. Am I coming across loud and clear?"

"Yeah."

Telling me twice is very fucking loud and clear.

"I'm glad to hear it," she says, and left.

She's in one of her cranky-about-nothing moods again. It's a good thing she's gone out or there'd be trouble at the ranch, her and me boxed up together for the evening. I ate and watched a movie with the sound turned way down and did some taping.

Update—12:17. Peggy came in and went straight to bed, didn't even poke her face in the living room. Tomorrow I'll phone Loretta and find out what happened. I bet it had something to do with the move to Arizona. The channel I'm watching is closing down for the night. Lots of jet fighters screaming across the sky and the flag waving and Marines saluting the land of the free and the home of the brave. I wonder if the jets have fiberglass wings. There's a message in this sign-off stars'n'stripes stuff, and what it's saying is, "Come and get us, Commie assholes! We're waitin' for ya!"

End update.

8

Peggy had to reopen the Wishee-Washee today, Saturday. I drove down with her, because she told me to get rid of all the cans in the basement. What there is down there is thirteen garbage bags full of empty Coke cans it took us about six months to accumulate, and now it's time to take them down to the can crusher outside Safeway. I hauled up the bags and crammed them in the trunk and the backseat, then we started out. Peggy's rigged for silent running again, so we had a quiet breakfast, and the loudest noise on the drive to the laundromat was the cans clinking and clanking in back of us.

"Pick me up at four," she says when I dropped her off. That's her regular quitting time on a Saturday, but the place stays open till eleven for everyone that does their own wash.

"Okay."

"And not one minute later."

"Yessir."

I gave her a real GI Joe salute but she didn't think it's cute. Screw you, lady. Us cabbies don't like customers that ain't got no humor, and the tip was lousy too. I drove to Safeway and parked as close to the crusher as I could, which was around a hundred yards away because the parking lot's so crowded it looks like the deck of an aircraft carrier on full-scale maneuvers. There were people lining up for the crusher same as me, so I had to wait awhile. I had just four bags with me. That's all I can carry at one time.

The crusher is this big blue metal box about fifteen feet by eight by eight with a hole to feed aluminum cans into, and the machinery inside crushes and crunches them into flat squares of solid aluminum that get taken away once a month maybe. You get fifteen cents a pound for your cans, but they have to be aluminum. The machine rejects steel cans, also stuff you might try to sneak in like aluminum foil and onetime baking trays, that kind of stuff. You try feeding that fake stuff into the crusher and it spits it right back at you. Finally it got to be my turn and I pulled the tape off the bag necks and started tipping Coke cans into the hole, *clinkety, clankety, bonkety,* then when it wouldn't take any more I waited for the crusher to start working, which it does about ten seconds after it quits receiving, then up it starts, *grind, grind, crackle, crinkle, crunch,* like a million pairs of false teeth getting snapped and busted. When the crusher quit I fed in more cans. That happened twice, then I'm out of cans. Some change came plinking into the little trough with the arrow above it and I scooped it out. $2.23. Then I went back to the car and got another four bags and stood in line again and fed them in and got $2.37, then I went and got the last five bags, very bored with the whole thing by then, also it's very hard to carry five bags full of cans. For the last bunch I got $3.21. Grand total for over an hour's standing in line $7.81.

I went into Safeway to grab the weekly eats, also to get some more bird seed. The squirrels finished up the first bag already. There's a whole shelf of bird seed, and I'm standing in front of it wondering if I should get the regular mix or sunflower seeds only, seeing as it's mainly squirrels that patronize my little backyard diner, and you have to keep the customer satisfied, then this voice behind me says, "Hello, Burris."

I turned around and it's Sandra's mom!

"Uh . . . hi, Mrs. Christensen."

"Getting the weekly groceries?"

"Uh . . . yeah."

"Me too. God, it's a chore."

I looked around but Sandra isn't there. Thank Christ for that. It's embarrassing enough just seeing her mom. I haven't been around to Harry's Highway Haven since Sandra told me we're through, a month ago now. Rick and Alice are very nice people, I mean it, but I didn't want to have anything to do with them now that I'm not dating their daughter anymore. It's like bumping into someone who had a death in the family just recently and you don't know what to say, only in this case it's *me* who's the corpse. But old Alice, she wasn't embarrassed at all, kept right on talking to me like I'm her next-door neighbor, saying how Rick's ordered a new sign for the motel, something eye-catching to grab business away from the million other motels out that way. She says Sandra wanted to change the name to the Bates Motel, yuk, yuk, but of course they weren't going to. It'll still be Harry's Highway Haven, but with a bigger sign.

Boy, can this dame *talk*. I just wanted to grab some seed and run, just wanted her to let me go, but she kept yakking, all the time waving her arms around like a windmill. Sandra told me one time her mom likes her own hands so much she's always waving them around under people's noses so they'll see how artistic they are, and she kids herself all the waving around is "expressive," not just showing off. Personally I think her fingers are way too skinny, with those long red stick-on nails and a very waxy look to the skin from wearing gloves full of special cream at night. But don't get me wrong—she's a very nice person, I just wish she'd quit gabbing and let me go, but what's the hurry, Murray, is how she looks at it, and keeps right on opening and shutting her mouth.

Then she touches me on the sleeve, because whenever someone does that to you, makes that fake-friendly gesture, you automatically look at the hand that's doing it, and obviously I hadn't been paying her terrific hands enough attention so she fakes this intimate little gesture, setting her hand down on my sleeve that way. It felt like a tiny pterodactyl roosting there, clutching at me.

"I just *remembered* . . ." she says. "The New Year's Eve *party!* Are you *doing* anything? Have you made arrangements with friends already, Burris?"

Is she kidding? I could fit all my friends in a toilet cubicle and still have room to take a squat.

"Uh . . . no, not exactly, I mean my plans are pretty fluid right now," I said, meaning they're like dishwater down a drain.

"*Wonderful!*" she says. "That means you can attend *our* little soiree. Don't worry, it's not for old fogies like Pete and *me*, ha, ha, ha . . . No, this is strictly for the benefit of Sandra's cohorts."

She's the kind of woman uses a word like *cohorts*. She's in the Art Appreciation Society, also the Buford Repertory Company. Last year she was Blanche DuBois in *A Streetcar Named Desire*. I didn't go see it. Sandra told me.

"It'll be fabulous fun, I guarantee it. We'll be keeping out of the way so *les enfants terribles* can do what comes naturally, within reason I hasten to add, and I know Sandra wants all her friends from school to be there. Howsabout making an entry in your social diary for the thirty-first. You won't regret it. There'll be some punch, and I mean punch with *punch*." She gave my arm a punch. "This is no Mom'n'Pop setup we're arranging, Burris. Of course we'll be holding car keys until our partygoers can prove they're capable of driving home without mishap. Rick doesn't want liquor there at all, but I told him everyone over sixteen in Buford will be swigging *something* on the night, so it may as well be under loose supervision rather than happening in someone's basement. A little bit of leeway and a little bit of responsibility, I think that's what's called for on occasions like this, don't you?"

"Yeah."

"So we can count on your attendance?"

"Sure."

"Terrific! I know Sandra's got you on her list. I'll give her the good news."

"Okay."

"Well, I have to battle my way through to the cheese counter."

She's the kind of woman won't eat cheese that comes in a regular packet, just plain ordinary cheese, no way, she's got to have dill and herbs and stuff in it. She'd just *die* if you found a lump of Kraft in her fridge. It's pretty funny when you think about it, I mean she helps Rick run a fucking *motel* for God's sake, which is a job about as intellectual and cultured et cetera as working *behind* the cheese counter. Any way you slice it, life in Buford is cheddar, not Roquefort.

"Nice talking to you, Mrs. Christensen."

" 'Bye now," she says, and gives me a final waggle of those long creepy fingers. She's got hands like Dracula's daughter.

I did the shopping fast as I could, checking that Alice wasn't in whatever aisle I needed before I went charging down it with my cart, pulling the usual crap off the shelves and clanging into other people's carts and saying, "Excuse me," a lot. I got what I needed in record time without seeing Alice again. She's probably still over at the cheese counter measuring the holes in the Swiss. Through the checkout, out to the parking lot with my sacks, into the backseat with them, ditch the cart in the recovery area, get behind the wheel . . . takeoff!

I drove home and put all the food where it's supposed to be, then tried to figure out what I'll do for the rest of the day. It's only 11:08 so I've still got the whole afternoon to fill in before I pick up Peggy at the Wishee-Washee. I put my feet up and had a Coke, my first contribution to the new mountain of cans we'll build in the basement before my next trip to the crusher. One small sip from a can, one giant slurp for Cankind.

I won't be going to Sandra's New Year's Eve party, punch or no punch. I can't decide if Alice was being generous or insensitive when she issued the invite. I think generous. She's kind of a phony but she's always ready to help people, like when I did my repeat semester she offered to help me with an essay on Hemingway, which was supposed to be all about Nick Adams, the kid based on old Ernie himself, an autobiographical character, and which all of us kids in school are supposed to identify with, being the same age as him. But I just couldn't get into those Nick Adams stories. What I did instead of reading them all was, I got this other book of Hemingway stories out of the library and it had this terrific story in it about a guy that asked a doctor to castrate him so's he won't be tempted by sex anymore, which he thinks is dirty, but the doctor won't do it and sends the guy away, and the guy is such a nut he goes and does it himself, but he's also kind of stupid as well as psychologically unbalanced and instead of cutting off his balls he cuts off his *dick* instead. Talk about *dumb*. Anyway, I liked that story a whole lot more than boring old Nick Adams who's all the time out in the woods pitching his tent and making sandwiches, ho hum. I didn't want to do the essay, with or without

Alice's help, and back then I still figured I'm headed for fame and glory as an actor, so I didn't bother writing one. Well, okay, I wrote a *little* essay on Nick Adams and handed it in. This is what I wrote, in its entirety, complete and unabridged— "Nick Adams. This guy likes to fish." I got an F–, surprise, surprise. I could've written a pretty good essay on the other character, the one who cut off his dick, but that wasn't on the curriculum. Not on the agenda, Brenda.

I hung around the house till 2:18 before I got sick of it and got in the Impala and drove back through town. I parked in a vacant lot a couple doors down from the laundromat then wandered around, looking for adventure as they say. Buford is not the place to go for adventure. For excitement we have Bowlarama, but check out your blood pressure before you go in, pal, because that much stimulation in one evening could seriously damage your health. Come to Bowlarama for life in the fast lane, ha ha!

I wandered down Oskaloosa, just walking slow and taking care not to step on all the ice and crap on the sidewalk, and I'm walking past the Cut'n'Curl Beauty Salon when I saw this old crippled lady getting wheeled out in a wheelchair. She must've been around seventy at least, and her legs were leaned over to one side like a couple of canes the way crippled people's legs are, and covered with a rug. She's got a parka on, powder blue, and under it there's a sweater with LET'S PARTY on the front. She just had her hair permed and it's clamped on her skull like a sci-fi sponge sucking her brains out, this real tight mass of curls, so many it didn't look real, more curls than a Greek statue's pubic hair. She's got dark glasses on too, so maybe she's blind, and she's being pushed along by someone I guess is her daughter, a middle-aged lady with silver snow boots and a pink pom-pom hat. They looked about as weird as anything I've seen, like they're in a movie, two hit men in disguise. The lady doing the pushing has got a shoulder holster under her coat and Granny's got an automatic weapon under the rug. They've been hired to ice the mailman just now coming out of the liquor store, but is he *really* a mailman, or someone putting a protection squeeze on the guy that owns the store? Yeah, that's it, and these two hit men have been brought in from out of town by the Storekeepers' Association to cream the squeeze artists before this thing gets out of hand. SMALL TOWN HIRES BIG GUNS.

I followed them down the street, watching the wheelchair's skinny tires slicing ruts in the snow and the pushlady's snow boots laying down tracks like an elephant would make, but I quit inventing stuff about them. It's just an old crippled lady that's maybe also blind, and her daughter or daughter-in-law, something ordinary like that. I'm not looking for drama and excitement at all. I'm looking for Lennie the Loop, that's what I'm doing, and like they say about cops and cabs, when you want one you can't find one. I wanted to see if he's wearing the cap I left on his doorstep. It was important somehow. And I wanted to hear him *talk*, wanted to ask him stuff about Vietnam and the Army and Carol Ann and the black Parisienne that looked like the Batmobile, all kinds of stuff. Lennie the Loop is the most interesting person in Buford, to me anyway. I wanted to get that hairy guy in a corner and make him *speak to me*, because what he knows will save my soul, I don't know why, but he's got to *tell me* what I want to know. Lennie's got *answers* in his head under the cap I cleaned for him, and all I need to be happy is to crawl inside Lennie's brain for a while and this big feeling of mystery about what he knows and what happened to him will get satisfied and go away. Lennie's got what I want, whatever it is, so I've got to talk to him, and *soon*. But first I have to find him. Maybe I should go back to the junkyard and see if he's there. Maybe not. He could be just about anywhere, a weird guy like that. I kept turning around to see if maybe he's behind me, but he never was.

The wheelchair ladies kept heading down toward Oskaloosa and Penley, which is where the accident happened, practically under their noses. This pickup coming down Penley collided with a Malibu that's moving across the intersection, which is one of those where there aren't any lights and all traffic has to stop and give way. The pickup was definitely the guilty party because he didn't even slow down, never mind stop and look, and he rammed the Malibu hard in the left side just behind the driver's seat. There's that sound of metal smashing metal that makes your heart stop whenever you hear it, and both of them went spinning across the road in different directions. The pickup slid into a ditch where there's a broken sewer or something getting fixed, which was boarded off and had flashing lights and all but the pickup slid straight through everything and both side wheels went down into the ditch and quit moving, and it's a lucky thing the guys working in the ditch were all further along it or they could've been hurt bad. Meanwhile the Malibu went sideways into a Dart that's parked by the intersection and came to a halt too, but it's the pickup that kept me looking at it because there's a god-awful howl from the back of it and I saw a wire cage about the size of a big TV set go tumbling over the side and onto the sidewalk in front of True-Value hardware, and the door got sprung open and out came this incredible animal, a bobcat, crazy with fright and spitting and rumbling, not knowing which way to turn. He's big as two big tomcats, with muttonchop cheek fur that curves out and down, and these big pointed ears like a bat and a stumpy tail, all grayish-red across his back, just the greatest-looking animal, all hunkered down with his big front paws spread wide and his back legs all set to spring every which way including straight up, so tense he's like a little furry bomb on legs.

People on the sidewalk just froze, partly because if the ditch hadn't been there the pickup would've slid right up on the sidewalk and maybe killed someone, so they're frozen with shock I guess, and on top of that there's this muttonchopped bundle of muscle and claws right at their feet, but only for a second or two, then he's streaking across Oskaloosa, heading right for me and the wheelchair ladies at the curb, and he's lucky there's no traffic moving because of the accident or he might've gotten run down when he came charging across that way, and even before he's halfway over I could hear him panting like a little engine, a kind of *hack! hack! hack!* way down in his chest, fright most likely, and then he's past us and disappeared down an alleyway, gone in the wink of an eye. *Plink!* No more bobcat. It all happened so fast the drivers are still in their cars with their hands on the wheel.

The lady pushing the wheelchair turns to me and says, "What was *that?*"

"Bobcat."

"But he was *little*."

"That's how they are—little."

"I think they're bigger than that."

This lady doesn't know the difference between a bobcat and a fucking mountain lion. Then the old lady in the dark glasses turns around in her wheelchair and says, "It was a *bobcat*. I saw one on TV. It's a *bobcat*. Get a policeman and tell him. That bobcat shouldn't be in a cage. It's illegal. They're wild animals and it's against the *law*."

Not only is she not blind, she's also very feisty for a cripple.

"Get a policeman!" she yells.

"There'll be one along in a minute," says the other lady, not looking very happy about the way Granny's kicking up a fuss.

"You!" says Granny to me. "Go get a policeman!"

"Huh?"

"There'll be one along in a *minute*. They always come when there's an accident," says the lady.

"I want that man charged," says Granny, pointing at the pickup, where the driver's just now climbing out of the cabin. "He shouldn't have wild animals locked up! They should lock *him* up!"

"Okay, all *right*," says the other one, and gives me this apologetic look. "Would you mind?" she says, meaning would I at least *look* like I'm going to fetch a cop.

"No, wait!" says Granny, and points at the alleyway. "Go and see to that poor animal. It's probably frightened half to death."

Okay, that I don't mind doing. There's a real crowd gathered around the Malibu and the pickup now, so I wouldn't be able to see much anyway. I went down the alley. It's got roll-down delivery doors facing onto it and some dumpsters and stacks of flattened cardboard cartons waiting to get picked up for pulping. There's a lot of peeling paint and naked bricks. Nothing comes through here except garbage and delivery trucks, so it doesn't have to look nice. But it doesn't look anything like a forest either, so I wondered where the bobcat went that he'd think was a safe place. Maybe he kept on running and went all the way through to Debbs without stopping, which means I'm wasting my time. I kept going anyway, looking all over the place, and when I'm just a third of the way down the alley a whole bunch of people came in after me to look for the bobcat too, and that just about finished it for me, I mean I hate being part of a group of people all doing the same thing, so when they caught up with me and asked if I saw him yet I told them I hadn't and let some other guys take the lead and dropped back till I'm the last in line. I just *hate* joining in anything.

By the time I reached Debbs the rest of the bobcat hunters were asking people there if they saw him, but no one had, so they turned around and went back up the alley, looking properly this time, but I've got a hunch old muttonchop Bob has gotten away somehow without anyone seeing. He'll get caught sooner or later, though. How can a bobcat plan its next move in something as weird as a town, with streets and buildings and cars instead of rocks and streams and trees? He'll be as confused as a cricket in a clock, and about as likely to get mangled.

It was late afternoon by then, and what with getting distracted by the accident and the bobcat I lost time that I should've been using to find Lennie the Loop. Already the sky's getting darker, with the sun sliding downhill fast somewhere behind the clouds. It might even snow again before dark. Looking for Lennie by wandering around town was just plain dumb. I had to get organized. I went back to the car and went through the glove compartment and found a piece of paper and a crappy ballpoint with practically no ink left in it. The paper was one of my old shopping lists, bread, coffee, eggs, et cetera, but the other side was empty so I used it to write Lennie a note.

> Dear Lennie,
> I have to talk with you if that's OK.
> > Burris Weems
> > (who brought your
> > cap back Friday)
> P.S. My address is 1404 Westwood Dr., 843-5104.

The plan is, I'll go out to the Bimmerhaus junkyard and see if Lennie's home, and if he's not I'll leave the note on his door so he'll see it when he comes in. Great plan!

I drove to the junkyard. The front gate's locked. Shit. The

great plan is stymied before it's even begun. The fact that the gate's locked doesn't necessarily mean no one's home, in fact a paranoid schizophrenic like Lennie would probably lock the gate when he comes *in* instead of goes out, so I have to get inside. The gate wasn't tall, no taller than the gate I climbed to get to the water tower on Crane Hill. I got over without any trouble and started along the tire ruts that lead to old man Bimmerhaus's trailer. When I came in sight of it I expected to see the Doberman come charging out of the kennel and choke himself on his leash, but he's not there. Neither is the tow truck, so the old guy's out on business and it looks like he took the dog along with him, like firemen in the old days had a Dalmatian in the fire truck with them for a mascot. Good. I hate Dobermans.

I went on past the trailer and worked my way through the yard to Lennie's shack. No light behind the one and only window, and the padlock's on the door. Shit again. Well, I came prepared for this, superbrain that I am, and I got out the note and folded it lengthwise a few times and stuck it through the padlock's hasp. Even a strong wind won't blow it out of there. Mission accomplished. I turned around to head for the gates and there's Dobey, ten feet away and blocking the only route out of there. Double shit.

He wasn't slobbering or growling, just standing very still with his head cocked a little bit to one side, like he's asking himself, "Should I eat this guy or not?" My skin goose-bumped from my scalp to my toes. If it had've puckered any more it would've bled. Jesus, was I scared. All of a sudden I had to take a leak too, probably a nervous reaction to the highly dangerous and potentially fatal situation I'm in. What to *do?* Maybe old Bimmerhaus just now came back and he'll whistle the dog to come grab some Dog Chow. But I would've heard the tow truck. The dog didn't get taken for a ride after all, he was here all along. How come he didn't come snapping at my boots when I climbed over the gate? It rattled plenty when I climbed over, so how come the killer with the ear-job didn't hear and come running to protect his master's valuable collection of rusted autos? Is this a watchdog or a pet? Maybe the party hats on his ears mean he can't hear so good. He didn't know I'm in the yard till he sniffed my tracks and followed. That must be the reason. . . .

Grrrrrrrrrrrrrrr . . .

I didn't move at all, but he's growling! If I try to take a leak he'll attack, maybe even *go for my nuts!* Hyenas do that when they've got their prey down, chomp off the nuts and start eating their way into the belly from there. I felt sick thinking about stuff like that. The Doberman still hadn't moved or growled again, so as long as I don't do anything dumb there's a chance I'll get out of this and still be able to have children. Sweat's pouring down my ribs now, even though the air's freezing. Why doesn't this dog with hair shorter than the nap on a suede glove feel cold and go make himself comfy in his nice cozy warm kennel? And it's getting dark. I can see the junkers silhouetted against the sky still, but when I look down the only things I can truly make out are the patches of snow under those black cliffs of Dodges and Plymouths and the white party hats covering Dobey's ears. Shit, shit, shit, *shit!* What am I gonna *do?* Wait a minute . . . dogs are supposed to react to the human voice, so if I can just sound masterful and unafraid maybe he'll wag his butt and lick my hand and do some typical doggy cringing stuff.

"Hey, pooch . . ."

Grrrrrrrrrrrrrrr . . .

Note for tomorrow—voice lessons. The situation is not improving, and yes . . . *yes* . . . it's started to snow. Fuck. Still, I've got my hat and mittens on so I'm okay freezewise. But that doesn't help my bladder. It really was uncomfortable inside me, my bladder, kind of agitating itself and getting all impatient, wanting me to go with the flow. No can do, bladder, not without risking death.

"Hey there, Dobey . . ."

Grrrrrrrrrrrrrrr . . .

"How they hangin', slimelips?"

Grrrrrrrrrrrrrrr . . .

"Dating anyone? Bet she's a real dog, ha ha."

Grrrrrrrrrrrrrrr . . .

"You bowlegged sonovabitch. You look like a faggot with those stupid little hats on your head."

He didn't growl!

"Also I heard your mother puts out for every mutt in town."

He's listening, it looks like . . .

"And your *sister*—boy, they had to spay her *twice*."

My voice must be getting stronger, that's why he's not growling anymore. He's responding to the firm sound of command, admitting I'm the boss and he's just a dog after all.

"And another thing, snotsnout, I've heard you're so dumb you cross your legs when you pee. Know what they call you down at the pound? Yellowfoot. Old Stinktoes. Piddlepockets. And the way you eat is a fucking disgrace. The last time I saw table manners like yours was on a hog farm, and next to you those porky guys looked *neat*."

I pointed a mitten at him so's he'll get the message. Big mistake. One second he was ten feet away, next second he's standing at my crotch and dripping slobber on my Red Wings, and there's this awful, *awful* sound coming out of him, kind of a low rumbling with an edge to it if you know what I mean. I froze. I turned into a statue. I stared straight ahead and imagined I'm on a beach and staring out to sea, watching these two little white triangles that aren't a Doberman's ear protectors, no sir, they're the sails of a schooner way out there on the horizon, and they're coming closer . . . closer . . . coming to rescue me from my little desert island with one coconut palm and a supply of empty bottles that I used to send out my call for help . . . help . . . help . . .

The snow's really coming down hard now and the sky's gone, but the sails are getting nearer . . . nearer . . . must've picked up one of my bottles that I pissed in . . . put a note in that says help . . . help . . . while the ocean laps at my feet, flecks of foam dripping from the ocean's lips onto my toes . . . Old Stinktoes . . . getting ready to pee down my pants if the schooner doesn't get here soon, but if I pee myself he'll smell it and know I'm afraid and he'll go for the place the smell of fear is coming from . . . pounce on my privates . . . gnaw my nuts . . . coconuts . . . I'm going nuts . . . the sails are further off than before . . . going the other way . . . and the sound of the ocean's getting louder . . . louder . . .

Bang!

The gates!
Roaaarrrr!
The tow truck!

The Doberman didn't budge, just kept right on growling way back in his throat. I heard the truck's brakes squeal when the old man stopped to close the gates behind him, *rattle! bang!* Then it went rumbling along between the stacked-up cars and stopped near the trailer. *Bang!* He's slammed the truck door. Now he's whistling for the dog . . . and Dobey still doesn't budge! Boy, this is testimony to superior training. My dick is practically twitching I'm so desperate to pee now. Come on, you stupid old fart, don't stand in front of the trailer whistling— *come look for Fido!*

Finally he started moving around the yard, calling out for the dog, calling him "Boy," because he hasn't got a name. "Where are you, boy? Come on, boy!" I'm almost crying now it hurts so bad. I have to imagine my bag of goodies is clenched like a fist, a tight fist, or else I'll let fly and rinse my Wranglers . . . Come *on*, you stupid old fucker! We're over *here*, for chrissakes! I'm in agony . . .

"Lennie? That you?"

He's here at last, but he can't see me properly, and I don't dare speak.

"Lennie?"

The dog's still right under me, I can hear it. The old guy must be half deaf if he can't hear it too . . .

"Dog . . ." I said, kind of slipping it out between my teeth.

"Huh?"

"Get-dog-off . . ."

"*There* you are, boy. C'mere. Come on, boy. *C'mere* when I say!"

The Doberman backed off. I practically fainted.

"Excuse me . . ."

I turned away and tried to unzip my fly, had a lot of trouble and figured it's because I'm wearing mittens, took them off, opened up . . .

"Aaaaaaaaaaaahhh . . ."

"Had you backed up, huh?"

"Yeah . . ."

Gallons of piss rushed out of me.

"Good boy," he says, and pats the dog on the head a few times, big heavy pats, bonking Dobey's skull hard, then he says, "Looking for Lennie again? You climb the gate?"

"Uh-huh."

I zipped up. The world was a good place again.

"He got the cap. I had a look this morning. Not on the doorstep."

"I was wondering if he got it."

"Well he did. I looked this morning and it wasn't there anymore, so he's got it all right."

"That's terrific, Mr. Bimmerhaus."

"Been stuck here long?"

"I dunno. It seemed like forever."

He gave the Doberman a few more pats on the head. I could barely see either of them, just heard the sound. It's dark as a cave between the auto stacks, and the snow looks like it's settling in for the night, coming down soft and silent.

"Cup of coffee'd be fine right about now. Get you some?"

"Thank you."

We went to the trailer and he slammed a kettle on the gas range.

"Have you actually *seen* Lennie lately?" I asked him.

"Nope, not since before Christmas. He's around, though. Puts his garbage in the trash can like a regular person, so he's around all right. I keep off his toes, don't go chasing after him."

"I was just wondering, you know. He's a mysterious kind of guy."

"Biggest mystery I ever come across."

He slammed a couple mugs onto the table. Mine's got parakeets on it. His is plain white. Jesus watched us from the wall.

"Were you out on business?"

"I was. Towed a pickup had an accident over to Duane's Body Shop. I get a little kickback from Duane. He's my cousin."

"Was it at the corner of Oskaloosa and Penley? I saw it happen."

"Naw, out along the Interstate. Ambulance was there too, but nobody got hurt bad."

"This guy had a bobcat in the back of his pickup and it got loose."

"Bobcat?"

"In a cage. When the accident happened he got loose."

"Bobcat in a cage?"

This guy needs caffeine very badly.

"Yeah, a bobcat in a cage in the back of a pickup, and it got away when the pickup smashed into another car."

"That's against the law, keeping bobcats. They don't allow it except in zoos."

"That's what everybody was saying that saw it."

"They'll make him set it free, you see if they don't. It'll be on the news, a thing like that. Or else give it to a zoo."

"No, it got *away*."

"Got away? Did they catch it yet?"

"I don't know. I didn't hang around."

"Thought that old bobcat'd get you, hey?"

"No, I just had other business to attend to, you know."

"Sure, sure," he says, like he knows deep down I'm a coward or something. He let out this very patronizing chuckle too. Other business . . .

"Shit!"

"Shit?"

I looked at my watch. 4:38!

"I'm supposed to pick up my mom at four . . ."

"You're late," he says.

"I can't wait for the coffee. I gotta go . . ."

"Sure," he says. "Can't keep her waiting."

"Uh . . . can you see me to the gate so the dog doesn't get me?"

"Sure can."

We went out and he says, "Let him smell your hand."

We would've been all night getting to the gate if I didn't, so I gritted my teeth and stuck my fingers in the dog's face. He didn't eat them. We got to the gate.

"Okay, thanks. 'Bye, Mr. Bimmerhaus."

"Chuck," he says. "Call me Chuck."

"I'm Burris."

"Boris?"

"Burris. I gotta go or she'll kill me."

"Drive slow or you'll kill your*self*," he says, like a wise old TV grandpa.

"Yeah. See ya."

I got in the Impala and drove back into town, slowly like he said, even though I wanted to plant my foot and make up for lost time. 4:43! Oh, shit, she's gonna kill me for sure . . . Fuck that Doberman! Fuck it with a chain saw!

9

Peggy was outside the Wishee-Washee. She could've waited inside where it's warm, but no, she's outside on the sidewalk in the snow, so I know she's in one of her crazy moods, making a martyr of herself like this just because I'm a few minutes late. Okay, fifty-eight minutes late, but she could've waited inside, right? I pulled up and kept the motor running. She didn't move, didn't even look at me so far as I can tell with just the light coming through the laundromat window. I revved a little just to snap her out of it, let her know I'm there, but she still didn't move. She's doing it deliberately, it's obvious. I hate it when she does stuff like this. I got pissed off and punched the horn a couple times. No reaction. I put the gears in park and got out. She's like a store-window dummy, not moving a muscle. I went over and stood right in front of her where she can't ignore me.

"I got held up. This dog . . ."

Wham!

I'm on my back in the slush on the sidewalk. My own mom decked me with a left hook! No, her palm was open so it was only a slap, but *what* a slap. Maybe if the pavement wasn't so slippery I wouldn't have gone down so easy, but down is where I went. It's very embarrassing to have that done to you in public, especially by your mom. I stayed where I was for a second or two, kind of surprised at what'd happened, then I got up. My hat fell off when I went down so I picked it up. It's got slush on it now, which I didn't like.

"It wasn't my *fault*. This Doberman had me backed up in the junkyard . . ."

She flung her hand back to hit me again, but this time I'm ready and danced out of the way, a kind of backward quickstep.

"I couldn't *help* it! If I hadda moved he woulda *bit* me! It was a *Doberman* . . ."

She marched right by me and went to the car.

"You coulda waited inside," I told her. "You didn't have to wait *outside*. A *normal* person would've waited *inside* . . ."

She got in the driver's seat and slammed the door. I heard the gears get shifted into drive. She's gonna leave me here! I went for the door handle but she floored the pedal and shot away from the curb like a dragster, the back end shimmying left and right before it got straightened out, then it's just a set of taillights heading up Covington. She drove off and *left* me . . .

The bitch! The stupid crazy *bitch!* God, I hated her guts, I really did. Just four nights back we took a Christmas Eve stroll together and threw snowballs at Jesus, Mary, and Joseph and ran all the way home laughing our heads off. This woman is definitely a lunatic. What kind of a way is that for a mother to treat her son! I was pretty close to tears if you want to know the truth. It was a very stressful situation.

What to do? I can't go home or she'll most likely hit me again, or give me the big freeze, and I can't stand that stuff. I checked my pockets. I've got a few bucks on me, so I won't starve. The best thing to do is go get something to eat, then keep away from Westwood Drive until she's gone to sleep. Okay, that's what I'll do. It's Saturday night after all, and Buford's main swinger shouldn't be at home with his nutty mother in any case. So it's onward and upward! Let the fun commence!

The fun commenced in Burger City, a very low-key beginning for the incredibly terrific time I intended having. I sat in a booth and munched my cheeseburger and thought about the mentally defective people that've figured in my life, like old Gene the queen last summer, and now it's Lennie the Loop and Peggy Weems. It's a strange planet, Janet, but yours truly will persevere.

What'll I do till I can go home? I marshaled my thoughts. I deputized my synapses. They couldn't think of anything, so I threw them into a brain cell, ha ha. Think, boy, *think!* What does a teenager do in Buford on a Saturday night? Goes to a party. Screws his girl. Gets drunk. I've got no friends, so no party. Ditto no girl, and I'm under the legal drinking age. My options were limited. I could always go see a movie.

I did it. I saw *Runaway Train*. Not good, not bad. Then I went in the theater next door and saw *Enemy Mine*. Forget it. When I came out it's only 9:03, so now what? Maybe Peggy's asleep and maybe she's not. I decided I'd wait at least another hour before going home, just to make sure. I don't feel like having another confrontation with a crazy woman like that. I like the quiet life. I bet I get ulcers pretty soon the way things are going, and I don't deserve them. Maybe I'll get hemorrhoids too. I think they're stress-related. Which would I prefer, ulcers or hemorrhoids? At least with ulcers you don't have to carry around an inflatable rubber ring to sit on. Good afternoon, Doctor. I'm not a vegetarian, so could you explain this bunch of grapes growing out of my ass?

Doctor . . . that reminded me. I know a head doctor, a shrink who can maybe fill me in on Lennie the Loop and Peggy too, namely Dr. Willett that I had to go see twice a week at the Juvenile Psychiatric Counseling Service after my suicide attempt last summer. What does a psychiatrist do in Buford on a Saturday night? Goes to a party. Screws his wife. Gets drunk in a bar, how would I know? What I *do* know is where he lives, because when I was seeing him I got this crazy notion I had to find out what kind of house a psychiatrist lives in, like has it got drawn shades and loudly ticking clocks and lots of couches or what? So I looked up his address in the phone book and took a stroll around there one night to see how it looked, and what it looked like was very ordinary, just the same as every other house on the street, which was Grobard Street. The shades were drawn like I thought they would be, but it was night after all, so that didn't mean anything. Now's my chance to find out about the clocks and couches. But you can't just crash someone's home on a Saturday night and expect him to be happy about it. Solution? Phone first, like they say in the commercials. I went in the phone booth next to the Tudor Rose Gift Shoppe and let my fingers do the walking. They walked as far as the W's. His name's on the same page as Weems, incidentally. I fed the slot and dialed.

Brrrr . . . Brrrr . . .

"Hello, 844-9124."

The doc's one of those people gives you the number straight off so's you'll know if you misdialed.

"Uh . . . hello, Dr. Willett?"

"Speaking."

"Uh . . . hi, it's Burris Weems."

"Burris?"

"Yeah, Burris Weems. You remember last July I hadda come in and talk with you about certain stuff?"

"I remember, Burris. How have you been?"

"Fine, everything's fine. I'm okay, but I'd like to talk about some other stuff with you if it's not impossible or anything."

"Sure, go ahead. Oh . . . you mean face-to-face?"

"Yeah."

"You want to make an appointment?"

"No, I thought . . . uh . . . I wasn't doing anything special tonight and I was wondering . . . uh . . . if you weren't doing anything special either . . ."

"You want to talk tonight, is that it, Burris?"

"Well yeah, if it's not too much of a big inconvenience or anything."

"As a matter of fact I'm doing diddly right now."

He's got a sense of humor, Dr. Willett, I wouldn't be talking to him otherwise.

"So I can come over?"

"Certainly. I could pick you up if you like. Where are you calling from?"

"Oh, that's okay. I can be there in around half an hour."

"I'll be expecting you."

"Okay. 'Bye."

He hung up. He's one of those guys that never says good-bye on the phone, which in my opinion gives the impression of not being too polite, but really he's a very nice guy, it just so happens he doesn't say good-bye on the phone. Plenty of people don't. Next time you watch a movie and someone's on the phone, see if they say good-bye before they hang up. I bet they don't. Me, I always say good-bye, Loretta too. Peggy doesn't.

I got there at 9:43, not too late for a social call I think. Not that this is a social call, I mean I'm here to ask his professional opinion relating to the weirdos in my life, so really I should be paying him for this. Too late now because I already rang the bell, which in a psychiatrist's house should make a sound like a very large gong echoing way back into the sanctum sanctorum or somewhere creepy like that, but instead it sounds like an everyday door chime. Psychiatrists probably like to pass themselves off as regular people. The door opened and there he is.

"Come on in, Burris."

"Thanks."

He took my hat and parka and mittens. I already stomped the snow off my boots before I came in. People are very particular about how you treat their carpets, especially this time of year.

"Let's go to the den," he says, hiking his glasses up on his nose.

"Okay."

He led the way. I could hear a TV in another room. He's got a wife, and a daughter who's away at college in Indianapolis getting taught how to be a shrink like her old man, but I guess she's home for Christmas, probably in there watching *The Snake Pit* or *Spellbound* or *Shock Corridor*, something shrinky like that.

"Here we are," he says, meaning the den. It looks like a very casual office, with books and files piled up everywhere and a desk. There's a big ashtray on the desk, about the size of those stone mortars Indian women used to grind corn in. The doc is a heavy smoker. Back in the summer we had to keep the windows open down at his office in the Juv. Psych. joint or we would've choked. I noticed he's got one of those little smoke-extractor gizmos here to keep the air clean. The rest of the house smelled okay so I bet his wife makes him come in here to inhale that stuff. I was very surprised to find out he's a smoker because I read somewhere it's an oral fixation which comes from not having been weened from the nipple, also some faggy stuff about sucking and all, so you'd expect a psychiatrist who knows all that deep analytical shit would be too embarrassed by it to smoke, but he does, like a house on fire. I don't. Boy, am I pure!

"Pick a seat," he says, and I parked myself on this nice

armchair and he took another one. He didn't sit behind the desk because he wants to keep the atmosphere casual, very sensitive of him I think.

"Now then, to what do I owe this pleasure?" he says with a smile to let me know he doesn't really talk that way. I already knew, but sometimes very intelligent guys like the doc spell everything out for people they think are dumber than them. But I wasn't offended or anything.

"Uh . . . there's a friend of mine and I'm kind of worried about him."

"What's the problem?"

I could tell he thinks the friend I'm talking about is me. I'd never do that dumb routine. Already he's lighting up a cigarette, a Marlboro. Somehow you'd expect that if a shrink *has* to smoke, he'd smoke Kools, but he doesn't. I can't connect Dr. Willett with the Marlboro Man you see on that big billboard next to Lawrensen's Garden Supplies downtown, the cowboy in the yellow shirt with a yellow bedroll tied on the back of his saddle, a color-coordinated cowboy. I heard real cowboys get hemorrhoids from all that bouncing in the saddle, but I bet the only rectal disorder the color-coordinated Marlboro Man has is from taking it up the old box canyon from other color-coordinated cowboys. The Marlboro Man is a jerk. Me, I prefer the Lucky billboard over by Dunkin' Donuts, this girl with her arm thrown across the top of her head and a cigarette at the end of it. LIGHT MY LUCKY is the caption, but with her arm up like that it looks like she's saying, SNIFF MY ARMPIT, or come to think of it, with those sexy eyes she's saying, LICK MY CLITTY or something. Cigarette billboards are junk, they really are. They should just show this big ashtray full of disgusting butts, and the caption should be, SUCK DEATH, SUCKER.

"The problem is he's crazy, harmless but crazy, a paranoid schizophrenic to be very specific about it."

"Hold on, Burris, it's inadvisable to employ psychiatric jargon unless you know exactly what you're talking about, and that takes years of training."

"It's not what *I* said about him, it's what a psychiatrist said."

"What psychiatrist?"

"Some Army psychiatrist."

"Army?"

"Or Marines, I'm not sure. No, old man Bimmerhaus said Army. Yeah, I'm sure."

"Are we talking about Lennie Bimmerhaus?"

"Right, Lennie the Loop."

"He's a friend of yours?"'

"Yeah, well, an acquaintance I guess you'd call him. You know about Lennie?"

"I think everyone in town knows about Lennie, I mean they know him by sight and reputation, but I doubt that anyone really *knows* him. I think Lennie may even be alienated from himself."

"Is that a regular part of being a paranoid schizophrenic?"

"What's your connection with him?"

"I saw him around town for years, like everyone else, and then I picked up his hat, and now I can't get him out of my head."

"I don't think I follow."

So I told him. I told him stuff I wouldn't tell my own mom. I think that's because I felt like I can trust the conversation not to go beyond these four walls. The conversation is being sucked into the smoke extractor along with the clouds from the doc's Marlboro. After I finished, Dr. Willett lit up his second cigarette and flicked the match into the big corn-grinder ashtray.

"Burris, I don't know that your interest in Lennie is healthy, considering."

"Considering what?"

"Considering that you have in the very recent past experienced a life-threatening situation, a *serious* one."

He's talking about you-know-what.

"Yeah, but so?"

"So the thing you should be concentrating on right now is the steady rebuilding of your own ego, your own sense of self-worth, not worrying about Lennie Bimmerhaus. Schizophrenics seldom improve, to be frank about it. If you keep running around town looking for answers from Lennie, who to my knowledge hasn't spoken a word in *years*, you'll allow your concern to degenerate into an obsession, and that's not healthy,

Burris. That's the kind of negative-feedback situation you should be trying hard to *avoid*. I'm not just talking to you now as a shrink, I'm telling you this as a friend. I like to think of us as friends. We shared a piece of your life last summer, and sharing makes for caring, both sides being agreeable."

He thinks I tried to kill myself because I flunked school. He doesn't know squat about Gene and Lee and Diane, the stuff that *really* put me over a toilet bowl in Harry's Highway Haven with Gene's pocket knife in my hand and my Sony around my neck to record any famous last words. He doesn't know *any* of that stuff, so if he thinks friendship is based on sharing, we barely know each other. Don't get me wrong—I like the guy or I wouldn't be here telling him about Lennie, but no way am I getting *that* palsy-walsy.

I pumped him for more information about Lennie's condition but he wouldn't do it, said Lennie wasn't a patient of his so anything he said would be in the nature of conjecture, and he never engaged in conjecture regarding an actual person, patient or not, unless he's talking with another psychiatrist. With a dropout-teenage-suicidal-type like me he doesn't talk shop, even if he thinks we shared a piece of my life last summer. He calls it professional ethics. But he did tell me some stuff about paranoid schizophrenics in general, and it turns out they're very fucking weird, and the latest theory is it's physiological in origin, which means they've got the wrong chemicals in their brains, or the wrong proportions of chemicals or something that scrambles their perception of things and makes them live in a different world to the one normal people live in. Everyone used to think they were just plain bughouse, but it's the chemicals so they can't help it, they really can't.

It got kind of complicated, but the interesting thing is that paranoid schizophrenic symptoms very often begin to show up in the late teens and get steadily worse. I'm not sure how old Lennie is, thirty something, but I bet he got drafted when he was eighteen like the rest of them, so maybe it wasn't Vietnam that made him crazy after all. Maybe he would've gone crazy *anyway* because of his screwed-up brain chemicals. I wish I knew what kind of shape my own brain is in, physiologically speaking. Maybe I'm developing paranoid schizophrenic symptoms a couple years early. I could be the youngest paranoid schizophrenic in America before too long, I mean I'm positive I don't see things the way normal people do. It's very worrying, frankly.

Then I told him about Peggy and how nuts she is. He met her one time in the summer as part of the remedial therapy or whatever, asking her what she thinks made me do what I did, blah, blah, but she just sounded like a very upset mom back then, so he hasn't seen the *real* Peggy Weems. But he wouldn't risk diagnosing her either, not without proper consultation, but he did say that cracking a joke one minute and slapping me in the face the next is not normal behavior, and she should go for some professional help very soon. "*Urgento Prontissimo*," he says, making a little joke, ha ha, then he wrote down a name and phone number and gave it to me.

"This guy is a colleague of mine, a very good man. See if you can get Peggy to give him a call."

"You don't want to see her yourself?"

"I'm a juvenile specialist, Burris. Dr. Barring treats adults. He'd do a better job than I could."

I guess he's got a point. If your Volvo breaks down you take it to the Volvo dealer, not Joe's Repairs. Everyone's a specialist nowadays. Would a podiatrist fix your sinuses? I put the name and number in my pocket.

"Well . . . uh . . . thanks for seeing me."

"Hold on there, pal. You're worried about Lennie Bimmerhaus and your mother, but how about yourself?"

"Huh?"

"Maybe I'm wrong, Burris, but your coming here late on a Saturday night with concerned questions regarding other people suggests to me that we have a classic example of transference on our hands."

He means what I'm *really* worried about is *me*. He was just about to explain it to me but I jumped in fast.

"Nah, I'm okay, honest."

"Sure about that?" he says, and gives me this very skeptical look.

"You bet."

"You're not worried about anything?"

"Nope."

"Mr. Gwynn tells me you let yourself get flunked out all over again."

Gwynn's the principal at Memorial High. I didn't like it that he's been making phone calls to a shrink about me behind my back. I *know* why I flunked out. I don't need to get analyzed for that, and I don't like the way Dr. Willett left it until now to admit he's had the phone calls from Gwynn. He should've said so first thing, soon as I came through the door, so he wasn't hiding anything while we talked. Boy, you can't trust anyone these days. My face must've showed how I feel, because old Willett says, "Now don't go getting mad just because the principal has shown concern for your future."

"I'm not."

"Everyone's on your side, Burris. No one's against you. No one wants to see you fail."

"Who's failing? I flunked out of school, that's all. School isn't everything."

"True, but it's a specialized, highly trained world out there. Foul up in school and you can say good-bye to any kind of professional training, unless you want to be a stock-car driver or a lumberjack."

"Well I don't, but I don't want to be a nuclear physicist or a brain surgeon either."

"I see. And what *do* you want to be?"

"Uh . . . excuse me, is this professionally ethical for you to be asking me stuff like this, like you're my vocational guidance counselor or something?"

I was very pissed. *Very* pissed.

"All of us exist within the social fabric, Burris. Mental disorders and general misery aren't just things that happen inside a patient's head, they happen in the *world*, the actual world all of us live in. I just don't want to see you make a bad choice at such an early stage in your life. You might end up paying the price forever. You're a bright kid, I know that. Your flunking out has got nothing to do with dumbness, I know that too, but what I *don't* know is *why* things are not going well with you right now. I suspect it has something to do with your mother's problems, and something to do with the fact that you walk with a limp, but I don't *know* because you won't tell me. You wouldn't tell me last summer and you're not telling me now, and I wish you would. That's the end of the lecture. How would you grade it?"

Boy, I wanted to pick up that ashtray and brain him, that's how I graded it. Who the fuck does he think he is, reminding me I walk with a limp! That's just incredibly rude, I think. Fuck *this* for a caper! I stood up.

"Excuse me, I have to go."

"Don't chicken out on me now, Burris."

"I'm *not* . . ."

"Sure you are. You think I'm an asshole for telling you the truth, but the *truth* is the very thing you need to *admit*. You've got the truth inside you, the *facts*, whatever they may be, and all you need to do is open up and let it all out. Don't knock the cathartic experience until you've experienced it. Listen, I let you get away with murder last summer. I knew you were holding back on me but I played it with kid gloves because of your situation—the police involvement and you just getting out of the hospital—and I fully intended getting to the bottom of things, Burris, but vacation ended and you went back to school and for a while there it looked as though you were a changed person, getting your grades, seeing your girl, putting whatever your big secret is *behind* you, so I let it lie. But I shouldn't have done that. I should've insisted you keep seeing me till I found out the *real* reason for your suicide attempt. I didn't do it and that was wrong of me, but now that you seem to be back at square one I think it's time we really got down to business. I'll listen to anything you have to tell me, anywhere, anytime. I'm paid by the state, Burris, so it won't cost you a dime, but it could cost you plenty later in life if you don't open up *now* and tell me what's on your mind."

"I haven't *got* anything on my mind . . ."

"You've got plenty, we both know that."

"Bullshit."

"No bullshit, pal. Why else would you want to be an actor if not to hide behind assumed faces and make-believe identities."

"Who says I wanna be an actor!"

"It isn't important who said it, the important thing is *why* you want to play roles that will only prevent you from confronting the truth."

"Who *said* it!"

"If you must know, Mrs. Christensen."

"Whaaaaaat! She's *crazy!*"

"She only repeated what Sandra told her, Burris. You told Sandra you wanted to be an actor."

"Bullshit. She's a liar."

"Why would she say a thing like that if it wasn't true?"

"Jesus, how should *I* know. Why don't you ask *her*."

I know how it happened. I remember Dr. Willett back in the summer telling me his wife is in amateur theater, which has got to be the Buford Repertory Company, there can't be two amateur theatrical outfits in a town this size, the same bunch Alice Christensen waves her hands around with. I just bet Sandra told Alice and Alice told Mrs. Willett that Sandra's boyfriend, the weird kid that was being analyzed by Dr. Willett last summer, has decided he's going to be an *actor* just like them, and Mrs. Willett told the story to the doc and now it's come back to haunt me, because being an actor is yesterday's news to me, and very embarrassing news too. Why the fuck did I *come* here tonight! Was I stupid or *what!*

And here's a scary thing—for about five seconds there I wanted to say yes to everything he said, yes I want to be an actor to hide behind faces that aren't my own, and yes the reason I want to hide behind those faces is because I've got this big *secret*, which is that I found old Gene who didn't know if he's a man or a woman, found him dead in his trailer at Green Acres with a bullet in his head and a gun in his hand, and I put him in the trunk of his car and drove him a thousand miles to show Lee and Diane what happened when they abandoned Gene the way they did, but I couldn't find them and I had to dump old Gene out there in the desert for the coyotes to chew on and it's been running around inside my head, the whole thing, like a dog chasing its own tail and I *can't tell anyone*, I just *can't*, because I'd get put in reform school or someplace awful for having done what I did, be cooped up with a bunch of dumbass delinquent bozos that'd push me around and dominate me for being a gimpy geek, maybe even molest me and stuff even if they're too dumb to know two plus two is four . . . *I will not get fucked up the ass by morons!* I will not let dumb people rule over me and do what they want just because I'm a geek. That will *not* happen *not* happen *not* . . . So I have to keep my mouth shut about Gene. Shut, shut, shut, shut, shut, shut . . . But that didn't stop me from wanting to spew all that stuff out at him, just to get it off my mind once and for all, get that monkey off my back before it turns into a fucking gorilla and squashes me under, so for about five seconds I figured I might just *do it*, spill the beans about everything and be done with it. Dr. Willett's a much sharper guy than I thought, and he deserves to know that he's right about me, kind of a reward for his smartness if you see what I mean. But I couldn't do it. The feeling was there all right, the temptation to *tell*, waiting on the end of my tongue, not inside me but not outside me either, like a sneeze that's almost ready to come flying out . . . but then it doesn't. I shut my mouth and the secret went back up through my nasal passages into my brain. I whipped it back up there fast and locked it in again, and now I'm shaking all over because I almost *told*, almost let the secret *escape!* But I didn't. It's under lock and key again, and now I'm melting the key, melting it down so the door to the secret can never be opened again, melting it like Spencer Tracy melted the key to the laboratory so he won't be tempted to go back in there and change himself from nice guy Dr. Jekyll into pukey Mr. Hyde again. Now it's just a hot puddle. No more key.

"I have to go now."

Dr. Willett's face dropped a little. He knew I was on the edge of telling him what he wants to know, but now he sees it isn't going to happen.

"Okay, Burris. I wouldn't try to force you to do anything you don't want to do, you know that."

I went to the door and opened it myself. He came along after me to the hallway and the front door. The TV was still on in the other room, very muffled with lots of dramatic music. I got my outdoor stuff on fast as I could with the doc watching.

"Don't forget what I told you," he says.

"Okay."

"The door is always open."

No it isn't. I melted the key.

"Sure. G'night."

"You take care, Burris. You want a lift home?"

"No, that's okay."

I left. I came very close to spilling my guts in there, but it didn't happen. I'm never going near Dr. Willett again in my entire life. He thinks I've got a secret? Let him whistle for it. The secret stays where it's at—locked up tight in my skull. Some people, they want your soul, they really do. They're like do-goody vampires, all set to kill you with kindness and understanding. Fuck 'em. Vampires can only come inside your house if you invite them, and I'm all through issuing invitations. Master Weems is not at home to anyone. *Slam!*

It's 10:27, still too early to go home, but maybe if I walk slow it'll take an hour and Peggy'll be asleep by the time I get to Westwood Drive. That's what I decided I'd do, walk home nice and slow and get in bed and put another day behind me. Sometimes I think I'm like a mole digging a tunnel under the ground, scooping away with my front paws and shoveling the earth past myself and shoving it behind me with my back paws. That's what I do with life, scoop a hole in front of me to make a little headway, then shove it behind me fast as I can, because maybe the next chunk I scoop'll have gold running through it. Hah!

Tramp, tramp, tramp. It's still snowing, but not as heavy. There's practically no traffic so it doesn't seem like a Saturday night at all. I guess most people stayed home and got themselves tucked up nice and warm in front of the VCR with plenty of booze and potato chips close by. Sounds good to me. I didn't look at the *TV Guide*. Maybe I missed a good movie tonight with all this drama and adventure happening to me. Frankly I prefer to keep that stuff on the screen, where it belongs. It felt good to be out of Willett's den, out of all that damn smoke. The air always smells good when it snows, like it just spilled out of a refrigerator that's been cleaned out, no food in it to go bad, just a nice clean refrigerator with this very clean cold air spilling out of it into my face. . . . Shit! I forgot to phone Loretta today and find out what happened when Peggy went around there yesterday evening. I'll do that tomorrow. I

bet it'll explain why Peggy was such a bitch to me this afternoon. If I had've phoned I might've been prepared for the
bitchiness. I'm gonna have to start writing notes to myself so I
don't forget important stuff like that. Hey, I left that note on
Lennie's door. I wonder if he found it yet. Maybe he'll call me.
Nah, I bet he doesn't. Still, if he knows I'm looking for him
maybe he'll make himself available for a brief conversation on
the meaning of madness and its role in everyday life. I bet he
could give lectures on that particular subject. Nah, he won't do
it, in fact he'll avoid me like I'm a leper, I bet. Expecting Lennie
the Loop to open up and act normal is like expecting Santa to
come down your chimney with a sackful of what it takes to
make you happy. He wouldn't stay long at my place. Burris,
you've been a bad boy. You dumped a dead guy in the desert
like garbage and you live off your poor mother like a parasite. I
was going to give you a Mercedes SL but instead I'm giving you
this broken shoelace, just to teach you a lesson. Shape up, kid.
Right now you aren't fit to fork hot reindeer shit.

It took more than an hour to get home. By the time I
stomped up the front walk it's 11:39. There's something on the
doorstep. Has Santa been here and left me something four days
late? It's my school knapsack. . . . What the fuck's it doing out
here? I picked it up, then tried to open the door, but it's locked.
I tried my key. No go. Peggy's gone and locked it from the
inside and set the dead bolt too, the stupid bitch! Okay, try the
back door. Around back we go, plowing through the snow.
Back door is also locked, and I don't have a key for it. Back to
the front porch, where I suddenly figured out what's happening
here. I opened the knapsack. Yep, there it is—a note.

> Burris,
> You are not welcome in my home
> tonight. Loretta will take you in.

Whaaaaaaa . . . ? She's gone even crazier than I thought,
gone and locked her *own son* out of his fucking home! What a
crazy cunt! There's a pair of pajamas in the knapsack, and a
toothbrush and some clean underwear and socks and a T-shirt
for tomorrow. She really means it! Also there's my Sony shoved

in there along with the rest . . . Jesus! Did she listen to what's on it? Is that why she's even crazier than she was this afternoon? Did she lock me out because she's heard me badmouthing her on tape? And what *else* did she hear? I played back the last few inches . . . Marines saluting and jet fighters soaring and the flag and the National Anthem . . . That's where I left off recording last night. She wouldn't have finished listening at that exact same spot. She doesn't know my secret. So why the hell did she put it in the knapsack? Maybe she picked it up in a hurry and thought it was my little Walkman. They're pretty much the same color. But why put it in with my pajamas? So I can go to sleep at Loretta's with music to soothe me I guess. Very thoughtful and considerate of you, Mother dear, but you forgot the fucking headset. Just as well—the headset's plugged into the real Walkman, and that would've started her wondering what this *other* little machine is. Narrow escape, definitely. It was dumb of me to leave the Sony lying around. From now on it goes into hiding whenever I'm not actually recording.

So now what do I do? I could try pounding on the door and screaming to be let in, but that'd only get the neighbors up, and I hate being the center of attention. I'll steal quietly away into the night, that's what I'll do, and fuck you, Peggy. Jesus, what a bitch. She's on the slippery slope for sure. Senility has come to grab her a few years early. Yoo hoo, Mrs. Weems! Here I am a few years early, come to turn you into a cranky, unreasonable, sour-faced old bag. Come now, Mrs. Weems, it won't be so bad. Most people won't even notice the difference in you, ha ha!

I hitched the knapsack onto my shoulders and left. I've walked miles already tonight but who cares? All this wandering around is good exercise, that's how I look at it. Who gives a fuck. But then a funny thing happened when I'm just a little way down Westwood. I'm passing Nonny the fireplug, and seeing him there with a pile of snow on his little red cap made me think about how we painted him up way back on that summer day in '76 and I got to call him Nonny, and it made me think about Peggy and me four nights back, running from that moron with baby Jesus on his lawn, running and laughing together . . . and tonight she locked me out of my own home

. . . *our* place. She shouldn't *do* stuff like that to me, she just *shouldn't.* . . . Fuck! Now I'm *bawling.* Is anyone around? No one, just me and Nonny. I felt *awful.* . . . Why'd she hafta lock me *out* for chrissakes! So I turned up late at the laundromat, so fucking *what!* It wasn't my *fault!* I had a Doberman slobbering over me and she didn't even gimme a chance to explain. . . . Why'd she lock me out?

Shaddap!

Quit squawkin', ya putz!

Ya nuttin' budda baby!

Ya nuttin' budda joik!

Okay, guys, I *hear* ya! Lemme alone already. I gotta walk on. So long, Nonny, and don't let any mutts piss down your striped pants. Boy, I really folded up *bad* back there. Nuttin' budda baby is *right.* No more of *that,* Matt. From now on I'm hard like a rock. You wanna get inside my head? Get yourself a sledgehammer. This nut won't crack! No way! Try any of that shit with me? Forget it! I'm made outa titanium. Bullets bounce off me like hailstones. Nuke me, go on, *nuke me!* I'll walk outa that fireball with a tan, Dan. I'll glow wherever I go, Joe. I'll never be without heat, Pete. I'm the Atomic Kid and you all better *stay away!*

I went to the park and found a bench. There's no one around. The Christmas tree's still here, but the lights got turned off at midnight, even though it's Saturday night. The city fathers are on a tight budget this year. I got out the Sony and talked into it for a whole hour almost. It's been a very heavy day. I'm sitting on my knapsack so my asshole doesn't freeze. A cold asshole could lead to hemorrhoids. I'm taking no chances. I've got my mittens on and the Sony's inside my parka hood, nestled up against my cheek. I had to thaw it out there before switching it on. Peggy must've put the knapsack out hours ago because that little machine was *cold.* But it works fine. I've been talking very softly, a whole hour of stuff that happened. Good thing it was almost a fresh tape. I've still got about half a side left so . . .

Something very amazing just happened. While I was talking I saw something move way over by the Christmas tree, and I shut up so it won't know I'm here. It came out from behind the tree very slow, very cautious. I thought it was a dog, but when it came right out from behind the tree and was silhouetted against the snow I knew what it was, no mistaking those pointed ears and tail that isn't there. He stood still, not looking at me, so he can't have heard me talking, just stood there with one front paw raised off the ground, still as a statue except for the ears that switched this way and that, scanning for sound but there isn't any to hear, just a very light snow touching the ground everywhere he listens. I didn't even breathe, didn't want him to hear me or see my cloud of breath, didn't want him to run away. He was frozen there, a little fugitive in a place he shouldn't be. I bet he was starving hungry and didn't know which way to turn, the poor little bastard. I wondered what I could do to help him, but there was nothing. How do you approach a wild bobcat and offer assistance? He hadn't moved, was still there with one paw off the ground, looking very lost and alone, and I still wasn't breathing, feeling kind of starved for air by then, but I knew if I let out a single breath he'd be gone. I didn't even blink. Everything was frozen except the falling snow, very fine and powdery so the bobcat is kind of smoky-looking, not a solid thing, like a photo that's only half developed yet, real but unreal.

I breathed. I had to. A cloud of breath like steam from a locomotive came out from my hood. He didn't see it! I breathed again. I'm tingling all over from fresh oxygen and from seeing the little guy out there by the switched-off Christmas tree with his radar ears picking up the sound of falling snow and silence, not even a single car in the distance to frighten him. He put his paw down. I wanted to touch him, to make sure he's really real and to let him know I'm on his side. I wanted to put him in my car and drive him home like I did with that dog on the day after Christmas, but I haven't got the car and he wouldn't get in anyway. If only he knew where he was he'd know to head southeast for the nearest edge of town, after which he could cross fields and stuff and sooner or later reach the State Forest where he'll be safe. But he doesn't know. He thinks he's on another planet a million light-years from home. They'll catch him, tomorrow or the next day. He's on human turf, not his own, so he doesn't have a chance. He's the last bobcat in America, running from the cage.

"Hey!"

I couldn't help myself. I wanted him to know I'm here too. His head's about the size of a giant Texas grapefruit, and it swiveled around and those big bat ears pointed straight at me. I could see his muttonchops hanging down like Yosemite Sam's mustache . . . then he turned and raced away, running in that humpety-backed way cats do, his spine going up and down, up and down, and the undersides of his back paws kicking up snow. Those little leather pads with the claws tucked away between them like switchblades were the last thing I saw. I loved that little guy and I made him run away. Well, he would've gone anyway. At least he knew I'm here, hiding out in the park same as him.

I feel very sad now that he's gone, also very cold. I've been sitting here in the falling snow too long. I wonder if Peggy phoned Loretta and told her to expect me. Nah, because Loretta would've told her not to be so stupid, and the knapsack wouldn't have been waiting for me on the porch. Shit! It's 1:07 and I still have to get to Loretta's. They're gonna be pissed at me for waking them up. I have to do it, though, or freeze.

This is Klondike Clancy strapping on his snowshoes and preparing for the big trek north. My sled is waiting, the dogs pulling impatiently at the traces. My lead dog is heroic Mukluk. Down, Mukluk, *down*, boy! Are we all set, team?

Yip! Yip! Yowl!

Crack that whip!

Mush!

10

I spent what was left of last night on the sofa at Pete and Loretta's. I didn't get much sleep because very early in the morning Chris and Angie came stampeding into the living room and started asking how come I'm here and where's Peggy et cetera. I told them I stayed out late and it wasn't as far to their place as it was to Peggy's, so I came here to sleep. They wanted to know where I was out so late at and I told them it was a very wild party with lots of dancing and music, which to them must've sounded like Sodom and Gomorrah because they're innocent, I thought, then Angie asks, "Was there dope and stuff?" I mean this kid is *nine*.

"No there wasn't any dope, and everyone drank Cherry Coke."

"Bull," she says.

I wonder if Pete ever hears her talk like this? I bet not.

"It's true, Cherry Coke and for those that really couldn't do without a shot of the hard stuff they had a secret case of Seven-Up."

"Naaaaahh, they didn't!"

"Yeeeaahh, they did."

"Seven-Up!" says Chris, very loud. That's his contribution to the conversation. He's very bright for four years old but he gets very excited about ordinary stuff like Seven-Up. Probably he'll grow out of it and start getting excited about girls in around ten years from now.

"Is Peggy gonna come pick you up?" asks Angie.

"I don't think so."

"I bet you were drunk and couldn't walk last night. That's why you're *here*!"

"Yeah, okay, you found out at last. Is anyone in the shower?"

"Daddy is."

Then Loretta came in and hustled them into the kitchen. I couldn't wait for the shower so I just climbed into the fresh duds Peggy put in my knapsack, then I went in and had breakfast with everyone, Pete being out of the shower by then. I was very hungry and had a double stack of blueberry pancakes. The all-American boy, that's me. I even had a glass of milk instead of coffee, but only because Angie bet me I wouldn't.

After breakfast the kids got sent outside to play with the kid next door who got a sled for Christmas and already was bored with it and was charging other kids a nickel a ride. I bet he's a big success when he grows up.

"I think we have to face facts," says Pete. "She's disturbed."

"You're telling me," I said, still feeling very pissed at Peggy.

"We'll go talk to her," says Loretta.

"I'm not going anywhere near her."

"Don't be silly, Burris. You can't stay here, there isn't enough room."

"I'm not going back there till she apologizes for what she did."

"Whoa, hold it," says Pete. "Don't go climbing on any high horses, not unless you want to fall off again."

"Excuse me?"

"I mean okay, you have to put up with some pretty screwy behavior from her, but she has to put up with some peculiar behavior from you too. Just don't go pointing the finger is what I'm saying."

"She locked me *out* and it was *snowing!*"

"But she knew you could come over here. Don't make it sound life-threatening."

"It's the *principle*. She's nuts!"

"No she isn't," says Loretta. "She just overreacted to you showing up late. She is *not* nuts."

"Overreacted! Boy, that's an understatement. If she deliberately ran me over with the car you'd probably say she did it because she's *upset*. And I *told* her what happened, the Doberman and all . . ."

"What were you doing down at the junkyard anyway?" says Pete.

"Looking for Lennie."

"Who's this Lennie, a friend of yours?"

"Not Lennie the *Loop*," says Loretta.

"Yeah, that's where he lives, down at the junkyard. I had his cap."

"His cap?"

"Yeah, I was returning his cap that he dropped a couple days back."

I didn't tell them he already had it back. That would've just complicated things. I couldn't have told them exactly why I'm still looking for Lennie because I'm not a hundred percent certain myself yet. You have to bend the facts a little under circumstances like these I think. I'm only bending them a little bit today. Some days I put U-bends in them.

Pete put both palms down flat on the table, like King Solomon making a big decision. "The only thing to do is talk it all out with Peggy and get things settled between you, okay?"

Loretta already said exactly that, but he probably wasn't listening. I'm still not crazy about the plan, frankly.

"I'm agin it."

"Pardon?"

"I'm agin it."

"Burris, we can't take you seriously when you talk like that. Are you practicing some kind of role or something? Are you pretending to *be* someone?"

"You mean am I *in character*?"

"Right."

"No, I'm just agin it."

Pete looks at Loretta, then back at me. Pete thinks *I'm* the one who's nuts. Pete thinks anyone who wouldn't want to work for the phone company is nuts, that's what kind of nut *he* is. Pete is a very ordinary nut. He's a peanut, and I'm a macadamia. Loretta's a cashew. Angie and Chris are a couple of acorns and Peggy's one of those walnuts you bust the shell open and it's all black and rotten inside.

Loretta drove me home. Pete stayed with the kids. About a year after his first wife left him she came back and said she wanted Angie and Chris, and he told her no way and she started hanging around the neighborhood spying on them and talking to them over the school-yard fence, stuff like that, and finally Pete had to get a restraining order from the courthouse to make her quit, which she did and moved to New Jersey with some guy, but Pete is still very worried she'll turn up someday and kidnap the kids, so he never lets them wander around town on their own. That's why he didn't come with us, and I was glad to be alone with Loretta.

"You don't really think she's nuts, do you?" she says.

"I dunno. Yeah, I think she is a little bit. She's been sucking the sauce a lot lately."

"Having a problem with drink doesn't make you nuts."

"But she's so *changeable*, up one minute and down the next. I don't know when I see her which one it's gonna be this time around. Do I get a laugh ready in case she makes some stupid joke, or do I get ready to block another left hook? It's not *normal*, the way she's been just lately."

"How lately?"

"Since you told her on Christmas Day you're moving to Arizona."

"It figures. You know she came to see us Friday night?"

"Yeah but she didn't say anything about it to me."

"Well she tried to talk me out of it. *Us* out of it. It was kind of sad the way she kept trying to make the move sound risky and foolish, and how Pete can't afford to make that kind of move. That got Pete upset and he told her he can't afford *not* to make it, and then she said he only wanted to move us down there to get away from *her* because he doesn't like her. That really got everyone shouting. Lucky the kids were next door with their friend."

"I don't think he *does* like her."

"That's not why we're moving."

"I know, but he doesn't like her anyway, and she knows it."

"Well there's nothing can be done about that particular problem. They just don't mix, those two. Anyway she calmed down after a while and apologized for having said it, and we all acted very civilized and had a few drinks and watched a movie together. That's when she went all silent."

"She does that to me too, just sits there and watches the tube and drinks, but you can tell she's not really *watching* it, she's somewhere else."

"Exactly what I thought. Pete didn't notice anything but I did, and you're right, she was sitting there thinking about something entirely different from what the movie was about."

"I think it's menopause."

"She's not old enough yet."

"I bet some women get it early. Or maybe she's senile *way* in advance of normal."

"That's ridiculous and you know it. She's just very unhappy."

"Who isn't?"

"Don't be flip, Burris. She's got problems. What we've been seeing are the symptoms of those problems. The drinking, the moodiness, it all fits."

"Problem number one is she's over forty."

"Don't be so patronizing. You'll be over forty yourself one day, and you won't want some smartass kid telling you it's a problem."

"I'm trying to see things from her point of view. Don't tell me women don't get worked up about being over forty. It's a problem."

"Okay, I'll accept that as problem number one."

"Problem two is her husband got wasted in the war."

"Check, and problem three is her boyfriend left her and went to Oregon with an eighteen-year-old girl."

"Did Mack get himself an eighteen-year-old girl? He's practically as old as Peggy! I thought he just left, went away on his own. How come I didn't hear about the girl?"

"Because it was none of your business, that's why. Peggy felt humiliated enough just by Mack leaving that way. Knowing he was with some girl half his age made her feel like an old bag."

"Shit. I didn't know about that."

"This may come as a big surprise to you, Burris, but the weight of what you don't know would sink a freighter."

"What's problem number four?"

"She works in a laundromat."

"Only in the winter. In summer she paints."

"You and I and Peggy all know her paintings are crap."

"Problem number five."

"Right, and problem number six is her drinking. Problem number seven is me leaving Indiana with Pete and the kids."

"Would Pete and the way she doesn't like him qualify as problem number eight?"

"Nope, you've got that particular niche all to yourself, Bub."

"Me? Am I a problem to mommy dear?"

"Don't be cute. You've got to figure something out, Burris."

"I'm working on it."

"How about we number *your* problems since we're in the mood for arithmetic."

"No thank you."

"One, you flunked school."

"Okay, okay . . ."

"Two, your girlfriend dumped on you."

"*Okay*, thank you very much indeed for that enlightening analysis I don't think."

"Would you agree those are your two big problems?"

"The first one, yeah, but not the second. That's no big deal."

"Taking it like a man, are we?"

"Sure, what's the problem? Easy come, easy go."

"Tough nut, huh?"

"You bet."

I was glad she didn't make my short leg problem number three. Loretta's smart enough to know it is, but also sensitive enough to know not to mention it, not like that bigmouth Willett. As a matter of fact I've got four problems. Number four is the same as one of Peggy's, namely Loretta leaving Buford. She knows about that one too.

"So you've got two problems and Peggy's got eight. I think that kind of tips the balance, don't you?"

"I guess."

"Don't guess—agree or disagree."

"I agree. She's got six more problems than me."

"So what are we going to do about it?"

"Uh . . . get her a face-lift and a stud to sleep with, register her with AA, get her a job on network TV as an anchorwoman and make me the cohost, and we'll get you and Pete a bigger home right here in Buford with the half million per year we pull in. No problem is too big if you just give it a little thought."

"Funny man."

"Thank you. Hey, what was the old man's division?"

"What?"

"The old man, what division of the Army was he in over in 'Nam?"

"I don't remember. I was only seven or eight when all that happened."

"Peggy didn't ever tell you later on, or maybe show you some Army papers and stuff?"

"No, nothing. Why?"

"Just curious. I mean he was our dad, so how come we don't know stuff like that? Exactly when and where was he killed, for instance?"

"I don't know. I just remember he was reported missing in action."

"So maybe he was taken prisoner, not killed."

"There's no record of that, and he didn't come home after the war."

"So you think he's definitely dead."

"Burris, get serious, of course he's dead. If you want the details why don't you write the War Department or the Pentagon or whoever."

"Don't you think it's kind of incredible that we don't already know basic stuff like that?"

"You know Peggy doesn't like talking about it."

"Yeah, but just the basic facts, you'd think she would've given us those by now."

"I think one of the reasons she didn't was so you wouldn't miss him so much."

"I don't miss him at *all*."

"There you are. It worked."

"You think she remembers?"

"Try asking."

"I will."

"But don't push it. If she won't talk, forget it, okay?"

"Okay."

We got to Westwood and parked by the curb. The Impala's

in the driveway, so Peggy's home. It's Sunday and she doesn't go to church or anything like that. Peggy in church would be like the scene in *The Valley of Gwangi* where the Tyrannosaurus Rex busts into the cathedral. Also she doesn't work on Sunday because the Wishee-Washee doesn't provide service washes on the Lord's day, you have to do it yourself, wash your sins away in the blood of the lamb, hallelujah and amen, brethren. I had my knapsack with me in case Peggy won't let me stay, in which case I'll have to stock up on a few items, like a fresh tape as well as clothes.

She let us in after Loretta rang the bell. I didn't look at her or say hello and she did likewise, just said hello to Loretta. I went directly to my room and shut the door. Let 'em yak together all they want. Include me out. I looked through the window at the bird feeder, and it hasn't even got squirrels hanging off it today. Then I saw it's empty. I forgot to fill it yesterday after I got back from the Safeway. I felt bad about that, so I went out to the kitchen where I put the new bag of seed, expecting Peggy and Loretta would be in the living room but they're not, they're in the kitchen too. They quit talking when I came in. I ignored them and got the seed and headed for the back door.

"Where are you off to?" says Peggy.

Big news, world! Burris Weems's mom consents to speak to him!

"Bird feeder."

"Glad I got it for you?"

"Huh?"

"I said are you glad you got a bird feeder for Christmas. You seem to be looking after your feathered friends."

"Yeah."

I went out back before she could make some more brilliant conversation. She probably only did it to make Loretta think she's a regular mother. Loretta's too smart to be fooled that easy. I stomped across the yard, kicking the snow plenty because I'm not in a good mood, and when I got to the bird feeder my mood got worse, because those fucking squirrels have got frustrated about there being no seed inside it and they've pulled pieces of wood off the roof and off the little ledges where the seed spills out to get eaten, just torn off these long splinters of wood for the sheer heck of it, the little shitheads! It must've been squirrels that did it, not birds. Nothing smaller than a condor could've done that much damage. It looks like a hurricane hit it. Fuck those squirrels! I looked up in the tree and there's two of the furry little pricks watching me. Tree rats, that's all they are.

I refilled the feeder for the sake of the birds, I mean they'll benefit from the seed that the tree rats'll spill on the ground when they swing on the feeder like Tarzan. The rats moved a little closer, wanting me to fuck off so they can start stuffing themselves, but I wasn't ready to go back inside yet. If there was another way back into the house I would've used it, but there's only one back door and it opens straight onto the kitchen, so I can't avoid Peggy. I could've used the front door, but that would've looked stupid. I didn't want to go back in, not till I'm prepared for it. It's not good to feel unwelcome in your own home. I was still pissed at Peggy even if she *has* got eight different problems. I think her biggest problem is she's a loser, but hey! where do I get off calling her that? I'm the biggest loser in town. Maybe it's hereditary.

I watched the rats watching me. Is there some way to booby-trap the feeder that'd get the rats without harming the birds? I guess not. They know it too, the little fuckers. They have to be punished. They can't pull my bird feeder to pieces and get away with it. They've moved even closer along the limb, not scared of me at all. The nerve! I stooped down very slow and made a nice fat snowball, then straightened up again, slow and easy. The rats hadn't moved. The one in the lead is only about four yards away. Come an' get it, chiselteeth . . . That's it, you cute fluffy little feller you, a little bit closer yet. . . . I put my arm back nice and slow, then *kapow!* I threw the snowball hard as I could. It missed the nearest one by about an inch and smacked into the trunk a foot or so from the second one. Boy, did those rats *move!* They stretched themselves all skinny and long and flew back up the tree like their tails were on fire. You could hear their claws on the bark all the way to the top—*tickety, tickety, tickety!* I hope they have heart attacks, the vermin.

I went back inside and stowed the seed bag away.

"What's this about you and Lennie the Loop?" says Peggy.

"Nothin'."

"Burris, answering 'nothing' to the question I asked doesn't even make sense. I'd like to know why you were down at the junkyard."

"Loretta must've already told you why."

"You were returning his cap, right?"

"Yeah."

"Why?"

"To keep his head warm. Mental cases need caps in winter just like the rest of us."

"Yes they do. I'm just surprised to see the samaritan instinct coming out in you."

"Well, you know, anyone who feeds birds is just bound to do stuff like that. St. Francis was very famous for returning stuff people dropped in the woods."

"Was he now?"

"Yeah, he was."

"I don't think I'm completely satisfied with that answer, Burris."

I didn't say anything.

"So I think you'd better tell me something else."

"Peggy, it's not that big a deal . . ." says Loretta, but Peggy hushed her just by lifting her hand a little bit. Loretta doesn't look too comfortable, like she regrets opening a can of worms by telling Peggy about me and Lennie. Normally she wouldn't let herself get hushed like that, but after the big lecture she gave me about how we mustn't upset poor old problematical Peggy I guess she feels she can't fight back directly, which I don't blame her for.

"I'd love to get that answer before lunch, Burris."

I still didn't say anything. If I had've opened my mouth I would've said something very crude I think, because I really hated her guts, I mean this whole third-degree thing was totally unnecessary in my opinion.

"I'm asking you because it disturbs me to learn that my son is associating with an insane person who wears the same clothes all the time and looks like a child molester."

"He isn't."

"Isn't what?"

"A child molester."

"I'm very glad to hear it. What *is* he?"

"Nothing."

"We have a bad case of the 'nothings' today, haven't we."

"Peggy . . ."

But Peggy hushed her again. If I could've spat acid in her eye I would've, I mean it. There's something inside me, a monster crawling up from my guts, coming up through my tubes and pretty soon he'll be in my mouth. Already I can't breathe properly because he's reached my chest and pushed all the air out. He's coming up fast, the monster, and part of me is afraid of what he'll do and part of me is very willing to hand my mouth over to the monster, tell it, "Say whatever's on your mind. Say *anything*. Go ahead, rip her to pieces." I know the monster can do this because it did it one time last summer. The monster made me pick up Peggy's pathetic velvet paintings and smash them over a chair. The monster liked that a lot. We had fun doing that, the monster and me. This time the monster will speak, but the aim is the same—get Peggy. She's asking for it, using that sarcastic tone. She's gonna get it, I swear. I don't know what the monster'll say because he won't tell me ahead of time. He invents stuff on the spur of the moment, then says it.

"Why are you hanging around this person?"

"He's my dad."

"What?"

"Lennie the Loop is my dad. He's your husband. He didn't get killed. Lennie got killed. My dad switched dog tags with Lennie. Everyone else died. Nobody knew the difference when they found him. He's not really insane, just watching what happens around town. He's watching you especially. He's wait-ing to see if you ever talk about him and what you'll say when you do. That's why he can't talk. He swore he wouldn't talk until you said something nice about him. He's been waiting and waiting. He looks like he does so you won't recognize him. Even old man Bimmerhaus thinks he's Lennie, but he isn't. He belongs to *us*."

Her face went white, it really did. I thought it was just an expression, "her face went white as a sheet" et cetera, but it really can happen, believe me, if the person is shocked enough, and it looks like the monster shocked her plenty, Loretta too. They're both staring at me like I just announced the countdown to the end of the world has started and the first number was ten, not a hundred.

"Oh . . . oh, you sick little bugger . . ."

"You asked me, I told you," says the monster. He's enjoying this, but he acts very deadpan, keeps his voice very flat, not like my voice at all. That's how I know it's the monster talking.

"Jesus, Burris . . ." says Loretta, looking about ready to puke. The monster did what she told Burris not to do. Monsters are like that.

Peggy says, "How dare you say such a thing about a man that died for nothing . . ."

"He didn't die. He lives down at the junkyard."

"Burris, cut it *out* . . ."

"He died for nothing and you think he's some demented bum . . . Oh, you awful little shit . . . You shitty little kid . . ."

"Peggy . . ."

"Twenty years old . . . Twenty years old and he died for *nothing!*"

She's screaming, I mean *screaming* at me . . . The monster took a powder. The monster left a big empty space in my chest. I'm very confused. What was it the monster said? Why is Peggy looking like she's about to bend the kitchen table out of shape with her bare hands? She's staring at me, maybe still seeing the monster that left so fast. What she said keeps on racing around in my head like Little Sir Echo—twenty years old! For nothing! Twenty years old! For *nothing* . . . Lennie Bimmerhaus isn't my old man. My old man is a few teeth and some bones in a rice paddy. He's dead. Twenty years old and he died for nothing. He died for nothing, just twenty years old. He died younger than his own daughter is today. Loretta's twenty-two and the old man died at twenty for nothing, in 1970, when I was one year old and Loretta was seven . . . that can't be right . . . wait a minute . . . seven from twenty is thirteen . . . *wait* a minute . . . he's dead at twenty in 1970 . . . Loretta was born in '63 . . . *wait* a minute . . .

They're both looking at me, not saying anything, just look-ing, and what they're looking at are the numbers clicking past my eyes like a checkout console, and they know the numbers don't add up. The arithmetic here is *impossible*, and I don't care anymore what the monster said, don't *care* how it hurt Peggy saying what it said, because Peggy said something I can see now she wishes she hadn't said—*his age when he died* which can't be twenty because if it was it means he was a father at *thirteen* . . . All this time I never knew how old he was, never asked, just assumed he was twenty-five at least, or how else could he be Loretta's father as well as mine? All this time no one ever told me any different and I never asked, never even asked what division he was in, never asked *anything* because it all happened so long ago it doesn't *mean* anything, and now the cat's out of the bag, a bobcat, very surprised to find himself where he is because he never expected to be let out of the bag, and Peggy's gone and shaken him out right over the kitchen table and now she wishes she could shove him back in the bag but she can't, because I've heard the secret number, the number that *doesn't add up!*

"You'd better tell him," says Loretta.

"No."

"Peggy, he *knows* . . ."

"Tell me *what!*"

"Take it easy, Burris. Peggy, are you okay?"

"Yes."

I can barely hear her, she's gone so quiet. The cat is a tiger.

"Tell me *what!*"

"You can cut out that yelling right now, mister," says Lo-retta. Loretta's in charge here. Peggy and I are too badly mauled by the tiger. "Take a seat."

"No."

"Okay. I suppose you've guessed."

"Yeah."

A lie. I couldn't guess my own weight. I couldn't guess what day it is. The cat's got my tongue. The cat is eating my tongue, eating his way inside me, looking for the monster. He'll eat that too.

"I felt the same way when I found out. Peggy didn't tell me

till I was eighteen. She wouldn't have told me then, but she let it slip just like today. We agreed you shouldn't be told because you had a lot of problems yourself back then. That was a couple of years after you broke your leg and it mended short and you had to wear that special boot. We both knew how miserable you were and didn't want to get you all upset knowing your father and my father were two different men. It was bad enough having no father around at all, but you were so close to us both we decided you'd only get screwed up if you found out I'm just your half sister. God, this sounds like a *soap* opera . . . Listen, it makes no difference who our fathers were, we couldn't be closer, right?"

The cat is a fucking saber-toothed tiger with fangs a foot long. Am I really hearing this? Two husbands for Peggy? Two kids, two fathers? I'm totally inside the cat. Completely eaten.

"Tell him all of it," whispers Peggy.

"Oh yeah, the embarrassing bit. Listen, kid, you think you've got problems to handle knowing we're half brother and sister? Hey, at least you're legitimate. This really *is* sounding soapy . . . Okay, look, Peggy was only nineteen when she had me. The guy did a disappearing act soon as he found out I'm on the way. No ring, geddit? Jesus, Peggy, I'm telling this all wrong . . . I'm sorry . . . Oh, shit. *Look*, Burris, I don't give a damn about being illegitimate, okay? I'm not just saying that. *Nobody* gives a damn nowadays about it. Look at half the movie stars in Hollywood, popping out bastards every other week. Who cares! Peggy was just a little ahead of her time. Our mom was a pioneer, Bub, a leader of the sexual revolution, and we can be proud of her, okay? Okay? Can we have the benefit of a reaction to all these incredible revelations, please?"

She waved her hand in front of my face. The cat is purring now that he's been fed. I had a cat and the cat ate me, the cat ate me by yonder tree, cat goes fiddle-dee-dee . . .

"Hey, guy, did you fall asleep while I went through all that complicated stuff? Want me to go through it again?"

It's hard to hear her over the purring. I can see her easy enough, way over the other side of the kitchen table alongside Peggy. They're both looking at me, looking very sick and worried. Loretta's got a smile on her face but it's not real. She's very anxious. If I stare at her unreal smile the rest of Loretta'll disappear and leave the smile behind, like the Cheshire cat. They both want me to say something. I feel almost sleepy. Being eaten by a cat does that to you. I could fall asleep right here where I'm standing, but I don't think I should. What I should do, I should answer Loretta. She and Peggy are waiting for an answer. The reason I feel sleepy, I think, is because the big thought in my mind before Loretta explained everything, the big thought howling in my head before she set me straight was, *She's adopted!* Yeah, I thought she must've been adopted, which would've explained her being seven when the old man got killed at twenty. I'm glad she's not adopted. I'm glad she's my half sister at least. That's a big relief. So she's a bastard, so what? It wouldn't even have occurred to me to think about it if she hadn't said about the guy disappearing without giving Peggy a ring. What's a bastard nowadays? Just one of the guys. It's even kind of glamorous, very unconventional, you know? Hey, I think I'm jealous. I wish *I* was the bastard in the family. That'd suit me fine, be the final piece of the puzzle that's *me*, the final stitch in the uniform I wear, the one that lets people know I'm a very weird person . . . *and proud of it!* But I didn't hold a grudge against Loretta because she got to be the bastard instead of me. How could I hold a grudge against my half sister? That'd be like holding a grudge against myself, and I've already got more than I need of those. Everything is okay. The cat's been fed. A fed cat is a happy cat. The meal wasn't what was expected, *bombe surprise* instead of Kitty Bits, but the facts have been digested, and digested facts are accepted facts. The time has come for me to say what I think about all this secret stuff that escaped into the kitchen when nobody expected it to. I have to put Peggy and Loretta at their ease. I'm at ease. The cat's at ease. They should be at ease too. I opened my mouth to pass judgment.

"Uh . . . wow."

"Is that all you can say, Bub?"

I thought hard.

"What's for lunch?"

They stared at me a couple more seconds then creased up, cackling like a couple of witches over a bubbling pot, slapping the table so hard the ashtray jumped. "What's for lunch!" They kept saying it to each other over and over and every time it made them laugh all the more, really screeching, I mean they were practically hysterical, which I think was because of all the tension beforehand instead of the incredible funniness of what I said. I bet the people next door figured someone over here is crazy, that's how loud the laughing was, but after a while they started gasping and holding their ribs from a pain in the gut from all that yuk-yuk-yukking.

When things got quieted down Peggy says, "We may as well go the whole hog." She said it to Loretta, who started looking worried again.

"The whole hog?" she says.

"He can take it. He's a big boy. Are you a big boy, Burris?"

"What whole hog?"

I'm very curious about this hog. Then it hit me . . . The cat's out of the bag all right, but it left a kitten in there, and the kitten's growing . . . *I'm* the one who's adopted! I don't belong to Peggy and Loretta, not even *half* belong! I'm *adopted!* Oh, no . . . Now I've got a pain in the gut just like Peggy and Loretta, but not from laughing, this awful pain, getting bigger, like it'll split me in two, neither half of which belongs to these women. . .

"See, Burris, the fact is . . . God, this is hard to say, even after the rest of it . . ."

"Go on," says Loretta in a voice that says, "Get it over with."

"See, Burris . . ."

The axe is raised. I lower my head onto the block. They've shaved my neck. They always do that, I don't know why. The drums are rolling . . .

"Your father, Burris . . . well, he wasn't married to me either, not until after you were born, anyway. I'm sorry, kiddo."

The axe falls. A bunch of flowers swats the back of my neck. Of *course* I'm not adopted. Why the fuck did I think it even for a second? Peggy gave a little shrug and put this dumb expression on her face. I could tell she's feeling kind of foolish. Loretta's touching her on the arm in a reassuring kind of way, female sisterhood and solidarity et cetera, and it almost made me start bawling to see my half sister touch my mom that way. I think I'm a little shell-shocked, but the good news is, not only am I not adopted, I'm an *actual bastard!* I don't need to be jealous of Loretta after all!

"That's another thing we decided we weren't going to tell you," says Loretta, then she looks at Peggy and says, "Boy, what a couple of blabbermouths," and both of them started laughing again, but not hysterical like last time, more like it's a relief to get everything out in the open at last. Then they quit laughing because they realized they haven't yet gotten my reaction to this latest startling revelation. Don't keep the ladies waiting, Weems. I peeled back my sleeve, looked at my watch.

"Anything else? I have an engagement."

It went down pretty well, didn't get as big a hand as the first time, but I should've expected a letdown after *that* extravaganza.

"You really don't mind?" says Peggy.

I took hold of my lapels like an old-time politician.

"Mother, I'm proud to be the offspring of your loins."

That went down pretty good too, but Peggy quit laughing after a few seconds and starts bawling her eyes out, so before you can say "Happy Families" Loretta and I are all over her like a bad case of poison ivy, being reassuring as hell, and pretty soon *all* of us are bawling our eyes out. I haven't been this close, this physically close to Peggy since I don't know when, and boy, she really stinks of cigarettes, especially her hair, but it doesn't matter, nothing matters because the cat that got let out of the bag was a friendly cat after all, a big grinning Cheshire cat with a smile that'll stay after the cat's gone away, that's how I felt.

"God, I need a *drink*," says Peggy.

We all had a stiff Southern Comfort. I don't know why drinks are called stiff, I mean they're liquid after all. A Popsicle is stiff. We had stiff drinks anyway. I felt great. I'm a *bastard*. Oh, boy!

I bet I was the only genuine bastard in Memorial High. If only I'd *known* I could've held my head higher when I was there. I'm not kidding, I felt proud as hell to be a bastard, I think because so many other things already separated me from your average kid that I only needed *one more thing* to push me over the edge into total social unacceptability, at which point you either have to retire to a cave and never look another human in the face, or else adapt to the circumstances and be *proud* to be different. See, the thing that made me unhappy at school wasn't just being different, but not being different *enough*. It's hard to explain, but having a short leg and being five foot three and trying to kill myself were enough to fuck me up at school, but if there had've been just *one more* disadvantage to my existence it would've meant I was *completely* beyond the pale, as they say, and I could've relaxed and accepted that *no way* was I ever going to fit in.

It's a big pity I didn't know all along I'm a bastard. I could've coped a lot better in the long run I think, with a thing like that to add to the rest of my problems. Push a guy far enough from the tribal fire and his shadow gets longer and darker and spookier, and he *becomes* the shadow, and everyone around the fire is kind of scared of him as well as despising him, because this long shadow-person isn't normal like they are and they feel threatened by him . . . like Lennie the Loop! Lennie is Buford's shadow-man, the guy that *has to be there* to make the rest feel normal. Lennie doesn't give a shit about fitting in with society, and that's why I dig him, because he's so far from the fire he doesn't care anymore, doesn't *need* the fire, and that's the route I've been taking all my life, I can see that now, moving away from the fire step by step so my shadow gets longer and spookier . . . and now I know who I am—I'm Lennie the Loop's apprentice. That's who I am. When Lennie dies I'll inherit his shadow like a cloak he's left me in his will, so what I said to Peggy about Lennie being my dad, it's true in a crazy kind of way. . . .

"Cheers!"

We had another drink. My head's got a carousel inside it, spinning and spinning around with the music playing and the lights and mirrors flashing, and the one and only rider, riding a black horse and going up and down, up and down is Lennie the Loop, staring straight ahead, very dignified with one hand holding the reins and the other inside his coat like Napoleon, mad Lennie, riding around and around while everyone points and laughs except me. I'm waiting to ride the same carousel on the same black horse when Lennie finally reaches for the brass ring, reaches and falls . . . and then it'll be my turn to ride around and around with those bright carousel lights throwing my shadow out over the crowd, turning it around and around like the single spoke of an invisible wheel, and when the shadow passes over the crowd they feel cold and fearful, but only for a second because my shadow passes on, around and around . . .

"Look at our boy. He's totally fazed by it all."

"No more booze for our boy."

I gave them a dopey grin to let them know I'm okay. They'd be very surprised to know that right smack in the middle of all this hands-on family-reunion stuff I'm thinking about Lennie the shadow-man, the lone rider, Lennie who doesn't have to say a word or do a thing to make the whole town know he's there, magic Lennie the sorcerer, and I'm the sorcerer's apprentice, I know I am, because no one else is fit for the job, no one else is so far from being ordinary, only *me*, and I'll take over from Lennie one of these days as shadow-man, the one and only, the guy way out on the edge of the firelight even when he's riding the rim of the carousel.

"Let's take a walk and wake the kid up."

"Burris, do you want to go for a walk?"

"Okay."

So we did. It wasn't snowing. We went down the street. At the corner of Ironwood and Mitchell there's a church with people going inside. Jesus, they looked funny, going in there to pray and get told what to do and what not to do, all because a bunch of dead guys wrote a book that's supposed to be the actual word of God. Unbelievable, but in they go to get the Word. They'd go crazy I bet if they didn't have the Book to hold on to. If it's not in the Book it *didn't happen*, and if it *is* in there it's *fact*, and if you don't believe it you're *doomed*, pal. So doom me, see if I care. I'm the shadow-man-in-waiting. I eat doom for breakfast.

Peggy points to a sign outside the church. "Lookit, guys, JESUS IS COMING."

"Great. Is he flying United or Pan Am?"

"He wouldn't do that. He'll be very humble and lowly and come by Greyhound."

"He should use Amtrak. They need the business."

Step aside, citizens, the Weems gang is in town.

11

When we got back from the walk the phone was ringing practically off the hook. It's Pete, wondering how come Loretta's been over here so long. "I *know* it's past lunchtime," she says.

"Tell him to get his own goddamn lunch," says Peggy.

"Be back soon" is what Loretta says.

"The beginning of the end," says Peggy, only half joking. She didn't want the party with her two bastard kids to get broken up. I didn't either, but Loretta didn't even take her coat off, just went and got her keys from the kitchen and headed for the front door. She stopped on the way to give me and Peggy a double hug, like we're the Three Musketeers or something.

"Just think," she says, "I only came over to borrow a cup of sugar."

But it didn't work. Peggy's upset that Loretta's going back over to Pete's place to her other family there, so she went all stiff with Loretta's arm around her. I could feel it even if Loretta's between us.

"Okay, guys, duty calls. Gotta go."

I went out to the car with her.

"She went all funny again," I said, Dr. Weems diagnosing the situation brilliantly as usual.

"I know. She was like a kite for a while there. Listen, do you truly not hold a grudge about all that dumb stuff we kept secret?"

"Are you kidding? I think it's very interesting, the whole thing."

"You know, Burris, sometimes you can be exactly what we want you to be."

"Too bad I'm not like that all the time, huh?"

"Go in and keep on being nice to her, okay?"

"Sure."

"See you 'round."

"Like a record."

Peggy taught us that when we were kids. It's something they used to say when Peggy was little. Loretta got in the car and I watched her drive away, then I went back inside. Peggy's in the kitchen smoking another nail and there's a fresh drink on the table in front of her.

"So what do you think about everything?" she asks me.

"I think it's very interesting."

"You don't hate me for not getting married until after you came along?"

"No, I like the idea."

"I just want to be sure you're not going to shut yourself away and brood about all this and not tell me how you really feel."

"I feel fine. I'm okay, honest."

"You're a very mature person sometimes."

"I agree."

"But not all the time."

"About this I'm being very mature, so will you please relax? Why not inhale on that cool, refreshing smoke and have yourself a drinky-poo."

For a second or two she thought I'm being sarcastic, then she laughed. "Sharp," she says, dragging on the nail, "very sharp."

"Was the old man sharp too?"

"To be honest, no. You get it from me. Like it or not, you're very much *my* kid."

"I like it, I like it. Let's not get paranoid here."

I sat down and reached for the bottle, but she moved it over to her side of the table. "A sharp kid doesn't cultivate a booze habit at age sixteen," she says.

"Okay, I'll go to my room and shoot up instead."

"You don't shoot up, Burris. You don't shoot up and you don't snort coke and you don't steal cars. You didn't even play hooky from school. You haven't got anyone pregnant that I know about. You never took up cigarettes and for all I know you haven't even smoked grass. You're the cleanest kid on the block, also the sharpest, so how come everything's gone wrong, honey, tell me that."

She never called me honey before in her life. She's had one Southern Comfort too many I think. She's looking very sincere and concerned, not faking it or anything. She really wants to know, but frankly I didn't feel like discussing personal stuff like that. What I wanted us to do is go watch the afternoon movie together and maybe sneak another little drinky-poo for myself, a pleasant Sunday with Mother.

"How come, Burris?"

"Beats me."

"There go the shutters. Whenever you don't want to talk about something the shutters come down over your eyes. I can actually *see* them coming down. After listening to me and Loretta spill the beans, don't you think you could spill just a little plateful of your own?"

She doesn't know that the kind of beans I could spill are the kind that'd sprout and grow like the ones in Jack and the Beanstalk, and they'd lift 1404 Westwood Drive and everyone in it up into the magic land of Juvenile Court and the County Detention Farm and fuck knows what else, so there'll be no spilling of beans by yours truly. She needed an answer, though. She looks a lot older than usual when she's worried, like now. When she's pissed at the world it makes her younger somehow.

"I think I'm screwed up because . . . I've got one leg shorter than the other."

"Oh, baby, you mustn't let a thing like that mess up your whole life. Did that what's-her-name take a hike because of that?"

She means Sandra.

"No, uh . . . we were intellectually incompatible. She was smarter than me."

Peggy got a few yuks out of that, then she got serious again. "You're a nice-looking kid. So what if you've got a little limp? Let me tell you something about women, Burris. Most of us couldn't give a damn about a thing like that in a guy, we really don't. We're superior to men in that regard. Most men want a Playmate of the Month. If she's got brains too, that's okay, but if not, still okay. Tits come first. It's pathetic. But women,

Burris, we look a little deeper. We see the *person*. Believe me, you could have a peg leg and a parrot and *still* get the girls so long as you keep that smart mouth of yours working. Forget the limp. A smart kid like you could talk his way into any girl's pants, excuse my delicacy."

"Yeah?"

"Yeah. It's funny, but Loretta's father was the talker, the original silver tongue is what that guy had. Your own dad was more of a listener."

"The first one . . . uh . . . talked his way . . ."

"Into my pants, right. And when you said *first* you were right. The oldest story in the book, and it happened to me. "Trust me, baby, it's okay, you won't get pregnant if we do it this special way." An eighteen-year-old today wouldn't buy it, not unless she's exceptionally dumb. Nowadays it happens to fourteen-year-olds. He had nice hair, very dark the way I like. So did your dad. You and Loretta both had dark hair like your fathers, very convenient for kidding you both along until I blabbed to Loretta. She took it the same way you're taking it. I'm very proud of you both."

"The guy split, huh?"

"Did he ever. He gets the bad news, he's *gone*. That's the second oldest story in the book."

"How come you didn't get married the second time, before I got born? I mean, not that I mind or anything, I'm just curious."

"I didn't want to by then."

"Yeah, but why exactly?"

"Oh, I don't know. The principle of it. I didn't like feeling I *had* to. Jerry was okay, I mean I loved him, at first anyway. He was a very quiet guy. His parents lived here in Buford but I met him up in Maine in sixty-eight. I was with a bunch of friends camping out and this guy, Jerry, came hitching down the road one day and hung around awhile and we ended up getting together. I had Loretta with me. He was very impressed that I took my kid with me to see Maine, and I liked him for that. Most guys would've thought I should be stuck at home with a kid just five years old, but Loretta was having a ball, he could see that. We stayed up there for a while. We picked apples for a living. Then I came to Indiana with him.

He said his parents wouldn't be very comfortable having me around if they knew we weren't married, so we pretended we were. He told them I was a divorcee and we got married up in Maine, and now he's brought his wife home to meet the folks, surprise, surprise. They trusted him so much they didn't even ask to see the license. We had a couple of cheap rings on. So far as they were concerned we were married. I don't think they were too happy about the instant family angle—Loretta—but they were pretty nice about the whole thing in the beginning.

"Jerry started working for his dad. They had a roofing business. Everything went along just fine for a while, then I started to see the real picture. Old man Weems and his wife didn't like me. They hid it pretty good at first, then they didn't bother anymore. I was twenty-four and their precious boy was only eighteen, so naturally they thought I cradle-snatched him. They couldn't believe he was crazy about me, nothing as simple as that. I was a cradle snatcher, period. They tried to do the right thing by us, though, even bought this place for us to live in. Jerry felt kind of guilty about the whole deal, pretending to be married, but he wanted to live here. He didn't like big cities and that was okay by me. He was a decent guy and I was happy with him most of the time, except when we went visiting his folks. Then I got pregnant. If you have daughters, Burris, tell them to use *two* kinds of contraception. One isn't safe. Jerry said we could sneak over the state line and get married without anyone knowing, but I said no, why should we? Everyone was being very hip about love and sex and birth back then. It was a very straight thing to do, get married just because you were pregnant. I didn't want an abortion either, so we kept on pretending we're married and looking forward to the happy event like a regular married couple.

"Then guess what happened—in sixty-nine the Army calls Jerry up for the draft. They don't take married men usually, not unless the Russians are dropping soldiers on Washington, so he went down to the draft board and told them he's a married man with one stepchild and his own kid on the way. Where's the license? they said. Prove you've got legal dependents and we'll give you a deferment. He came home looking pretty sick. He knew they wouldn't accept a marriage license dated *after* they issued his draft notice. It was too late. We were so *dumb*. We should've figured it'd happen. Vietnam was *the* topic, morning, noon, and night. You couldn't turn on the TV without seeing the war."

"So that's when you told him to go up to Canada."

I already knew this part, kind of.

"I told him and *told* him. I *pleaded* with him. He wouldn't listen, even when I really blew my top. He'd just turn away and leave the house. He went and told his parents the whole story. They were pretty disgusted with him for lying to them about us being married. Naturally they blamed *me* for everything. His old man went down to the draft board and argued with them all day, but it didn't make any difference. Jerry asked me again to marry him but I said no, why should we if it wouldn't change the draft board's mind? What would the point be? We had a lot of fights about that. I told him it's like locking the stable door after the horse has already gone, but he still kept at me to get married. I think in his mind he figured getting married would somehow square things with his family. We weren't even *happy* together by then."

"Why didn't he want to go to Canada?"

"He was a regular down-home boy at heart, just didn't want to leave the town he was born in, something . . . *dumb* like that. And I think he had this notion that if he couldn't fix things between his parents and him by marrying me, he'd do it by going ahead and letting the Army take him. The old folks were real flag-wavers, you know? They didn't want their boy to fight, but they thought we were over there for a good reason, so they'd give him up if the government wanted them to. Jerry wouldn't do what I wanted. I called him a lot of very nasty names. He didn't deserve them I guess. He was just a guy who loved his parents and wanted to make good in their eyes. I tried one last thing. I went to the head of the draft board downtown and begged him to let Jerry off, really *begged* him, and you know what that fat old prick said to me? He said, "You should've thought of that before you went and had your fun, Miss Hippie." Had my *fun!* Miss *Hippie!* I wanted to *kill* him. He was some local bigwig with a Polish name, something starting with a Z, a real superpatriot, and he looked at me like I was the whore of Babylon. No way was he going to defer a guy that hung around with a tramp like me, that's the way he saw it."

"What an asshole!"

"You said it. So Jerry went in the Army. He said he still wanted to marry me but I said no again, because I didn't want to do anything that would've made his parents feel better about the situation. I blamed *them* and old Zee-something, and they blamed me, so sixty-nine was a very bitter year. Jerry did his basic training. They trained them up and shipped them out like frankfurters to get chewed up in Vietnam, all those eighteen- and nineteen-year-olds. He got leave before his unit shipped out. I couldn't recognize him. He had this awful shaved head . . . I'd never even *seen* his ears before . . . I cried and cried. You and Loretta cried too, because I was. We got married right here in town. He said if he got killed he wanted me to have an Army widow's pension to help bring you and Loretta up on, so I did it, I married him. At least it was only a justice of the peace that did it, not some Holy Joe like his parents would've wanted. They didn't even get invited. We just up and did it. I felt numb all through it, Jerry too. We couldn't even make love properly before he went back to the Army and got shipped out.

"He used to write me these very sweet, very dumb letters about missing me over there. I had to force myself to write back, I mean I couldn't think of anything *real* to say, anything *sincere*. I still loved him, in a way, but not the way I would've if he'd done the smart thing and made a run for Canada. I would've respected him for breaking the stupid, *stupid* draft laws and telling his parents to go fight the war themselves if they believed all that death-or-glory bullshit. God, I hated them. They were nice, average, backbone-of-America types, and I hated them. But I think I hated the draft board guy more. I looked him up in the phone book. He was the only Zee-what-ever-it-was in there, and I had this plan to set fire to his house. Just a fantasy. I sat in here and changed your diapers and watched the war on TV and tried to explain to Loretta where Jerry was, and waited for him to get killed. If I'd really loved him I think I would've believed he's not going to be one of the dead ones, the way wives always think. But I didn't think that.

I knew he'd stop a bullet, and . . . listen, Burris, I'm telling you the *truth*, and you *mustn't hate me for it*. I had this idea in my head that any man . . . *foolish* enough not to run to Canada was *asking* to get killed. I'm sorry. That's the way I was thinking all through the end of sixty-nine and into seventy. I think I was getting to be a little bit more of a basket case every day, writing those stupid letters to him and acting the role of the patient, suffering Army wife. I hated it, *all* of it. I didn't go see his parents once, not *once*, I hated them so much, and they didn't come over here, not even to see you, because they hated me too. I felt like I'd sold myself to middle America just because Jerry was a nice guy, that's all, just a nice guy."

She lit another cigarette. She forgot to stub the first one out, so I did it for her. She sucked that smoke down like it's all that's keeping her alive.

"I think I ended up hating myself most of all. I mean I ran away from home in sixty-two, before it got to be the 'in' thing to do, and I knew I'd *never* live the way my own parents did, believing all the dopey things everyone believed in, you know, God and country. It was all going to be different for me, oh *yes*, and what happened? I wind up in the heartland with two kids and a husband I don't even love fighting a stupid, *shitty* war thousands of miles away. Sometimes I thought I'd run away again, escape from the whole deal, even leave you and Loretta behind, go find another place to live, in another state with another man, someone on the wrong side of the fence like me. But I didn't do that either. I kept on doing what I was doing, the all-American mom, the patsy with the apron and the vacuum cleaner and the milk formula. Once, *just* once, I thought I'd kill myself. That's why I never gave you a lecture about what happened last summer. That's why I didn't push you for answers the way I might've done, or get in your face generally about it, then or now, because I know how you must've felt to do what you did. I don't know why you did it, but it's got to be more than just having a limp. Anyway, I know how you must've felt, and it's the most awful feeling in the world, honey. It was bad enough I should feel that way at twenty-five, but no one as young as you should have to feel like I felt, no one . . ."

She's leaking tears again. I can't tell if they're for her or me. I got her a kitchen towel and she blotted herself dry, then had another shot of Southern Comfort. We must be too far north. She's getting no comfort that I can see.

"Then it happened the way it happens in the movies. The doorbell rings. Try very hard to understand this, Burris. It was almost a *relief* . . . I'd waited all that time for it to happen, and it happened. I could quit waiting. He wasn't officially dead, just missing in action, but it didn't even occur to me that he might still be alive. Don't hate me for this, but . . . I hated the way the Army told me there was a reasonable chance he was captured. I didn't want to hear that. I wanted it to be over, finished with. I've never told anyone that before, not even Loretta. If you were a regular everyday kid I wouldn't have told you either, but you're not, you're very much *my* kid, and we don't look at the world the same way other people do, am I right?"

"You bet . . . uh . . . yeah, definitely."

"His parents wanted to believe he was captured, not killed, but his number or whatever was never handed over by the VC. They didn't accept he was dead until seventy-two. They never said so, but I know they accepted it because they were killed about then in an auto crash, and in their will they left everything to some cousins in Iowa. They didn't leave anything to Jerry because I would've got it as his widow. So they knew he was dead when they changed the will all right. They didn't leave a cent for you, kiddo, their own grandson. I think they made themselves believe you weren't Jerry's kid, that's how much they hated me. They weren't thinking too clearly by then. Jerry's death, or disappearance or whatever you want to call it, it twisted their thinking, maybe even made them a little crazy. The old lady had a terrible skin rash she was so upset by everything. Jerry was their only kid. They were too old to cope with losing him that way. That war . . . that war screwed *everyone*. Poor Jerry. All he had to do to live was give Uncle Sam the finger and run for the border. Canada's just a long day's drive from here. He could've done it easy, taken all of us up there and come home again after Jimmy Carter's amnesty. But he just couldn't do it. He let the old red, white, and blue wool get pulled over his eyes. Mom and Pop and Uncle Sam, they wouldn't let him, so he died along with all the rest. Now you know."

Now I know. What can I say?

"Thanks."

She gave me this lopsided look.

"It's a load off the old mind," she says.

We didn't talk for around a minute. I got antsy. She's looking at the wall. That's *my* job.

"Wanna watch a movie?"

"Sure," she says, and we picked ourselves up and went into the living room. She brought along her booze and cigarettes. The movie had already started but we watched it anyway. We both saw it before. Peggy had a couple more shots and fell asleep. I got up and turned the sound way down so there's just this murmuring to keep her company, then I went and looked in the phone book. Two Zalewskis, three Zaritskys, five Zimmers, two Zinsmeyers, three Zucarellis, one Zurowski, two Zweigs. Zurowski is the one, the fat old prick. He'll be older and fatter and prickier now. He called Peggy Miss Hippie. She must've been pretty wild-looking back then, no bra I bet, and hair all down her back. Poor old Peggy. Zurowski Martin, 5102 Carriage Hill Dr., 843-1131. I bet his pals call him Marty. Marty the prick. This guy put my dumb old man in the Army. You prick, Marty Zurowski. I put the phone book back on the stand in the hall. Now what? It's 2:37. I decided I'd give Lennie the Loop one more try.

I got the keys and drove across town to the junkyard. The gates were closed but not locked, so I went on through. When I came in sight of the trailer the Doberman ran at me but stopped a yard or two away, growling. I expected him to be tied to the kennel because the tow truck's here, which means old Bimmerhaus is home. The dog quit growling but wasn't about to move anyplace else, so I told him, "Look, you know me. I was here twice before, remember? You even sniffed my hand last time. Take another sniff." I took off a mitten very slowly and put out my hand. He came forward and sniffed it. "Atta boy. Is Lennie home?" He didn't know. I went past the trailer and kept on till I got to Lennie's shack. The note I left jammed in

his padlock is gone, but the padlock's still there. Lennie is out.
I went on back to the trailer and knocked on the door but no
one opened it. I can hear the TV inside, so maybe I should
knock louder. I did it, but still no one answered. I went around
to the side window and stood on the propane tank and looked
through. Old Bimmerhaus is asleep in front of the tube with a
whole regiment of empty Budweisers around his boots. I got
down and patted the dog. He's still got those dopey ear protectors on. I didn't touch them in case his ears are still sore from
getting clipped. He's an okay dog when you get to know him.
"Now what?" I said, but he wasn't big on suggestions. "Escort
me to the gate, Rex," I told him, and he did. "You're a
gentleman," I said, and shut him in. I got in the car and
drummed the wheel awhile. In the glove compartment there's a
map of Buford. I took it out and looked at the index. Carriage
Hill Dr. E7. I turned it over. E . . . 7 . . . my two fingers
met. It's out past the edge of town. Ignition . . . Drive . . . I'm
on my way.

I kept telling myself this is a bad idea. What could I do,
punch the old prick out? He probably won't even know who
Jerry Weems was anymore. Weems? Weems? Oh yeah, the
dipstick with the hippie girlfriend, tried to worm his way out of
the draft. Weems the worm, didn't want to do his patriotic
duty, sends his slut girlfriend along with a belly like a basketball to ask if we can't please give him a deferment. Did I tell *her*
where to go. You know what? They weren't even married, got
a family started and not even married, how *about* that. Army's
what a guy like that needs to straighten him out.

I got there faster than I figured. Carriage Hill Drive is about
a mile outside the city limits. It runs off the main road opposite
a little gas pump and store. I turned onto it and kept driving.
There aren't too many houses along it, but the ones that are
there are very big and fancy, with lots of untouched woods
around, acres of trees with their empty branches all feathered
along the skyline and nothing marking the snow underneath
but animal tracks I bet. You have to pay plenty for big houses
like these with all those acres of privacy around them. They're
about a quarter of a mile apart, most of them with long drive-
ways and fake old-fashioned architecture so they look like the

kind of place George Washington would've lived in, apart from the three-car garage with the weathercock on top. Zurowski's place was the ninth one along, which doesn't explain why it's number 5102. Rich people probably figure single-digit numbers don't have class, so they make sure the zoning laws or whatever let them have nice long numbers for their fancy mailboxes that are painted like little red barns, very cute I don't think.

I drove right on by. I chickened out. Big rich houses are very intimidating. Parking the Impala in front of 5102 would've been like pulling up outside the White House in a garbage truck. I chickened out and kept driving. I passed a fire road it looked like, leading off Carriage Hill Drive on the left, then there were no more homes. The Zurowski place was the last. Ahead of me is trees and more trees on both sides. I went on another mile, then turned around and drove back, telling myself I'm a coward for coming all the way out here and then chickening out, but then I came to the fire road again and swung onto it without even thinking twice. It's on the same side of Carriage Hill Drive as the Zurowski place, and only a couple hundred yards from the edge of his lawn. It went up a little rise so there's a slope on the left, in the direction of Zurowski's.

I stopped and parked on the edge of the road, which on this side has got a drainage ditch alongside it, with woods on the far side. I couldn't pull too far off the road or I would've ended up in the ditch. Where I'm parked is blocking the road some, but there aren't any tire tracks so it isn't used except in the summer I bet, because who needs fire roads in winter? It isn't even paved, just a dirt road so fire trucks can get to a blaze in the woods.

Engine off. I got out and crossed the road, then started down the slope. It's a pretty steep grade and I took it slow, planting my boots sideways like a skier, and it didn't take too many steps till I'm under the trees. Did you ever notice how when you get among trees everything suddenly goes quiet? The branches swallow everything up. In winter it's quiet as can be because there aren't any leaves to rustle in the wind, and today there isn't any wind anyway. So it was very quiet. Every step I took sounded like Godzilla trampling Tokyo. The only tracks I saw were bird tracks, I don't know what kind. It was very beautiful in there with snow over everything, clean white snow, not the brown slush town snow turns into after a while. I stopped a few times just to look at it, the snow and the trees. Not even a twig moved, like the woods are frozen solid. There was one old tree that fell over and pulled its own roots out of the ground about a hundred years ago I guess, so it's dead as stone and covered in snow, all the roots like frozen snakes in the air. It felt very good to be in that place, but I'm there on business, not pleasure.

Finding Zurowski's wasn't hard, I just headed in the general direction of the place in relation to the fire road and lucked out after ten minutes or so. The trees thinned out and I snuck up behind the last one and there it is, the back of the house. There must've been at least a dozen windows, upstairs and down, so I stayed behind the tree with just a little bit of my head poking out. The big back lawn has got two interesting things on it, a satellite dish and a greenhouse. Maybe they can't get a cable hookup way out here, and they wouldn't want to spoil their chimney cluster, which isn't even real chimneys, I bet, by bolting a TV aerial to it, no sir, not classy, so it's a satellite dish for Mr. Zurowski and family. It's the solid kind, not the latticework type, painted creamy yellow. It looks like a giant fungus pointed at the sky. The greenhouse was a big one, at least fifty feet by twenty. They must have a complete jungle in there. I can't see through the glass because it's all beaded on the inside with moisture. All I can see is greenish shapes. It must be like the Amazon basin in there.

Okay, I've seen the enemy camp, so what did it get me? I haven't got the guts to go around the front and ring the doorbell even, so why did I come out here? Old Zurowski isn't going to fall on his knees and beg my forgiveness for his big crime, in fact he'd most likely call the cops. And let's face it, what does it *mean* to me that the old man got sent off to Vietnam and blown away and I got brought up without a father? It doesn't *mean* anything. I never knew him so I never missed him. So I didn't have an old man to practice one-on-one with, shooting at the basketball hoop over the garage door like every American dad and kid are supposed to. We haven't got a garage or a hoop, and I don't like basketball anyway. Maybe he would've wanted to go fishing like TV dads always do. I wouldn't have liked that, sitting in a dumb rowboat for hours. He would've wanted to take me to the ball game. I *hate* ball games. Ball games are what practically *everyone* likes, so I'm just naturally obliged to hate them. He would've wanted to watch football on the tube, rooting for the home team or the state team or whoever and keeping me from watching the movie on the other channel. I would've hated him for that. He would've expected me to be macho. I'm not. I haven't got it in me. Never had it, never will. I would've been a big disappointment to the old man, and ditto likewise vice versa. It would've been lousy having a father. It's been tough enough just having a mother, frankly. Maybe old Zurowski did me a favor, sparing me all that father-son buddy-buddy crap. It would've been very cringe-making to get called Champ and Tiger and have this guy always punching me on the shoulder and pretending to box with me and dragging me out in the backyard to toss the old baseball around. Fuck that for a caper. Taking everything into account, I'm better off for not having had a dad. That's what I think, even if some people would say I'm sick to think that way. Too bad, Dad.

Zurowski was a prick to my mom, but what's he done to *me*? Nothing. And somehow I couldn't see that he was a prick to my old man either. The old man should've done what Peggy wanted him to, run for the border, but he wasn't prepared to break the rules. Zurowski was just the guy in charge of the rules, probably a very stupid guy, I admit, but who else would you expect to have in charge of stupid rules? Jerry Weems didn't have to obey those rules. Uncle Sam isn't God. He made a choice, I mean he chose not to choose, if you see what I mean. Zurowski didn't get the old man killed. The *old man* got the old man killed. I can see why Peggy hated Zurowski for calling her Miss Hippie and all, but I can also see why Peggy didn't have a whole lot of respect for Jerry Weems after he got on board the Army bus and let himself get driven off to boot camp and the war. He didn't have to do it. He could've run. Calling it a patriotic duty to go fight in 'Nam doesn't mean a thing, not to me, I mean when Hitler and Tojo told *their* people to get into uniform they called *that* patriotism, right? I wonder if the old man ever asked himself if there was a good reason for the war. I bet not. I bet most of those guys that got drafted didn't ask that question any more than those millions of Krauts and Japs asked themselves. The Big Boss says go fight, so they go fight, and everyone back home acts very surprised when the body bags start arriving on their doorstep, and even more surprised when the war gets lost by us, the *good guys!* How can the good guys lose? they ask themselves. I bet the Krauts and Japs thought *they* were the good guys too. The whole thing makes me want to puke.

I took another peek at the back of the house and the satellite dish and greenhouse, then followed my tracks back to the fire road and the car. I got in and stared at the dash awhile. It's getting dark now, that time when even though the sun's low there aren't any long shadows because the sky's too cloudy. Time to go home. I got out the map. It doesn't have the fire road marked on it, so it's kind of risky to drive on ahead without knowing where I'll come out, or if it's a dead end maybe, and if I have a breakdown no one'll ever drive along here and give me a lift back to town. I'll have to turn around and go out the way I came in, which is also risky because it's a narrow road with a ditch on one side and a slope on the other, and the Impala is kind of long and wide and needs a football field to turn around in, but I'll have to do it.

Ignition. I put the car in gear and moved out slow, swung across the road, turned the wheel and reversed, turned the wheel the other way and went forward, turned the wheel back again and reversed. I had to do that five or six times before I got turned around. In a car that big on a road that small you can only move about two feet either way before you have to stop. Any more and I would've gone into the ditch or down the slope. It was very tricky but finally I did it and headed on back to Carriage Hill Drive, just a few hundred yards, turned right and a half minute later I'm passing by Zurowski's driveway and mailbox. So long, Zurowski, you old prick! The past is the past. I've got my own problems. Revenge is something that happens in the movies.

When I got back home it's well and truly dark. Peggy was awake and wanted to know where I went. "Just for a drive," I said. We ate supper without much talking. I did the dishes while Peggy kind of wandered off into the living room. She's got a new bottle of Southern Comfort in her hand. She wanted to play records, which I wasn't in the mood for so I went to my room and put a fresh tape in the Sony and yakked my head off. Today is probably a big milestone in my life, but it's funny, I don't feel all that different for finding out all that stuff. I think I must be a very adaptable person.

Peggy's got the volume way, way up. It's one of her favorites—*Sixty Fabulous Hits from the Sixties*. I didn't go out and ask her to turn it down. There wouldn't have been enough room out there for me and Peggy *and* the Beach Boys and the Turtles and the Byrds and Wilson Pickett and Sonny and Cher and the Supremes and the Lovin' Spoonful and the Mamas and Papas and all the rest. She's listening to Herman's Hermits now, *I'm Into Something Good*.

I doubt it.

12

It's hard to remember dreams unless you're woken up in the middle of one. I was dreaming I'm in the cockpit of the old Sabre jet in the playground over in Belvedere, the one I used to climb inside when I was a kid and pretend I'm a hotshot pilot hero. I'm in there flying the jet, I mean really flying it through the air because this is a dream, and I look out at the clouds and I see this face right next to the cockpit and it's Lennie the Loop with his hair and beard whipping around in the wind way up there, and he says *without moving his lips*, "Your mother wants you," and I looked where he's looking, which is across the other side of the cockpit, and he's right, Peggy's there with her hair blowing around, telling me to "Get up, Burris. Wake *up* . . ."

"Wake *up!*"

I sat up so fast I almost knocked her teeth out with the top of my head. I looked around for Lennie but he's not there. Daylight's coming through the window shades. I can smell the booze on Peggy's breath she's so close, a very sickly smell that cuts through the smoke in her hair even.

"Huh?"

"Get up. We're going to Washington."

"Huh?"

"We're going to Washington. I thought about it all night. Get up."

"Washington?"

"To the memorial."

"The *war* memorial?"

"I've got breakfast ready. Move your butt."

And she walked out before I can ask any more questions.

The *war* memorial? She's flipped. It was pretty clear what happened. All that true-confessions stuff yesterday has pushed her into a guilt trip over thinking the old man was a clown for letting himself get drafted and killed. She's thought that way since '69, a long time to think of your husband as a clown, so now she wants to make amends. It's crazy. It's too *late*, also the wrong time of year. I did what she wanted and got up. She's in the kitchen dishing out poached eggs.

"We can't go now," I told her.

"Why not?"

"It's winter. The roads are icy. Washington's hundreds of miles away."

"The Interstates'll be open. Eat."

"Today's Monday."

"So?"

"You're supposed to go to the Wishee-Washee."

"Screw the Wishee-Washee."

"Old Blangsted'll fire you."

"Screw old Blangsted too."

"He'll fire you and we won't have any money anymore."

"Then you can go get a job and support me like a good boy should."

"Why do we have to go *now*?"

"Why not? You'll eat faster if you shut up."

She only fixed breakfast for one. The remains of her own breakfast are in the ashtray. She's living on smoke and do-good daydreams.

"I don't think this is very smart."

"So don't think it. All you need to do is share the driving."

"This is dumb."

"His name's on those black walls. I want to read it."

"You'll have to spend hours and hours looking for it first. The names aren't alphabetical."

"There'll be someone there to help us find him."

Notice that? Find *him*, not *it*. All there is in Washington is his goddamn name, not the man himself, not even his ghost.

"Come *on*," she says. "Eat!"

"I'll get indigestion."

"So we'll pick up some Tums."

"This is gonna cost a couple hundred bucks in gas and motels."

"I don't care. I've made up my mind."

"Did you tell Loretta yet?"

"She'd only try to talk me out of it. Anyway, he's not her father, he's yours."

"Yeah, and I don't think it's a good idea."

"Burris, I don't *care* what you think. Eat! Pack a bag and let's *go*."

I ate. I packed a bag. This is *double* crazy. She's only doing it because she played all those old sixties songs last night. I put my Sony in the bag along with the other stuff. Crazy, crazy, *crazy* . . . She's already outside in the car, honking the horn to make me hurry up. If I didn't know better I'd say she was high on speed or something. She's really got a bug up her ass about this Washington thing, a brainwave that'll swamp her unless I'm there to bail her out. Letting her do this crazy thing on her own would be like giving matches to a baby. This lady has to be chaperoned for her own good. There's the horn again.

I locked the front door. She's revving the motor to get it warmed up. I dumped my knapsack in the backseat and got inside next to her and she backed out into the street practically before I got the fucking door closed. Uh-oh, crazy person behind the wheel, Neil. We took off down the street like there's a posse after us.

"Can we go slower on account of the law and the ice, please?"

She slowed down a fraction. The Rand McNally highway guide is on the seat between us. "Sixty-four east to pick up Seventy-nine north," she says, "then we hop across on Route Forty and pick up Two-seventy all the way down to Washington. With luck we'll be there tomorrow night."

"Terrific."

"Where's your spirit of adventure, kid? This'll be the first time you've been out of state in your life."

Except for my summertime jaunt down to New Mexico and Arizona, which she doesn't know about and never will, Jill.

We stopped at the drive-through Instabank and Peggy shoved her plastic in and the machine spat three hundred bucks at her, the most it'll give out in one day to one person. She dumps it in my lap. "Take care of it, Mr. Treasurer." We got a tankful of gas at the Exxon station, then we're heading down Pinskey to the junction with I-64 and swinging onto that big wide eastbound lane with the Impala giving itself a sixty-miles-per-hour hernia. It sounded like there's a bunch of elves under the hood banging on the engine block with metal coat hangers.

"How long since you had it checked out?"

"Stop worrying."

"This is a bad time of year to get stranded."

"Buster Brown wore a frown, like a 'nana upside down."

That's what she used to say when I was a little kid and I got in a temper about something. I used to wear Buster Brown shoes, see, and a 'nana is a banana in case you didn't already guess. It's only 9:07. Peggy turned on the radio, AM not FM, natch. This is the Weemsmobile after all.

"I love music when I drive, don't you, kiddo?"

"Love it."

We hammered along at a steady sixty like everyone else. No one drives fifty-five, not even little old ladies, the kind that drive big old Eldorados and are so tiny you can't see their heads over the windowsill or their hands on the wheel. Whenever you see an Eldorado with no one driving, it's a little old lady, usually called Bernice. If it's the husband driving you can generally see his hat. The husbands are always called Elmer. Whenever you see Bernice and Elmer together it means they're driving to see a relative in the hospital in another town.

The heater doesn't work too good so we kept our parkas on. Peggy hummed along with the radio with this big smile on her face. She's totally daffy.

"Why are we *doing* this?"

"We should've done it a long time ago. Don't give me any grief, Burris. I'm going to Washington and you're going with me."

"*Jahwohl, mein Führer.*"

Daffy as a daffodil. She's got the light of righteousness in her eyes. The only thing that'll stop her is a nuclear strike. *Mrs. Weems Goes to Washington.* Weems Junior goes along for the ride. I sat back and let the elves take us there. Also I put on my seat belt. You never know, Joe. I told Peggy she should do the same.

"Do it for me, please. I'm keeping both hands on the wheel like a careful driver should."

I leaned over and buckled her up, like strapping a baby into a high chair so it won't fall and break its dumb head. This lady needs looking after.

She drove for almost four hours, then we stopped for eats at a Bob's Big Boy outside Lexington, Kentucky. After we finished I waited outside by the plastic statue while Peggy took a dump. Bob's Big Boy has got snow on his kiss curl. Finally she came out. "I almost fell asleep in there," she says. "You better do some driving."

Which I did, with the radio off. She fell asleep next to me. I don't think she slept at all last night, probably kept awake by her Big Idea. She's in the grip of guilt, which is a very strong thing. The grip of guilt made me drive Gene home in the trunk of his car, and the grip of guilt about the way I had to dump him in the desert has kept my lip buttoned ever since. Guilt made me come along with Peggy, because I know I haven't behaved like a good boy should, flunking out of school and letting her feed me without giving a nickel back. By going to Washington she wants to wipe out everything that's gone wrong for her since '69, like a Catholic that hasn't been to confession in all that time and all of a sudden rediscovers her faith. It's a big illusion in my opinion. Nothing gets fixed with one stroke. Nothing gets fixed, period. You just learn to live with broken things and maybe build a few new things that'll also get broken by and by, you can bet on it. This is the philosophy of Burris Weems. I do not seek converts, but if you wish to know more just send me five dollars and a stamped, self-addressed envelope. Don't forget the zip code, gang.

I drove and drove. I like driving. The elves didn't get any louder or lose their rhythm. Peggy being asleep was the next best thing to being alone. The highway stretched out ahead of me like a set of rails. The car practically steered itself across Kentucky, past all those snowed-on fields and woods and hills and barns. We crossed the state line into West Virginia at 4:11. I wasn't doing any thinking at all, just driving, driving, driving

. . . but I wasn't negligent in the control of my vehicle, no sir. I was a very alert zombie, if you know what I mean.

At 4:37 I pulled off the Interstate and stopped in the parking lot of a McDonald's. I had to nudge Peggy to wake her up. "Where are we?" she says, and I told her. She looked at me like I said we're in Katmandu. Boy, she was really asleep there for a few hours, way down at the bottom of the sea, and now she's surfaced and wonders if she can swim and how she got out here in the first place.

"Are you hungry?" I asked her.

"No," she says, but I don't think she really knows.

We got out of the car and went inside. She could hardly walk, she's so cramped up from sleeping. She acted like she didn't know what anything is, ordinary things like the walls and plants and lights, and the customers too. I put her at a table by the window and got in line for burgers and brought them back on a tray. She's staring at the tabletop like there's a battle plan drawn on it. I dumped the tray and sat down. She stared at her burger like she never saw one before. I started eating, but she didn't.

"Are you okay?"

She nodded at the burger. People were looking at her. They figured she's drunk or doped out, and I don't blame them. Her hair's like a bird's nest in a storm, all sagging over to one side where she leaned her head against the car window for so long. She stared out at the dark awhile. It's almost night already. She didn't say a word while I ate my burger. I never saw her look so lost. She's a million miles away. Pretty soon it was black as black outside. What the fuck were we *doing* so many miles from home?

"Don't you want your burger?"

She shook her head. There's a little kid watching us. His mom made him quit because it's rude to stare at funny-looking people. That's us—funny-looking. We're a pair. Peggy's still watching the night and the empty playground outside the window. It's cold and dark out there.

"You want to go?"

She got up, didn't bother to answer, just got up real slow like an old lady with arthritis or something. We went out to the parking lot and got in the car. She didn't offer to drive so I got behind the wheel again. "How much longer before we start looking for a motel?" I asked her.

"Take me home," she says.

"Huh?"

"Home. Take me home."

The dream busted wide open while she slept her way across Kentucky. It flew out her ear when she wasn't awake and watchful to keep it inside her head. Now it's gone. She's not even trying to get it back, I can tell.

"Okay."

I drove across the street to a Mobil station and tanked up again, the third time since we started. The Impala is a gas hog. Then we got back on I-64, heading west this time. Washington is somewhere back of our taillights. We won't ever go there now. You only plan a thing like this one time. If it falls apart, that's *it*. You put the plan in the garbage, another broken thing you'll learn to live with.

"I couldn't do it."

Peggy's way over on the other side of the seat, hugging herself.

"I didn't think it was a very good idea in the first place."

I said it gently as I could, not wanting it to sound like, "I told you so," more like, "We're doing the right thing now, heading home."

"I couldn't do it," she says again. "I couldn't have stood there with all those others, those Army vets and people who lost someone in the war. I would've felt like a hypocrite. I've seen them on the news, crying. I couldn't do that. Last night I thought I could. Now I know I can't. They'd know it too, everyone else there. They'd see me not crying. I'll never go anywhere near that awful place. I don't fit in there, not with all those people that keep voting assholes into office and believing what they're told because the man that tells them lives in the White House. I thought all that believing crap ended with Nixon, but it didn't. It's back. Not thinking, just believing. We're outnumbered, honey. The dumb people are in charge all over again. Everyone's gone back to believing. Believe, believe, believe, that's all everyone wants—to believe in the U.S.A.

Tell them it's just another country and they'll tear you to pieces, those knee-jerk patriots. The U.S.A. is God's country. They need to believe it. Not me. I don't subscribe. Am I crazy?"

She's looking at me. It's a serious question.

"No."

It's what she wants to hear. I mean it too. She's not crazy. If she is, then I'm crazy too.

"Thanks, kid," she says.

"You're welcome."

"You want me to drive again?"

"In a little while."

"We're strange people, Burris."

"Yeah."

We took turns, driving and napping, driving and napping, hardly talking at all. We could've stopped at a motel, but both of us knew it'd be better if we made it all the way home again without stopping over someplace. That way it'd seem like we hadn't ever gone on this big mistake of a trip. It's a strange way to think, but we're strange people.

At around midnight we got back to Buford. That's around *fifteen hours* of driving. We went inside, kind of beat. Peggy turned on the lights and looked around the living room. "Maybe we should've kept going," she says. I didn't say anything. We burned all that gas and rubber so she could get everything straight in her head once and for all, and as soon as we set foot inside the old homestead she's doubting herself all over again.

"Fix me a little drink will you, Burris. I feel like shit."

I made us both one. She didn't raise a fuss.

"I'm sorry," she says. We're on the sofa, looking at the dead TV out of habit. When you're on the sofa that's what's in front of you—the tube.

"What about?"

"The wild-goose chase."

"It doesn't matter. Now I've been out of state."

"It'll always be a mess," she says, meaning Jerry Weems and the war and all.

"Yeah, I guess so."

"You know what depresses me? Knowing I'll always have

this hate inside me. I can't make it go away. It'll always be there. I can't do anything to stop it, and you know what depresses me the most? It depresses me that I hate *myself* as much as I hate all those people out there who don't feel about things the way I do. I hate myself for getting caught up with people that weren't like me and never could be. I can't forgive myself for that. When I think of the war that's what I think of—the way I compromised myself. I don't think about the thousands of dead soldiers and burning villages and innocent victims and grieving families. I don't think about any of that. I just think about how I made a fool of myself by getting involved with the kind of people and situation I never should've gotten involved with. It's a very selfish kind of hate, just a tiny portion of a huge tragedy, but it's the only part that's truly real to me. Do you see what I mean?"

"Yeah, I think so."

"I wish I could kill it, have myself hypnotized or something so I don't remember any of it. Imagine what would happen if I went and told people I hate myself because I'm ashamed I married someone who did what his government told him to do and got killed doing it. They'd think I was sick, or a Communist or something. Do you think I'm sick?"

"No."

She's like me—different from the rest. I don't know how come we argued all these years when we see things so much the same way. She had another drink but kept the bottle near her so I can't have another one too.

"Listen, Burris, I'm talking seriously now. Sometime in the future I'm going to go crazy. They're going to put me in a hospital."

"You're *not* crazy. If you were you wouldn't *say* you are."

"It's way down inside me, honey. One of these days it'll come all the way up and I'll eat the rug and fill my pants, all that crazy stuff. It'll be the rubber room for old Peggy."

"Bull."

"No bull. I'm getting old, and when you're old you're supposed to be able to look back and feel good about what happened in your life, and I won't be able to do that, I mean I'm very proud of you and Loretta and the way you turned out, more or less, but it doesn't make any difference. I'll look back and only be able to see what a big mess I made of things, marrying Jerry, taking up with those other guys, Mack and the ones before him, every one a no-goodnik, but what do I expect if I'm dumb enough to take up with guys like that? Jerry was the only decent one, and look what he was dumb enough to let happen to him. It's all been a mess, everything to do with men. I bet there's people around here that think I'm just a whore. I bet they think that. Is that what you think? I bet there's times you think your mother's nothing but an old whore. You can be honest with me. I won't blame you for thinking it even if I never thought it about myself. I've made a mess of everything but I've never been a whore. I've *liked* all the men I've slept with, even if it turned out later they were selfish jerks. *Liking* them, that's my definition of what *not* being a whore is. That doesn't make it any less of a mess, though."

She took another big gulp of Southern Comfort. She's not even looking at me anymore while she talks. She's talking to the walls and the carpet and the TV screen.

"So it isn't going to work out for me, the old-age thing, and I'll go crazy, I know it. It's just waiting inside me till it's time to come on out and show the folks how crazy old Peggy really is. You'll have to be grown-up by then. I couldn't stand it if I went crazy and you were still just a kid. You'll have to be a man when it happens, so you aren't connected with me anymore. I want to be alone when it happens, with you and Loretta out of the way. You've got to grow up and start looking after yourself so I can let myself go crazy and forget everything. Promise me you'll do that for me, so I know I only have to keep from going crazy a little while longer."

"You're not crazy or *going* crazy or *anything*, so will you please quit saying it. Just *quit* it!"

She held up her hands, smiling this spooky smile.

"Okay, okay. I'm not going crazy. I made it all up. It's a bedtime story I made up. Now I'm going to bed. Thank you for driving me home."

She made it sound like we went on a date across town, not across three states. "Good night," she says, and picked up the bottle and took it to her room and shut the door. She won't be going to the Wishee-Washee tomorrow either, not if she took the bottle to bed with her. I wish she had've left it behind. I'd like to knock myself out with a few shots. I'm wide-awake. All that driving and drama and I'm still wide-awake. It's what Peggy just said that's woken me up. She was serious. She really does think it's only a matter of time before she goes crazy, which doesn't mean she *is* crazy, but it makes me think she's got a bigger problem with the old man and Vietnam et cetera than I ever guessed. It's fucked her over completely, it really has, and only a small part of it is political. The big part, the important bit—that's personal. I have to admit she's right about people's reaction if she told them she's ashamed to be the widow of a vet. They'd burn her at the fucking stake.

I got the Sony out of my knapsack. I've told it all this stuff. It's a neat machine but it doesn't have any answers. I went to Peggy's door and listened. She's asleep. No wonder Mack left her if he had to lie next to that snoring all night. That was a cheap shot. I shouldn't have said that. I wonder if things are better for Peggy when she's asleep, or if she has crazy dreams. It isn't fair that she has to feel like shit. Apart from being a pain in the neck sometimes, Peggy Weems is not a bad person. From what she said, the one and only bad thing she did, she did to herself—she married this very average-sounding dork called Jerry Weems, a decent guy but not very independent, and she's hated herself for it ever since. I bet they would've gotten divorced if he hadn't been killed. An unusual person shouldn't ever team up with an ordinary person. Miss Hippie met Small-Town Sam, and I'm the result. I take after my mom. Lucky for me. Imagine being *ordinary!* The old man would've been an embarrassment to us both. That's why Peggy hates to see Loretta with an average guy like Pete. It's like history repeating itself. Well, it's out of her hands. They're moving away and she can't stop them. When Loretta goes I think Peggy'll let herself get a little bit closer to the edge. Maybe when I'm twenty-one and out of her hair she'll push herself over, because there won't be anything left to keep her where she is. She'll fall down and down, and be grateful for it. Do I really think this? I don't know. If there was something I could do, I'd do it. Getting a job won't do it. That'd just be giving a face-lift to a head that's got so much pressure inside it there'll come a time pretty soon when it just has to explode. No more head. Peggy'll fall over the edge and never have to feel anything again except the feeling of falling until she drops dead in a mental ward someday with drool running down her chin and her eyes looking at her lap.

I can't stand thinking about this stuff, and the walls are full of it. I'm going for a drive. Five hundred plus miles already today . . . yesterday, and I'm going for a drive?

Ker—razy.

13

Guess where I drove. No, not to the junkyard. I drove out to Carriage Hill Drive and pulled onto the fire road and parked where I parked Sunday afternoon. I don't know why I went there, I just did. I sat in the car for a while, but it's too cold for sitting still so I got out and crossed the road and went down the slope into the trees. Peggy keeps a flashlight in the glove compartment for changing tires in the dark, and I took that along with me but didn't really need it to find my way, because the tracks I made on Sunday are still there. It hasn't snowed since Saturday.

I went crunching along through the woods. The moon's pretty close to full, and every now and then the clouds moved away and let it shine through. When that happened the snow turned almost blue-white, and the tree trunks went black. It got so bright for a few seconds I expected the snow to sparkle, but it just got very bluish. I don't know why I had to see the Zurowski place again, I just did. I wasn't thinking about Peggy, or anything really. I was just a pair of eyes in the woods following this line of mushy footprints in the snow. Sometimes a chunk of snow fell off the trees near me and plopped onto the ground. It made a sound like when you hit a puffed-up comforter with the flat of your hand, soft on soft. The air was very cold on my face. It felt like I'm looking at things through a wooden mask. If somebody saw me they wouldn't know it's me, because I've got this wooden mask on.

I came to the back lawn. The satellite dish was there, and the greenhouse. There weren't any lights on in the house. It's way past one o'clock. I guess they don't watch the late show. I stood awhile, wondering why I'm here and what I'll do next.

My feet got cold just standing there so I went on across the lawn, which had no marks on it at all until I stepped out on it, and I walked across to the greenhouse. It's very big from up close, bigger than the house I live in. The flowers and plants in there have got more room than human beings. I went around the side of it till I got to the door. It's locked. I wanted to see those flowers. I took off my hat and held it against a pane of glass just above the door handle and gave it a quick punch. The pane broke and fell inside without very much noise at all. I put my hat back on and reached through and fiddled with the lock till it opened, then I went in and closed the door behind me. When exactly did I turn into a criminal—when I stepped through the door, when I broke the pane, or when I thought about taking off my hat and using it to muffle the sound of breaking glass? Whatever, I'm a criminal now. It sent the blood humming through me, made me feel dizzy and very *alive* at the same time, a thief's rush.

Right away I had to take my hat off again. It was hot in there, which I knew it would be, but not *this* hot, like I walked into a room full of cotton wadding soaked in warm water. I wandered along the aisles looking at the plants, hundreds of them. I can't see too well in the dark but the smell of flowers was so strong it's like walking past the perfume counter in a big department store with a lot of women dabbing stuff on their wrists. I flashed the light a couple of times just to see what kind of flowers they were. They looked very fancy to me, orchids I think, weird shapes on stalks like some kind of intelligent life-form, not like plants at all. I bet they're worth plenty. I went all around the place, up and down both aisles. The smell was making me a little bit sick, frankly.

Then I saw a thermometer on the wall. I took a close look at it with the flashlight, just a second or two of light, because I wanted to know exactly how hot it was in there, and it's ninety-three degrees. I had my parka off by then, and my mittens, in fact the sweat was really pouring off me. There's pipes all along the aisles that are hot to touch, hot water pipes to keep the temperature way up. I looked at the thermometer again, and this time it's only ninety-two. It's falling because of the cold air coming in through the broken pane. Then I saw the wire going behind the thermometer. I followed it along to the doorway, where it goes down the side of the door and into the ground, and I started getting worried because what it is, I think, is an alarm connected to the house, so if the temperature in here drops below a certain point a bell or something rings in the house and the Zurowskis'll come charging out to fix whatever's wrong so their precious orchids don't die. I stuffed my hat in the hole to stop more cold air from coming in. I didn't want to leave yet, or be disturbed. I'm still trying to figure out why I'm here.

I walked up and down the aisles some more, then there's a hissing sound and it started to *rain* in there, a very fine rain, like mist almost. It's coming from little spigots along the roof supports, like a built-in firefighting system in an office. This place is fully automated. The Zurowskis don't even have to go around with a watering can. The misty rain only lasted a minute or so. All the plants looked shiny under the moonlight coming through the glass, shiny and wet and strange, like a plastic jungle. I took another look at the thermometer. The hat worked, because it hasn't dropped below ninety-two. The shirt's sticking to my back and my feet are on fire inside my boots. My socks are practically squelching.

Near the door there's a cupboard. I opened it up and there's packets of stuff in there, special plant food I think, and some forks and trowels and other gardening stuff, all arranged very neatly. I picked up a pair of pruning shears. I bet they cut fresh flowers every day and take them into the house and put them in fancy vases to make the place smell wonderful. I worked the shears in my hand. They've got a spring to keep the handles apart. I went over to the wire connecting the thermometer with the alarm in the house and cut it. *Snip!* Now it can get cold in here and they won't know. Every plant could shrivel with frost and die, and they wouldn't know, would just keep right on snoring while their very expensive orchids turned to tissue paper. I could make that happen. It seemed like a good idea, a worthwhile project. I got kind of *excited* about it. Yeah, I thought, I'll kill all the plants, thousands of bucks worth! That'll teach Zurowski to send my old man off to war and set my mom up for a fucking mental ward!

I took a closer look at the overhead pipe system that links the spigots. They're all joined to one main pipe that comes out of the ground over by the door, just a few feet from the alarm wire. There's a timer set into the pipe. It's set for sixty minutes. Every hour the plants get sprayed for one minute to make them think they're back home in the jungle. I examined the heating pipes too. There's a tap wheel on each of them at the end nearest to the door. I turned them all off and waited five minutes, then touched the pipes. Yep, cooler than they were now that the hot water isn't circulating anymore. Then I put my parka back on and set the spray timer to zero. It started spraying. It'll keep spraying till someone shuts it off, because the time is always zero. The plants'll think it's the monsoon. I pulled my hat out of the empty door pane and put it on, then went outside. I left the door open, in fact I packed some snow along the edge to keep it that way, because there might be some wind later on and I don't want it to blow shut. The greenhouse is filled with misty rain. With the sprayers spraying and the heat pipes off and the door open the temperature should drop a couple of degrees every minute, at least. In an hour or so every plant'll be covered in ice. That'll teach you, Zurowski. I hope some of your orchids are prizewinners, priceless even!

It was so easy to do, almost *too* easy. It was a very casual crime. I felt good about it anyway, easy or not. There's so much spray in there now it's drifting out the open door. I put my mittens back on, ducked back inside, and smeared any fingerprints I might've left on the pruning shears and timer and taps. I should've done that earlier, but I'm only an amateur at criminal activity. When I came out again the spray on my hat and parka froze in a couple of seconds. I looked like I'd been frosted, like a window all crystal-covered.

I walked back across the lawn, past the satellite dish and into the woods. I felt very, very good about what I did. The pride is back, Jack. You know the expression "icy contempt"? That's what I've showed Zurowski. I icy-contempted his greenhouse. I did a little dance under the trees, I really did. I felt *terrific!* I kicked up snow and capered around like a total idiot. Boy, I wish I could see old Zurowski's face when he looks inside the greenhouse tomorrow. It'll be the *white* house! Serves him right, the old fart! Draft my dumb dad, willya? Bet you wish you hadn't now, ha ha! Call my mom Miss Hippie, huh? Well take *that*, ya prick! I hope you break down and cry when you see what I did to your fucking flowers. I'm glad I did it and I'd do it again. *Kick* that snow! *Laugh* that laugh! Then this white thing came out of the trees and rushed at me. It's an owl, a white owl, and it doesn't make a sound, quiet like a ghost with its legs hanging under it all fluffed out with white feathers like those bloomers ladies wore a hundred years ago, then *whoooosh!* he skimmed over my head, and when I turned around he's already gone, vanished into the woods. I never saw a real owl before in my life. It made me shiver all over. A white owl. *Whoooosh!* and he's gone. I only saw him for two seconds.

All of a sudden I felt very weird, like my legs'll give way under me any minute now, and it made me panic. I started running, running back along my tracks, blundering along like a blind man, and all because an owl spooked me, I mean I felt excited at seeing him, not scared or anything, but he made me panic somehow and my legs *have* to run, have to take me away from here fast as they can, run, run, *run!* I made it to the slope and went up it with my mittens on the ground, the way a monkey runs up a palm tree. Now I'm on the road, and there's the car. I fumbled the keys out of my pocket and got in.

Now for the tricky part—turning around. I did it okay on Sunday, so no cause for alarm here. Ignition. Headlights. I started the same back-and-forthing as last time, a few feet at a time, spinning the wheel this way, that way, inching my way around till I'm halfway there, meaning the Impala's at right angles across the road, and I must've gotten a little too confident at the way things are going okay, because I reversed too far and the fucking back wheels went sliding down into the drainage ditch behind me. *Shit!* I gunned the motor to get out, but all that happened was the front of the car slid to the right and the right front wheel ended up in the ditch too, so now there's three wheels out of four off the road. I switched off the engine and killed the lights, then got out to see how bad it is.

Pretty damn bad. The car's tilted at around thirty-five degrees down into the ditch. No way can I get it out with just the horses under the hood. I can't tell if there's any damage to the side panels that are touching the ditch's far side. It went in the ditch slowly, so there wasn't much impact. Why am I worried about the bodywork on Peggy's crummy old car? I should be worried about getting out of here before daybreak, when old Zurowski'll find his greenhouse in a mess and call the cops and they'll follow my tracks directly here and arrest me for breaking and entering and malicious damage and Christ knows what else. *Double* shit! What an *idiot* to back up too far like that. I could cut brush and put it under the rear wheels like they always do in the movies, but I haven't got anything to cut brush with, and I'm not going back to Zurowski's for the pruning shears. It wouldn't work anyway, not with the car tipped so far over. It'll have to be towed out, and it has to happen before daybreak. It's 2:06 now. I know a tow-truck operator, but it's at least nine miles to old Bimmerhaus's place. What an *idiot!* The master criminal breaks into the impregnable vault and steals the fabulous diamond, then slips on the marble floor and breaks his fucking hip and gets arrested by the janitor the next morning. What a lousy fuck-up of a dopey plan for revenge. Burris Weems, the Moriarty of the Midwest.

Wait a minute . . . The service station down where Carriage Hill Drive meets the main road into Buford. I passed it twice on Sunday, coming and going. Was there a phone booth outside, across from the gas pumps? Think . . . was there? Was it next to the store entrance? Or was that a Coke machine? Try to remember . . . I can't, I *can't* remember . . . How far to the main road from here? Two miles, minimum. What choice have I got? None. I started walking back along the fire road to Carriage Hill Drive, turned right and kept going. A few minutes later I passed Zurowski's driveway with its little red-barn mailbox. Fuck you, Zurowski. If there's no phone at the service station I'm sunk. You'll put me behind bars, which means you killed my old man, turned my mom into a mental case, and me into a jailbird. Cancer'll be too good for you, pal. There just better be a phone there or else . . . I'm scared shitless, frankly. Even more than the anger in me, there's this fear. I don't want to be caught. Jesus, that'd be embarrassing, having my name in the paper and on the local news. WOULD-BE SUICIDE BECOMES VANDAL—REVENGE MOTIVE MISFIRES—MOTHER HOSPITALIZED—

SISTER DENIES RELATIONSHIP. There better be a phone or I'm dead, Fred. They'll send me away to a juvenile prison filled with tough guys that carved up other guys in school or raped the girl next door. They'll rape *me* as soon as I set foot in the showers. It always happens. Everyone knows it. The warden sees it as part of the punishment. I'll get gang-raped in the showers and the doctors'll have to sew my rectum back together again like a split sail. That phone better be where I want it to be . . . and in working order! What if it's been vandalized? Some coneheads do that for fun, smash public phones. Shit, it better not be smashed, that phone I don't even know is there . . . *crunch, crunch, crunch* . . . I'm walking as fast as I can. The next house can't be too far away now. They were around a quarter of a mile apart, the houses along here. Zurowski's was the ninth and last. Why couldn't it be the first? Then there wouldn't have been a fire road alongside it and I wouldn't have gone snooping around his back lawn and busted into his greenhouse and blitzed his daffodils and driven into a ditch and got my asshole reamed from here to breakfast . . . *crunch, crunch, crunch* . . .

I passed the homes one by one, all nine of them, and every house I passed made me more and more certain I wasn't going to get away with my little greenhouse caper. Why did I even *do* it? I didn't ever intend to tell Peggy about it, so she wouldn't get any secondhand satisfaction from what I did, so why the hell did I do it? *I'm* the mentally unstable member of the family, not her. Compared to me she's as solid as Mt. Rushmore. I'm kidding myself when I say I'm smart. No one smart would've done what I did, wrecked that nice greenhouse and then backed his car into a ditch just a short walk away from the scene of the crime, with a nice set of footprints leading directly from one to the other for the cops to follow . . . and why didn't I take the Impala's license plate with me when I left it there, and any other stuff its ownership could be traced through? *Idiot!* If I can't get old Bimmerhaus out here to help me I'll have to go back and do that, remove the license plate and various stuff from the glove compartment, which'll take forever and put me right back at the center of things where I don't want to be, and dawn'll be that much closer by then, giving me even less time to make a getaway before the cops arrive, and I'll be on foot and they'll track me . . . No, leave it all there, just walk home and go to bed and in the morning look out the window and say, "Hey, Peggy, the car's been stolen!" That way the cops'll think the same bunch of joyriders that stole the car also pulled the greenhouse job . . . but the car won't show evidence of hot-wiring, which is the only way thieves could've driven it away from our place, so the cops'll *know* it was me, Burris Weems, who did the dirty deed . . . unless I convince them Peggy left the keys in the dash through forgetfulness, an open invitation to theft, very foolish of her, Officer, but she's been under a strain lately . . . Zurowski? No, never heard the name before. Yes, it's sad that vandalism and theft are on the increase. What these young offenders need is a public whipping . . . and there's the service station up ahead!

The place is dark. I can't see yet if there's a phone booth. I ran till I got right up close. The gas pumps are locked . . . and that square shape over there is only a Pepsi machine. Shit! Fuck! Now I'll have to walk all the way home and do the biggest con job of my life to make the cops think I had nothing to do with any of this. I passed the front of the store, one of those tiny outfits where they have to charge you twice what you'd pay in a supermarket, just to show a little profit and stay alive. Why did I think there'd be a phone at a pathetic dump like this? Wishful thinking is all it was. I walked on by, my boots weighing a ton I'm so depressed and scared. But then I turned around for one last look . . . and there's a phone booth against the wall that's furthest from Carriage Hill Drive! I *did* see it on Sunday! My subconscious kept it filed away for emergencies, and this is definitely one of those.

I ran back to it and yanked the door open. The overhead light's busted, but I had my flashlight. The phone book is swinging on its wire like the answer to all the world's deepest questions about what everything means, life and death et cetera, the book of deliverance from my earthly woe, Joe. I scrabbled through it with mittens and flashlight, found the number, and searched my pockets for some cash. Wouldn't that just be the limit, to find a phone and not have twenty cents. I had a quarter, so I put that in the big slot and dialed. I didn't mind losing the extra five cents.

It rang . . .

and rang . . .

and rang . . .

Click.

"Yeah?"

"Uh . . . Mr. Bimmerhaus?"

"Yeah?"

"Uh . . . hi, it's Burris Weems, Mr. Bimmerhaus."

"Who?"

"Burris Weems, you know, who brought Lennie's cap back."

"Boris?"

"Burris, yeah, and I've got kind of a problem, Mr. Bimmerhaus, sir . . . "

"What the hell time of night you call this!"

"I know it's late, but . . . uh . . . there's this problem that came up . . ."

"You know what time it is?"

"Yessir, and I'm very sorry to wake you up, but there's this emergency that needs to be taken care of . . ."

"What emergency?"

"My car went off the road and into a ditch, Mr. Bimmerhaus, and I need your truck to haul it out."

"In a ditch?"

"Yessir. I can't get it out on my own."

"Why the hell can't it keep till morning?"

"I'm . . . uh . . . not at liberty to say, but it has to be gotten out tonight. It's very important, honest. I can't leave it there till morning or I'm in big trouble, frankly, Mr. Bimmerhaus, and I thought to myself, who's the only guy I can trust to get me out of this very dangerous situation, and you're the guy I thought of, Chuck."

People like it when you use their first name. I'm employing psychology here, very insincere but totally necessary I think.

"Dangerous situation?"

"Yessir, Chuck. I can't leave that car where it is or repercussions'll happen. It has to be gotten out tonight or the repercussions will occur, definitely."

"Whose car is it?"

"My mom's."

"You take it without telling her?"

"Well, yeah . . ."

"You banged it up pretty bad, is that it?"

"No sir, it's not hurt too bad that I can see, but it's in a ditch and I can't get it out without a tow truck."

"Well so long as it's not hurt too bad she's not gonna whomp you too much. You tell me where it is and I'll go get it in the morning."

"But it has to be gotten out *now* . . ."

"See, Boris, I charge double after dark. It's regular policy. All operators work for double the rate after business hours."

"Okay, but you have to come do it now . . ."

"We're talking eighty bucks, Boris. You got eighty bucks?"

"Well, not in my actual pocket right this minute, no sir, but you can trust me for it."

"That's not the way Bimmerhaus Towing Service operates, boy. I work on a strictly cash basis. No dough, no tow."

"You can trust me for it, Chuck, honest, I just don't happen to have it on me at this very moment. I can get it for you tomorrow, easy."

"From your mama?"

"No sir, my sister. She'll give me the cash."

"That way your mama won't know, is that it?"

"Well, yeah . . . more or less."

"Where's the car at?"

"It's on a fire road that leads off Carriage Hill Drive."

"You anywhere near it?"

"No sir, I'm at a service station where Carriage Hill Drive meets the main road into town, I forget the name of the road."

"That'll be Lackland Road."

"Yessir, I think that's it, Chuck. There's a pay phone here."

"You stay put till I get there."

"Okay."

He hung up. He sounded kind of pissed about getting woken up, but there's eighty bucks in it for him so I don't know why he's bitching. I hung up too, and strolled around the place a few times, keeping warm. What a fucking mess, but it looks like I fixed things, except for the cash. How am I going to ask Loretta for that much without telling her what happened here? I'll have to lie for it. I'll think of something plausible. Jesus, it's cold. No snow in the sky, though. If it'd only snow my tracks'd be wiped out and the cops probably wouldn't even know the Impala's stuck on the fire road, and I could get Chuck to do his towing thing in daylight for a reasonable forty bucks. But it isn't snowing, so it'll have to be the Big Fib. That's life. I'm not so scared now that I know Chuck's on his way. I'll be out of here with the car long before old Zurowski finds his greenhouse turned into a refrigerator overnight. I bet it's happened already, the transformation, all that spray frozen over the plants and flowers. I looked at my watch. Well over an hour now since Operation Deep Freeze began. It'll be fridge city for sure.

Not being scared anymore made me feel better about the crime. A crime that you get caught for is something you shouldn't have done, but a crime you get away with is a big thrill. I'm not sure where morality fits into the picture. I think morality only gets brought in if you get caught, or if someone gets hurt. Is it true that plants feel pain? I didn't think of that. I bet they panicked when they felt the change of temperature. Hey, who left the goddamn door open! Turn the heat up, willya! I can't feel my leaves anymore! Sorry, guys. Consider yourselves more tragic victims of Vietnam, like all your cousins over there that got defoliated by Agent Orange. Freezing is quicker I bet. They say that revenge is a dish that tastes best when it's taken cold. That's what I did tonight. I took sub-zero revenge. It tastes okay.

It took old Chuck almost half an hour to climb into his truck and drive on out here. He pulled up at last and I got up in the cabin with him and we started down Carriage Hill Drive.

"Sorry to get you out of bed, Chuck."

"Me too," he says, still pissed. Maybe I should call him Mr. Bimmerhaus again, show a little respect for his aged person et cetera.

"What were you doing out here anyway? Got friends out here?"

"No sir, I just happened to be passing through, and I went

down this very narrow fire road and went over the side into a ditch. I thought it was a shortcut back to town."

"You want to keep away from fire roads in this kind of weather. No one goes down 'em from November till March. You could die down there and wouldn't no one know about it till spring."

"Yeah, it was a big mistake."

We drove a mile or so without talking.

"Fancy houses along here," he says. "Millionaire's row."

"Yeah."

After another silence he says, "They got that cat."

"What cat?"

"That bobcat you told about. Got him this afternoon. Police cornered him back of K-Mart and he run across the road and got hit by a Buick it looked like. That's what they showed on the news."

"Aww, shit . . . Is he dead?"

"You bet."

So he didn't make it after all. I knew he wouldn't. I felt awful, like it was somehow my fault. "Here's the road," I said.

He hung a left and a minute later we reached the Impala.

"Won't be too hard by the look of it," he says.

We got out. He kept the truck's engine running while he walked around the car—the three sides of it that aren't jammed against the side of the ditch that is. Then he unhitched the towline and paid out about ten yards of wire and went down and hooked up the Impala's front end. "Stay clear of it," he says, and goes back to the truck and throws a lever on the winch. The slack got taken up and the car started coming out of the ditch. It came straight ahead for a yard or two at first, then the front got slewed sideways up onto the road as the wire got shorter, and a second or two later the back wheels are up on the road too. Chuck threw the lever back and put some slack in the wire. "Start her up," he tells me, and I did. The engine worked fine. He unhitched the gear and stowed everything away.

"I can't turn the truck around," he says, "so we'll go on ahead. It comes out along Bellflower. Follow me close so I know you haven't gone off the edge again."

"Okay."

He got in the truck and we started off along the fire road with the trees reaching up tall on both sides and the headlights punching through the dark. I kept my own lights low so I don't blind Chuck in his rearview mirror. I believe in driver courtesy. But while we're driving along I started thinking about what'll happen when the cops follow my tracks away from the greenhouse. They'll see how my car slid into the ditch and how a truck came along and hauled me out. There'll be no mistaking those double-tired truck tracks. And the cops'll ring around town asking all the tow-truck operators if they hauled a car out of the fire road that runs off Carriage Hill Drive, and when they ask Chuck he'll say he did, and they'll tell him what I did, which makes him an unwitting accomplice to the crime. He won't get prosecuted because he'll say he didn't know about the greenhouse, and they'll believe him because he's got an honest-John look to him, even got a picture of Jesus in his trailer, so he'll be okay. But I won't. He'll put the cops straight onto me when they ask whose car it was he hauled out. They'll ask him that before they tell him what I was doing out there, the cunning sonsabitches. He'll put my head in the noose without even knowing it. But maybe he'll be glad about that when he finds out what I did. Why doesn't it *snow* and cover all those footprints and tire tracks and make my life easier? Why can't we have a good strong blizzard beginning the minute I'm home and safely in my nice warm bed? Everything would be fine if only it'd *snow* dammit!

But it won't, I know it won't. Fate doesn't work that way for Burris Weems. So now I have to make a decision. I need to clue old Chuck in and hope he sees things my way and keeps his lip zipped when the cops call. It's a pretty big risk, telling him what I did, because he's the law-abiding type I think, and he'll maybe figure I'm just some punk teenage vandal that should get thrown in the slammer until I learn some respect for the property of honest citizens. That's what he'll be inclined to think, an honest-John guy like him. I'll have to be very persuasive, stress the Vietnam angle, mention Lennie a couple dozen times, another victim like my old man, which is pefectly true I guess, but I felt like a total hypocrite planning this stuff out in my head while I'm driving along behind old Chuck's tow truck.

There's no other way, though. Weems the weasel will worm his way out.

The fire road ended at Bellflower like he said and we both turned left for Buford. When we got to Harriman Road I could've hung a right and headed on home, but I didn't, I followed Chuck all the way back to the junkyard and parked while he got out to open the gates for himself.

"Lose your way again?" he says. He thinks I'm an idiot.

"No. I have to tell you something."

"You can't get the eighty bucks, right?"

"No, something else."

"Uh-huh. Get the gates."

He got back in the truck and drove on through. I closed the gates and followed along to the trailer. He killed the engine and climbed down. The dog was there, wagging his no-tailed butt for a welcome. "Come on in," says Chuck. We went inside and he started making coffee.

"What's this important thing that isn't about the eighty?"

"It's . . . uh . . . about what I was doing out on the fire road."

"You weren't just taking a shortcut, huh?"

"No sir, I went out there deliberately."

"To do what?"

I told him. The coffee was ready by the time I finished. He sipped at his but I couldn't—too hot.

"Why tell me?" he asks.

So I told him that too. The coffee's cool enough to drink by then, and we both slurped away for a little while. He's thinking hard, I can tell. So far I hadn't used Lennie's name, which I was proud about. But I'll use it if I have to.

"You want me to tell the cops I didn't do any towing."

"If you don't mind . . ."

"You must sure hate this Zurowski."

"Yeah."

"That was in sixty-nine, you said?"

"Yes sir."

"Lennie went in the army in seventy-two. Was this same feller head of the draft board then?"

"I dunno. But probably."

Hypocrite!

"'Course, Lennie didn't raise objections. Me neither. That was before Watergate and all that crooked stuff came out about Nixon. That burned me. I disbelieved it at first. You don't expect the President to act like that. Then when he quit the job I believed it all right. Lennie, he didn't come out of the Army hospital that first time till the war's over and Nixon's gone for good."

I didn't say anything. He's thinking the way I want him to think. We slurped a little more. This is real coffee, not decaffeinated. Old guys like Chuck, they like caffeine in their coffee and plenty of tasty tar and nicotine in their unfiltered cigarettes and a hearty helping of good old-fashioned fat in their T-bone steaks.

"And your mom's a sick woman on account of it all."

"She's mentally unstable and needs a psychiatrist, but we can't afford one."

"That's too bad. A woman shouldn't have to bring up a kid on her own."

"Two kids."

"She must hate this Zurowski guy too, him being responsible for sending her husband away."

"Yeah, she does, but she's a very law-abiding person and wouldn't like it if she found out what I did. She'd call the cops if she found out. That's why I can't ask her for the eighty."

I'm hoping if I play my cards right old Chuck'll tell me to forget the money for the sake of our mutual grudge against Zurowski or Nixon or whoever. I'm in trouble if he doesn't. Loretta can't afford to give me eighty bucks just like that.

"It's been pretty hard on the whole family. My sister's not mentally well either, and . . . uh . . . last summer I tried to kill myself."

"You what?"

I took off my wristband and showed him the scar. Very low, Weems, just the *lowest*.

"You shouldn't have done that, boy. Nothing's so bad you need to kill yourself over it. There's always people in the world that'll help you if you just ask."

"Yessir, I know that now. Tonight's a good example I think,

I mean the way you got out of a warm bed and came and helped me with the car and all. I'm very grateful about that. Stuff like that makes me believe what you just said about people helping you when you're in trouble. It was downright decent, if you don't mind my saying so, Mr. Bimmerhaus, sir."

He didn't mind. He soaked it up like a kitchen towel. I saw that eighty bucks shrinking away to nothing inside his head. He likes thinking he's a big samaritan, which if he does what I want, he is.

"Tell you what, son," he says. "If the cops call me up I'll tell 'em I stayed in all night. I don't approve of what it was you did, but I can understand the way your mind was working when you went ahead and did it. I'll tell the cops I stayed in, mainly out of concern for your mother. I'm not going to be the one that puts a sick woman in the hospital on account of some rich man's flowers. I've got no time and sympathy for a man that sat behind a desk and sent young boys off to a war that was dirty and dishonest and lost before it started. I won't concern myself with that kind, but I still think it's wrong, destroying private property that way. Don't you ever do anything like that again, hear me?"

"Yessir, I do. Thank you."

"I guess it's time both of us were in bed like honest men."

"Yeah, I guess."

I stood up. We went outside.

"Is Lennie home tonight?"

"He's home, but don't you be pestering him about did he get his cap or not. He's got it because I've seen it on him."

It was frustrating knowing Lennie the Loop that I wanted so bad to talk to is just fifty yards away in his shack, but what could I do? The Doberman went with us down to the gate. Old Bimmerhaus says, "See if you can get that eighty to me before the year's out," which I think is supposed to be a joke, because 1985 ends in about nineteen hours from now. The old prick wasn't going to cancel the debt out of admiration or understanding or solidarity after all, the greedy bastard. *Eighty bucks*, and he didn't even need to tow me away or anything, just hauled me out of the ditch in around one little minute! Eighty bucks for *that!*

"Uh . . . okay, I'll get right on it."

"You do that," he says, "and don't go stomping on any flower pots meantime."

Another pathetic joke. This old fart slays me, he really does. He shut the gate behind me and locked it. *Fuck* him! How am I gonna lay my hands on that kind of cash before midnight . . . and I started banging on the gate to get him back again, because I just now remembered I've got Peggy's cash that she got out of the Instabank yesterday morning before we started out for Washington, got it right there in my pocket, over two hundred forty bucks after gas and burgers.

"Mr. Bimmerhaus! Mr. Bimmerhaus!"

I heard his boots coming back, and he unlocked the gate. "Now what?" he says. He really thinks I'm a lobotomy case.

"I've got the money right here."

I pulled out the wad and showed him.

"Why didn't you say so before?"

"I forgot."

"Son, if I forgot I had that much money in my jeans I'd have myself committed to a retirement home. Let's have it."

I peeled off four twenties. I had to squint close to see which bills were which. He shoved them in his pants, then says, "Son, I'm not going to ask you if you want to change your story about what you were doing out at the Zurowski place, but I'll be watching the news tonight and if there's nothing about a greenhouse and something about a robbery instead, you and me'll have to have another little talk. I believed all that about the greenhouse and why you did it, and I'd hate to find out I swallowed a lie."

"I *didn't* lie . . ."

"How come you've got that kind of money on you?"

"It's my mom's. She got it so we could go to Washington . . . to the war memorial."

"War memorial?"

"We went yesterday . . . "

"You went to Washington and back yesterday?"

"Well, just part of the way . . . then we turned back."

"I'll be watching the news," he says, and slammed the gate. I should've told him about the Washington trip while we were inside. He doesn't believe a word of it. Well fuck *you*, Chuck. The news'll make an honest man of me and then you'll feel like a turd for making insinuations like that, you old prick! Greedy old prick!

I went to the car and got in. Now that I've paid old Bimmerhaus off I only have to explain to Peggy how come the money she trusted me with is eighty bucks short. With any luck she'll be too mental to notice anyhow. Did *I* say *that*? Boy, I really am a slime.

I drove home and went inside. Peggy's still snoring. I got everything down on tape while it's fresh in my mind, the second taping I've done tonight, I mean this morning. I'm up-to-date now. What a crazy story! I still haven't figured out a way to cover the missing cash. I'll sleep on it. Devious guys like me can always figure something out, no matter what.

Signing off to grab some sleep.

Even the wicked need their rest.

14

I woke up late, surprise, surprise, and the light coming under the shade was gray. There's no sound at all coming from inside the house or out back in the yard, just no sound at all, and that's how I knew it's snowing, because when it snows it covers *sound* as well as *things*. A quick look out the window. Slow-motion snow drifting down without any wind to swirl it around. It made me feel peaceful and calm to watch it falling without a sound in the yard. You can almost let yourself get hypnotized by falling snow. I watched it awhile with an empty head, then I saw that something's missing out there, and what it is is the bird feeder. It's gone.

I got dressed and laced up my boots and went out back, and there it is in the ground, already practically covered in snow. Those fucking squirrels went and swung it completely off the hook, the little shits! It's lying there with the roof off and one of the clear plastic sides half out of its slot. No seeds left, natch. They must've gotten mad because I didn't refill it since Sunday. I went back inside and got the seed bag and put the feeder back together again, then filled it and hung it on the hook. I can't see the vandals anywhere. Maybe it's too cold for them today. Peggy's wind chimes drooped on the back porch like a mass hanging of little men, one of those outlaw roundups they used to have. You are cordially invited to a necktie party at the state prison. I wonder if I'll end up like those little hanged chimes. Nah, the snow's already covered my tracks by now, and Chuck'd lie for me anyway. I paid him eighty bucks to do it.

A quick walk around to the front yard. The Impala's there, so Peggy's still at home. It's 1:42, so she's lost her job for sure.

I bet old Blangsted phoned here plenty of times yesterday, trying to find out how come she's not down at the Wishee-Washee feeding the machines. Big loss I don't think. I'm not even worried anymore about no money coming into the house. Peggy's right, it was a shitty job and she's better off without it. The car's right side panels were kind of dented and dinged where they hit the side of the ditch, but nothing too bad, which is just as well because Peggy let the insurance lapse.

I went down to the mailbox. Maybe we've won a million bucks. Nope, just the light bill and some junk mail. I looked up and down the street. Nothing's moving except Mukluk from a couple doors down. He looks very happy to be out in the snow. It's what huskies were made for. I walked up the street to say hi, because Mukluk is a pooch I admire, a very laid-back guy with ice-blue eyes almost as spooky as Lennie the Loop's. I got to him just as he lifted his leg and pissed over Nonny. Thanks, Mukluk, thanks a bunch, pal. The piss melted away a little patch of ice from Nonny's stripes and showed the faded red, white, and blue. Nonny is definitely looking shabby these days. Maybe I should repaint him with a tuxedo or something.

"Hey, Mukluk, hey, boy."

He let me pat him a couple times, then he's off down the street to piss on more fireplugs and trees. I went back to 1404 and kicked snow off my boots before I went inside. Peggy's still in bed but awake, because when I knocked she says, "Come in." In I went. She's got the shades drawn still and no light on, so it's kind of dark in there. She's sitting up with pillows behind her and her hair looks like it's had ten thousand volts run through it.

"Hi," I said.

"Hi yourself."

"Want some breakfast?"

"No thanks."

"My treat. Toast, coffee, OJ, you name it."

"No."

"Not feeling good?"

"I'm never going back there."

"Back where?"

"I quit."

"Yeah, you told me yesterday."

"I'm not a quitter by nature," she says, "but I quit."

"Right. We've got cinnamon toast. I can even make French toast if zat is Madame's wish."

I said that last bit in a French voice to see if she'll smile, but she didn't. Then I saw she's got her hands in her lap, and in her fingers is this little shot glass, and in the glass is a very generous shot of Southern Comfort. I can smell its tangy smell from where I'm standing, in fact the whole room smelled boozy and ashy and sweaty.

"No," she says.

"It's no trouble."

"I don't want anything."

"I understand Madame perfectlee. Ze toast, she will not arrive."

Still no smile. She took a snort instead. Isn't that the definition of a drunk, someone who drinks before breakfast? Peggy Weems is a drunk. My mom the lush. This isn't good.

"Hey, was the name of the guy Zurowski?"

"What?"

"Was his name Zurowski, the guy that was head of the draft board back in sixty-nine, the guy you asked to give the old man a deferment?"

"No."

"Huh?"

"No."

She took another snort. Now the glass is empty, but there's plenty more left in the bottle on the bedside table. How many did she have already to screw up her brain and make her remember wrong?

"Zurowski," I said. "It has to be. He's the only one in the book. You said a guy with a Polish name that starts with a Z, the only one in the book. That's Zurowski."

"No. I don't remember, but it wasn't Zurowski. It was more unpronounceable than that. What about it anyway?"

"I looked in the book. He's the only one. He's the guy that did it."

"Burris, I don't want to talk about any of that stuff, please. Yesterday was a mistake. I was wrong. We shouldn't have gone. I'm sorry I dragged you along and thank you very much for driving and putting up with me being stupid about everything, but I don't want to talk about your father or the war or *anything*, if you don't mind. I think it's time we put that stuff behind us, don't you?"

"Sure, but Zurowski had to be the one. I checked it out."

"For the final time, it wasn't Zurowski."

"How do you know that if you can't remember what it *was*?"

"I'm getting annoyed, Burris. Today's my official quitting day. I'm having a little celebration, and I don't want to get in an argument over something that doesn't even matter anymore. End of chapter, okay?"

She poured the glass full again. She's the one having the breakfast of her choice, but I'm the condemned man, because she isn't drunk yet so she means what she says about Zurowski, but it *has* to be him. He's the *only one* in the book, just like she told me, the only Polish name with a Z that doesn't have at least one other the same as it in the listings, the only one that fits the bill in the entire Z list of the 1985 local phone book, the very latest edition so it *can't* be wrong . . .

1985

1969

'85

'69

"Shit . . ."

"Did you say shit?"

"Excuse me . . ."

"Don't say shit to your mother."

"I hafta go . . ."

"What's the matter with you?" she says, but I'm already gone.

I got the keys.

I took the car.

I drove to the library.

I went inside.

I asked the lady, "Have you got a Buford phone directory for 1969?"

"I'll have to get it from the back room," she says. She knows me because I come in here a fair amount. She thinks I'm a very nice boy because I'm always polite and I actually read books. She went out back and got the phone book and handed it over. "They didn't put a color picture on the cover back then," she says.

"Yeah. Thank you."

I went to a table and sat down. I've got the shakes. I know ahead of time what I'll find. I turned to the Z's. There wasn't so many as nowadays, and there's only one that's on its own—Zajaczkowski. There's no Zurowski at all.

ERROR

ERROR

SYSTEMS MALFUNCTION

ABORT

ABORT

I looked at the names over and over. Nothing changed. This is the book of my life, filled with all my mistakes and crimes and sins, rows and rows of alphabetical wrongdoing. Let your fingers do the walking, you'll walk the fuckers right down to the knuckle.

How could I be so *dumb???*

Hi, I'm Burris Weems. I've got a cabbage in my head.

I ruined someone's greenhouse.

Thousands of bucks.

Malicious and Unprovoked Vandalism with Deliberate Intent to Cause Grief.

Twenty years.

Take the cell key, give it to Dr. Jekyll, have him melt it down.

I created a monster. It looked like the ordinary, everyday me, but it had *no brain at all!!!*

Shit!

Fuck!

Idiot!

I can't help having no brain. There's a demon in my skull. It tells me things that aren't true, and I *believe* it . . .

Thousands of bucks.

Twenty years.

Twenty thousand bucks.

A thousand years.

JUVENILE OFFENDER CONVICTED—INSANITY DEFENSE FAILS—
"DUMB, YES—CRAZY, NO" SAYS JUDGE—ORDERS KEY MELTED.

I took the phone book back.

"Thank you," I said.

"You're very welcome," says the lady.

"Happy New Year," I told her.

"Thank you, and a Happy New Year to you too."

She'd barf in my face if she knew what I just found out.

I drove home again. Conditions were not good for driving, so I took it very slow. I didn't really want to reach home. I felt like a ship that slipped its anchor and is drifting around on an ocean of snow. No one can see me. I'm even invisible on radar. At the corner of Grant and Westwood I looked in the rearview mirror to make sure no one's tailgating me, and I saw my face. My eyes were all screwed up tight and I didn't even know it. I looked like someone just ran a sword through me. I deliberately had to unclench my eyes.

I felt very strange by the time I parked in the driveway. I went inside. Peggy's still in bed.

"It was Zajaczkowski," I told her.

"Say again?"

"Zajaczkowski."

She thought about it a while.

"Could be," she says.

"It *was*. He's the only one in the sixty-nine phone book in the Z's who's on his own. There was only one Zajaczkowski here in sixty-nine. He's the one that *did* it. Wait a minute . . ."

I went and looked in the '85 book again. No Zajaczkowski. I went back in Peggy's room.

"He's dead or moved away now, but he was the one."

"Okay, so he was the one. I believe I asked you to drop this particular subject just a short while back. Do you remember me asking you to do that little favor for me? I'm asking you again, very politely, Burris, to *cut it out*. Am I getting through?"

"Yeah."

"I'd like to be alone now, please. I'm on vacation from the world and I want to enjoy it."

I left her there and closed the bedroom door behind me. She wants to be alone? She'll be alone. I want to be alone too. I want to get to the bottom of how it feels to be a vandal and a fool at the same time. The bottom is a long way down. I went in my room to tape and to find it, that far down bottom where I'll know exactly how it feels to be *me*, the particular me I am today. I'd rather be just about any other kind of me, frankly, except the suicidal me that came rushing up from under last summer. That's a me I don't want to see again, ever. Who is this new me? I'll tell you something for free—he isn't surprised to learn how dumb he is and how wrong a move he made, not really surprised at all. Is this because I don't expect very much from myself? That'd be kind of sad, to *expect* myself to fuck things up, but it can't be denied that fucking things up is what I'm good at. I'm Professor Emeritus of Foul-ups, the Dean of Dunces. *Do You Sincerely Want To Be Stupid?* Just send five dollars to me, Burris Weems, and I guarantee I'll reduce your brains to mush. *Tired Of Success?* Five small bucks will fix your wagon but good. I did the wrong thing. I can't tell anyone. Another big secret for me to sit on. That's two big secrets in one year. At this rate I'll have a whole clutch of them under me by 1990, secrets as big as ostrich eggs rolling out from under my stupid butt and smashing open all around me so people will stop and point and hold their noses because the secrets smell like shit, only multiplied a million times. I did the *wrong thing*. I'll never get to heaven, Kevin.

I lay on the bed and stared out the window. The sky was filled with snow, a whiteness that isn't near and isn't far, it's just *there*, always falling and always quiet. I felt like I could've floated right out through the window and across the yard and up into all that whiteness and kept on rising through it forever, up and up till the cold white of snow turned into the white heat of sunlight. I'd rise so high I'd get burned, and down I'd fall again, this charred hunk of burger falling down through the snowy sky till it hit the yard—*whap!* I'd lie in the yard and the snow would cover me like a white wool blanket, cover me over till there's nothing left to see, just this white mound that could have anything at all under it. They'd look for me everywhere, and I'd be right there in the yard. They'd never find me. I don't want them to. Leave me alone. I won't go to the Zurowski place and own up and apologize. I'm too scared. I'm a coward.

It doesn't bother me to know that. It's what I've always suspected. I have this burning need inside me to escape punishment. Show me the scene of the crime, document the circumstantial evidence, point the finger at me . . . I'll shake my head and tell you I was playing poker with the mayor when it happened. No way will I confess. It isn't worth it. Peggy and Loretta would have pain all over again, the same way they had it last July. I can't do that to them. But that sounds too noble. The real reason I won't own up is because I'm a coward like I said. This is an official news bulletin—Burris Weems is a coward, a shitty little coward. It's not surprising that I'm a failure at everything. I'm *supposed* to be. That's what I was made for. Cowardice sits very easily on my skinny shoulders. Lucky for me cowardice doesn't have a lot of width to it. Cowardice is a narrow thing. Cowardice is skinny and low and mean and stupid, like a hungry snake eating its own tail. I can feel it inside me, the snake, squirming around in there, eating itself, getting stronger and weaker at the same time. It'll still be alive way after I'm dead, getting younger and younger every time it sheds its skin. The snake is inside me. The snake is me. I am the snake, Jake. *Hissssssss* . . . I'm falling asleep. Being guilty makes me tired. Temporarily suspending operations while our aerial is adjusted. This is Radio WEEMS signing off . . .

Another crazy dream . . . I only remember the last part. It's the end of the world because the button was pushed. The concrete slabs roll back and the missiles sniff the air. They're all set to fly. Ten . . . nine . . . eight . . . preignition . . . seven . . . six . . . five . . . and they're beyond cancellation now . . . four . . . three . . . two . . . *Ignition!* Clouds of smoke spew out of the underground silos and there's a red-orange glow down there in the bottom of those concrete tubes as the nose cones start rising above the ground a few inches at a time, the slowest missiles in the world, because they aren't missiles at all, they're Lennie the Loop, every one of them, rising out of the silos very slowly, a million Lennies stiff as light poles, rising into the air with smoke and flame around their boots . . . then Lennie starts leaning to one side, all of the Lennies, leaning like there's a force-ten gale pushing them over, and they lose their balance on their flaming boots and fall out of the air before they're ever truly up there, fall over and down like old brick chimneys and explode—*Whooooooomp!* All of them do that, all the Lennies. Not a single one makes it into the air. They all die in flames, and a four-star general in the bunker next to me says, "Well you said it'd happen, and it did." There's a bell ringing somewhere. "They should shut that thing off," he says. "There's no danger anymore. You can wake up now."

And I did.

It's the phone!

I practically fell off the bed, then ran through to the living room. The house is dark because it's already dark outside. I slept right through what was left of the daylight.

"Hello?"

"Two deep-dish pizzas with extra cheese and mushrooms, please."

"Hi, Loretta."

"I rang you guys three, four times yesterday. Where were you?"

"Uh . . . the phone must've not been working."

Did she phone the Wishee-Washee too? I'm asking myself, but she didn't, because the next thing she says is, "Have you guys got plans for this evening?"

"Uh . . . no, just staying in, I guess. How about you?"

"There's a phone company party we might drop in on. Is Peggy home yet?"

I looked at my watch, squint, squint . . . 5:07.

"Uh . . . no, she's not."

"Tell her to give me a call when she comes in."

"Okay."

I couldn't tell her Peggy quit the laundromat and is probably dead drunk in the bedroom right now. It's like Peggy quitting the Wishee-Washee has got something to do with me ruining Zurowski's greenhouse, like it's all part of the same fucking mess, which is a very dumb way of thinking because the two things have got nothing to do with each other, but that's how I felt, like we're accomplices or something.

"I'd invite you both," says Loretta, "but it's supposed to be for employees' families only. I told Pete that in-laws are family, but he said it means immediate family, not relations. It's kind of pathetic, I think."

She's embarrassed about us not being able to come along, I can tell.

"That's okay. We'll make out."

"How's it been with you two since the big Sunday revelations?"

"Fine. Okay. No difference, as a matter of fact. You should've told me I'm the illegitimate heir to the throne or something, you know, a big dramatic deal. Something like that would've made a difference I bet, but not this ordinary stuff."

"Sorry to disappoint you, Bub. Tell her to gimme a buzz."

"Will do."

" 'Bye now."

" 'Bye."

Click.

Maybe the phone woke Peggy up. I snuck along to her room and peeked in. Total darkness with snoring coming out of it. I closed the door. 5:09. It's New Year's Eve, Steve, and I haven't even had breakfast yet! I went in the kitchen and ate like a pig. Then it's 5:30 and time for the local news. I switched on the tube. Stuff about the weather. Stuff about how the Buford City Council is getting ready for 1986 by having all its records transferred to computer discs. Fascinating. More stuff about the weather. Yawn, yawn. Some footage of an accident at the corner of Keilor and Dogwood. Nobody got hurt. Stuff about driving carefully tonight if you're going to a party, and not drinking too much or you'll have an accident on the way home. C'mon, c'mon . . . A bunch of people around town wishing the camera a Happy New Year, special messages and good wishes for '86, all that junk, and then it's the bit I've been waiting for . . .

"Vandalism on a grand scale here in Buford on this last day of nineteen-eighty-five," says Wesley Wright, our local TV newsman, a real dork. They're showing the Zurowski place, the front of it at first. "It happened on Carriage Hill Drive sometime in the night but wasn't discovered till this morning, a greenhouse that used to be the pride of its owner, Mrs. Betty Zurowski, now a miniature ice palace." Now it's the backyard with the greenhouse, and the camera goes through the door and looks inside, where all that water coming down from the spray nozzles froze the way I knew it would and made stalagmites and stalactites of shining white everywhere, with these green shapes under it all, the drowned orchids, frozen like a prehistoric rain forest that all of a sudden got hit by the ice age and preserved forever the way it was. "This was no malfunction of the greenhouse's spray system," says Wesley, and we move in for a close-up of the alarm wire I cut, "but a deliberate act of vandalism. Without the temperature alarm in operation Mrs. Zurowski had no way of knowing her prizewinning orchids were being sprayed non-stop, the temperature in the greenhouse plummeting by the minute. The heating system was turned off . . ." Close-up of the tap wheels, frozen in the off position. ". . . and the spray system set to work continuously." Close-up of the timer set at zero. Then there's this old lady with a handkerchief in her face, crying all down her cheeks. Wesley asks if she knows why anyone would do a thing like this, and she shakes her head and says she doesn't know, it just doesn't make any sense, and cries some more. Boy, did I ever feel like a turd. Wesley started saying some more about it but I turned the set off and sat there squirming around like a dog with fleas, squirming with guilt, frankly.

The phone again!

"Hello?"

I was expecting it to be Wesley Wright, asking for an exclusive interview. Guilt makes you think strange things.

"Boris?"

"Uh . . . yeah."

"You watching the news?"

"Yessir, Mr. Bimmerhaus."

"That was a big mistake you made, son, the husband being dead like that."

"Pardon me?"

"You watch the news or not? There's just the widow left. Husband died six months ago."

I turned old Wesley off too soon, it looks like. Shit! Chuck has to be smoothed over, and fast.

"Oh . . . well I didn't know that, Mr. Bimmerhaus. I wouldn't have done it if I'd known he was dead already."

"There's just the wife left now."

"I don't know what to say, Mr. Bimmerhaus."

"Maybe next time you'll think a thing through instead of jumping right in the way you did."

"Yessir, that's good advice."

"There's no point in upsetting old ladies if it's their husband that didn't give your dad a deferment."

"No sir, I really regret it."

"You run a risk whenever you take the law in your own hands the way you did. Things can go wrong, like this."

"Yessir."

"There's no point."

"No sir, no point. I guess I goofed."

"I guess you did. There's this nice Zurowski woman crying her eyes out and she doesn't even know why it happened."

"I feel bad about it, Mr. Bimmerhaus."

"You think maybe she'll connect it to her husband being on the draft board all that time back?"

"I doubt it, Mr. Bimmerhaus."

Seeing as he was never on it, seeing as his name wasn't Zajaczkowski.

"It's a real fouled-up deal, Boris."

"Yessir, I guess it is."

More than you'll ever know, Chuck.

"I hope you learn something from this experience."

"I definitely have, Mr. Bimmerhaus."

I've learned not to turn a big car on a narrow road in the snow.

"The cops didn't call me."

"No sir, I figured they wouldn't when it started snowing. The tracks would've been gone."

"Maybe it's a good thing. If they had've asked me about towing someone and I knew what I know now about the husband being dead, maybe I'd change my mind and tell 'em what I know. You never should've done this, Boris."

"No sir."

I'm waiting for him to apologize about accusing me of stealing that wad of cash from the Zurowskis, but he didn't mention it, probably figures a dickhead like me doesn't deserve apologies.

"You can't get revenge on a dead man," he says.

"No sir, I can see that now."

"You should've phoned him up and talked to him before-hand. That way you would've found out he's dead."

"I should've done that all right, Mr. Bimmerhaus."

"Well, I just hope you learned something from this experience."

"Yessir."

"They didn't say on the news if she had insurance. You think she had insurance?"

"I dunno, Mr. Bimmerhaus. I think rich people always have insurance."

"I hope so. She looked like a nice woman."

"Yessir."

"She was very upset."

"I'm very ashamed about it."

"Well, it'll be a lesson for you."

An eighty-dollar lesson.

"Yessir, a very important learning experience."

"It's a bad way to start the new year."

I didn't say anything. If I say anything it'll only start him off again.

"You there, Boris?"

"Yessir."

"I said it's a bad way to start the new year."

"Yessir, it is. I regret all of it. How's Lennie?"

"Huh?"

"How's Lennie, okay?"

"He's okay."

"Wish him a Happy New Year for me, willya."

"What?"

"Wish him a Happy New Year, and a Happy New Year to you too, Mr. Bimmerhaus."

"Yeah," is all he says.

"Well thanks for calling, sir."

"I just wanted you to know what you did."

"Yessir, I appreciate your concern, I really do."

"Just don't do it again."

TEENAGER GOES ON GREENHOUSE VANDALISM SPREE—SAYS PLANTS ARE EVIL

"No sir."

He hung up. About fucking time.

"Who was that?"

Peggy came in the room looking like a ghost in her long nightgown.

"Wrong number."

"Don't tell lies, Burris. You were talking for a couple of minutes. I heard you."

"It was Loretta. She wants you to call back. I didn't tell her you quit the laundromat."

"Why not? What difference?"

"I dunno, I just didn't tell her."

She took the phone off me and started dialing. I went in the kitchen. I could hear her talking, but not what she said. She talked for maybe ten minutes, then the phone went *smack! ping!* onto the cradle and she came stomping through to the refrigerator and got herself a big glass of orange juice, probably because she's dehydrated after all that lonely boozing. Then she sat down. We're on opposite sides of the table.

"Your sister's mad at me."

"You mean my half sister."

"Don't go fussing with terms, Burris, I'm not in the mood ."

"Did you tell her about the Washington trip?"

"No, about quitting. She thinks it's irresponsible. Do you think it's an irresponsible thing to do?"

"I don't see why you should stay there if you don't like it."

"You've changed your tune since yesterday. "Where's the money going to come from?" you said."

"That was yesterday."

"In that case we think the same. We are of one accord, chum. But Loretta thinks different from us. She would've agreed with us before she married Pete. He's changed her. She doesn't know it yet, but he's changed her. Pretty soon she'll be too ashamed of us to invite us around, and she won't call here anymore. We're not invited to the party tonight, did you know?"

"It's only for the phone company families."

"That's what she *says*, but is it *true* I'd like to know."

Peggy's still drunk, even if she slept for hours. Her hands look wrong with a glass of that bright orange stuff between them. It should be brownish-gold Southern Comfort. She knocked back a mouthful and pulled a face. She thinks it should be Southern Comfort too.

"I'm not staying inside the house on New Year's Eve, no way."

"Uh . . . you going out somewhere?"

"You bet. How about yourself, your friends throwing any parties?"

Big joke. She knows I don't have any friends.

"Nah. Where you going?"

"Out of this damn house. It's like a coffin."

"But where, specifically?"

"Specifically, Frankie's Red Room."

That's a downtown cocktail lounge Peggy used to go to when Mack was her boyfriend. She hasn't been there in a while. They get a very weird clientele at Frankie's Red Room. Anyone in Buford who's a little bit weird ends up at the Red Room sooner or later, Peggy says. She also says she's got a bar stool reserved for me there for when I'm old enough to drink legally. She says I'll fit right in, ha ha! She'd be disappointed in me if I turned out normal, she's so weird and screwed-up herself, which is why she doesn't make as big a deal out of me being a useless bum as other mothers would. I have to be honest about that, I mean I get a pretty good deal around here, foodwise, rentwise et cetera. But that doesn't mean I wanted her to go to Frankie's Red Room. People go to the Red Room to find someone to go home with. My mom is fixing to get laid and wake up in 1986 with some guy's head next to hers on the pillow. I hope she goes to his place, not back here. It was bad enough listening to Peggy and Mack pounding the bedroom to pieces, I mean I *liked* Mack, but I don't want some unknown bozo coming in the house tonight to fuck my mother. So I'm being selfish, I can't help it.

"Why there?"

"I know the people there. I want some company. This place is like a prison."

"Well I'm staying in."

"Suit yourself. Won't you get miserable stuck in here on your own?"

"Probably."

"Burris, are you trying to lay a guilt trip on me? Do you not want me to go out tonight? Don't you think I should be allowed to have a little fun? I'm over twenty-one."

"Way over."

Uh-oh. Mistake. She's giving me the dagger eye.

"It's my life," she says, kind of hissing between her teeth. "If I were you I'd make a New Year's resolution. I'd promise myself not to be such a little stick-in-the-mud where the happiness of my old lady was concerned. My *very* old lady who still has some zing left in her and isn't *quite* ready to flop down in her grave so you can shovel shit . . . shovel earth over her poor old miserable wrinkled *body*. I'm going *out*, so get used to it, okay?"

"Okay."

"And I also wouldn't stay in this place tonight. It isn't right, you sitting here watching the crowds in Times Square on TV at midnight. What kind of New Year's Eve is that?"

She knows me through and through. That's what I would've done.

"Okay, I'll go out too."

"Good. Neither of us should be stuck inside tonight. I'm taking the car, so you'll have to walk to wherever, or I'll give you a lift. Where did you say?"

"I dunno yet, but it should be me that has the car because you'll just get drunk at Frankie's and kill yourself on the road and then I'd be an *orphan*."

She thought that was pretty funny, even laughed.

"Awwww, does da widdle feller not wanna be a norphan?"

"No."

I don't like it when she does funny voices. *I* do the funny voices around here.

"Good point, kid. I *will* get drunk and maybe killed. Tell you what, you can be my chauffeur for the end of eighty-five, how about that?"

"Chauffeur?"

"You drive me to the Red Room, then the car's yours for the rest of the night, so long as you promise me *you* won't get drunk or stoned and pile it up. Deal?"

"Deal."

We shook hands on it. She was in a good mood, not like when she came in after hanging up on Loretta.

"I'll need some drinking money. Where's the bundle I gave you yesterday?"

My guts turned upside down inside me. She's gonna find out . . .

"What bundle?"

"I gave you three hundred bucks for the Wasington fiasco."

"Oh yeah. We spent a bunch of it on gas and stuff . . ."

"Let's have the rest."

I emptied my pockets. This very crushed fold of bills got dumped on the table and opened out slowly like a stop-motion flower in one of those nature shows on the tube. Peggy picks it up and counts it.

"A hundred thirty-three? Where's the rest?"

"We spent it. The car's a real gas-hog . . ."

"Burris, the car *guzzles* gas, it doesn't gargle and spit it out. We did *not* spend a hundred and seventy bucks on gas yesterday."

"There were burgers too."

"Including burgers."

I went through my pockets again with this deep frown on my face. She's watching me very closely with a suspicious look in her eye. Peggy Weems is part-time crazy, but she's no fool.

"Quit pretending. Where is it?"

"Uh . . . I think I've lost it."

"You think you've lost it."

"Yeah, it looks that way."

"That's not the way it looks to me, Burris. It looks to me like you spent that money without my permission, eighty or ninety dollars. What have you done with it?"

"Nothing. I lost it."

"You didn't. You spent it. On what?"

"I didn't spend it."

"Then where is it?"

"I *lost* it!"

"You *didn't!* And don't raise your voice to me! Where-is-that-money!"

"I dunno."

"You *do* know, and we're not budging from this table until

you tell me. And that *doesn't* mean you'll keep me in here all night, Burris. I'm going out, and before I do I'll know what happened to that cash. I want to know *right now* what you did with it."

"I lost it."

"You did *not* lose it."

"I did *too* lose it."

We traded daggers across the table, then Peggy says, "Burris, I just want to *know*. I'm sure you had a reason for spending it the way you did. You're an intelligent kid and you wouldn't just blow ninety bucks for no reason."

"Eighty."

Mistake . . .

"Eighty," she says, very suspicious. "Exactly eighty?"

"Approximately. I've lost approximately eighty bucks."

"You mean you spent it."

"No, I mean I lost it."

"Eighty bucks."

"Right. Eighty bucks. Approximately."

"You didn't lose it, Burris."

"Yes I did lose it."

"No."

"Yes."

We weren't shouting or anything, just talking quietly like an old married couple discussing the weather across the kitchen table.

"Are you going to tell me now, or are you going to tell me later?"

"I can't tell you what didn't happen."

"I know you're lying, Burris."

"No you don't, because I'm not. You just *think* you know."

"I know what I know. I know your face. You're covering up, and not very well. What happened to the money, Burris? I just want to know what happened to the eighty dollars *approximately*. You know we can't afford to have that kind of cash go missing. I'd like you to tell me straight out what you spent it on. I won't punish you. You're too big to spank. I just want to know what happened to the money so I can enjoy New Year's

Eve without this big mystery hanging over my head. Is that too much to ask?"

"No."

"So what happened to the money?"

"I lost it."

"*You did not lose it! You spent it, you little shit! Don't lie to me!*"

Boy, she went crazy right in front of my eyes. She leaned so far across the table she pushed the orange juice over with her tits and it went everywhere. She's breathing through her mouth she's so worked up. I was pretty scared, frankly.

"Are you going to stick to that story, Burris?"

"It's what happened, honest. I lost it . . ."

"I'm giving you one last chance to tell the truth. You won't be punished, but I have to know the truth. I'll give you one minute to think about it."

I looked at the table. I couldn't look at her eyes. All those little daggers were sticking out of my face where she planted them, hundreds of them. I look like a porcupine. I wanted to tell her about Chuck Bimmerhaus and the tow truck, but that would've meant explaining how come I was out on the fire road, and even if I tell her I was just riding around she'll read in the news tomorrow about the Zurowskis' greenhouse and put two and two together and then I'll look very dumb. I already felt dumb about old Chuck knowing Zurowski died six months ago, so I don't want anyone finding out Zurowski not only wasn't alive to feel bad about the greenhouse, he wasn't even the one that deserved punishment for being head of the draft board. I'd love to know when that prick Zajaczkowski left town. I bet it was years ago. What a fucking mess.

A minute is a long time when no one says anything and all you can do is think about what a total idiot you are, a very long time, stretching like a rubber band, stretching and stretching till it's let go to squash me *splat*! like a fly on the wall. I can't tell her, I just can't. I'm not ashamed to be a criminal vandal as such, just ashamed for being dumb. When you're a five-foot-three gimp with a suicide scar on your wrist you need to believe you're smarter than anyone else, or you've got nothing to keep you going, no ego food, and finding out you're *not* so smart is a bad enough break without other people finding out too, so I can't tell her, which is a shame because I'd like to, really I would, just to get it all off my chest, but I can't do it. The big secret about the greenhouse and the wrong man will just have to sit inside me alongside the big secret about old Gene last summer. They'll keep each other company inside me. A minute really is a long time when no one says anything and all there is to do is stare at the spilled OJ on the table . . .

"Well?"

I looked up. Will I tell her anyway? She's my mom after all. "I lost it."

She looked at me a long while.

"Okay, chum. Now we know where we stand. In eighty-six one of us is going to kill the other, I swear."

She's exaggerating because she's pissed at me for not breaking down and telling the truth. She hates it when I'm as strong as her.

"Clean this table," she says.

I got a sponge and mopped up the juice, and while I'm doing it she went in her room. I squeezed out the sponge in the sink, then did the same as her and went in my room. What a way to end the year. I bet I've had enough traumatic experiences in 1985 to last till 2000. Too much has happened in one little year. I bet there are people who had absolutely nothing happen to them from January through December, the lucky sonsofbitches. I put a new tape in the Sony and picked up from where I left off when I fell asleep this afternoon. It's been a very heavy day so far, even if I slept through most of it, and it's only 6:47 now! When it rains in the life of Burris Weems it's a fucking cats'n'dogs-can't-see-your-hand-in-front-of-your-face-so-Noah-go-build-your-ark type downpour . . .

There goes Peggy's door . . . Now the front door . . . *Bam!* Now I hear the car starting up. I guess I won't be doing any chauffeuring after all. I hope she's not going directly to Frankie's Red Room. She needs to eat something first. I need to eat too. I'm starving again. First stop, the kitchen, for frozen pizza. Then it's on to the madcap delights of New Year's Eve and a joyful ringing in of the first day of 1986.

In Times Square.

15

I watched the network news. I couldn't concentrate. I don't think anything very important happened in the world today, but I can't be sure. After the news I watched some other stuff, channel-hopping, not really seeing what I'm staring at. It's New Year's Eve and I'm alone in the house with a half-eaten pizza and the tube for company, a very pathetic situation even for a loner like me. Sometimes enough is enough. Robinson Crusoe toughed it out on his own for years like a real hero, but life was a whole lot better when Friday came along. You know what old Rob's first words were when they met? "Thank God it's Friday!" Yuk yuk!

Over to the window. It's not snowing anymore. I hope Peggy made it to the Red Room okay. It really is red in there, she says, red ceiling and walls and even this tacky red carpet on the floor, and the lighting is red and yellow. You can only tell what you're drinking by the taste, according to Peggy, because all drinks look red in there, like blood. Make mine a type-O cocktail, bartender, and don't forget the cherry. Red red red. She calls it the Womb Room. She's probably in there right now, throwing red Southern Comfort down her throat and cozying up to skinny men. She only goes for skinny guys. She'll wind up with someone for sure. She's in the mood for fucking. Me, I haven't thought about sex for days and days. I read somewhere that tension and worry kill your sex drive, and now I know it's true. I'm very worried about everything that's happened this past week or so. I've worried my sex drive into neutral, maybe even reverse. A guy my age is supposed to have jizz practically coming out his ears he's so goddamn horny, but my prick is too worried about other stuff to even lift his head. He just looks at the floor and worries about stuff. He thinks he's about ninety-five years old, my prick.

More TV. Hop, hop, hop. What the fuck am I watching? The programs go in my eyes and out my nose. Five seconds after I've seen something I forget what it was. Usually that just happens with the commercials, but tonight it's happening with everything. What it means is—I don't want to *be* here. I want to be out *there* having fun on New Year's Eve like everybody else. I want to be slapped on the back and told, "Hey, Burris, glad you could make it! The party can really let rip now that *you're* here, pal." And everyone turns to look at me and they all smile and wave and yell my name and jump up and down and wet their pants because *I'm* there. What a fantasy! I bet if I went to a party they'd stop me at the door after I rang the bell and say, "Weems . . . who the fuck invited *you?*" And after I walked away they'd wipe my greasy fingerprint off the doorbell. Boy, am I miserable. This is just terrible, gang. I hafta get outa here . . .

8:53. A little over three hours of 1985 left. I can't sit here on my own and cross from one year to the next in this fucking awful room with the tube laughing at me. I won't do it! I'll put on my Eskimo rig and take a long walk. Even if I have to be alone, at least I'll be alone away from here. Anyplace is better than 1404 Westwood Drive tonight, I kid you not.

So that's what I did, got suited up and went walking. I took the Sony with me so I can make a few philosophical reflections when the hands on my watch meet at twelve, something like, "Thus passes one year into the next, without observable change," or how about, "The passage from year to year was accomplished with less drama than the passing of darkness to dawn." I think that's got kind of a classy ring to it. I should be a speechwriter. Four score and something years ago we are gathered here to celebrate this day of infamy, asking not what your country can do for you, but what you can do for painful hemorrhoids with just one call to the number on your screen, but hurry hurry hurry while stocks last, because America is not sold in stores, so just send $9.99 for a piece of America, or charge it! No COD's accepted.

Crunch, crunch, crunch. There are parties happening behind these windows, I can hear them, all that laughing and talking and music. They don't know I'm walking by. It's a good night to end the year, clear and bright, a little above zero they said on the weather report. I'm following a very familiar route. Guess where I'm headed. I'm going to school. Yeah, that's right, good old Memorial High, down on the corner of Tamarack and Griffith. I've walked this route a million times. I could do it blindfolded. It takes twenty-seven minutes, usually. Make it a little longer on account of the snow. Burris Weems is on his way to school with his Sony tucked inside his parka hood. Burris Weems talks to himself, everyone knows that, but is it surprising with a family situation like his? Everyone knows the mother is man-hungry, and the sister was the same before she finally got married. Some example they set. No wonder the kid turned out such a loser. Everyone knows he'll try to kill himself again before he's eighteen, and he'll succeed before he's twenty. Everyone knows, everyone knows . . .

And there it is, Memorial High. Not a light showing in the whole place, not a footprint in the snow along the walks and across the lawns and quad. Memorial High is dead. I sat on a bench and listened to the rope thwacking the steel flagpole in the wind. *Thung, thung, thung*, it goes, very hollow and sad. There's no flag up there, just the rope and the pole with the moon and a few clouds behind, also a couple of stars. This'd be the place to kill myself if I wanted to, right here under an empty flagpole.

> *Ever on to greater deeds,*
> *Our limit is the sky—*
> *We're Indiana's bold new breed*
> *From Buford Memorial High!*

That's from 1961 when they built the place. I think the principal's wife wrote it. Or maybe it was the janitor. What a poem! Doesn't it just choke you up? It's supposed to be very moving. My bowels are very moved every time I hear it. I never saw anything like a bold new breed while I was here, just kids trying very hard to be exactly like each other. I would've tried to be one of them too, I admit it, but I couldn't because

I'm a gimp, so I'm automatically different. You can't be a high school hero unless you're on the football team or you're a track champ or whatever. That's the way it is in High School U.S.A. Heroes get the girl, they really do. No others need apply. No shrimp gimps wanted. I'm feeling very sorry for myself, which is pathetic. I should be grateful I was never in any danger of turning into an ordinary guy. That would've been the pits. I'm Burris Weems, small-town social leper, and that's the way it *should* be. I *like* it like that. Fuck you, Memorial High! Fuck you, prom kings and prom queens, and fuck every member of the Bravos, which is the team. Some of those guys are good enough to turn professional in a few years. They'll make a million bucks and get the chance to advertize razors. Talk about *fame!* Pass me the puke bag. Fuck you all, because I'm feeling very pissed off tonight at the whole world. To be honest, I guess most of the kids here are basically okay people, but they aren't like *me*, so they're from an entirely different zoo. They think they're outside the bars looking in at me, and I think I'm on the outside looking in at them. They'd think I'm crazy if they knew what I think. Well, they won't get the chance, because schooldays are gone days. No more school for our hero. No more nothing. It's all behind me now. The happiest days of your life. Horseshit. Only if your face fits, pal. Fit that face. Smile for the yearbook . . .

Sherilu Darcel is fun to be around and sees a future for herself in veterinary medicine. We know you'll make it, Sherilu! Danny Patruchik knows what he wants—a shot at Hollywood. We've got the popcorn warm, Danny! Jeannie Isacksen is guaranteed to do one thing—succeed with style! Burris Weems can be described in one word—indescribable! Just kidding, Burris . . .

Sure you were, wiseass. Am I offended? Nah. If the shoe fits, wear it. I've got seven-league boots on my feet. Everyone else has sneakers. Eat my dust, creeps! I'm going places you never heard of! Okay, I haven't heard of them yet myself, but they're out there somewhere, those places . . . No they aren't. The whole world is like Buford, only bigger. Why would things be better somewhere else? They wouldn't, is the answer. This *is* the world, right here where I'm sitting. So why am I bitching? Am I sick? No. Am I in a wheelchair? No. Am I

blind? Nope. Am I deaf? Huh? Speak up! Ha ha! Get serious.
Am I a dope addict? No. Am I mentally retarded? No, I'm a
genius compared to most of 'em in this dump. *So what am I
bitching about!* Things aren't so bad, considering. So I don't fit
in—big fucking deal. Who *wants* to fit! Not me. I'm A-okay
and worth my pay. I'm feeling good the way I should. Feeling
fine and it's no crime. Feeling great—how 'bout a date! Nah,
no dates for me, not since old Sandra told me to get lost. She
used to be my currant date, but now she's raisin the roof with
another guy. Not funny. Nope, not funny at all . . .

Hold the phone!

I gotta party!

Sandra's old lady gave me an invite in Safeway last Saturday!
Up off the bench. What's the time? 9:48. It'll take me an
hour to reach Harry's Highway Haven, maybe more, but I'll
have at least an hour of partying before midnight, and who
knows how long after! Wait a minute . . . Mrs. Christensen.
said I was on Sandra's list, but Sandra didn't phone me to
confirm it. Suspicious. Maybe her old lady was just being kind,
inviting me on the spur of the moment like that. Maybe when
she got home and told Sandra what she did, Sandra gave her
the old "Mother, how *could* you!" routine. Yeah, I bet she did,
and that's why she didn't phone me to confirm that I really *am*
on her goddamn list. Why would she want me there at her
New Year's Eve party anyway? It doesn't make sense. It'd just
be embarrassing. Mrs. Christensen was definitely way out of
line, giving me that invite the way she did, I mean I'm sure she
meant well by doing it, but Sandra won't want me around.

Shit! I got excited for around eight seconds there . . . But
wait just a fucking minute now . . . I *did* get an invite, right?
Right. So I've got a legitimate right to show up at the motel and
shake a leg with the rest of them, right? You bet I do. Sandra's
probably counting on me being too chickenhearted to show up,
I just know it. She'll count on me not having the nerve after she
didn't phone me to confirm it, the bitch. Well she's got a big
surprise coming her way because I'm *gonna* show up whether
she likes it or not, so *there!* Nyaaaaaahh! I'm acting like a little
kid. I have to calm down. Am I really going to do it? Yeah,
why the fuck not. It's New Year's Eve and I'm sick of being on

my own. I'm going to Sandra's party even it I have to gate-crash it. Signing off till later.

Some party I don't think!

What a waste of fucking time!

Begin at the beginning. I got to Harry's Highway Haven at 10:56. There's a whole bunch of cars outside but I don't know which ones belong to the motel guests and which ones belong to the people at Sandra's party. I bet her new boyfriend Paul is here. I wondered which car is his. Maybe the Charger with the rear end jacked up like a cat in heat. Nah, too garage mechanic with greasy jeans for Sandra. How about the Bronco 4x4 with the THIS VEHICLE INSURED BY SMITH AND WESSON sticker. Nah, too baseball cap and Miller beer. The Trans Am maybe? Nah, she'd think the eagle on the hood is tacky. Ahah! A 300 ZX, all shiny new, a real yuppie rocket. I bet Paul's dad bought it for him. Paul's dad is something big in real estate. Yeah, that's his car, practically guaranteed. It makes Peggy's Impala look like a tramp steamer, and I haven't even *got* Peggy's Impala. I'm riding up to the old corral on Shanks's mare, hobo Joe with no place to go. Will there be room at the inn for the weary traveler? Frankly I'd like to sit down. My bad hip is killing me after all this stomping through the snow.

Harry's Highway Haven has got a function room attached to it just like hotels sometimes have, even if Harry's is just a motel, but it only gets hired about twice a year. I bet that's where the action'll be tonight. It's around back, but I thought I better do the polite thing and kind of announce myself at the office like I'm a customer wanting a room.

So I did, I went in the office, which has still got Christmas decorations all over, very colorful and bright, and Sandra's dad Rick is behind the counter. He didn't know it's me till I pulled back my parka hood and took off my fur hat. I already took the Sony out of the hood. It's safe in my pocket. He looked at me a moment, then he recognized me.

"Hi there, stranger," he says.

"Hi, Rick."

It was hard for me to talk because my face was kind of frozen.

"Haven't seen you around in a while, Burris."

"I've been busy, you know."

"Sure, everyone's busy this time of year, don't I know it."

We both know it's bullshit about me being busy. What have I got to be busy about? Like the old song says—"I'm busy doin' nothin'."

"So how's life been treating you lately?" he wants to know.

"Oh, pretty good I guess."

"That's some hat you've got. You kill it yourself?"

"My sister gave it to me."

I want him to tell me to take my parka off and come on through to the party. I can hear the music from here, the Fabulous Thunderbirds I think. Sandra didn't have any Fabulous Thunderbirds in her collection when I used to come around here, so it's probably a Christmas present, or maybe Paul or one of her other friends brought some tapes along. Rick's looking at me with this smile on his face, like he's waiting for me to explain what I'm doing here, and I started thinking maybe old Alice didn't tell him about the invite she gave me in Safeway, just told Sandra. This is very embarrassing, but I've walked a long way to get here and I want *in*.

"Sorry I'm late," I said, and started unzipping my parka and kicking snow off my Red Wings.

"Oh, you joining in the swingin' soiree?"

Yep, old Alice failed to inform her hubby that their daughter's old flame is stopping by for fruit punch. Boy, that really burns me! Some people have got no regard for other people's feelings.

"Yeah, Mrs. Christensen told me on Saturday to come on over tonight."

"For the party," he says, wanting to get it straight.

"Yeah, for the party."

I want *in*. No one's gonna turn me away from the door tonight, pal. I'm in a very aggressive mood, I don't really know why, I only know I want *in*. I quit stomping my boots to let him know the next move is up to him. His smile isn't so big now. I don't think he believed me about the invite but what can he do, call me a liar? He'll check it out with wifey soon enough.

"Well, come on through," he says, and lifts up the counter to let me by. "I have to stay on duty awhile yet, but I'll be back there in time for the big countdown. You know the way?"

"Sure."

"Dump your stuff in the first room on your left."

"Okay."

Which I did. There's more coats piled up in there than a Salvation Army thrift store. I shoved my hat and mittens inside my parka and dumped it in a corner, then I went along the corridor a little further to where the function room is and opened one of the double doors and went in. There must've been around a hundred people in there. Alice told me it was a party for Sandra's friends, but the partyites are all grown-ups, not a single person my age. Shit! What kind of scene have I wandered into? That stupid Alice . . . What a cheesebrain!

"Hi there, Burris."

Aww . . . shit! It's Dr. Willett! He's very red in the face and his glasses are on crooked, so he's plenty drunk. I guess even psychiatrists have to let it all hang out once in a while, but it's embarrassing bumping into him here.

"Hi, Dr. Willett."

There's a break in the music between tracks. It's definitely the Fabulous Thunderbirds.

"Nobody said you'd be here," he says.

"Rick and Alice didn't want to build up too much excitement and anticipation, you know."

His face folded up like a squeeze box and he pumped out a string of creaky laughs. He's got a load on for sure.

"Is Mrs. Willett here?" I asked him.

Frankly I don't care if she's here or not. I'm making conversation.

"Uh . . . yes, over there somewhere," he says, and sloshed his drink at the far wall. More music, very loud. Everyone's shouting like crazy and dancing around. I'm the only sober person in the room I bet. They're all thirty and forty years old, all Rick and Alice's friends. I can't see a single teenager, not even Sandra. I'm positive Alice told me it was a party for Sandra's friends, but what the heck, who wants to talk to a bunch of geeks I already spent too much time with in class anyway?

"What kind of booze are they dishing out, Doc?"

Did I really say that? Too many old movies, Weems. Get modern.

"Oh, a bit of everything, I think, but you'd better take it easy, Burris. I don't think the Christensens want to be responsible for any underage drinking."

So much for Alice and her fruit punch for *les enfants terribles*. That dame . . . that *woman* is a certified ding-dong. No wonder Rick gave me a funny look when I said I got invited. Everone here is twenty years older than me! What a stupid, goddamn foul-up!

"Did you think about what we discussed on Saturday night?"

"Huh?"

"About the possibility of dropping by and discussing what's on your mind."

"Oh yeah . . . I don't think I've got anything on my mind as a matter of fact, Dr. Willett."

"Call me Keith."

"Uh . . . right."

He really wants to find out what makes me tick. It'll never happen, not till the sea gives up its dead, Fred.

"Now come on, Burris. How about a New Year's resolution that says you should start eighty-six with a clean slate, just wipe out all that crap swimming around in the old noodle, let it out and feel all the better for getting rid of it. How about it?"

The old *noodle*? He's drunker than I thought. I bet if he had've called the human brain a *noodle* back in shrink school they would've run him out of there before you could say Sigmund Freud. And calling my psychological disorder *crap* sounds pretty unprofessional to me. I could probably have him fired for saying stuff like that, even if he did it outside office hours. But I won't. I'm not that kind of guy.

"There's nothing on my mind, Dr. Willett. Keith. I'm okay."

"Still worrying about Lennie Bimmerhaus and your mother?"

"No, they're okay too, I think, probably partying it up tonight like everyone else."

"It's something, isn't it," he says, looking around at the party. He practically spun himself off his feet doing it, but then he kind of swiveled back to me. "Seriously now, Burris, you and I need to talk. I'd hate to think that you won't open up because I'm a shrink, and I'm forty-three, but really I don't think that's the problem, do you? I think you're the kind of kid that's already gone way beyond peer pressure, so the typical teen reaction won't be yours, am I right? Frankly, Burris, I've got a feeling that if I could just get you to trust me a little there's nothing we couldn't accomplish, psychologically speaking. Each of us has a demon inside, and you can feed off the demon or let the demon feed off you. Van Gogh and Beethoven had demons, and both of them fed off their demons to produce works of genius, but poor old Vincent couldn't keep the demon from feeding off *him* at the end. I'd hate to think of you being consumed by your demon, Burris. It's unnecessary. You can tame the demon, make it eat out of your hand, make it *work* for you, but first you have to admit it's *there*. That's what I was trying to tell you on Saturday, that if you'd just relax a little and speak freely . . ."

"Burris, my *God*, is that *you?*"

It's Alice, and she's so drunk she makes Dr. Willett look sober. He wasn't happy about being interrupted that way, and you could see the big effort it took him not to tell the hostess to fuck off while he's trying to do something important, namely finding out about my demon, which I don't plan on introducing him to anyway, not in a million years. My demon is chained up in the dungeon where he belongs.

"Let's see . . . did I invite you? I think I did, didn't I? When *was* that?"

"Saturday, in Safeway."

"God, *yes*, that's *right!* Oh, Burris, I suppose you're looking for Sandra, aren't you. She isn't here, wouldn't even join her mother's friends for ten *minutes*. God, we had an argument about *that*. I told her she didn't have enough friends to make opening the function room worthwhile, you know how picky she is about who she associates with, so I told her there'd be a few of *my* friends to fill out the space a little, and didn't she just bitch about *that*, my God, until Rick told her if she doesn't want any adults around she can just find herself another party, that's all, and she *did* and took all her little friends *with* her, ha ha *haaaa!*"

Alice is the kind of lady that squeals when she laughs, when she's drunk, anyway. I'm nodding my head up and down to show her I understand how come Sandra and her buddies aren't here, and she grabs my arm the same way she did on Saturday and says, "I should've told you sooner. I forgot, I *forgot* . . . God, that girl has some things to answer for. How about it, Keith, is analysis worthwhile for willful little bitches . . . *oops*, little minxes? I mean I *believe* independence shouldn't be crushed in the young, but honestly, there has to be a line drawn *somewhere*, but *where* is the line to be drawn, do you think? I'm just *asking*, sweetie. You don't have the meter ticking, do you? Ha, ha, *haaaaa* . . ."

"There's nothing wrong with her, Alice. It's a typical clash of wills. It happens in every family, enlightened or not, so don't worry about it. Ten dollars, please."

"Ha ha *haaaa* . . . Anyway, Burris, you're stuck with old fogies only, unless you can find out where Sandra is. Do you know Paul's house? She might be there. God, Keith, she might be doing *anything*, I mean we've had the usual mother-daughter chat about sex and there's no real problem there, but the *drugs* that seem to be flowing these days, peddled right there in *school* . . . Were you ever offered drugs in school, Burris? Is it true you can't walk down a corridor without some pusher getting in your face? That's what I really worry about, Keith, the drugs. If she wants to smoke a little grass who am I to say her nay, I mean I'm no *hypocrite* for God's sake, but cocaine and angel dust, no *thank* you, not for flesh and blood of *mine*. Were you ever offered anything like that, Burris? Please be honest. We worry about it all the time, Rick especially."

"Uh . . . nobody ever offered me anything like that."

"Are you sure? It won't go beyond this room, I *promise*."

She's leaning very close to my head so I can hear her over the music and shouting that's going on, and I can see right down between her tits. They're kind of flat, but she isn't wearing a bra or anything because her dress hasn't got straps, or maybe she's wearing one of those strapless bras, it's hard to tell for sure. Anyway, there's this very shallow valley showing, but the funny thing is it's not her tits I ended up staring at, it's the little dip between where her collarbones meet, nowhere *near* her tits, which doesn't make a whole lot of sense even to *me*, but what I wanted to do was kiss her right there between the knobbly bits where her collarbones end, right in the little hollowed-out bit that kind of shivers when she breathes and talks and laughs, and this is *Mrs. Christensen* I'm talking about, Sandra's *mom*, which makes me think I must be kind of perverted or something, wanting to kiss Sandra's mom's collarbones and all, but I couldn't help it and that's the truth.

"You can tell us and it won't go further than these walls, will it, Keith."

"This is *your* parental paranoia, Alice, not mine. Burris and I were discussing something entirely different."

"I dunno anything about drugs, Mrs. Christensen. All I ever did was smoke a little weed, frankly, and that was just getting passed around, you know, I mean I've never paid cash for anything. Nobody ever offered me stuff in the corridors."

It's true. I was such a big nothing at school even the pushers didn't bother with me, like there's a bubble around me that goes where I go, and on the outside of the bubble in letters I can't see from inside is a message: DON'T WASTE YOUR TIME— TOTAL ZERO WITHIN.

"Well at least that's *something*," she says, and the little dip between the ends of her collarbones got taken away. "We've got fruit punch and various other poisons, but don't do anything I wouldn't do, okay, Burris?"

"Sure."

And she went away and I'm stuck with the doc again. I turned back my sleeve. It's only 11:09! I feel like I've been here forever. Maybe it's just as well Sandra went somewhere else for New Year's Eve, I mean Paul would've been with her and I wouldn't have liked to see them together.

"How long till eighty-five is behind us?" says the doc.

"About fifty minutes."

"And what's a young person's prognosis for eighty-six? I think the patient will continue to sicken while the doctors continue telling him he's improving. They'll do that right up until it's time to pull the plug."

He answered his own question before I even had time to think about it. I bet he's been waiting all evening for someone to ask him what's ahead in 1986, but no one did, so he had to ask himself. It was fairly witty I guess, what he said, but it would've been wittier if I thought he made it up right on the spot, which he didn't, anyone could see that. It made me feel a little bit sorry for him, and it's kind of disturbing when that happens, I mean he's a college man with a degree and a big intellect et cetera, but here he is on New Year's Eve with clever stuff to say and no one'll give him the chance to say any of it because they're too busy boozing and bopping and trying to make out with each other's husbands and wives I bet, so the doc has to get little old me in a corner and ask *me* what *he* wants to be asked, but before I can open my mouth he says what he's been busting to say all along about the patients and the doctors. It's very sad in my opinion.

"Yeah, I think you're probably right."

"The thing I find really unsettling," he says, "is Reagan's popularity, even with young people. How would you rate the President, Burris?"

"I dunno. He's kind of friendly but dorky I guess."

"An amiable vacuum, you mean. I don't think I could be even *that* charitable. I'd have to call him a benign menace. To cure the world's ills you have to *understand* the world's ills, and he doesn't."

"My mom'd agree with you about that. She calls him Robot Ron."

"Is she a Democrat?"

"She's a nonaligned anarchist."

He let out a whinny like a horse, he thinks it's so funny. I didn't think it was so great myself. I've done better, frankly.

"I'll have to remember that," he says when he quit whinnying, then he says, "It's comments like that that make me think you're holding out on me, Burris. Your average kid around town wouldn't know what the hell an anarchist is unless he saw a video about it. I really want you to think about what I've said, the New Year and the clean slate. There'd be no stopping you if you'd just rid yourself of whatever it is that's bugging you, and believe me, I know something's bugging you. Every week I talk with kids that have difficulties over something or other, and some of them I know I can help, and some of them

I'm pretty sure I can't, to be honest, because I can't extract them from their current negative environment and place them in a nurturing, progressive one, I mean, to be blunt, their parents are either repressive monsters or just plain stupid. But not one of those kids is like you, Burris. I don't want you to be the big one that got away. I'm not trying to flatter your ego, talking to you man-to-man like this, just telling you how I feel. Psychiatrists have feelings too, ha ha . . . Incidentally, what I'm doing at this moment would probably be termed unprofessional by certain of my colleagues, but I'm not concerned with their opinions, I'm concerned with you, you and your future. There's no limit to what you could accomplish with a mind as sharp as yours."

"*Our limit is the sky.*"

"Exactly. The sky's the limit . . ."

"You two are very engrossed, I must say."

It's a lady with a drink in her hand who's come up behind Dr. Willett.

"Burris is my pet project," says the doc. "Burris, I don't think you've met my wife. Libby, meet Burris Weems."

She doesn't look like a psychiatrist's wife. I expected she'd have glasses and short hair and be kind of frumpy, but she's got plenty of hair and a pretty nice figure too. Jesus, I'm getting horny for all these old ladies tonight! Is there dope in the air or something that's making me feel this way? I can't smell any, but I'm definitely getting a hard-on. I had to drag my eyes off her chest, frankly. She knew I was looking at her boobs, I could tell by her eyes, which have got a message in them that says, "Maybe you've got my dingaling of a husband fascinated by your warped little mind, pal, but *I* know you're just another little pudknocker with pimply fantasies about older women."

"Hi," I said.

"Nice to meet you at last," she says.

Sounds like the doc's been gabbing about me over the breakfast table. I don't know how I feel about that. I mean it *is* kind of flattering to be talked about, but at the same time I don't think I like the idea of these people that I don't even really know—and who for sure don't know diddly about *me*—these people talking about me *behind my back*, if you see what I mean.

"Yeah. I hear you're a thespian," I said.

She looked at me. She's wondering if it's supposed to be some kind of smartass play on words or something, which if I'm as smart as it sounds like the doc's been telling her I am, I could certainly be doing, but which I'm actually not, being a smartass I mean, I'm just saying the first thing that came into my head and being a little too clever about it maybe. I think I just should've called her an actress and everything would've been okay, but I called her a thespian and she doesn't like me for it. Her eyes are telling me, "Eat my shorts, you precocious little fart." I definitely haven't made a friend.

"There are a few of us here from the playhouse," she says, which I guess means the theater. She said it in a very snotty voice, so I know I'm right about the message in the eyes. The doc jumps in and says, "They're doing Ionesco."

"Great," I said, even if I never heard of him.

"*Rhinoceros,*" says Libby, like it's a perfectly normal word to say to someone.

"Terrific," I said.

She's still giving me that nasty look, not sure if I'm putting her on or not, so I said, "I bet you need plenty of buckets and scoops for that one," and old Keith pretty near busted a gut over it, but Libby doesn't see the joke, or else thinks it's a joke on *her*, which if she does it means she's one of those people who are too sensitive. She gave Keith a look that says he's acting like an idiot, and when he saw it he quit laughing, like turning off a faucet. I don't think she respects him. Just a hunch. It made me like him more. I bet if he cracks a joke around the house she just gives him that pitying look and he clams up like he did just now.

"Are you interested in the theater?" she says.

"Nah, not really."

"How about the movies?"

"Yeah."

"Can you recommend anything?"

I could very easy recommend she go take a squat. She doesn't like me, not one little bit. I think it's partly because her husband, who she thinks is a dickhead, *does* like me. Well I don't like you either, lady. I bet she thinks she's a real fucking intellectual. I tried to remember the dumbest movie in town.

"*Invasion U.S.A.*," I said.

"You recommend that, do you?"

"Yeah, I do. It's definitely a great movie. You'd love it."

"I'll make a point of seeing it," she says.

Bullshit she will.

"There's Mike," she says to no one in particular, and walked away. Mike was probably there for the last half hour, but she made out like she just now discovered that *Mike* is *there*, which means she can quit talking to morons like me and the doc. Good riddance, bitch-face. Boy, I'd hate to be married to *her*. Old Keith kind of looked at his drink for a moment, then he says, "They're expecting a good audience."

Did *that* ever sound lame. I figured he's embarrassed because his wife came across like a real nut-pulper and he knows I don't like her for the very good reason that she's unlikable. This poor guy is expected to help kids work out their big mental problems while he's married to *her*? It must be tough keeping his mind on the job. If I was in his shoes I'd be all the time thinking up ways to murder Mrs. Pulpnuts without getting caught. Divorce'd be too easy. What a bitch, I mean it. Old Keith is standing there swirling his drink around. His wife killed the conversation stone dead. I bet come midnight she winds up kissing someone that isn't her husband, maybe Mike.

"Uh . . . is your daughter here?"

"Kate? No, she's out with some of her old Buford friends."

"She's gonna be a psychiatrist too, right?"

"Strictly speaking, a psychologist."

"You must be pretty happy about that."

"Yes, it's gratifying. I think I'll just freshen this up."

And he walked away. I waited for him to come back, but he didn't. I felt sorry for him, I really did. He can't talk any more to a crummy kid like me because his wife came over and made him feel stupid, which is a big shame because he's an okay guy, the doc. Feeling that way made me want to get out of there fast. No way am I staying around till midnight. I don't belong here.

I kind of slid out the door and collected my parka from the coatroom. If I had've known what coat was Mrs. Willett's I would've laid a turd in the pocket. Then I went out through the side door, the one that only opens from the inside that you take whenever there's a fire or whatever. I didn't want to talk to Rick again, which I would've had to do if I went out through the office. I didn't want to talk to anyone, just wanted to walk. I walked away from Harry's Highway Haven, then past all the other motels and the burger joints and gas stations along this stretch of the Buford Thruway.

The Sony's inside my hood again. It knows what happened at Harry's. It's 11:59 now, and I'm headed away from town. I've been walking and talking and not looking where I'm going, and now it's too late to be with people for the big countdown just one minute from now. Maybe it was deliberate, the route I've taken, I mean subconsciously speaking. Can the subconscious do deliberate stuff? The doc could've told me. What I mean is, maybe deep inside me there's a kind of compass that steered me *this* way instead of some other direction while I walked and talked, because where I'm headed is the auto junkyard. Where Lennie lives. I stopped and thought about it. I won't get there in time for the countdown, but if he's there I can for sure by God wish him a Happy New Year pretty soon afterward. I'll do it! I'll go see Lennie the Loop and back him into a corner and kill the bastard with kindness and greetings, whether he wants 'em or not. It's time the two of us came face-to-face. No more pussyfooting around. I started walking again. I know where I'm going now. I'll do some rehearsing too.

"Hi, Lennie. Happy New Year."

"Happy New Year, Lennie."

"Shake, Lennie, and a Happy New Year to ya."

"Put it there, pal. Hey, a Happy New Year, I mean it."

None of them sounded right.

I couldn't think what he might say back to me.

If he's there.

I'm a-comin', Lennie!

16

Crunch, crunch, crunch. I'm off the Thruway and cutting across a stretch of empty land, just snow and brush and junk that got dumped here. This route'll get me to the Bimmerhaus place quicker. Car horns way over on my left. More car horns right across town, also some kind of siren somebody rigged up. It's midnight. So long, '85. As years go, you sucked. Hi, '86, got anything nice in store for me? Yes? No? Wow! Somebody just let rip with a couple shotgun blasts. Is that legal, discharging a firearm within the city limits? More horns, and the siren's still howling. I bet everyone's smooching from Harland Heights right across to Firbank, kissy kissy kissy. Happy New Year, darling. Same to you, lover. Get that tongue in there. Shit, now it's rifle fire! Somebody's opened up with a hunting rifle, or maybe it's a big handgun, a Magnum maybe. What a fucking bunch of nuts. Still shooting. No one wants to be the last to fire. The cops'll probably ignore it, tonight being what it is. The siren's quit now. It must've been a real ear-buster up close, like the three-minute-warning siren on top of City Hall, the one they test at noon on the first Monday of every month, the one that's supposed to give us time to say our prayers before the missiles start coming down. *Kaboooooooooooooommmmmmmm!!!* Special bulletin—World War III began today at 12:03 Eastern. It ended at 12:05.

The shooting's stopped. They probably emptied all their clips at Halley's Comet. Where the fuck *is* that thing? I don't even know where to look. What we need is a big neon arrow in the sky. No more car horns now. Everything's quiet again. 1986 is here. It's official. Big deal. So what. All that matters is

I'm on my way to see Lennie the Loop. I'm kind of excited about it, frankly. That guy . . . that guy has been crowding my head for too long. We have to talk. He's not dumb, he can talk to me, tell me what I want to know, like how he got like he is. Was it the war? Was it coming home and finding his car mangled and his wife dead? What happened, huh? We've got a heavy date, Lennie and me. Awww, gosh . . . I forgot the corsage already. Will Lennie be peeved and not talk to me all evening? Will Lennie put out on our first date? Will there be something to tell the guys in the locker room tomorrow? Will it work out the way I want? Will Bill thrill Jill, or will Jill chill Bill? Stay tuned for the answers to these and other burning questions after a brief pause for station identification and these words to the wise: Moms, are you tired of leaky diapers? You are? Then quit wearing them for a shower cap and put 'em on the fucking baby, ha ha! Enough of this unseemly laughter. The task before us is enormous. Who put that enormous task there? *You* did, Simkins? Well put it back in the enormous task bin, idiot! All kidding aside, gang, it's definitely confrontation time for me and Lennie, time we buckled on our guns and took that long walk down Main Street. Will quiet Lennie let his pistols speak for him? Or will the new gun in town, Kid Weems, be faster on the draw? Draw your own conclusions while you can, sports fans, 'cos the Bimmerhaus Saloon ain't but a 'baccy spit away now, and soon the lead's a-gonna fly, fly, fly . . .

Shutting down for now.

I'm back.
Incredible scenes.
Total weirdness.
Where was I?
Yeah, getting close to the junkyard. It was 12:48 by then. I tried the gates but they're locked, so I climbed over. They rattled some when I dropped into the yard, and two seconds later the Doberman is crouched in front of me, snarling. "Hey, pooch." He quit snarling and straightened up. This is a mutt with a memory. "Lennie home, huh? Let's go see."
We started through the yard. There was enough moonlight

on the snow covering all those junked autos to make them look like they've been sugar-frosted. Chuck's tow truck wasn't there, so he's most likely out celebrating with a bunch of other old farts. I went on through to Lennie's shack, and there's a light in the window! Boy, the ticker practically jumped out of my chest when I saw it. He's home! Lennie the Loop is actually *home!* I stopped about five yards from his door, scared all of a sudden. What the fuck am I *doing* here? I don't even *know* this guy, this paranoid schizophrenic person . . . What if he opens the door and takes my head off with a machete? What if he tells the dog to take my throat out? This is *crazy* . . . I'm getting outa here . . .

Hold it, chickenshit. Lennie's harmless, everyone knows that.

The biggest risk you run is getting told you've got no manners for presenting yourself unannounced at this hour of the night. You might wait weeks to catch him at home again. You want to talk to the guy, right? So knock on the fucking door, coward. *Do* it!

I did it, went up to the door and knocked. I could hardly breathe, I'm so worked up. The dog was sniffing my boots, smelling all the streets I walked down tonight. My hip hurts bad. C'mon, Lennie, let me in so's I can take the weight off. But he didn't open up. I knocked again but he still didn't answer the door. Then I figured what's happening, which is that he's probably in there crouched in a corner, scared shitless because someone knocked on his goddamn door. Regular, ordinary stuff like hearing a knock at the door is most likely something old Lennie isn't used to, being a nut case living in the middle of a junkyard like he is, so he doesn't know what to do. I think *I'm* scared? Imagine how Lennie feels, trying to bore a hole through the shack's back wall with his head. I should've thought of this before, should've known you don't just walk up to the home of someone like Lennie the Loop and expect him to answer the door pronto like you're from the gas company or whatever, no sir, you have to take into account the fact that the occupant of this shack is not your regular guy, he's a paranoid schizophrenic Viet vet that hardly opened him mouth in ten years, so all the ordinary rules don't apply, not in a situation like this. So what do I do? Elementary, my dear Watson—one opens the door oneself.

"Lennie? Are you in there, Lennie? It's Burris Weems, the guy that left the note on Saturday. Uh . . . are you gonna open the door? It's cold out here."

No answer, no footsteps, no nothin'.

I turned the door handle.

It opened.

I went in.

No Lennie.

There's a Coleman lamp on a little table in the middle of the room, and over in the corner there's an Army cot, very rumpled and untidy, and in the other corner there's a chemical toilet, not screened off or anything. There's a propane heater in there too, kicking out lots of heat. But no Lennie. I pulled back my hood and took off my hat and mittens. I already closed the door behind me. It's real quiet in there, just the lamp and the heater giving out this very soft *hissssssss*. There's a hunk of crappy carpet on the floor to hide the boards, and over against the wall there's three of those big metal-edged chests like you put your stuff in if you're going on a long ocean voyage. How come if Lennie isn't here he left the lamp and heater on? It doesn't make sense.

Then I noticed the walls. When I first came in I didn't really look, just thought it was some kind of weird wallpaper design covering them, but it isn't wallpaper at all, it's a million different pictures of naked women stuck all over the walls, and not just Playboy centerfolds either, I mean most of them are beaver shots from very raunchy magazines that don't care if the model is pretty or not, just so's she'll open out like a clam for the camera, even pull herself wider open than she'd normally be with her legs apart so you can see right in there, like something out of a medical book.

It made me feel horny for about ten seconds, then it made me feel sick almost, like looking at pictures of beef carcasses split open and hung on hooks in some meat-packing plant, carcass after carcass, all the same, all turned inside out practically. It was ugly, definitely ugly, and the worst part of it was that most of the pictures were peppered with little holes all around the vaginas, so it looks like there's swarms of insects crawling out from inside the women, very creepy until you see what it really is, namely dart holes. I looked around for the darts and they're clustered in a picture over on the other wall, a very fat girl on her back with boobs that spilled sideways like sacks of flour they're so huge, and stuck right there between her legs are these plastic darts, three red and three blue. She's smiling between her legs at the darts stuck there. Just about every girl in all those overlapping pictures had dart holes in her boobs or vagina.

Lennie the Loop is sick. I couldn't figure it, all this pathetic stuff on the walls. Why's it there? Two girls are playing with each other in one of the pictures and he stuck so many holes in them they look like they've got a disease, and a few feet away there's another lesbian picture all spattered with holes the same way, only this one has also got the girls' eyes gouged out. And next to it there's another one the same, in fact the closer I looked the more obvious it was that more than half the pictures were women doing stuff to each other, and most of them had the regular dart holes in their privates plus their eyes blacked out with so many dart holes they're not even there anymore, like tattered masks across their faces. I don't understand *any* of this. Is he a sex maniac or what? Does Lennie have a sex life? He looks kind of unclean, so who'd fuck him? Even a hooker would think twice I bet, and if he tried raping someone he'd be identified right away. No one else looks like Lennie.

I looked around the room again. Apart from the stuff I already told about, there's nothing. It's like a prison cell in here. I'm sweating inside my parka, but I won't take it off. I'm getting out of here pretty soon. This is a sick place, a sad place. I could see Lennie lying on his Army cot and staring at all the naked women and opening his pants and jizzing all over himself, then picking up his darts and flinging them where his dick could never go . . . *Thunk!* A crotch. *Thunk!* A tit. *Thunk!* An eyeball. Poor old mad masturbating Lennie, jack-off sicko pervert feeb. I bet deep down he must really hate women to do this stuff to pictures of them, and maybe he hates lesbians most of all, or else he's turned on by that stuff the way some guys are, but that still wouldn't explain the dart holes. No, this is not regular turn-on territory, it's sick city. It stinks in here. It stinks of old dirty clothes and jizzed sheets and propane, and I bet the chemical toilet needs emptying too. Has old Chuck ever been in here? Does he know about all this sick stuff? He'd hate it, I know he would. I guess Lennie keeps the door locked so tight even his old man doesn't know what kind of a snake pit this place is.

Up until a few minutes ago I kind of thought Lennie and me might be . . . you know, kindred spirits or something, but not anymore. I was kind of sorry for him because of the way people hate him soon as they lay eyes on him. If this was a movie I'd discover when I came in here that it's all fresh and clean and the guy that everyone in town thinks is a mad dirty lunatic is really a very wise and humble guy, practically Jesus, living this very strange life of the mind in the middle of the junkyard with lots of books on philosophy and religion et cetera, a real-live American saint too good and holy to lead a regular life like the rest of the world. But this isn't a movie, it's real, and Lennie's shack is just as disgusting and weird as Lennie looks, worse even than everybody suspects. This place is a shithole.

You know what I was? I was disappointed. More than feeling sick and disgusted, I felt very disappointed. Lennie isn't anything like I thought he'd be. Let's face it, I *wanted* him to be some kind of wise and humble and misunderstood guy just like he'd be in a movie where the ending would have this moral that people shouldn't judge a book by its cover, blah blah. I wanted to be the only one in town who knows the real and actual truth about Lennie Bimmerhaus, all the stuff the Army shrinks and even his old man never found out. I'd know it all because Lennie would trust me, shy and humble and wise Lennie the junkyard hermit, a poor guy screwed up by the war, another victim of lousy politics and patriotism and dumbness. That's how it should've been, the big discovery inside Lennie's shack, but it isn't, it's a boot shoved hard in my face, a stinking shitty boot grinding my eyes out because my eyes didn't see what they wanted to see. I knew there wouldn't be any cheese-wire loop in here, or a human-hair blanket, none of that schoolkid crap, but I never expected these crucified vaginas and punctured tits and missing eyeballs, no way . . . and I bet I know why it's like this! I bet I know why! Lennie's wife *did* cheat on him while he was away, but with another *woman!* He must've found out somehow, and finding out his car was wrecked on top of the news about Carol Ann must've flipped him out. Could that be it? I want to know for sure. I have to figure out the why and the wherefore even if Lennie's just a pathetic animal I don't want to meet anymore. I have to know *why* he's the way he is. Carol Ann a lesbian . . . I bet it would've hit a guy like Lennie—who was just a hotted-up car fan and typical small-town ding-dong—hit him like a freight train. His *wife?* A *lesbian?* Maybe she wrote him a Dear John. Maybe he found out that way. Dear Lennie, when you come back I'll be gone. It's better with a woman than it could ever be with a man, especially you. Maybe she mailed the letter and was on her way home when she got creamed by the Mayflower truck like old Chuck told me, or maybe she was on her way home from having terrific sex with her lady friend and wasn't concentrating, part of her mind on her purring pussy and part of it on the letter she mailed to Lennie in 'Nam just yesterday . . . I'm making all this stuff up, making movies in my head. Maybe nothing like that happened at all. Maybe what made Lennie crazy was just bad chemicals in his brain after all. He's just a sad fuck-up of a guy that can't fit in anywhere, can't even get loved by anyone because he hates women, that much I'm sure of, because no one who thinks women are okay could've done what he's done to those pictures, all those hundreds of mutilated paper ladies, real Jack the Ripper stuff. I wanted out of there.

But then I got this feeling, this feeling when I looked at the three chests. I had to know what's in them. Carol Ann's letter maybe? They're big and blue with fake brass edges, three of them in a row. Three blue boxes. What's inside them? Maybe two of them are empty, and it's box number three that has the holiday in Hawaii and the living-room suite and the Panasonic TV and the Chevy Monte Carlo in it. Lennie's not here. I can *look*. I went over and hunkered down in front of the middle one. If there's an answer here this is the one that'll have it—the chest in the middle, don't ask me why. I opened it. Clothes. Smelly old clothes and underwear and socks. Doesn't he know you have to ventilate stuff like this? I closed it again and opened the one on the left. Magazines. Not snatch magazines like you'd expect. *Wheels. Motor. Street Rod. Car.* A whole chest full of them. I picked one up. It's from 1976. He *hoards* these things. He's a kid. He looks like Rasputin but he's a teenager still, with a grease mark across his brow and chrome and torque and horsepower on his mind. Maybe the magazines are hiding something. I dug right down deep, but there's nothing else in there, just glossy paper covered with souped-up street machines, triple carburetor dragsters from outer space with bikini girls draped all over their hoods. The girls haven't been stabbed. Lennie probably had too much respect for the cars they're lying on.

Chest number three, the one on the right. I opened it up. Model cars. Plastic assemble-it-yourself-with-glue models. Hot rods, natch. They were good, very carefully done. There were squared-off jitneys from the thirties, and those tapering bombs from the forties with the big fenders, and long, wide boxes with fins from the fifties, all of them different somehow from the regular assembly-line product, I mean they had weird paint jobs in colors out of a psychedelic rainbow, crazy colors that hurt your eyes, so bright and strong they're tacky, if you know what I mean, and they had engines that poked up through the hoods or else were exposed completely, *chromed* engines, even chromed exhausts, and they sat low to the ground like they're getting set to spring like cats, and the roofs were lowered too, so the windows are just long slits like you'd expect machine guns to poke out of, and the wheels were fat racing wheels that put plenty of tread on the road. Fantasy machines. Lennie's substitute for teddy bears and Raggedy Anns, definitely regressive in my opinion.

This shack isn't real. It's a lunatic's castle with a moat around it of trashed autos and a doggie dragon to bar the way, and inside it's a treasure cave for a twelve-year-old, a pathetic kid who jabs and stabs at those big luscious pink things called women that live way out beyond the moat where he doesn't belong. It's the sickest, saddest place in town, and apart from Lennie I'm the only one who knows.

Confession time. I wanted to steal one of his model cars, not just because he's done such a terrific job of putting them together and painting them and all, but for a souvenir, something I could take away with me and look at every now and then to remind myself how I spent five minutes inside the crazy man's castle and lived to tell the tale, none of which is any excuse for thievery, but I wasn't thinking about right and wrong at the time, I just *wanted* one of those beautiful little cars. He's got dozens of them in the chest, all piled one on top of the other like the junked autos outside, but these aren't squashed and I bet he takes them out and puts them back very, very carefully so he doesn't chip the glitzy paint jobs. Dozens of them, so he won't miss just one I bet, and even if he does he won't know it was me that took it. But I'll be smart—I'll take one from way down on the bottom so maybe it'll be weeks before he figures out it's gone.

I started taking them out, nice and careful, and putting them on the floor around me, and pretty soon I'm down into the guts of the chest where he keeps the tubes of glue and cans of paint, aerosol cans so the models don't have brush marks on them. He must spray the parts before he glues them together. I picked up one of the cans, and I'm just about to put it down on the floor when *bam!* the door opens behind me and I knew the crazy king is back in his castle . . .

Jesus . . .

Shit . . .

I looked over my shoulder, cranked my head around to see. It's the only part of my body I can move. The rest of me is frozen. It's Lennie the Loop all right, standing in the doorway and looking at me like he can't believe there's a real-live human being inside his off-limits hideaway. He's got one foot inside and one foot outside, frozen like me. We must've stared at each other for half a minute, not moving, and my heart's tripping and stumbling to keep up a regular beat I'm so scared and guilty, so scared I have to drag air into myself so my lungs don't quit. I've been crouching next to the chests so long my legs are numb. I'm just a pair of eyes that are fixed on Lennie the Loop, a galloping heart and a hand closed around an aerosol can. That's all there is of me. The rest has vanished. I'm a dead man.

He came in and shut the door. He did it slow and never once took his eyes off me. Jesus, he looked dangerous. He's wearing the black wool hat I laundered for him, and that long black hair is hanging down both sides of his face and beard. He's wearing wool gloves, gray I think, and the same old overcoat he always wears. He's long and skinny as a clothespin, but it's the eyes you have to watch, the no-color eyes with the tiny black pupils in the middle like they were put there by an ice pick. Those eyes burned holes in me like laser beams. I'm a dead man for sure. He'll kill me for monkeying around with his stuff, for *being here at all* . . . But he's taking his time, just standing there with the Coleman lamp throwing light on him from waist level so there are dark half-moons under his eyes and his mustache threw a shadow up across his cheekbones, and those eyes are like flamethrowers burning me to cinders where I'm squatted in front of the treasure chest he caught me looting. He's the pirate king and I'm the sneaky bastard he caught trying to nab his gold and pearls in the secret cave. So now I have to die. I've made his treasure dirty by touching it and he has to kill me to make it clean again. It's only fair. I'm guilty as hell. He'll kill me dead for what I did, it's just a matter of time, maybe seconds, maybe a whole minute before I die. Maybe if I say I'm sorry . . . but I can't talk. My tongue's rolled itself back into my throat like a snail backing into its shell, wanting to be as far from the threat as possible. It's clamped so far back there I can hardly breathe . . . and Lennie's moving . . . moving across to the Army cot and kneeling down . . . reaching under it . . . straightening up again . . . with a gun in his hand!

It's a pistol, big and black and heavy-looking, but I don't know what kind. I'd really like to know what kind of gun is going to blow me away a few seconds from now, I really would. It's even bigger and squarer than the old Army Colt that private eyes used to carry, not lean and mean like a modern automatic, more like a machine pistol. Is he gonna blast me to pieces? I wanted to tell him someone'll hear the noise if he blasts me with a machine pistol without a silencer, and he'll get caught and get the chair for murder, but I couldn't tell him, couldn't get a word past that rolled-up wedged-tight tongue of mine hiding so far back in my mouth it's practically in my throat, a big fat cowardly worm all curled up and waiting for the end, the burst of flame, the firing pin tapping like a type-writer gone crazy, the string of ejected cartridges pumping out the side, the bullets jumping all over me, killing me a million ways, killing me to death, and now he's lifting the gun . . .

aiming . . .

right between my eyes . . .

Lennie

no

please

right

between

the eyes

. . .

Smack!

I felt it hit, just one bullet, right between the eyes like I knew it'd be, and my face is wet with blood and I went hard against the chest with the impact and fell off my feet that I couldn't even feel anymore, I've been crouched so long, fell off them all the way to the floor and lay there on my side with the bullet in my brain and the aerosol can in my hand still and waited for the black curtains that mean I'm dead. But they didn't show. I figured maybe it's because my life hadn't flashed before my eyes yet the way it's supposed to, every little thing that ever happened, so I waited for the speeded-up movie, the Big Fast-Forward, sixteen years in sixteen seconds, but the show's on hold, all I can see is the dirty carpet a couple inches from my nose, and my nose is . . . orange!

Huh?

I waited for the movie and the curtain. Still zip. What kind of dying *is* this? I want it to be *over*, want my suffering to *stop* . . . but I'm *not* suffering except for pins and needles in my legs from the blood racing back into them now that they're stretched out on the floor somewhere at the other end of me, and there's a sticky feeling from the orange blood all over my face and I'm *still* not dead . . .

But I'm *bleeding* . . .

But my blood is orange . . .

I told my hand to reach and touch my face. After a while it

did it. No hole in my forehead. No blood. Orange paint. He hit me with a paint pellet . . . The gun in his hand is an air pistol that fires paint pellets, the kind of gun those weekend survivalists use, those idiots who like to charge around in the woods, blasting away at each other without anyone actually getting killed, just scoring hits that get totaled up at the end of the day. Bang—you're dead. Retire from the field of fire and give your camouflage jacket a rinse to get that nasty orange stain out. New, all-temperature Cheer will do the trick, and *Mmmmmmm*, smells good too . . .

A splat gun . . .

You prick Lennie . . .

You fucking *asshole* . . .

I could *kill* you for that!

I got up. He didn't fire again, kept the gun aimed at me but didn't pull the trigger. Maybe it only fires one pellet at a time. Maybe he has to break it open and put a new pellet in and pump up the air chamber again. But he kept it aimed at me anyway, like it's a real gun and he's got the drop on me, the dopey idiot bastard. I really hated him for making me think I was truly going to *die* . . . My tongue unrolled like a red carpet and hit my teeth.

"Very fucking funny," I said, but it came out like a frog-croak.

He just kept the gun aimed at me, secret-agent cowboy-hero gunslinger, Lennie. What a pathetic sonofabitch. Am I supposed to still be scared, or what? I didn't know *how* to feel. I had anger and fright and guilt and shame all swirling around inside me, a real gut-churning mess that wanted to puke itself up. Get out, that's what I had to do, get out before anything weirder than what already happened happens.

My hat and mittens are over on the table. I took a step . . .

Ker-runch!

I trod on a model car.

I didn't *mean* to . . . Jesus, now he'll *really* kill me . . .

He's looking at the floor where one of his pride and joys is just shattered bits of colored plastic, silver and turquoise. Is he mad or full of grief? I can't tell. Out. Right now. I went to the table and grabbed my stuff. I'm not looking at Lennie anymore.

If I back away from him like he's a hungry tiger he'll know I'm scared. That might be a bad thing. Bluff it out. Turn your back on him like he's no threat at all. Go to the door without looking back. Do it now.

I did it. Now I'm at the door. I have to open it. Problem—hat and mittens in one hand, spray can in the other. Put one down. The can. It's been in my fist a fair few minutes now. My fingers kind of locked onto it when Lennie came through the door, a nervous reflex I guess. I should put the can down so I can open the door, but there's nothing near the door to put the can on, and I don't want to stoop and put it on the floor because that'd somehow make me look weak, don't ask me why, and I didn't want to just drop it, because that might look kind of insulting and push Lennie over the edge, if he's anywhere near it, which I don't know for sure, and he'll come at me with his bare hands, or maybe club me with that fucking air pistol, so I can't do that either, and in the end I just shoved the can fast into my pocket, hoping Lennie doesn't notice, is still staring at his smashed car so hard he's hardly aware of me at all—stashed it in there and opened the door and left and closed the door behind me. I'm alive!

The dog was there, like he's been waiting all this time for me to come out. The first thing I did was go to the nearest rust heap and scoop some snow off the fender and rub my face to get that orange paint off. I rubbed and scrubbed till I couldn't feel my skin anymore, then I headed for the gate, walking slow so the Doberman doesn't get all excited and start chewing my butt off. We got to the gate. "Happy New Year," I told the dog. Then I climbed over.

I'm out of there. It's a good thing I already paid Chuck his eighty bucks. No way am I ever going back. What a crazy fucking thing to happen, like a dream. I can't even figure out what it *means* or anything, just run action replays inside my head, from the time I opened the shack door and went in, to the time I opened it again and went out. Totally insane, the whole thing. I'm telling the Sony everything on my way home, and you know what?

I'll be glad to get there.

17

Wrong again, Weems.

I just played back that last bit about being glad to get home. How dumb can you get. It's 3:07 now. You'll never guess where I am. The thing is, when I got home the Impala's parked in the driveway, so Peggy's home before me. It was around 2 A.M. by then. I went in, and the first thing I heard was voices from her bedroom, so she found a guy all right. Shit! Strangers in the house I *don't* need, not tonight. I stood in the living room wondering what to do.

"Burris, is that you?" she calls out.

Who the fuck else would be coming through the front door with a key?

"No!" I said. Shouted, as a matter of fact. I was mad.

I went out again, straight back out into the night. I'm not having some guy I don't even know fucking my mother in the next room while I'm trying to sleep. She might at least have gone to a motel if the guy doesn't have somewhere to take her. There must be an empty motel room *somewhere* in Buford tonight. Sometimes I think Peggy's got no class at all. Okay, I'm a big boy and I know the facts of life and I don't think she should stitch herself up just because she's over forty, but I just don't wanna *listen* to it! Not tonight!

So I'm out on the street again after maybe sixty seconds inside my own home. Isn't that something? Life's a real crock sometimes. I should get myself one of those T-shirts with that terrific message on the front: LIFE'S A BITCH—THEN YOU DIE. That just about sums it up. You can keep your Philosophy 101 and a million books on library shelves, that T-shirt says it all. So I'm on the street again, standing outside 1404, wondering what to do now. The town is quiet, Westwood Drive anyway. I started walking. I've walked miles and miles tonight and gotten nowhere.

Then I saw Nonny. He's standing on the curb like always, little Nonny, the patriotic fireplug, a heavy metal nephew of Uncle Sam. I went over to look at him. He's got a cone of snow on his red cap but he's smiling anyway, little Mr. Optimistic. Let it rain, let it shine, I'm okay because I'm American-made, stars and stripes and stripes and stars. Piss on me and see if I care, I'm American-made so it rolls right off, piss and crap, whatever you lay on me it don't make no never mind, pardner, 'cos I'm a product of the Yew Ess Ay, which means I'm rustproof, practically indestructible, pal, that's why I keep right on smilin' through, because if I quit, if I quit smiling for just *one second* and admit I'm no better than a fireplug from Tashkent or Timbuktu, if I do that for even a *fraction of a second* the whole damn street'll disappear and the world'll split in half and that'll be the end of *everything* if America quits smiling at itself, because without America what kind of world would it be, I'm askin' ya, no kinda world at all, buddy, so I'm a-keepin' this here smile *whatever*.

No hydrant, no world.

Maybe.

Maybe not.

I took out Lennie's spray can and shook it. Nonny, your days of stars'n'stripes are over. You've been this way since '76. Loretta and me, we painted you. Now it's '86 and I'm gonna *un*-paint you, so hold your breath, little guy, 'cos here comes the rain . . . I held the can up to the streetlight so I can read the color on the label. Gold Flake. Okay, Nonny, you're gonna shimmer and shine from now on. I squatted down next to him and brushed the snow off his pointy little head. We smiled at each other. So long, Nonny. I started spraying.

The cap went first, then the smile. I drowned him in a golden mist, worked my way around him, still squatting, spraying and spraying. I must've looked like a chimpanzee. I kept that button down and the paint hissed out nonstop, covering old Nonny from top to toe. 'Bye, 'bye . . . and hello, Goldie. You're a yellow fellow that's looking mellow. I emptied the can, gave him a double coat to keep out the cold. It'll probably look lousy in daylight, but right now he looks like he's worth his weight in . . . you guessed it. The streetlight made him glow, almost, and the little flaky bits in the paint glinted like frost crystals. Gold Flake, what a color, just about the tackiest you can buy, except maybe for Cherry Flake, the kind of colors you see on very cheap drum kits. No more Nonny. I've killed him off. The street didn't disappear. The planet kept spinning. Goldie marches to the beat of a different drummer. I dumped the empty can in the gutter. So I'm a litterbug, so sue me. Tonight I don't care.

I walked away.

I walked and walked. I climbed Crane Hill. I climbed the water tower. I sat on the warning light. The night's still clear. I can see all of Buford. Twinkling light, way below me. I'm waiting for the sun. The new year doesn't truly begin till sunrise. I'm waiting for the new year. Meanwhile I'm keeping watch. Something's coming from the east. Maybe angels, maybe missiles. Maybe just the edge of dawn. I'll be here when it comes. I bet it's sad and gray. I should've kept the can. Saved some of that Gold Flake. When the new day comes it'll need help.

I'd raise my can.

I'd paint it gold.